# *IF MEMORY SERVES*

# TANYA GOODWIN

## A MITCHELL MORRIS ROMANTIC THRILLER

Published by
Mitchell Morris  December/2012
A Division of Celeris Publishing Group, Inc.
Port Richey, FL

Mitchell Morris is a registered trademark
of
Celeris Publishing Group, Inc.

ISBN-13: 9781937629359
ISBN-10: 193762935X
Library of Congress Control Number: 2012913318

# IF
# MEMORY
# SERVES

## TANYA GOODWIN

**A MITCHELL MORRIS ROMANTIC THRILLER**

# Chapter One

$T$ara's beeper blared, rousing her from the hospital's call room bed. She had just closed her eyes after delivering two boys, one girl, and a set of twins, one of which dallied for thirty minutes, enjoying the roomy womb for himself. She glanced at her pager. The labor and delivery extension followed by 911 scrolled across it. Her heartbeat rocketed.

Cinching the ribbon of her blue scrub pants around her waist, she stumbled out of the call room and bolted down the hallway, followed closely by the clapping of rubber-soled shoes scurrying across the linoleum tiles of the labor and delivery unit. Catching a glimpse of the night shift nurses' backs dashing into labor room five, Dr. Tara Ross ran into the room behind them. Smoothing her rumpled short brown hair, she assessed the chaos.

*"No,"* the laboring woman screamed. She rolled from side to side on the labor bed. Her arms were wrapped across her pregnant belly, her sweaty blonde hair plastered to her pale cheeks.

"Oh my God," Tara mumbled. She recognized Alexis Kent, the woman that left her practice against medical advice.

"I can't get an IV in. She's completely out of control, and her veins are collapsed," the charge nurse said.

Another nurse scooted a fetal heart monitor along Alexis's belly. "I get 120 beats per minute, Dr. Ross."

Tara palpated Alexis's rigid abdomen and then checked her pulse -120. The nurse had heard the maternal pulse, not the fetal heartbeat.

Another nurse glanced at the Dinamap monitor. She darted her eyes toward Tara. "Her blood pressure is 80/50 and her pulse ox is down to 95 percent"

Alexis shut her eyes and lolled her head against the pillow. Her pallor camouflaged her body among the white hospital sheets.

Tara licked her parched lips. She feared this would happen. With two prior cesarean sections and this baby in a breech position, she had advised Alexis to have a repeat cesarean section for her, and her baby's, safety. Despite Tara's deep concern and multiple conferences with Alexis and then pleas, Alexis left Tara's obstetric practice, desiring a home birth with a lay midwife.

Tara stroked her patient's damp forehead. The woman's eyelids fluttered open. "Alexis, you need to have a c-section immediately. The baby is in distress, and you may be bleeding internally. I need to deliver your baby now."

She glanced at the waiting nurses. "Let's roll her back to the OR!"

A nurse tightened the rubber tourniquet around Alexis's arm and took one last jab into her antecubital fossa. Drops of dark red blood dripped from the hub of the 18 gauge IV catheter.

"I'm in," she called and handed the blood-filled syringe to a lab tech for a stat type and cross.

The Chief of Anesthesiology at Brewster Medical Center poked his head into the labor room. "Alexis, Sweetheart, I'm here." Panting, he ran over to her and cradled her head in his hands. "It's going to be okay," Dr. Robert Upton told his daughter and leaned over to kiss her forehead. Then, banging the side rails, he yelled, "Let's go people."

The on call anesthesiologist stood in the doorway. "I'm all set in the OR, Dr. Ross."

He turned to address Alexis. "Alexis, I'm Dr. Morris," he said calmly. "I'm going to be your anesthesiologist." He then turned and introduced himself to Alexis's husband, Bradley.

Bradley, pressed against the far wall of the labor room, stared straight ahead, clutching his toddler daughter with one arm and gripping his little boy's hand with the other.

Tara touched him on his shoulder. "We'll take good care of her."

Bradley blinked and nodded. His lower lip trembled.

The nurses gave the wheeled hospital bed a shove and rolled the bulky bed toward the door. The black wheels of the bed shimmied and squealed around the corner steering like a rickety grocery cart. Tara ran along one side of the bed, Dr. Upton along the other.

Barely conscious, Alexis no longer screamed. Her body jostled between the side rails. It was only when the bed bumped the doorframe as the nurses pushed it into the OR, that Alexis stirred briefly, and then shut her eyes again.

Alexis's midwife trotted behind the rumbling bed, frantic. "She didn't want to deliver at the birthing center so I came to her house. Her cervix had dilated to five centimeters without a problem. Then she just ...started screaming. I knew something was wrong. Bradley carried her to the car and rushed her here. I'm so sorry."

Tara quickly put on her scrub hat. "We'll talk about this later. I need to get in the OR."

Dr. Edouard LaCroix burst through the steel double doors of the OR hallway. "I got here as fast as I could, Tara." He turned toward Bradley and Dr. Upton. "I understand you're scared, but Dr. Ross and I will do our best for Alexis." He glared at the midwife and said nothing.

Tara gently pried Robert Upton's curled fingers from the bed's metal side rails "Dr. Morris is a good man. I know you trust him. Stay with Bradley and the children in the waiting room. He needs you, right now. I promise I'll tell you what's happening."

He nodded. "Thank you."

Tara and Edouard, armed with scrub caps, masks, booties and a prayer, stood at the scrub sink.

Edouard wasn't a tall man, but muscular. His bright blue scrub cap matched his intent eyes behind the glass of his oval wireless frames. He tucked stray brown wavy hairs under the band of his cap and gazed into her bloodshot eyes.

"You look exhausted."

"It's been a crazy night. And it's about to get crazier."

"Darling, you warned her. You can't control everyone and everything. Tonight will end. He shot her a reassuring grin. "Then you can sleep it off ... in my bed."

Tara and Edouard had practiced obstetrics together for six years now. They had practiced dating for the last six months.

He wanted more — *now.*

But she needed room to breathe, to contemplate the complications of intimacy with a business partner, hesitant to enter into a committed relationship after her recent divorce. And then there was Abbie, her fifteen- year-old daughter, to consider.

The scrub nurse methodically counted the instruments and lap pads while another painted Alexis's belly with a Betadine-soaked sponge until it gleamed deep maroon.

Tara and Edouard unfolded the sterile blue drape over Alexis's body, her rounded belly jutting through the oval cut of the covering, the tackiness of the Betadine solution sticking to the edges.

Dr. Morris injected a sedative and muscle relaxant into Alexis's IV and then quickly inserted her breathing tube. "You're good to go."

Tara pressed the silver blade of her scalpel to Alexis's skin, incising a vertical cut from her navel to just above her pubic bone. Being an emergency Cesarean, there was no time for cosmetic consideration. She and Edouard toiled their way through the fascia and entered the peritoneal cavity. Their eyes met. They blinked at each other. They immediately recognized what was right there, in their hands. The placenta was shoved out of the fractured uterus — a tiny hand flopped across it, bathed in a sea of dark green amniotic fluid. She pushed the baby's hand back into the torn uterus and extracted the limp little girl, grasping her feet.

"I have a ruptured uterus here with placental and fetal expulsion," Tara called to the neonatologist. "Meconium. Floppy baby coming your way!"

She handed the tiny girl to the neonatologist, dreading she was giving her a dead baby. The pediatric specialist performed the obligatory resuscitative measures.

She shook her head. "Sorry, Tara."

Tara and Edouard struggled to control the bleeding, but Alexis's torn uterus could not be salvaged. Her hemoglobin had dropped to a dangerous six. Alexis grew paler with each passing minute, and the anesthesiologist squeezed the fifth pint of blood into her IV.

Tara looked at Edouard. "We've tried everything." Droplets of sweat dotted her forehead. "We can't go on much further. She's bleeding out. She needs a hysterectomy."

"I agree. We don't have any more options."

Tara glanced at Dr. Morris over the brim of her surgical mask. "We're going overtime. How's she doing?"

"As long as the blood's coming, then we're holding."

A lab tech entered the OR and handed the anesthesiologist three more bags of blood. Tara spied Robert's face through the crack of the OR door as he peeked into the room. She knew he wanted in there, it was his daughter she was working on. Hell, she would want the same thing if this were *her* daughter. But he was family. This was no objective case for him.

Tearing her gaze away as blood cascaded down the blue drape covering Alexis's body, Tara reached up and adjusted the OR light, focusing it on her operative field, the glare from it glinting dully off the bloodied tools.

No baby cried.

Robert, Tara was sure, had to be alarmed. He knew what it meant, not to hear his grandchild take its first breath.

Her chest heavy at the thought of relaying the somber news, Tara called out from beneath her blood-spattered surgical mask, "Robert, I'll be right out."

She glanced at a nurse, "I can't leave the OR now. Get Robert and Bradley in a private area to wait. I'll speak to them as soon as I can."

"Will do, Dr. Ross. I'll get them ready. That is if there's ever a ready."

The neonatologist left the OR too, with the baby girl swaddled in her arms while Tara and Edouard completed Alexis's surgery. After the emergency hysterectomy, the nurses and the anesthesiologist transported Alexis to the Intensive Care Unit. Only Edouard and Tara stood in the OR now.

He whispered in her ear, "You did the best you could in a tough situation. Let's go talk with Robert and Bradley. Then we'll go back to the call room."

She squeezed his hand. They ripped off their bloody gowns, gloves, and surgical booties and then left the maroon spattered room—bumping right into Robert Upton.

"Robert, come with me and we'll talk. Where's Alexis's husband?" Tara asked.

"We're all in the waiting room."

"Are there other people there?"

Robert shook his head. Tara swallowed hard, seeing tears welling up in his eyes. "No, not tonight," he replied.

They walked together to the surgical waiting room. Bradley sat solemnly in a chair, staring at a wall while his children slept on the sofa, blissfully oblivious to the whole ordeal.

Tara pulled up a chair and sat across from Bradley. Edouard stood quietly behind her.

She rested her hands over Bradley's fingers, which were tightly folded into a blanched ball. "Bradley, Alexis had a complication. Her uterus ... womb ... ruptured." She paused and took a deep breath. She had to tell him. "Your baby girl did not survive."

Bradley sank his head into his hands and sobbed. No one spoke for several minutes. Minutes that felt more like an hour.

Bradley composed himself enough to say, "Okay, go on."

"When her uterus ruptured, the placenta—or afterbirth—became detached. The baby could not survive without the oxygen supply of the placenta."

"When did that happen?" he asked.

"I don't know, but it had been a while."

"How's Alexis?"

"Alexis needed several blood transfusions, but despite all our efforts, we had to proceed with a hysterectomy in order to save her life. She's in the ICU. Her bleeding is under control, but she'll need close monitoring."

"Thank you for saving her."

Robert rubbed his eyes. "This is so hard for all of us. You did the best you could, Tara. And that has kept my daughter alive."

Tara drew a deep breath, stemming the tears so close to pooling in her lower lids. "I'm so sorry, Bradley, Robert."

"Thank you," they said softly and in unison.

Bradley grasped Tara's hand. "When can I see Alexis and the baby?"

"Alexis is still sedated. She's in the intensive care unit. I can take you to a private room where you can spend time with your daughter. Would you like to do that?"

"Yes," he said. He turned to Robert. "I'd like you to be there too."

"Absolutely," Robert replied. He hugged his son-in-law.

Bradley scooped up his sleepy children.

Tara opened the waiting room door and ushered them into an empty patient room.

"I'll be right back," she said. Clicking the door closed behind her, Tara paused. Her head buzzed, and her stomach tightened with anxiety.

She returned, carrying the lifeless babe, wrapped in a white cotton blanket, a pink knitted cap crowning her tiny head. Tara placed the infant into Bradley's arms.

"She's so tiny. So beautiful," Bradley murmured.

Robert peered inside the blanket and gazed at his granddaughter. "Yes, she is beautiful."

They took turns holding her, sobbing into each other's arms.

Tara shuffled to the call room. Her eyes burned, and her legs felt brick heavy. The door was ajar. Edouard sat on the edge of the bed, patting the mattress, beckoning her to sit next to him. The metal frame groaned as she sank into the bed and scooted to his side, too exhausted to cry. She shut her eyes as Edouard's placed his hand on her shoulder. The pang in her chest squeezed her hard. She shifted on the bed, pressing against him, praying for comfort that never came.

"I'm so sorry you had such an awful night." He leaned into her and kissed her head. "Happy New Year."

"Shit. It's New Year's Day. I completely forgot." She licked the saline from her lips.

"Get some rest. We'll have plenty of time together at the Vegas conference."

Tara tapped her forehead with the palm of her hand. "*Oh,* the conference. I can't go. I'm wiped out, and I just put the house up for sale. The divorce…he… took everything I had."

Including her fifteen year- old daughter, Abbie—she prayed that was only temporary.

Her ex, Theo, had insisted she sign off on Abbie's passport to Greece to visit his parents. Her own parents deceased, she wanted Abbie to know and love her Greek grandparents. Christened Abigal Katerina Christopoulos, Tara had always wanted her daughter to embrace her Greek background from her father's side. She had passed down her own Russian ethnicity to Tara. She hoped Theo was doing the same, and not whisking their daughter away in revenge. Her heart squeezed. *He wouldn't keep Abbie from her*!

But truthfully, this was a good time as any for her daughter to go. She'd hit a financial sinkhole. Broke, Tara was finally forced to sell her dream, house, and although she was chronically exhausted, sleep offered her no relief from the turmoil in her life.

She had kissed Abbie goodbye, vowing she'd get a new place for them by the time she returned from Greece. Abbie had written her a note before she left, telling Tara that she couldn't wait to see her Yiayia and her Papou, but she also couldn't wait to get back to her mother with hugs, kisses, and photos from her grandparent's remote island home. Tara wondered how her daughter would live without texting and Facebook, but her stomach churned too, at the thought of not hearing from Abbie over the next three weeks. She was marking the days on her calendar until Abbie's return, "X" ing out all the ones that had passed since she left.

Tara rubbed her eyes, yawned, and leaned on Edouard's shoulder. "I have to deal with the realtor, and I sent my boxes to Marielle's place in Brooklyn." *That is, what she had left,* she thought. "I promised to spend some time with her. She wants me to stay with her a while."

"I thought you were moving in with me."

"Eventually Edouard. I need some time away. I want to get this right."

"It *is* right."

She wasn't as sure. He was pushing her, and she was starting to resent him. Not a way to start a relationship. He was distant with Abbie, and her daughter wrinkled her nose at him every chance she got. Tara doubted Edouard's house would be the right place for her.

He stroked her cheek. "Go home and get some sleep, darling. You've barely slept this whole month. All hell seems to break loose when you're on call. In fact, take the next two weeks off. You haven't taken a vacation in over two years. Relax. Stay with your friend, Marielle. Nora Grayson, the new OB, comes in on Monday. I'll arrange for cross coverage so she won't feel overwhelmed. Quit feeling guilty and enjoy your vacation."

*He's right, God, I need the break. Two weeks!*

Between the two of them, their practice couldn't keep up with the patient load, especially since most of the women demanded to see a woman physician. She found she couldn't say "no" to many of them, when they came in for their labors, and she was delivering their babies, despite Edouard being the physician on call. Although it bruised his ego, he consistently slept better than she did.

She gave him a quick peck on his lips.

"Have a terrific time at the conference. We'll finalize our plans when you get back. I'll miss you," he said.

"I'll miss you too."

# Chapter Two

Monday, January 2, Noon

Tara squeezed through the New York City subway turnstile, catching the hem of her jacket around one of the bars. Trapped for a few seconds, she grimaced as a fat woman grumbled behind her. Her pulse quickened as she desperately yanked to free her jacket. The bars finally ratcheted closed, sending Tara stumbling out. The woman shoved past her.

Tara trudged up the cracked concrete stairs, squinting her eyes as she exited the dim subway station. She had exited the 72$^{nd}$ Street and Broadway station on Manhattan's Upper West Side and now stood in Verdi Square, at least that's what the green park sign claimed. The whipping winter wind slapped her cheeks as the departing train rumbled beneath her feet. Tara furrowed her forehead.

*This isn't Brooklyn! What on earth am I doing here?*

The pulse in her neck throbbed beneath her scarf. She drew a deep breath. *Don't panic.* Glancing around her surroundings, disoriented, Tara finally spied something familiar – the black and white marquis to the dance studio where she took ballet classes Mondays, Thursdays, and Saturdays.

But where was her dance bag? She shook her head.

*What day was it?*

Tara rushed past Fairway Market, the grocery store she'd stopped into so many times before, to grab an apple, some nuts, and a bottle of water after class to snack on the train home.

*Home? Why the hell couldn't she remember where that was?*

Despite the bone-chilling cold of the afternoon, a bead of sweat trickled down her back. She loosened her jacket, unzipping it away from her neck.

Her heart raced and her breathing accelerated, the quick puffs disappearing into the cold, gray sky.

*I don't understand. Why did I take the train here? And why am I having such an off day?*

Swirls of frigid gusts nearly knocked her to the sidewalk. She huddled in a street corner, barricading herself from the assaulting winds. Tara opened her wallet. She had twenty-five dollars, one credit card, and a stamped Metro North train ticket—Brewster to Grand Central printed at the bottom. Then she looked at the address on her driver's license.

Her mouth had gone dry.

The Brewster address made no sense. How could that be? When had she moved from Manhattan? Her head ached, her fingers tingled beneath her mittens, and her ears began to ring so loud that she couldn't think.

*Breathe, Tara. Breathe.*

Something strange was happening. Something she couldn't stop.

Detective Lieutenant Jeffrey Corrigan rubbed his temples. He rolled two aspirin tablets between his fingers before popping them into his mouth, gulping the bitter pills down his throat with his stagnant glass of water. Stacks of files littered the top of his desk.

The media were clamoring for information about the college kids shot at the Starbright's Coffee Shop.

He had the perp who knifed his girlfriend, waiting for him in interview room three.

Drug dealers were killing each other on Manhattan's Upper West Side.

The list went on and on. His head throbbed, his stomach grumbled, and his copper-rimmed glasses slid down the bridge of his nose.

"Damn it. I've to get these fixed," he muttered and pushed them back up.

Did you say something, Boss?" Laurie Styles, his young P.A.A, asked as she trotted into his office. She inched closer to his desk

Jeffrey pushed back in his chair. "No. I'm just mumbling to myself."

He liked Laurie, but she sometimes hovered — too often and too close for comfort. But, she was efficient and kept him organized. He certainly didn't want to lose her.

Just last week, he studiously avoided her for days, after declining her dinner invitation. He gently reminded her that dating within the house was taboo, and that included police administrative assistants. Besides, after a messy divorce like the one he'd just been through, he had sworn off romantic entanglements of any kind.

"Looks like you're having a tough day. I'll get you a cup of coffee," she said.

He sighed and stretched his long arms behind his head. While he relished being commander of Manhattan's Upper West Side homicide squad, today the job just sucked. He raked his fingers through his straight, sandy-blonde hair. Two weeks past due for his haircut, it grazed the collar of his shirt, flirting with regulation.

She eyed him speculatively. "I'll check your schedule and make an appointment with your barber." Before he could protest, she was gone.

The monthly CompStat meeting was a week away, and he'd need a trim before the brass came down on him, his hair, *and* the spike of homicides in his precinct. He glanced at the sleeves of his white cotton shirt, amazed at the straight creases. He pressed his shirts every Saturday night, an iron in one hand and a bottle of Guinness in the other.

Jeffrey shuffled the piles of paperwork on his desk, hoping the illusion of order would inspire him to tackle his review of open cases before his boss showed up. His day was complicated enough without the captain in his face. He furrowed his brows. The mood of the two seven soured every time Captain Ray Scardino was in the house. And today of all days, the captain was planning to saddle him with a 28 year-old neophyte detective with minimal street smarts.

Laurie stepped over his big black Oxfords. "Here's your coffee."

His feet stuck out like an obstacle course for her to navigate around. He curled them back under his desk, banging his knees in the process. "Shit," he whispered rubbing his knees.

"Let me take your glasses before they hit the floor." She held out her hand. "I'll shove some of these files over to make room for your coffee. Do you want me to get your glasses fixed?"

"No, thank you," he said but did not relinquish his glasses. "You're always taking care of me. I appreciate that. I'll get them fixed, one of these days."

"It's no problem. I'll gladly do it. I know *you* won't get around to it."

He relented and handed Laurie his glasses. Then he yanked open the sticky top drawer of his desk. A bottle of aspirin and a roll of antacids nearly ricocheted out.

*Ah, here they are.* He plucked out his old readers; wire framed aviators that he also never got around to fixing. The left rim brushed over his eyebrow, the right side sagged below the other, and the bridge totally missed his nose. He tossed them on his desk.

Laurie giggled. "I'll get them fixed by the end of the day."

"Thank you."

"You're welcome. Now drink your coffee before it gets cold."

Jeffrey smiled, raised his coffee mug, and sipped. The heat slid down his throat and soothed his stomach. He closed his eyes, reveling in the brief relief. He didn't want to deal with anything else. He didn't have the time.

Tara tugged the braids of her knitted hat, pulling it snug to her head, and walked north on Broadway. Maybe, if she kept walking, she'd snap out of it. A few feet away, a woman in a long grey woolen coat and wearing a pale pink Tammy hat with a matching scarf exited a building pushing a winterized baby tram, a zipped plastic shield protecting the baby inside of it.

Tara's heart pounded. She picked up her pace and strode up next the woman.

She pleaded with the woman. "The baby's cold. Warm her! Warm her!"

The woman stopped and scrunched her forehead. "Excuse me?"

"The baby's cold. She's not moving."

"Okay, lady. It's a boy. I don't know you. Mind your own business, you crazy bitch."

The woman opened the door to a bakery and dodged inside, shoving the tram in first. Joined by another woman, they peered out the glass window at Tara, pointing at her.

Tara jerked her head away and hurried across Broadway to Amsterdam. The driver of a yellow cab beeped his horn.

"Hey lady, watch where the hell you're going!"

She skittered onto the sidewalk and pulled her hat even tighter over her ears.

Why did she say that to that woman? And she walked right in front of that cab! *What's wrong with me?* She took a deep breath and walked on.

Tara's stomach growled. She'd searched for a café, one with WiFi. That way she'd get out of the cold, grab some lunch, and perhaps something on her computer would jog her memory, piece this whole misadventure together.

Just as she approached La Vita Cafe, a man slammed into her sending all 110 pounds of her airborne. He grabbed her around her waist. Her boots clattered on the icy sidewalk as she struggled to regain her balance.

"Whoa, I got you," he said.

*Where did he come from?*

The man pulled her closer preventing her butt from smacking the snowy pavement. She gazed up at him.

Tall and slender, he looked polished in his charcoal gray coat and tweed cap. She was surprised that he didn't slip in his black leather boots, hidden beneath his sharply pleated black trousers, and land smack next to her. A gust of wind flipped up his dark brown bangs. Then she noticed his eyes, one blue, and the other one hazel. She tried not to stare, but there was something odd about him. His eyes narrowed when he smiled. She shuddered.

"It's my fault. I'm so sorry. I wasn't looking where I was going. Are you okay?" He loosened his grip.

Tara dusted snow from her sleeves. "Yes, I'm fine. Thanks for the save."

But he was staring at her laptop case, and her pulse spiked in warning. *He collided with me on purpose!*

"How about I buy you a cup of coffee? It's the least I could do since I nearly knocked you over. Come on. A hot cup of coffee on a freezing day would do us both some good."

Tara hesitated. The guy was overly ingratiating to her in a weird way, and he bordered on persistent. She had to get away from him.

"Thank you for offering, but I already have plans for lunch. Have a good day."

He nodded. "Oh I will. You, too."

She nodded back to him and tugged up her coat collar. The less conversation between them, the better.

Picking up her pace, she strode to Amsterdam Avenue and 71$^{st}$, eager to look back to see if he followed her, but decided against it. Lunchtime approached, and despite the bitter weather, people were everywhere, walking swiftly to warm themselves in nearby restaurants. She couldn't tell whose footsteps crunched on the snowy sidewalk behind her. It could be anyone. Tara gave in. She had to look.

Making a fast 360, she assessed her surroundings, but the creepy man was nowhere in sight. Her heart slowed. Now for a bite to eat and to boot up her laptop.

She dodged into La Vita Café and shut the door, pushing the draft away. A line had already formed at the counter. Tara waited, shifting from one foot to the other, the snow from her boots melting around her.

The line moved.

She stepped over her puddle only to land in the slush of the person ahead of her. Tara sighed. At least there was safety in numbers. She glanced to her right. Two uniformed New York City policemen sat at a back table, drinking coffee, their backs to the wall. *Oh, thank God.* She was safe here. She thought about asking them for help, but they'd think her crazy or high. The man hadn't followed her inside the café, and she had no proof he was stalking her. Perhaps she was overreacting. The guy was weird, but probably harmless. Finally, it was her turn to order.

Tara bought a cup of coffee and a bowl of chili, choices that would heat her insides down to her frozen toes. Meandering around the lunchtime crowd, she found an empty table and sat. She pulling off her hat and fingered her short brown hair loose. Placing her purse and laptop case on the chair next to her, Tara sipped her coffee.

She smiled at the two teenage girls about her daughter's age, sitting at the table next to hers, giggling and texting between bites of their burgers and fries. A knife fell from their table and clattered to the floor. Tara watched it bounce on the tiles until it stopped.

*Hurry. Pick up the knife. You can save her!*

A waiter scooped it up.

Tara jerked her head and blinked a few times. She gripped the edges of the table until her pulse slowed. *For Pete's sake. It was only a knife.*

Tara had just stuck her spoon into her chili, when the man she thought she had evaded put his hand on the back of the empty chair across from her.

"What a pleasant surprise catching up with you like this," he said.

"Uh, yeah."

"May I sit?" Before she could decline his offer yet again, the man sat, holding his cup of coffee. "I apologize if I startled you. By the way, my name is Ted. Ted Larkin."

"I'm Tara."

"Nice to meet you, Tara…"

She looked straight into his face. *I'm not falling for that.* ."Just Tara."

His lips pressed into a smile. "Okay, just Tara."

*God, he was persistent.* She'd gulp her coffee and get a few spoonfuls of chili in her belly, and then she was out of here she decided.

"May I at least buy you a second cup of coffee? It's freezing out there."

"Yes, it is, but I'm okay here. I'm almost finished. I need to get back home. My husband is waiting for me."

Maybe this jerk would get the message and move on.

The man leaned past her and stared out the café window. Tara turned around to see what he was tracking, but all she saw were people bustling along the snowy Upper West Side sidewalks.

As she turned back, she caught him purposefully knocking over his cup. Coffee splashed onto the table, flowing over an edge, and dribbling onto her laptop case.

"Oh, I'm so sorry, "he said.

Tara sighed and grabbed napkins, but before she could pat dry her case, his hand was already there, resting over her bag.

She clutched it to her side, not wanting him to touch it. "I'm sure they'll get you another cup." Tara stood and glanced at her watch. "I'm late. I need to go. I hope you enjoy the rest of your lunch."

Tara pushed her way through the lunch crowd, bolted out the door, and headed back to the subway station. She'd get on a downtown train. Maybe she'd recognize the stops. And most importantly, she had to ditch that man. *Ted Larkin. Hmmm. I bet that's not even his real name.*

Tara jogged toward the 72 st. Station. Then she heard his voice. She ran faster. Panting, and her throat gone dry, she was almost to the station's stairs.

"Hey, Tara. Wait up!" Larkin grabbed the back of Tara's jacket. Her body jerked back as he yanked her laptop case.

*"Give it to me,"* he hissed.

21

"No! What the hell are you doing? Piss off! "

The handles of the black case began to slip from her hand. She clasped her fingers around them, squeezing as tight as she could. Surely, if she clung on, someone would come to her assistance.

He bared his teeth; a wolf primed to attack. His knuckles sped to her face like a torpedo. She turned her head, bracing for the impact. Surprisingly, she felt no pain as the blow struck her left eye.

He wrested the case from her.

People screamed as Tara tumbled down the stairwell, the thunder of feet echoing in her head.

"Stop, NYPD!" the men called.

Tara lay crumpled at the bottom of the stairs.

A woman yelled, "Hold it right there, Larkin. You're cornered."

Tara heard scuffling. Out of the corner of her right eye, she saw the man kick the woman in her stomach. They rolled down the stairs, straight at her. She closed her eyes, bracing herself. Someone landed on top of her.

"Get off me, damn it," she yelled. She flung her right hand back and slapped someone across the face. When Tara rolled over, she couldn't help but notice the woman's red cheek, her handprint blazing across it.

*Oh, no.*

Larkin righted himself and laughed. "You have nothing on me, detective."

He hurled Tara's laptop in front of an approaching number three train. It splintered into pieces on the rails, releasing a cloud of white powder that disappeared into the dank subway tunnel as the conductor sped the train through the stop.

Two male plainclothes detectives tackled him to the ground and handcuffed Larkin's hands behind his back. One reached under his coat. "I got his gun," he yelled.

The woman handcuffed Tara. "I'm Detective Shear. It's over, lady, let's go.

"I'm so sorry I hit you, detective."

Her own eye stung. She couldn't imagine how the detective felt. Tara tried to touch it but couldn't since her hands were restrained at her back.

Tara's heart pounded making her eye throb harder, "Go where?"

"The police station."

# Chapter Three

Monday, January 2, 3 p.m.

*T*he iron gate squeaked to a close, the bolt latching loud enough to echo down the hall.

"I'll have to put you in this holding cell, but it won't be for long," Detective Shear said.

Tara shifted on the wooden bench and tapped the concrete floor with the balls of her feet. She glanced up at Liz, searching her face for any hint of anger. She'd really screwed up now. "I 'm so sorry, Detective. Honestly, I didn't mean to hit you."

"I know. We'll get you moved out of here and get this situation cleared up."

"Thank you, Detective Shear." Despite accidentally slapping Detective Shear, the detective had been nothing but courteous and genuinely concerned about her. Tara trusted the young ponytailed but professional officer.

"You're welcome, Dr Ross. Someone will be down shortly to get you and tend to your eye."

Another woman waiting in the cell yelled, "Hey, when's someone gonna come and get me? I can't get no sleep in here. I gotta work all night."

Liz rolled her eyes. "He'll be coming for you eventually, Sugar. He always does."

Sugar swung her legs onto the bench and rolled onto her belly exposing her bare rear end. Her pale skin popped from the diamond cut outs of her vinyl fire-engine red dress and her spiky platinum hair grated against the black faux fur of her jacket. Her smudged mascara and faded red lipstick aged her beyond her years. She leered at Tara. "What are you looking at?"

Tara shook her head. There was no point in arguing with the hooker. She glimpsed at Sugar sprawled out on the cell bench making herself at home, sure that the hooker had seen the inside of a holding tank several times before.

"Hey! Tell Ray to hurry his brass ass down here and get me out."

Liz shook her head and walked away, calling to Sugar over her shoulder without giving her as much as a glance, "I'll be sure to tell him."

"Yeah, when we getting out of here?"

"Shut up, Doris," Sugar yelled.

"No. *You* shut up," Doris hollered back.

"Both of you, shut up," Liz bellowed.

As Liz walked away, Tara clung to the iron bars, leaning her forehead against them. She'd give anything to leave with the detective. Tara bit her bottom lip. She didn't belong here. Not with these two. She wanted to call someone but didn't know where to start. Her shoulders sank. *I need to get out of here!*

Sugar rolled over and farted. Tara wrinkled her nose and scooted into a corner as far away as she could get from Sugar's derriere. She stopped smack across from Doris who sat with her legs apart. Doris belched. The alcohol hit Tara in the face. She reared back, repulsed.

Sugar snorted. "You can run, sweetie, but you can't hide."

Tara refused to answer her. Instead, she strained to read the faded print on Doris's dirty tee shirt, but all she could make out was, Welcome to Cape Cod.

Doris cackled. Her belly jiggled over the constricting waistband of her navy blue spandex tights. She banged her brown work boots together flicking caked mud right onto Tara's brown suede boots.

25

"Good shot," Tara whispered.

Tossing her unkempt brown curly hair, Doris asked, "Got a cigarette?"

"No, Doris. Miss Uppity here don't got no cigarette for you. Now shut the hell up. I'm trying to get some sleep," Sugar said.

Doris insisted. "Got a cigarette?"

Tara crossed her arms. "No, I don't smoke."

Doris whined. "But I want a cigarette. Won't someone give me a cigarette?"

Sugar smacked the bench with the palm of her hand. "For God's sake, zip it Doris. You're not getting no cigarette."

Tara corrected her. "She isn't getting a cigarette."

Sugar smirked, giving her the middle finger salute. "Well la–dee–da."

"Hey ladies, keep it down in there. Doris, you know there's no smoking here," the sergeant called from his desk.

Tara pressed her palms to her ears. *Yes, please both of you shut up. My head is about to explode.*

Liz Shear stood at the doorway of Jeffrey's office. "I'm aware you're having a busy day, but I need to talk to you. Got a minute?"

"For you, always. Come in. Sit."

So far, he'd managed to keep it secret that they had dated for a month, even though it seemed so long ago now. Even Mike, his right hand man and best friend, didn't know.

It happened shortly after his divorce and Liz's transfer to the two-seven narcotics division. Though initially attracted to each other, there was no spark when they touched. She had admitted the same.

Liz sat facing his desk, her brown hair neatly combed back in a ponytail, her make-up natural. A gold detective's shield hung around her neck, resting between her breasts.

Jeffrey admired her. She was attractive, smart, and as bold as any of the guys. The best marksman in her squad, she could shoot the dick off of a gnat.

"I hear your day hasn't been that great," he said.

"Well, if freezing my ass off on a park bench, falling down concrete stairs, getting slapped and nearly shot constitutes a bad day, then yeah I'd say my day's been crap so far."

"What can I do for you?"

"I have this woman in lock up. I don't want to charge her. She's no criminal. She was just scared. Can you get her out of there and get her story? I ran a check. She's clean. She's a doctor."

Jeffrey raised his eyebrows. "A doctor?"

"Yeah. Crazy isn't it? She got caught up in the sting on Larkin, a cocaine supplier on the Upper West Side. He had a .45 ACP on him that ballistics matched to the bullet found in Bogo's head. We can get Larkin for a string of charges, but you get him for homicide."

"Mike caught the Bogo case. Get with him about Larkin. There's another supplier out there competing with Larkin. Too bad Bogo can't tell us with who he was double dipping. With Larkin out of circulation, the other supplier is going to get busy."

Liz nodded. "Hopefully we can get him before he adds to your CompStat woes."

"Definitely not going to be a quiet month. I'm going to need two aspirin and a Guinness before next month's statistics meeting."

"I feel for you." Liz stood and placed Tara's file on Jeffrey's desk, tapping it. "Thanks for doing this."

"All right. I'll go down and take care of the good doctor."

He pushed his chair back and sighed. A tall stack of papers on his desk surrendered to gravity, falling to the floor in domino fashion.

"Great," he muttered. He scooped up the folders and dumped them back on his desk.

Liz stifled a laugh as she left his office.

Jeffrey followed her out, lumbering down the hallway, grumbling. "Why can't narcotics bail out the misguided doctor? Oh, yeah," he sighed. "My precinct. My problem."

He pedaled down three flights of stairs, his mind alive with questions. By the time he had reached the holding cells, his neck veins no longer bulged, and his breathing had eased considerably.

*How'd a doctor get into this mess?*

He straightened his tie, approached the sergeant's desk, and leaned over, his long arms easily spanning the top. "Hey, Sam. I'm looking for a woman."

"Aren't we all? We have a couple of fine examples you can pick from this afternoon. You want one with panties or no panties?

He laughed. "I'd go with the panties."

"Just so happens, I have one left. Cell number two, corner pocket. Name is Tara Ross. Has quite a shiner there. Can't vouch for the panty thing."

"Thanks Sam."

They walked over to the cell together. Sam unlocked the door. Jeffrey peeked in, all the way to the far corner of the holding cell where Tara sat huddled, her left eye swollen shut.

"Tara Ross?"

She tilted her head up and looked at him, her good eye open. "Oh, thank God! A lawyer."

He smiled. "I'm not a lawyer. I'm Lieutenant Jeffrey Corrigan. I'll take you to my office, and we'll get this straightened out."

He stretched out his hand to her. Tara's fingers relaxed in his palm. Jeffrey's pulse picked up a pleasant pace. The petite doctor was hardly what he had expected. She sure gave Liz a solid smack and put up a decent fight with Larkin. Even with her bruised eye, he couldn't help but stare at that little curve of her upper lip. This was by far the best part of his day.

"Come with me," he said.

# Chapter Four

Monday, January 2, 3:30 p.m.

"*L*et me take a look at that eye," he said.

Tara pushed back into her chair, leaning her head back. She looked up at him. Her good eye met his gold belt buckle and tip of his shamrock tie. She traced the tiny green clovers up to his face. He seemed to stretch for miles.

He cupped the back of her head and whispered, "Tilt your head back further."

His breath warmed her cheeks. Her right eye focused on his hazel eyes.

"That's quite a shiner you got there."

"It doesn't hurt." She was lying. It hurt like hell.

"This is cold, and it may sting a little." He gently lowered an ice pack onto her bruised eye.

"Ow!"

He jumped back. "Did I hurt you?"

"No." She took a deep breath. "I'm just having a hell of a day."

"Yes, you are. Are you hungry?"

"I'm starved." She'd only had three spoonfuls of her chili before that cretin parked his ass uninvited at her table.

"I haven't had lunch either. I'll get us both a sandwich, and we'll talk."

While he was gone, Tara gazed around the room. Stark white plaster walls surrounded her. She stood and circled his desk. No picture of a wife or kids decorated it. Tara walked over to the wall and stared at a framed picture of Jeffrey, looking about in his twenties, outfitted in his uniform and police cap. A police academy graduation? Two older men flanked him, both with huge smiles on their faces. One looked to be his father. Tara could tell by their similar facial features. She had no idea who the other man was, but everyone in the photo appeared overjoyed. They must have been so proud of him. Tara noticed there were no women in the picture. No mother? No wife or girlfriend?

There was the sound of footsteps in the hall. She rushed back to the chair and plopped into it, wincing as the wooden frame groaned, praying he didn't catch her spying around in his office.

"All we had in the fridge were turkey sandwiches. Is that okay? I can call out for something else. Uh...it's no problem." He set a wrapped sandwich down in front of her and offered up a cup of coffee.

*What a nice guy to go through all this trouble.* With his white shirtsleeves rolled up, she stared at his muscular arms as he held out her drink. Her eyes wandered to his waist and then lower. The man could definitely fill out an everyday suit. Her insides warmed, and she hadn't even sipped that steamy cup of coffee he brought her yet.

"No. Turkey's fine. Thank you."

An attractive, full figured woman walked into his office. She glimpsed at Tara and raised her eyebrows in surprise.

"Lieutenant, here's the report on Larkin as you requested."

"Thanks Laurie."

She left his office, glancing sideways at Tara before she closed his door behind her.

Jeffrey smiled at Tara. "Laurie is the precinct administrative assistant."

"Ah, she seems...nice." *She certainly made it clear that I don't belong here.*

He winked at her. "Laurie's just not used to seeing a woman in my office."

Tara politely grinned back. *Especially not one in trouble with the law.*

He sifted through the pages. Tara tapped her toes at every crinkle. She gripped the chair handles.

"I had no idea who he was. I did slap Detective Shear, but it was an accident. I swear. I thought she was that horrible man trying to hurt me again. I am deeply sorry."

The last thing she wanted to do was go back into that cell.

Jeffrey cleared his throat. "So you had no knowledge of the cocaine in your laptop case?"

"*Cocaine!* What?"

He glanced up from the pages fanned on top of his desk. "What I'm saying is *you had no knowledge of the cocaine in your case. Right?*" He grinned. "Just nod."

"Oh yeah. Right," she said nodding.

"Well, Dr. Ross," he said pushing away from the desk. "It's clear to me that you had no connection with this drug dealer. You were, unfortunately, a victim of circumstance."

"Please, call me Tara." *Why doesn't doctor sound right?*

Jeffrey smiled. "All right. And please, call me Jeffrey."

That wouldn't be hard. For a lieutenant, he was hardly daunting, at least with her. She'd give it a try, see how that fit. Tara leaned forward in her chair. "Jeffrey then, I honestly don't know how those drugs got into my case." She paused. "Wait a minute. When we were in that cafe, he spilled his coffee. I bent down to clean off my purse. I bet that's when he planted that cocaine."

"Most likely. He must have been on to our tail and needed to get rid of his coke, at least temporarily. That's why he picked you, grabbing your laptop case figuring he'd get away with it on the train. When he realized he was cornered, he dumped the evidence. There are no charges against you Dr. Ross...Tara. I'm sorry about your laptop and your eye. Now please stay with me, and let's enjoy our lunch."

She'd enjoy nothing more. A man who'd made her feel safe for the first time today and decent food. Even the ache from her eye was beginning to wane.

Tara bit into her sandwich. A slab of turkey squeezed from the bottom and plopped into her lap.

"Oh my!" Her face warmed. *I'm such a slob! He had to have noticed that.*

Jeffrey dropped his unbitten sandwich onto the paper plate and grabbed a napkin. "Here," he said, extending it to her.

She laughed. What else could she do? Clearly, he noticed. Tara plucked the piece of turkey from her lap and dabbed at her jeans.

"I can't finish a meal without wearing at least a third of it." She smiled at him and brought her coffee cup to her lips. Tan droplets cascaded down her chin and dribbled into her cleavage, disappearing beneath the "V" of her black sweater.

Jeffrey grinned and jutted out another napkin. Catching himself just short of patting her chest, he knocked over his cup of coffee. A river of java flowed between his files.

*"Damn."* He grabbed the folders, plunked them on the floor, and blotted his desk with the remaining napkins.

Finally, a man who competed with her own clumsiness, she mused. As she helped him wipe up the coffee dribbling from the edge of his desk, their arms twisted. Heat spiraled up her cheeks. His face reddened too. They pulled their hands back to their sides.

Jeffrey cleared his throat and handed her plate back to her. "Please, finish your sandwich, and if you can wait a while, I'd like to take you home."

*Home? I'm not actually sure where home is. How am I going to explain this to him when I don't know why I'm like this? He's going to think I'm a lunatic. I'll just smile and nod. If he takes me home, maybe I'll recognize something, the house where I live. That just might do it. I don't have a choice. I can't stay here. I don't even know if that credit card in my wallet is any good.* She curled her toes in her boots. "Sure" she said, praying she'd not get the chance to embarrass herself.

"Great. I just have a few more things to finish up here before we leave."

A man yelled, "Unhand me. I want to see Lieutenant Corrigan."

Jeffrey put down his sandwich, again. "Wait here, Tara. And keep that ice pack on your eye."

He ran down the stairs, his long legs easily skipping over a few steps. "Hey," he said to the homeless man. "How's it going?" He motioned for the desk sergeant to let him through.

"Lieutenant Corrigan, I tell you, it's as cold as a witch's tit out there and the shelters are full up. The desk sergeant wouldn't let me up to see you. Can I stay here? Please help me out. I need a place tonight, and I'm hungry."

"Come upstairs with me, Charlie. I'll get you squared away."

Charlie stuck his tongue out at the desk sergeant and then scampered up the steps.

His frequent appearances at the precinct annoyed the all too busy sergeant who usually ushered the homeless man back out the street. But Jeffrey always made sure the man had something to eat and a clean set of clothes and a place to sleep when he came to the precinct.

Charlie trotted ahead of Jeffrey and ducked into his office. Jeffrey bolted in behind the homeless man, fearing the ragged man would startle Tara.

Charlie rounded Tara's chair and pleaded, "Are you gonna eat that?"

She dropped her sandwich, this time onto the paper plate balanced on her lap.

"No. No," Jeffrey admonished him. "That's Tara's sandwich. Come with me to the kitchen and I'll get you something to eat."

"Very nice to meet you, Tara," Charlie said. "I had no intention of stealing your sandwich."

"I knew you weren't going to take it. I'm sure Lieutenant Corrigan will get you one just as tasty."

"I like her!"

"Yes, me too. Now come to the kitchen with me." He winked at Tara and mouthed, "Thank you."

She mouthed back, "You're welcome."

Jeffrey and Charlie caught Detective Herb Malik in the kitchen with a cannoli stuffed in his mouth.

"What? The P.A.A. in anticrime brings me cannolis," Herb said. Pointing his chubby finger at Jeffrey he added, "And don't tell Ophelia. She's got me on this low carb diet. It's killing me. I got to have cannoli."

Jeffrey grinned and rubbed the corner of his mouth, gesturing to Herb to wipe the cakey white filling from his lips. "I won't tell your girlfriend. Do me a favor and stay with Charlie for about 20 minutes. I got the sister of the woman who was knifed to death coming to make an ID. And I got a woman in my office."

"She's a looker," Charlie interjected.

"Yes she is. And I don't want her to leave without me."

Herb wiped his mouth and waddled over to the coffee maker. He tipped the carafe over his Styrofoam cup. "It's about time. What's it been? Two years since your divorce?" he asked.

"It's not like that." Jeffrey kind of wished it was. "I have to go." He plucked the last remaining turkey sandwich from the fridge and handed it to Charlie.

"Thanks, Lieutenant Corrigan."

Jeffrey clapped him on his shoulder. A puff of dust flew from the homeless man's worn, gray tweed coat. Jeffrey shook his cold alabaster hand. "We'll get you a place to stay, Charlie. Herb give the man some hot cocoa. And give him one of those cannoli."

"My cannoli?"

"Yes. Ophelia would be proud of you."

"I guess. Here you go Charlie. Enjoy."

"Thanks."

"I wonder if they make a low carb cannoli," Herb muttered.

With a mouthful of turkey sandwich, Charlie sputtered, "Nope, they don't."

Jeffrey hustled past Laurie's desk, hurrying to meet the deceased woman's family.

"Boss," Laurie said, loud enough to get his attention. He skidded to a halt and backpedaled toward Laurie.

"Yes."

She smiled and held up his glasses. "I got your glasses fixed."

He took them from her. "Thank you. You've gone beyond the call of duty."

"You're welcome," she gushed.

He popped his head into his office. "How are you doing, Tara? Can I get you anything else?"

"No thanks. I'm good. Looks like you're real busy. You haven't even taken a bite of your sandwich."

"I'll get around to it. If you're still hungry, please help yourself to mine and to the cannoli in the kitchen. I have to take care of something. I'll be back." *Damn right, I will.* Oddly attracted to the mysterious doctor, Jeffrey couldn't wait to get back to her.

Jeffrey greeted the woman's grieving family and expressed his condolence for what was surely a gruesome death. He wanted to choke the monster that had fractured the defenseless woman's skull with his fists and then stabbed her thirty-two times.

After the deceased's sister tearfully identified the callous killer in a line up, he thanked her and gave the family his card, reassuring them that he would keep them apprised of the upcoming proceedings. He watched them leave crying, their shoulders shaking.

*One less asshole on the street, hundreds more to go.*

He zipped by Laurie's desk, stopping long enough to ask her to get Father Kiernan on the phone and then plunked down into his chair directly across from Tara. "Did you help yourself to a cannoli?"

She patted her lips with a paper napkin. "Yeah, I snuck one. I have a sweet tooth."

"So do I. One of my detectives is on a diet. We're actually doing him a favor."

Tara laughed. "We wouldn't want to let him down, would we?"

Jeffrey smiled. "Absolutely not!"

He raised the sandwich to his mouth, teeth poised to sink into it when he heard Laurie call out, "I got Father Kiernan on line two."

He dropped the sandwich on his plate and picked up the phone. "Hello Father. They're good. Yes, I'll try and make it next Sunday." He glanced at Tara, smiled, and shrugged his shoulders. "Father, I have a favor to ask you. I have a homeless man who needs shelter for tonight. I can't send him out in this weather. Terrific. I'll sleep better tonight and I'm sure he will too. Yes, I'll send your regards to Johnny and Evie. Goodbye Father Kiernan." He hung up the phone. "My sister regularly attends Mass there. My brother only goes because of his kids and because his wife makes him. Me—twice a year."

"Christmas and Easter?"

"You got it."

"How about your family?" she asked.

"Well, there's my sister, Evie, my brother, Johnny, my dad, Joe, and Frank, my dad's former police partner. We consider him family. We've all known him since we were little."

"How about your mom?"

"Died of breast cancer when I was twelve." A lump rose in his throat. He took a gulp of his coffee to shove it back down.

"I'm so sorry. I was looking at your police academy picture. No wonder she's not next to you." Tara smiled at him. "I'm sure she was there with you in spirit, proud of you."

Jeffrey rubbed his eye. "Thank you. How about your folks?"

Tara shook her head. "My parents are no longer living. Prostate cancer. Heart disease."

He set his coffee down on his desk and leaned in towards her. "Oh, so sorry."

"Thanks."

Jeffrey arched his eyebrows. He had to know. "Husband?"

"Divorced."

"Me too. Two years." He grinned. *Well, that clears the way.*

He'd quickly eat, get his day wrapped up, and then he'd take her home. Jeffrey glanced out his office window. Snowflakes swirled in circles. He'd get her home safe, and even if he got stuck in the storm on his way back then it would be worth it. He didn't think it possible, but something inside him was screaming Tara was the one. He better eat fast.

Just as he opened his mouth to bite into his sandwich, Laurie yelled out, "May Day. May Day. Captain Ray Scardino in the house."

# Chapter Five

Monday, January 2, 4:20 p.m.

*J*effrey threw down his sandwich.

Captain Ray Scardino was his immediate superior. His boss. But unlike Jeffrey, Ray Scardino had risen through the ranks with minimal street experience. Jeffrey strongly suspected he had a patron. He was a "house mouse" that excelled at test taking and the ultimate ass-kisser. He also was a disaster at crime scenes, contaminating every case he could get his grimy hands on. Jeffrey did his best to keep Captain Scardino away from the scene, while the Captain did everything he possibly could to stay in Jeffrey's face.

He leaned against the doorframe of his office, bracing himself for Scardino's untimely visit.

Ray Scardino strode past Laurie's desk. Accompanying him was Paul Rivchak, the 28 year-old, newly minted detective with barely five years experience in uniform.

Paul strutted up to Laurie's desk. The blonde, blue-eyed detective flashed a pearly smile. He extended his hand and said, "Hi, I'm Detective Rivchak."

Laurie's voice quivered, and her hands trembled. "I'm Laurie Styles, the P.A.A. Let me know if you need any help. I'm here for you…uh…to assist you."

Paul grinned. "Good to know."

"Oh, brother," Jeffrey whispered.

Laurie cleared her throat. "Lieutenant Corrigan, Captain Scardino is here with Detective Paul Rivchak."

"Yeah, I see."

Paul winked at Laurie.

"Laurie, have Detectives Price and Malik come to my office," Jeffrey called as he walked away. He returned to his desk, rubbed his temples, and shifted in his seat awaiting his captain's appearance.

Captain Ray Scardino stepped into Jeffrey's office and stood, Napoleonic, with arms crossed at his chest. He reeked of Old Spice, and his dark blue tie hung sloppily over his crinkled white shirt. Tufts of tightly curled black hair sprouted from the rim of his undershirt.

"Lieutenant Corrigan, this is Detective Paul Rivchak. I'm placing him under your command," Scardino said.

"Good to have you aboard." Jeffrey shook Paul's hand. They stood eye to eye. At 6 feet 2, they towered over Ray Scardino. The rest of his squad entered his office. "These are Detectives Mike Price and Herb Malik." They all shook hands. "And sitting quietly in the corner is my friend, Dr. Tara Ross." Tara nodded and politely smiled. He hoped one day, he'd be able to call her more than a friend.

Mike Price glanced at Tara and then back at Jeffrey. He squinted and furrowed his brows. Jeffrey shook his head at Mike, his signal for "I'll tell you later."

"Detective Rivchak, I'm going to partner you with Detective Price. He'll get you up to speed. Detective Price, show Detective Rivchak his desk and introduce him around."

"Sure thing, Lou." Lou being an informal short for lieutenant, their boss.

Scardino's eyes roamed over to Tara. Jeffrey gritted his teeth. *That slime bag.*

"And who is this beautiful lady here?" He walked over to Tara and leaned, just so, glancing into her cleavage "Oh, she has bruised eye."

Jeffrey bristled. Before he could wedge between his lewd captain and Tara, she recoiled, jutting out her hand keeping him a respectable two feet away from her face.

*Good for her!*

She gave him a firm but abrupt handshake. "Hello, Captain Scardino."

He grasped her hand but distanced himself from her. "I must be going. I need to get an informant of mine out of lock up. But she's hardly as classy as you."

"Sugar? I remember her. She asked for you by name," she said.

"How do you know Sugar?" Ray Scardino asked.

Tara grinned like Cheshire cat. "We spent a little time together earlier this afternoon."

Jeffrey interrupted, "Tara was mistakenly caught up in a sting operation. Larkin assaulted her."

"That bastard. We're all better off with him locked up," Scardino said.

His captain stood in the doorway, partially blocking Laurie's entrance. She pressed her back to the doorframe and sucked in her stomach. He lightly brushed his arm against her breast.

*All right, that's it. Get the hell out of my office! Out of my precinct!* Jeffrey wanted to pounce on his pathetic boss, force him to apologize, but instead he stepped in front of Scardino, shielding Laurie from his captain's future advances.

"Lieutenant, Father Kiernan is here to pick up Charlie. He found a space for him at a shelter."

"Great news."

"Corrigan, quit wasting our resources on the homeless. Let other people do that. Besides, they know where the shelters are. They know how to manipulate the system," Scardino huffed.

"Manipulate the system?" Jeffrey asked, trying not to raise his voice at his boss.

"Yeah. Quit jamming us up on non-priority matters. I'm sure you've got some open cases you need to be working on. And I'll be back next week for your CompStat numbers. Not looking like a good month for you."

*Screw you.* "Yes Sir. I'll have them ready by next week."

"Remember, you're the C.O. of the squad. No more of that bleeding heart bullshit. Delegate. Delegate. Delegate. Especially if you want to be up for captain. Seventeen years on the job. I shouldn't have to remind you how to be a boss."

*My seventeen to your twelve, asshole.* "Yes, point well taken, sir."

Father Kiernan was lingering at Jeffrey's door, and then finding a break in the conversation, ventured inside.

"What's up Padre?" Scardino mocked.

"Good day, Captain," Father Kiernan said.

"Well it's not a good day for those of us who work more than one day a week. What I wouldn't give to work only on Sundays." Scardino turned to Charlie and said, "For Christ's sake, get a job."

On his way out, he tripped over his shoelace and stumbled for about ten feet before catching his balance.

Tara burst out laughing.

Jeffrey joined her with his own guffaws. He snorted. "Serves him right." *This woman is too funny!*

"The Lord works in some non-mysterious ways," Father Kiernan echoed his sentiment perfectly.

# Chapter Six

## Monday, January 2, 4:45 p.m.

$\mathcal{M}$ike rapped on Jeffrey's door to the tune of *Shave and a Haircut*. Jeffrey grinned and knocked back twice on his desk — *Two bits*.

"I see our illustrious captain has left the premises. Lieutenant, can I speak to you in interview room one?" Mike asked.

"Sure thing." Jeffrey winked at Tara. "I'll be right back." He scurried down the hall after Price.

He found him, pacing in the interview room. Mike smoothed his thick, wavy brown hair and traced his fingers across his mustache. "So what's up with Alice in Wonderland? Looks like she dropped down one hell of a rabbit hole."

"Give her break, eh? She's had a traumatic day. I got her out of lock up. She's clear. Liz confirmed she's an OB/GYN in Brewster."

"A gynecologist? Now that's my dream job. Naked women all day long."

"I'm sure they don't look at it that way."

"The only naked women I see are all dead. I don't even get to see Amy naked anymore. It's a shame too since her tits are enormous now that she's pregnant."

Jeffrey gave him a disapproving look.

"Well, it's true. She's huge! Due next month."

Jeffrey sighed. Since their childhood, his best friend lacked a filter between his brain and his mouth. His Id reigned supreme over his Ego and Superego.

Mike rested his hands on his hips. "What are going to do about Dr. Tara?"

"I'm going to drive her home. And then I'm going to ask her out."

"You're a fool to drive *Dr. Who* home in this weather. It's starting to come down hard. And what do you know about her anyway?"

"It'll work out. *I hope.* "So did Liz bring you up to date about Larkin?"

"Yeah. He lawyered up. No surprise there."

He tapped Mike's arm. "Congrats again."

He was eager to get back to his office. Back to Tara. He stopped at Laurie's desk. She was gathering her coat to leave. "Laurie, I want to thank you for today."

"You're welcome Boss. I like Detective Rivchak. He'll be a great addition to the squad. Oh, and your lady friend is still waiting for you in your office. Good night."

"Yes, he will. Good night, Laurie." He still had his doubts about Paul's ability. At least Laurie's careful attention was now on Paul, and thankfully no longer on him.

He dashed into his office. "I'm sorry to keep you waiting. It's been a hectic day."

"You've had a tough day, and I don't want to add to it. I can find a hotel for the night.

"It's no problem, honest. I want to take you home. And a hotel bed is no replacement for the comfort of your own bed. It's freezing out there. Let me help you with your jacket."

He lifted her down jacket from the back of her chair. Pint sized compared to his monster of a coat, he fumbled with the sleeves. His arm shot clear through them trying to pull them right side out.

Tara giggled.

Jeffrey shook the cantankerous jacket free. "My son's in college. It's been a while since I've dealt with miniature clothes!"

"Looks like you've wrestled with it well."

He helped her slide into her jacket. "Boy, you're tiny, but uh...in a good way. Here's your purse. I'll get my coat, and then we'll be off to Brewster. I'll have you home in a little over an hour. I noted that your driver's license shows you live at 210 Pebble Road?" Jeffrey plopped her hat on her head. He overshot, partially covering her swollen eye. "Oh, I'm sorry. I hope I didn't hurt you. Let me fix that." He readjusted her hat.

Tara gently patted her eye. "Much better. Thanks"

He opened doors for her all the way out of the station house as his dad had always taught him, finally opening the passenger door to his black Mustang. Making sure her feet were tucked in and her seat belt buckled, he shut the door and proceeded to get in too. She had given him an odd look when he mentioned her driver's license. It wasn't expired, and she had no traffic violations on record. But still, there was something there, he knew it. Was she being evasive? He'd explore that later, but tonight, priority one was getting her home safe. It was 14 degrees now that the sun had set, and plops of large snowflakes showered the windshield. The nor'easter predicted was approaching rapidly.

Jeffrey pulled his car out of the precinct lot. The tires spun as the car turned the corner, his car fishtailing into the street. He jerked it back into control, holding out one hand over Tara in protective mode. His heart pounded. "Are you okay?"

She pushed back into the seat. "Yeah fine."

He drew his hand back to the steering wheel and glanced at her. *She looks pale, even with that bruised eye. Crap! I must have scared the hell out of her.*

44

A patrol car pulled up next to them, its blue and red flashing lights coloring the snowflakes pummeling the vehicle. The officer got out of his vehicle and trudged towards Jeffrey's car, his black boots sinking into the snow and his head lowered as icy flakes pelted his plastic covered cap. The officer inched up the muffler around his neck.

Jeffrey cracked his window. A gust of window blew flakes into his Mustang that landed on his lap and onto the dash.

"Good evening, Lieutenant Corrigan. If I were you, I'd get home soon, sir. They're closing down 684. No Interstate travel tonight. The Hutch is still open though."

"Thanks, officer. You better get back in your car. This blizzard is getting ugly."

The officer rubbed his leather-gloved hands together. "And it's gonna get uglier before it's all done. Drive safe."

"You, too, brother" The officer swatted at swirls of snow all the way back to his vehicle. He eased the patrol car away.

Jeffrey leaned back in his seat and strummed his fingers on the steering wheel. He looked at Tara. "Well, it looks like we're not going to make it to Brewster tonight after all, at least not in this car. We can try to find you a hotel, but with the roads closed, our choices may be limited. Your call. Although, I live in White Plains, thirty minutes from here, it will probably be an hour tonight. I live alone, and I have a spare room. You're welcome to stay at my house tonight. I know you don't know me well…"

Tara smiled "You seem pretty harmless and, I can't remember ever seeing a storm this bad in the city. Okay. I'll trust you. We'll go to your place since our *choices are limited* tonight."

Her sense of humor made her even sexier to him. But he'd be a gentleman. As much as he wanted to touch her hand again, he'd take it easy. Wait and see whether she was as intrigued by him as he was by her.

"All right. We're off then." Jeffrey started the car and headed for the parkway. "I'll crank up the heater." Jets of warm air blasted through the vents. "Warm enough?" he asked.

She smiled. "Absolutely."

He had no idea how long she had been walking around the frigid streets today, but he read in Liz's report how Tara had run, huddled with head down, to the subway stairwell, braving the whipping winds and that asshole Larkin. She deserved a warm car on a night like this. He glanced at her, bundled up in the front seat of his Mustang, petite and nearly lost in her winter jacket.

She yawned.

"Tired?"

"I'm whipped. It's been a long and bizarre day for me, not to mention your day. Boy, that captain of yours is a jerk."

Jeffrey chuckled. "Yeah, he is. But you handled him well. " He turned his attention to the snowy road. "I have to go slow, but don't worry, we'll be to my house soon. Go ahead and rest."

An hour later, he had made it off the parkway, stuttering the car down the exit ramp.

"Almost home now."

But she didn't respond. His heart lurched. Maybe her injury was more serious than he thought.

He took his eyes off the road briefly. Her lips were slightly parted. Her breathing paused at times—a purr more than a snore. He took a deep breath. *I guess she's just exhausted. After the day she had, I could understand.*

When he made a sliding turn, her head flopped against his shoulder.

"Tara. Tara. I can't shift."

She didn't budge.

He gently pushed her off his shoulder. Her head lolled past the seat back and thudded onto the passenger door window. Grabbing her jacket and nearly running into a snow bank, he yanked her upright. His heart raced. She merely snored in response. *That's all she needs—a black eye* and *a bruised head.*

Finally home, the Mustang's tires crunched over the snowy driveway. The porch light flashed on, illuminating her somnolent face. He got out of the car and eased the door shut, taking care not to jangle his keys, although he doubted that would make a difference. She was sound asleep.

Jeffrey trotted to the front door, turned the key, and opened it. It groaned in protest. He reminded himself to get some WD 40, again. He strode to his son's room. With James at college, he'd put Tara in that room.

Pushing the empty bedroom door open, he fluffed two pillows and pulled the covers back. On his way out, he turned up the thermostat making sure she'd keep warm and comfortable all night.

Returning to the car, he slowly opened the passenger door. His long arm easily reaching her seat belt buckle, he clicked it open.

She didn't stir.

He lifted her out of the car and cradled her in his arms as he carried her through the house. If he hadn't felt her chest rising and falling, he'd swear she was dead.

She sighed softly as he laid her on the bed.

Slipping her hat and jacket off and inching her boots from her tiny feet, he covered her with his son's old comforter. The full sized bed seemed too roomy for her somehow, and her brown hair poked out beneath the blue blanket.

He clicked off the light and left the door ajar. Then he shuffled into his living room and dropped, free fall, onto the tan leather sofa. He had just reached into his pants pocket to retrieve his cell, when the phone began to vibrate. It was Mike.

"You didn't make it to Brewster, did you?"

# Chapter Seven

*T*ara kicked her legs and punched her fists beneath the blue blanket. Her flailing body only complicated matters, trapping her further under the sheets. She stopped struggling and took a deep breath. Now would be a good time to remember why she was waking up in a strange bed. Tara patted her body.

"Okay, clothes still on."

She bolted straight up in bed and whipped around to see whom she had slept with. No one was there, nor any telltale dents in the pillow or bed sheets. She flopped back into the bed and flung her arm across her face.

"Ow!"

Then she remembered her bruised eye.

And then Jeffrey.

Glancing out the window, she hoped to get her bearings, but all she saw was a wall of white crystals, clinging half way up the glass pane. *Now* she recalled the snowstorm, and that she left the police station with Jeffrey. She'd decided to stay.

"This must be his house."

The buzzing of an alarm clock echoed into the hallway.

48

*Where is that coming from?*

She untangled herself from the bed sheets and tiptoed into the hall, following the buzzing sound straight to his partially open bedroom door. She tilted her head and craned her neck. Her heart fluttered guiltily, but she had to peek inside his room.

Jeffrey rolled to his side and silenced the alarm clock. He flipped off the covers and rocked out of bed. Clasping his arms above his head, he maneuvered them back between his shoulder blades, twisted at the waist, and yawned.

The wooden floor creaked as Tara backed away. His head jerked toward the door, his eyes gone wide. They stared at each other. Heat rose to her face. Jeffrey's ears turned crimson too. She had caught him in his underwear, and now she was staring at his junk, his boxers tenting his morning erection.

Tara spun on her heels, averting her gaze. "Oh, I'm so sorry. It was an accident. I certainly didn't mean to walk in on you. Um...I heard the alarm go off."

Pulling a sheet to his waist, he stammered, "Uh, n...no problem. The kitchen is at the end of the hallway to your right. I'll...I'll be there in a minute."

"Sure. Uh, take your time," she said, struggling to keep her eyes off him. She grinned. *Man, I slept in the wrong bed.*

Tara pattered through the hallway toward the kitchen, trying to contain her voyeuristic smile. She ran her fingers along the eggshell white walls, feeling little skips, little holes, where pictures used to hang.

*Were they from framed wedding photos and family portraits? Why did he take them down?*

The kitchen was small but tidy. No dishes were in the sink, and the white and gold-flecked countertops were eerily shiny for a single man's abode. The cabinets were honey oak, but everything else was bone white, too bland for her taste. His kitchen appeared to be recently renovated, but barely used.

Then she spotted the bulging bag under the lid of his trashcan. She glanced around then lifted it. Folded cardboard pizza boxes were crammed against the sides, empty soda, and beer bottles piled in between them.

*That explains his immaculate kitchen. The man lives by takeout.*

She replaced the lid and then sat at the kitchen table, waiting for him.

Jeffrey padded into the kitchen shortly after. His bare feet thumped across the tiled floor. Dressed in faded jeans and a gray cotton tee shirt, he sported an unshaven, bristly face.

"Did you sleep okay?" he asked. "The room was chilly so I turned up the heat. Was it warm enough?"

"Just right." Her brain may be on break, but her eyes were working overtime. *Hot damn!* His jeans hung loose on his manly, square hips with just enough slack in the back to acknowledge a firm butt beneath. His gray tee shirt emphasized his full chest, muscular arms, and solid abs. And those were the longest legs she had ever seen on a man.

She recalled running in Central Park when she lived on the Upper Westside of Manhattan. Tara couldn't help but notice Jeffrey had that runner type body. *When was the last time I ran?*

"Do you run?" she asked.

"Um, yes, I do. Whenever I get the chance. You should come with me sometime. I would enjoy the company."

"It's a date," she said, curious to see whether she was still in shape.

"Okay then. I'm going to keep you to that, once the snow stops and melts off. By the looks of it, that could be next year!" He grinned from ear to ear. "Would you like breakfast, Tara?"

"Yes," she nodded.

"How about scrambled eggs with a little hot sauce?"

Tara propped her elbow on the table and pressed her chin into her palm. "Scrambled with a little heat would be great."

Looking straight at her and smiling, he said, "A little heat is good."

He reached into the cupboard and pulled out a frying pan, placing it on the burner. Tara eyed Jeffrey's behind as leaned into the open fridge. He must have retrieved half a dozen eggs in that huge palm of his. Her mind wandered to what else was huge, recalling his morning salute with a big smile. Cracking a few eggs into the frying pan, he whistled as he stirred them around, adding a smattering of hot sauce. She stared at his hips, shifting side to side, as shook the pan. The eggs weren't the only things sizzling.

Jeffrey switched off the burner and turned to face her. "Get it while it's hot!"

Tara reached beneath the table and steadied her knees with her palms. The kitchen was definitely getting hotter. "Wow. That looks delicious." She glanced at his trashcan. "I had no idea you could cook."

He grinned. "Only on special occasions."

Her knees quit trembling but now her stomach fluttered. Was she a special occasion? With Jeffrey going all out for breakfast, he certainly made her feel that way.

Jeffrey scooped the eggs onto two plates and brought them to the table, placing one in front of her. He loaded bread into the toaster, pressed the coffeemaker onto brew, and returned to the fridge, pulling out a carton of orange juice, butter, and jam. The toaster ejected the bread and the coffee pot beeped. "Toast's up." Yanking the two hot slices from the toaster, he tossed them onto the plates and then sat down at the table, directly across from her. He paused to catch his breath.

Tara arched her eyebrows. "I'm impressed. I feel like I'm the guest of honor. I could get used to this."

Jeffrey smiled, picked up a forkful of eggs, and paused. "Your eye looks better today. The swelling has gone down."

She raised her hand and covered her eye, "I must be quite a sight."

He took her hand away from her face and gently squeezed it. "You look fine. Eat your breakfast before it gets cold."

*This guy's a keeper.* She dug in and lifted a forkful of scrambled egg, which promptly fell off her fork and landed on her sweater. Smack on her right breast.

He laughed softly. "Good catch."

It then slid off her breast and dropped onto her lap. *Oh God, not again.*

He teased, "Ah, almost. Bounced right off the rim."

"I warned you that I have an eating disorder."

They laughed and then wolfed down their food, just as cops and doctors do.

When they were done, Jeffrey cleared the table and then sat back down. "I have to go to the station house for a few hours. My brother, Johnny, has a four-wheel drive SUV. He's picking me up this morning. He called me earlier. According to the news, the roads to Brewster are still closed. I'm sorry, Tara. Whenever the roads are passable, I'll take you home. I promise."

Tara fidgeted in her chair. Her mouth had gone dry, and she licked her lips. She had to confess. "Jeffrey, you don't understand. I haven't been entirely honest with you. I know that my license has a Brewster address, but...I don't remember anything about the place. I don't know what's happened. I wouldn't recognize my own home."

"What do you mean you don't remember anything? Since when?"

"Bits and pieces, but everything since I was in Manhattan, yesterday." Tara exhaled. "Since Larkin... I don't know what's going on."

Jeffrey reached over and ran his fingers through her hair, pressing in gentle circles around her scalp. "Hmmm, I don't feel any bumps." His lips tightened. "I should have taken you to an emergency room."

"What for? I swear I didn't hit my head, and my black eye is superficial. I recall standing in Verdi Square, trying to figure out why I came to the Upper West Side instead of Brooklyn. Where I was headed in Brooklyn? *That* I don't know."

He placed his hand over hers, blanketing it. "That explains why you've been a bit vague, I suppose."

His hand was warm and his hazel eyes soothing.

"I'm scared, Jeffrey."

"Well you're safe here, and everything will be okay. I know someone at the station house who can help you—Dr. Leo Kane. His specialty is post-traumatic stress disorders. I'll arrange a meeting with him. And I honestly think we should get you physically checked out. I'll ask Leo about that too."

Jeffrey stroked her hand. His extra reassurance slowed her pulse. Giving her hand another pat, he pushed back from the kitchen table and stood.

"I'm going to take a shower and head into the city. I have cases to review, and I have a new detective to keep my eye on. Give me fifteen minutes to get ready. Meanwhile, go through your purse. See if you have anything that I can track for you today, receipts, etc. Is there anyone you want to call?"

"No. My ex husband took my daughter, Abbie, to visit his parents in Greece. They have a house on a remote island. Only local phone service and no internet."

"I have son, James. He's a freshman at Columbia. Stays in the dorm."

Tara rubbed the back of her neck. "I hope he doesn't mind I steal his room. What if he comes home?"

"Nah." Jeffrey shrugged. "Even when he comes home, he's not truly home. But don't worry. He was just here over the holidays."

Her palms moistened. She narrowed her eye. "Holidays...?" *Why couldn't she remember which one?* She waited a few seconds for him to respond, but then blurted triumphantly, "Christmas!"

"Yeah. James left New Years Day."

Tara stared at the kitchen table. A memory tugged at her mind.

*"I'm so sorry you had such an awful night."* He kissed me. *"Happy New Year."*

A hand rested on her shoulder.

"Are you all right?" Jeffrey asked.

Tara blinked and gave a quick shake of her head. "Y...yes, I'm fine. And thank you for everything, Jeffrey. A place to stay and a fabulous breakfast."

"No problem. I want to help you. Boy, I guess it's a good thing I couldn't drop you off in Brewster last night."

Tara swallowed hard past the lump rising in the back of her throat. "Do you think I'm a freak?"

He shook his head. "No. We'll solve this. It's what I do best."

Tara heard the water running in the bathroom followed by the whoosh of the showerhead. Picturing him naked in the shower distracted her from her mission to solve her memory dilemma. She focused back on emptying her purse. Tara looked at her driver's license. Yes, apparently she lived at 210 Pebble Road in Brewster, New York. She was also a safe driver and an organ donor. In her wallet, she discovered the $15 remaining after spending money on a lunch she hadn't finished at La Vita Café—thanks to Larkin—a Visa card, five punches on a ten trip Metro North ticket, and a Metro Card. In a smaller compartment, she discovered a Chapstick and an iPhone. A dead iPhone. No charger! *Damn it!*

Jeffrey returned to the kitchen. His face freshly shaven; he wore a light blue shirt, a navy pinstripe tie, and navy trousers. Dressed up. Dressed down. Didn't matter. She couldn't fathom why he was alone looking the way he did.

He leaned over her shoulder. They were cheek to cheek. Tara inhaled. Her heart skipped. He smelled shower clean. Tara couldn't help but move in closer, and Jeffrey made no effort to pull away from her. They both paused.

Jeffrey cleared his throat. "So, what was in your purse?"

She shoved the cards and iPhone across the kitchen table. "One credit card, a Metro Card, a Metro North ticket, and one very dead cell phone."

"Since you're not a suspect of any crime, I can't legally run your credit or cell phone records. I can reach out to some guys in transit, and we may be able to check your Metro Card for the stations and times where you last used it. Unfortunately, I haven't been able to find my iPhone charger for weeks. I use the one at the station. I'll bring it home and then you can check your contacts."

He slid on his glasses and glanced at the Metro North ticket. "We know you got on the train at Brewster station. Hang tight. I'll do what I can today. I'll call you later. Take it easy today. Rest. When I get home, we'll shape up a plan. Okay?"

"Okay," she said, but all she could think was that she was damn lucky to have landed in his precinct.

"In the meantime, stay here, as my guest. There's plenty of room. I'll write down my office extension at the station house and my cell number. You can call me anytime. I'll show you where some bath towels are, and if you need to do laundry, the washer and dryer are downstairs in the basement. Make sure you leave the door to the basement ajar. It doesn't lock if it closes, but it shuts pretty tightly. Help yourself to whatever you like in the fridge or pantry. My laptop is in my study. It's actually the 'everything room' and a mess. Cleaning that room has been on my project list forever. Just haven't gotten around to it yet."

A horn beeped in the driveway.

"That's my brother. I gotta go."

He smiled and touched her cheek. "I'll see you later."

Her skin tingled beneath his hand. "Bye," she said, softly. She missed him already.

She heard the crunch of tires over snow and then headed into the living room. Kneeling on his sofa, Tara peered between the beige drapes of the large window, watching Jeffrey get into the waiting black SUV. She squinted but couldn't make out his brother's face. Then the vehicle backed up and disappeared behind the snow banks.

Jeffrey was gone. Now she could do some detective work of her own.

# Chapter Eight

Tuesday, January 3, 8:30 a.m.

*S*he reached between the leather cushions of his couch and retrieved a TV remote and a pair of stiff, white sport socks. "Gross!"

Then she discovered his sweatshirt and running pants, strategically stuffed behind a throw pillow. Tara chuckled at his "man cleaning".

She gathered up his clothes, and picked up an empty candy wrapper crumpled on top of a December issue of Runner's Magazine, strewn across the coffee table. As she stepped forward, a wooden plank beneath her foot creaked, the sound echoing in the stillness of the house. Her palms glistened with sweat and her skin tingled. An ugly shiver crept up her spine. She jumped, nearly dropping the bundle of clothes. *What a scaredy-cat.*

"It's just the floor, silly … just the floor."

She bunched up the clothes and headed to the basement. Hopefully, the egg on her sweater and jeans would wash out. The egg on her face was a different matter altogether. At least he laughed with her.

She twisted the knob of the basement door. It squeaked open. Tara stared at the wooden stairs that pitched into a dark abyss. She hated basements. Cold. Dank. Anyone could be lurking there.

"Oh, get a grip, Tara. Turn on the frickin' light and go."

She patted the wall, blindly feeling for a light switch.

"Got it."

She plunked down the stairs, step-by-step. The washer and dryer stood under a small window, next to the boiler.

Cold air stung her nose. She shivered in the frigid basement. Following the chilly draft, she found the culprit–a window, cracked open high above the dryer, with its awning loosened, and the frame poking outside. Snow had burrowed in through the crack.

She set the clothes on top of the washer and climbed onto the dryer. The frozen powder nipped at her fingers as she shoved it from the sill and bolted the window closed.

After sliding off the dryer, Tara tossed the clothes into the washer. She smacked her palm to her forehead. She was wearing the clothes she needed to launder.

She stripped. Dumping her clothes into the machine, Tara poured detergent into the washer and pulled the cycle knob. She shivered as she waited for the machine to chug into action and then bounded up the stairs, naked, her hands folded across her bare breasts.

Tara leaned into the basement door.

Nothing.

She jiggled the doorknob "Oh crap. The door closed."

He'd warned her to keep it ajar.

*Don't panic. You're only trapped, naked, in a man's basement.*

She shoved and shoved against the door, but it was too formidable of an opponent for her.

*Okay one more time.*

Blam.

The balls of her hands vibrated in pain as the door gave way.

She slammed the cantankerous door shut and ran down the hallway, skidding to a stop at the bathroom door, waiting for her heart to find its natural rhythm.

*I'm already naked. And a shower would feel good.*

57

Tara scurried into the bathroom on the balls of her feet. Although she was home alone, she closed the door out of habit.

Turning on the shower, she stepped into the tub. The hot water drenched her hair and her body went limp under the spray. She moved closer to the showerhead. The water rolled over her shoulders, massaging them into submission. Prancing in her bare feet, she let the hot water tunnel under her feet, to warm her soles. An hour had passed since Jeffrey had taken his shower, but Tara could smell him, breathing in his lingering scent.

She shut off the water and wrapped herself up in a thick towel. Tara drew a deep breath, bracing herself before descending those stairs to the basement, again. This time she wouldn't be outsmarted. She left the door cracked open, placing a rolled kitchen towel between the weighty door and its frame.

The cold concrete floor bit at her bare feet. She flung the clothes from the washer to the dryer, started it and then bolted up the stairs, and slammed the door, then stood there, panting.

*What the hell am I running from?*

While the clothes dried, Tara searched for something to wear. She crept into Jeffrey's bedroom. He wouldn't even have to know, and he probably wouldn't care, she thought.

His bed was unmade. Covers pulled back. His pillow indented where he had rested his head. She walked over to his dresser and opened the top drawer, taking out a pair of white sport socks. Then she rifled through his underwear until she felt something hard and bulky beneath his briefs. She pulled the object free.

"A gun!" Tara picked it up and palmed it. She pointed it toward the mirror, holding the revolver in both hands and spreading her feet as she'd seen on every cop TV show. Tara grinned at her reflection. She narrowed her gaze trying to look tough, parodying how Detective Shear or Jeffrey would look.

"Gotcha Larkin!"

Tara lowered the gun. *I better put this back and hope Jeffrey doesn't notice I've messed with his gun.* She quickly buried it under a pair of Calvin Kleins.

Tara then picked out a pair of blue pinstriped boxers and shoved the drawer closed.

The next drawer down, she found a plain white tee shirt. Now she had a complete ensemble.

Tara donned the socks, boxers, and tee shirt. Her feet flopped around in the socks and the tee shirt drooped to her knees. The boxers fell straight to the floor.

Holding up the baggy underwear with both hands, Tara high stepped to the kitchen, careful to not trip over his floppy oversized socks. She shuffled around until she found a safety pin in a drawer and secured the waistband.

*Clap-Clap. Clap-Clap,* coming from the basement.

"Oh God, not that basement window again."

She twisted the doorknob but stopped, tilted her head and listened. Footsteps crunched in the snow. Someone was walking around the house. She ducked into the closest room, the bathroom, and shut the door, wincing as it clicked closed.

The wooden floorboards creaked. The thick black edges of men's shoes paced along the bottom crack of the door. She held her breath. The shadow disappeared.

The phone rang. No one picked it up. No voices.

It seemed like an eternity, but the phone stopped ringing. Tara exhaled. She paced in the bathroom, hesitant to venture out. She put her ear to the door. All was quiet. She couldn't spend the whole afternoon secluded in his bathroom. Tara grabbed the doorknob only to hear a car pull up and the slam of a car door. The front door groaned. Footsteps thudded down the hallway, growing louder as they approached the bathroom door.

*He's back.*

Tara jerked her hand from the knob, curled her fingers into tight fists, and gritted her teeth. *I should have run into his bedroom and grabbed that gun. Too late now.*

She searched for a weapon and settled on the first thing she saw of substance. Tara snatched the toilet plunger. Then she waited, braced for the attack, her pulse pumping.

The glass beveled knob rotated and the bathroom door creaked open.

She waited until she saw just enough of the man and then swung the plunger. It smacked her attacker squarely at his waist.

Jeffrey jumped back. "Hey! What the hell..."

Tara lowered the plunger. "Oh my God. I'm sorry, Jeffrey. I thought you were him."

Jeffrey wrinkled his forehead and raised his palms. "Who?"

"The guy who broke in." Tara narrowed her eyes. "Maybe it was Larkin."

He shook his head. "No, Tara. Larkin is in lockup. But someone was in my house? Put that plunger down and stay here."

Tara knitted her eyebrows but complied. She'd run and get the gun from his dresser drawer, but then she'd have to admit she'd discovered it. It was bad enough that she nearly took him out with a plunger.

"Jeffrey placed his hand over his 9 mm Glock holstered at his side. He had told Tara she'd be safe in his home. Whoever was lurking around, he'd find him. He slunk down the hall. Nothing was missing. No signs of forced entry. Then he found the note in the kitchen. Jeffrey chuckled as he read it, especially at the comment about fixing the basement window. He tacked the note to the refrigerator and returned to the bathroom. With a big grin on his face, he leaned against the doorframe.

"Tara, it's okay. The intruder was my dad. He stopped by to pick up his heating pad. He must have left it here over the holidays. My dad has a key to get in. He didn't know you here. And you didn't know who he was. I called, but you didn't answer."

Tara folded her hands across her chest. "You could have warned me."

Jeffrey dug his hands into his hips. "I *would* have, but I didn't know my dad was coming over. He didn't call me." *He smiled and crooked his at her. "Come here."*

His tee shirt covered her hips, and his boxers were crumpled around her ankles. His socks flopped around her feet like diving flippers. Tara shuffled toward him. "I was doing laundry, and I needed something to wear in the meantime. I hope you don't mind I snuck into your dresser."

"Not at all," he said. He laughed. "You look better in them than I do."

Jeffrey hugged her close. He had come in from the winter wind, and she was so warm. His mind hummed, and his heart pounded as her tiny body purred in his embrace.

And then it happened. His hands dropped to her behind.

He jerked them away, tucking them back to his side and took a step back, his face hot. "I'm sorry. I, uh, didn't mean to…"

"It's all right. Honestly, I'm not offended."

He grinned. "And Tara, if anyone other than my family or I bust in, next time, use the plunger's wooden end. Smack your attacker between his legs. Right in the balls. When he's bent over in agony, knock him upside the head. Then run like hell and get out."

Tara nodded. "I'll remember that."

Jeffrey moved her hand away. "Your clothes are probably dry by now. I'll go downstairs and get them." He left the bathroom, jogged down the hall, and then descended into the basement. He called up, "How about I order pizza?"

"Pizza would be great. And thanks for getting the clothes. Your basement freaks me out."

"It *is* rather uninviting. One of these days, I'm going to build it out. Make it livable. And fix the window." His words climbed the stairs with him.

He brought the laundry basket, full of clean clothes, up from the basement. "Thanks for doing my laundry too. You didn't have to."

"It was no problem. It didn't make sense to run a load with just my stuff. I only have the one outfit."

Jeffrey smiled and bunched up the boxer's at her waist, securing them with the safety pin that had sprung open and was now dangling from the waistband. He leaned back and nodded. "Perfect."

The doorbell rang, and soon, Jeffrey returned to the kitchen carrying a steaming cardboard box. They sat in his warm white kitchen, slurping their slices of gooey cheese pizza. Tomato sauce dribbled down her chin and dripped onto her borrowed white tee shirt.

Tara grabbed a napkin and dabbed at the spilt sauce cascading between her breasts.

He winked. "Now that's a darn shame!"

She gazed downward. "I'm sorry about the stain."

"Don't worry about it. I have two-dozen white tee shirts, at least. I'm good." He pushed back his chair. "I'll be right back." He retrieved a tee shirt from James's room and brought it back to her. "Try this one on. I think James last wore this when he was twelve. It might fit you better."

Tara took the shirt and trotted back into James's room. She returned wearing a clean shirt. She kept Jeffrey's boxers on and pulled the floppy socks up, the heels poking out from the back of her calves.

His pulse climbed. *Only she could look so damn sexy in an outfit like that.*

They devoured the rest of the pizza without further incident and then retired to his living room, where they sat on the sofa a respectful distance apart.

"Hey! There's the remote. I've been looking for that," he said.

She smiled. "It was under the cushions. Along with your mildewed socks. And I found your sweatshirt and running pants stashed behind a pillow."

"Excellent detective work. You got me. Guilty as charged."

Cheryl had constantly harassed him about his messy habits. After the divorce, he moved away from the city and her. Best thing he ever did. Lived as he pleased.

But now, with his beautiful and mysterious houseguest sharing his quarters, he planned on reforming. Unlike Cheryl, he didn't mind Tara ribbing him about his wayward housekeeping, and she, in turn, took it in stride when he teased her about her wayward eating.

*God, she's fun to be around. I've got to pray for more snow.*

Tara yawned. "I'm exhausted. I don't think I'm going to make it past ten o'clock. Goodnight Jeffrey."

"See you in the morning." Jeffrey could only hope he'd see her every morning. He was falling that fast.

She stood and stretched, then headed to James's room.

"Sleep well."

He watched her shuffle down the hall in his oversized socks and underwear. Even in baggy clothes and with a bruised eye, she had that sexy, "pixie" thing going on. James's bedroom door closed behind her.

Lonely without her company, Jeffrey retired to his bedroom. He stripped down to his maroon and black plaid boxers, set the alarm, and dodged under the covers. Punching his pillow with his fist, he tossed beneath the sheets. For the first time in two years, he felt the emptiness of his bed. Tara lingered in his thoughts. As he dozed he dreamed of her next to him. He reached out to caress her…

"Suction! Suction! Damn it! I can't see the bleeder!" she screamed.

Jeffrey bolted up in bed and flung off his covers. Shit!"

He burst through James's bedroom door and found Tara, wide-eyed and clinging to the sheets at the edge of the bed.

# Chapter Nine

Wednesday, January 4, 3:00 a.m.

"Tara. Tara. Wake up. It's only a dream. You're okay."

She flailed her arms. Her eyes strained to open. Jeffrey sat at the edge of the bed, holding her firmly and rocking her.

"It's all right. It's all right," he whispered.

She sank into his embrace and rested her head against his warm skin. His heart pounded in her ear. It took a full minute for her pulse to slow in tandem with his declining heart rate.

He wrapped her in a blanket and carried her to his bed. Cocooned and safe, he brushed her bangs from her damp forehead.

"What happened to you, Tara?" he asked.

The alarm buzzed.

She murmured, "What?"

Jeffrey flung his arm toward the nightstand and banged the blaring clock. His chest bare, he bunched his blanket at his waist.

Tara glanced beneath her sheets, to see what she was, or wasn't, wearing. She sighed. *Still in his underwear.* She clutched her blanket to her breasts.

"Nothing happened," Jeffrey said. "You had a terrible dream and nearly fell out of bed. I was worried you might hit your head so I wrapped you up and brought you in here."

"Oh." She wasn't sure whether she was relieved or disappointed. "I'm sorry I frightened you."

"You were screaming something about suctioning. A bleeder? I think that's what you were yelling. Do you remember any of that, Tara?"

Tara shook her head. "No."

But she did remember. *She was in an operating room holding a surgical needle holder loaded with chromic suture. The woman was bleeding. She couldn't stop it.* Tara shuddered. She just wanted to forget the whole nightmare.

"Do you feel better now?" he asked.

She clutched the blanket to her chest, her heart still thumping. "Yes, thank you."

"Well, as long as you're okay." He levered himself into a sitting position. "I have to get going. I have an important meeting to go to this morning, so I won't be at the precinct until this afternoon. Call my cell if there's an emergency."

Tara looked away out of courtesy as he swung out of bed, avoiding embarrassing him like last time, but she did manage to glimpse at his backside. He *was* wearing something below the waist. Boxers. Nice boxers.

"I'll write the number on the back of my card and leave it on the kitchen counter."

"I'll be fine. Don't worry about me. I'll try not to bother you."

"I didn't mean it that way. Trust me, you're no bother. I like having you here."

Warmth snaked from the tips of her toes to her scalp. Her heartbeat eased from a thump to a flutter. The kind of flutter you get with that first drop while seated in the front car on a rollercoaster.

"All right," she said. "I like being here."

After a few minutes, Jeffrey returned to her bedroom, looking crisp and official in a pressed white shirt and dark trousers. His suit jacket accentuated his broad shoulders and his detective badge gleamed on his lapel.

Tara pushed up in his bed, pulling the blanket with her. "Wow! You look great."

"CompStat meeting today at One Police Plaza. I get the pleasure of bosses and brass grilling me about my precinct stats. Up there defending my actions in front of the "mighty" and my peers. It's not been the best month, and it's my week to be scrutinized."

Tara nodded. "I can relate. During my training, we had hospital rounds that would tighten any sphincter. The attending physicians would interrogate us, spouting out a barrage of questions tailored to unnerve us, mercilessly stumping us in front of nurses, med students, and other resident physicians. And, as though that wasn't bad enough, we had morbidity and mortality grand rounds that would practically assure a slow and painful death to the presenter. Drug reps would bring coffee and doughnuts. We used to call it "Death and Doughnuts." Tara shook her head in disbelief. *Whoa! How did I remember that? That happened years ago.*

He sat at the edge of the bed and squeezed her hand. "Sounds awful. But, hey, you just remembered something from your past. That's progress." He cleared his throat. "By the way, I need you to come down to the station house this afternoon to ID Larkin. We're holding him on several serious charges, including homicide. I've arranged for my dad to come pick you up at two this afternoon. He drives a black sedan. And he would like to meet you *properly*. He feels terrible about the other day. You'll like him. And don't worry. Larkin won't be able to see you. I'll be there along with the assistant district attorney. Afterward, I'll take you out to dinner later. Do you like Greek food?"

She grinned. "I do."

"Great. Well, help yourself to breakfast. I gotta run. See you later." He hesitated a few seconds but then kissed her on her forehead. "Goodbye."

She wasn't sure which one of them was crazier. Theirs was the weirdest chance encounter. But she wasn't going to fight it, and he wasn't resisting their growing attraction either.

Once he was gone, Tara slid out from the warm blanket and shivered. Hurrying into the bathroom, she showered, not dawdling under the water. She stepped out of the tub and dried off, wrapped the towel over her breasts and tiptoed over to the sink.

Tara looked into the mirror at her plain face and bruised eye that had morphed into an ugly rainbow of brown and yellow. Maybe she could pop into Duane Reade Drug Store on the way to dinner and get some make-up to hide it. Nothing she could do about it now. At least he had a blow dryer. She fingered her hair dry, and pattered in her bare feet into her room. She smiled. He'd waited until she'd gotten up and then laid out her clothes on the bed; her bra and panties tucked under her jeans and sweater.

She dressed and ventured into his study. Flipping through a stack of papers on Jeffrey's desk, she pulled out his iPhone charger, the one for which he'd been searching for months, and pumped her fist in victory. *Yes!* Still giddy from his kiss, she plugged in her iPhone and scrolled through her contacts. *Marielle! Of course! I remember! I remember! My best friend! You're on a roll!*

Tara tapped Marielle's number. She answered on the second ring.

"Oh my God, Tara I can't believe it. I was so worried. Where are you?"

Tara closed her eyes and sighed. Her heartbeat climbed. "Marielle, I'm so happy to reach you, too. Listen. I have to tell you something. Ready?"

"Yeah, sweetie. What's wrong?"

She'd have to blurt it out. There was no way around it

"Okay, long story short," Tara began, "I completely forgot about our plans, but not because I didn't care. I ran into some... difficulty." Tara paused and swallowed hard. "Marielle, I can't remember some things. I ended up on the Upper Westside of Manhattan, met up with a drug dealer, got assaulted, then I hit a cop, and landed briefly in jail with a hooker and a crazy woman." She was talking too fast, and probably sounded like a lunatic too, but she forged on. "But on the bright side, Lieutenant  Corrigan bailed me out. Because of the snowstorm, I'm stranded at his house in White Plains."

Silence.

"Marielle, are you there?"

Marielle's breathing crackled through the phone. "Did you hit your head, Tara?"

"No, I just have a black eye."

"You're not making complete sense here, Sweetie."

"I know it sounds crazy, and I'm frustrated, too. Some things are coming back. But there are these gaps."

"I can't even imagine how you must feel. Take a deep breath. This isn't something we should discuss over the phone. I need to see you."

"I'll be at the 27th Precinct around two thirty this afternoon."

Pause. "I'm coming to get you. I'll be there at three. And where would I find Detective Corrigan?" Marielle asked.

"His office is on the third floor, homicide division."

# Chapter Ten

Wednesday, January 4, 8:30 a.m.

"Good morning, Lieutenant. I put a cup of coffee and a bagel on your desk. Also, Detectives Price and Malik would like to speak to you," Laurie informed him.

"Thanks. Send them in." He sipped his coffee, bit into the bagel, and crooked his finger at Mike, who now peered into his office.

"Where's Herb?" Jeffrey asked with his mouth full of bagel.

"Ah come on. You can't see Malik behind me? I may have put on a few pounds, but there's no way I'm bigger than Herb," Mike teased.

Mike stepped to the side, revealing. Herb, whose cheeks were puffed out from the glazed doughnut he had stuffed into his mouth.

"What's up guys? I need to leave for One PP soon," Jeffrey said.

They pulled up their chairs across from Jeffrey's desk and sat. Mike crossed his legs, resting his hand on his ankle. He grinned. "That's precisely why we're here—to save your ass," Mike said.

"Save my ass? And how are you going to do that?"

"I'm so glad you asked Lou. I'll let Herb make your day first."

Herb swallowed down his doughnut. "Thanks to your approval for overtime, I have the coffee shop killer on the way to central booking. Got a decent look at him from their surveillance tapes. I caught him in a bodega on Amsterdam and 86th next door to his apartment building. I brought him in and showed him the tapes. Got a signed confession." He leaned back in his chair proudly. "And here's the best part, I recovered a .22, stashed in a dumpster, three blocks north of the coffee shop. The ME found .22 caliber bullets in both vics. Ballistics confirms weapon match. Apparently, he owed Larkin a grand, and didn't want to get capped like Bogo, so he hit Starbright's and shot the kids to work off the debt." Herb dropped his report on Jeffrey's desk.

"Nice work!"

"And here's *my* news," Mike said. "You're going to like this. I have an informant who says that Larkin boasted about gunning down Bogo, as an example to others who are past due on their payments. Here's my report. Now go kick some CompStat ass."

Jeffrey waved Herb's report in victory. "Great work. Nabbing the perp within 24 hours of a high profile case is just what we needed. You've made my day, Herb. I'm going to call for a press conference this afternoon. I want you there to take the credit."

"Hey! What am I? Invisible?" Mike blustered.

"Detective Price, stellar work as usual." He clapped Mike on the back. "I can always count on you."

"Yeah, I know. Now, get going, Lou. And we'll have Larkin available for the line up this afternoon. Tara *is* coming?"

"Dad's bringing her here around 2:30. He'll drop her off, and then take Frank to his doctor's appointment at Sloan."

"I love when your dad and Frank come by. They have the greatest stories about how they worked their cases back in the day. I want to be just like them when I grow up," Mike said with a smile and a triumphant swing of his fist.

"I hear they still carry their .38's?" Herb said.

Jeffrey grinned. "They sure do. See you guys later."

Jeffrey whistled as he drove away from One Police Plaza. The CompStat meeting was a success. His presentation was smooth and succinct and clinching the Starbright's case was a real coup. The chief of D's had even congratulated him and wished him luck on his upcoming captain's exam. He couldn't wait to tell Tara about the meeting.

*Ah, shit. I have to call Leo.* He voice dialed Laurie's extension "Hey Laurie. Can you please call Dr. Kane and see if he can meet me in my office at fifteen-hundred."

"What shall I tell him this is in reference to?"

"Tell him that I need to speak to him about memory problems."

"Ah ha, okay. I'll tell him," Laurie said.

"I'm on my way back now."

Not more than a handful of minutes later, he parked his Mustang in front of the station house. The snow was melting, and his black loafers sank into brown slush. The wetness seeped into his socks, but he didn't care. He bounded up the stairs—two and three at a time—to the third floor.

Tapping Laurie's desk, he said, "I'm back. Any messages?"

"Yes, Boss. Dr. Kane can meet you at 3 p.m. as requested. You have a press conference about the Starbrights case at 1:15. Larkin will be in lineup at 2:30. Your father called. He said the roads are clear, and he should have Dr. Ross here by 2:30."

Detective Rivchak sauntered over to Laurie's desk. "Lieutenant, I'm told congrats are in order. I heard Detective Malik got lucky."

*Does the man work?* Scardino had surely saddled him with one conceited prick.

"That wasn't luck, Rivchak. That was skill and hard work. Why don't you go talk to Detective Malik about it? Congratulate him. Pick his brain about the case, and some of the others that he's solved. He's a good man to look up to."

"Sure. I'll do that," Paul said sarcastically and wandered away.

Jeffrey let his irritability with Paul slide away. He had to hurry if he wanted to make the press conference. He dropped his briefcase on his desk and sprinted over to narcotics. Hopefully Liz hadn't left for lunch. Now it was his turn to ask for a favor.

He rounded the corner and burst into her office, leaning over her desk and said, "Liz, I need your help."

# Chapter Eleven

Wednesday, January 4, Noon

*L*iz looked Jeffrey straight in his eyes. "Sure. I'm having a pretty good day myself. No one's shot me or thrown me down a stairwell ... yet. So, what can I do for you?"

"I'm going to Loehmann's during lunch to buy Tara—Dr. Ross—some clothes. I haven't been able to get her back to her house yet. You know, female things. I don't know what to get. What sizes? What styles? I never shopped for Cheryl. I have no experience with women's clothes. What size bra do you wear?"

"Excuse *me*?"

Jeffrey's cheeks warmed. "I didn't mean it that way, Liz. I'm not interested in your breasts."

Liz chuckled. "No. No. You never were."

"Liz, please? We're square, right?"

She nodded and smiled. "Yeah, we are. Okay, I wear a 34 B."

He wrote 34 B on his note pad.

"Tara's a little fuller so I'd say 34C?" she guessed.

Jeffrey wrinkled his forehead, scratched out B, and then wrote C. He glanced back up at Liz. "How about panties?"

She waved her hands. "I gotta stop at bras, Jeffrey. I don't feel comfortable discussing my panties with you."

"Size, Liz. What *size*?"

"Go with small or medium. It all depends on her style and her personal preferences. Call her up and ask her. Haven't you looked inside her bra and panties yet?" She winked at him.

"No. She did laundry the other day, and I did lay out her clean clothes on the bed."

"Woo hoo. In the bedroom already! Hard to see the labels when her underwear's on the floor."

"Get your mind out of the gutter. She sleeps in James's room. Well except," he paused and cocked his head. Liz's eyes went wide. "Except last night. Anyway, I tucked her underwear under her clothes when I laid them out this morning. I didn't look at the size labels. It felt too intrusive."

"You need a little intrusive in your life, Jeffrey. You need it badly," Liz teased.

"You and Mike are a lot alike, you know that?"

"Yeah, well, we both look out for you. And that's where it ends. I'll let it go this time, but never again mention my name in the same breath with Mike Price's. You better get going. You got some shopping to do. Good luck, Lou."

"Thanks for your help, *Detective Shear*. And for everything else."

"You're welcome," she said with a smile.

Jeffrey had never been inside Loehmann's, but it had always looked like a good store to find women's clothes. He pushed open the door. Dazed by the jungle of women's clothes, he rode the escalator down to the first floor and rounded a corner, landing in the lingerie department.

"Let's see, 34C. Where the hell is that?" Jeffrey proceeded to the racks of bras. With so many to choose from, it was all so confusing. He only had an hour, so he had to pick *something*.

He sifted through the bras, on the alert for any tags with 34C. Still unsure, he curled his hands around the cups of a bra labeled 34C, gauging the correct size for Tara by feel.

"Humph." The woman next to Jeffrey glared at him.

He grinned at her. "Great sale today, huh?"

She grabbed her little girl's hand, and they hurried away. The little girl looked back at Jeffrey with one of those typical kid, couple-of-teeth-missing smiles. He gave the little one a quick wave and turned his attention back to the bras.

He reached into his coat pocket and pulled out the list Liz had helped him make. He stared at the sea of bras, all pointing at him.

"Can I help you, Sir?" A busty saleswoman in a cream cashmere sweater and a pencil skirt appeared at his side.

"I need a bra. Uh, 34C," he stammered.

She chuckled. "A 34C isn't going to fit you honey. You need our Big Gal line."

"No! No!" He shook his hands. "Not for me. It's for a lady friend." The saleswoman glanced at his ring finger. He held up his left hand. "See? I'm not some creep. I'm not married. And no, I didn't remove it before I came here."

She nodded. "Okay then. So, let's see. Underwire or wireless? Padded or unpadded? Solid or print? Front or back closure? Straps, strapless, or racer back?

"Uh, I dunno!" He handed the saleswoman his list.

Her eyes scrolled down it. She snickered "You really don't know what you're doing!"

Jeffrey shook his head. "Help me, please."

"No problem. Let's see..." She chose four bras in a brisk and efficient manner. "These are nice. I recommend basics: full size, underwire, in either white, beige, black, or pale pink."

"Fine, I'll take all four. I'm pressed for time. Now show me your panties."

She waggled her finger at him. "You're a lively one, aren't you?"

"I need some, uh, medium-smalls."

The woman grinned. "They don't come in medium-small, son. Either small, or medium. Bikini, hipster, briefs, boy briefs, thong, sheer, cotton, lycra/poly blend, solid or print?"

*Oh man. Here we go again.* He stood dazed, with four bras straddling his forearm.

"Never mind. I'll pick out a few basic items. Describe her to me."

"Caucasian female. Five feet one. Short brown hair. About 110 pounds."

"You a cop?"

"Yes ma'am."

"Figures."

Jeffrey clutched the assortment of women's undergarments to his chest, struggling to catch a pair of panties before it fell to the floor.

The saleswoman chuckled. She relieved him of his clumsy grip, placing the lingerie in a shopping basket.

"Thanks." Basket in hand, Jeffrey stared at the escalator.

"You look lost again," the saleswoman said.

"Uh, yes mam." Heat rose up his neck. "I'm obviously not particularly good at this. My lady friend also needs some...uh...regular clothes."

She grinned. "Your lady will need socks, pullovers, sweaters, and some jeans. I have an idea of what will fit her based on your description."

Jeffrey didn't argue. With her help, he hoped he'd be finished in under an hour and back to the station. Paperwork had never looked so good, but anticipating Tara's surprise made every humiliating moment absolutely worthwhile.

The saleswoman shot through every department in the store plucking items from the racks and dropped them into his basket. Jeffrey picked up his pace just to follow her.

"That's it," she said finally.

Jeffrey wiped the sweat from his brow with the back of his hand. "Oh, thank God. Give me a criminal any day"

"Ah, it wasn't so bad. You're a pro now. Now you can come back and do it all on your own."

"Uh, maybe." *I hope not.*

The saleswoman rang up Tara's new wardrobe. "Keep the receipt. Those are all exchangeable, except the panties." She handed the shopping bag to Jeffrey. "You're a nice guy. I'm sure your lady 'friend' will be pleasantly surprised."

He grinned ear to ear. "I hope so." Jeffrey thanked her, grabbed the bag, and bolted for the door.

Jeffrey walked into his office and put the shopping bag on the floor next to his chair. Mike and Herb sat at Jeffrey's desk, devouring their slices of cheese pizza. Two slices waited on a paper plate for him.

Jeffrey collapsed into his chair. "Thanks guys. This will hold me over until dinner, at least. I'm taking Tara over to Niko's tonight." He was greeted with catcalls and whistles. Sometimes he felt like the station house was more of a frat house. "So what's been happening here since I've been gone?"

Mike grabbed a napkin and wiped tomato sauce from the corner of his mouth. "The perp who stabbed his ex-girlfriend to death was picked up and is on his way to Rikers. I've spoken with the family, and they're relieved, to say the least. Trial date is sometime in April."

Herb added, "And he'll have company. Our coffee shop shooter will be riding with him to Rikers. Trial date isn't set but will be soon given the media attention."

Rivchak picked that moment to walk into the room. "Hey, what's up?" He reached over Herb's chubby fingers and grabbed the last slice of pizza from the box. "Carbs man, gotta watch those carbs," he chided, in a blatant alpha move.

Jeffrey gritted his teeth

Paul generated tension within the squad, and he wasn't going to tolerate discord. Jeffrey couldn't wait to see how Paul functioned at his first homicide. Perhaps humility would settle him down.

"Well what do we have here?" Mike teased.

Before Jeffrey could snatch the bag away, Mike was already nosing through it. He yanked out the pale pink bra and slid it on over his shirt. Herb rifled through the panties.

"You got these panties at Loehmann's?" Herb asked. "I'll have to stop by and get some for Ophelia. Maybe she'll be so grateful that she'll cancel her convention trip next week, and I won't get stuck bird sitting." Herb looked stricken by the thought. "Lou, if I do get stuck with that damn bird, can I bring him here? He can't be left alone because he needs at least three hours of attention. Ophelia doesn't trust anyone else."

"Does he fly?" Jeffery asked.

"No. His wings are clipped. He sits on his perch, watches people, and talks when the mood strikes him. It should be one or two days max."

"Okay," he said warily. "But keep him over by your desk. And don't let Scardino see him."

"Thanks," Herb breathed in relief.

Liz Shear peeked into his office. Chewing on his pizza, he motioned for her to come in. "Hey, Liz. Come in and have a seat. Want some pizza?"

"No thanks. I already had my lunch." She took one look at the grown men parading in Jeffrey's office like fools twirling women's undergarments around their fingers. She shook her head. "Wow, this reminds me of my junior high homeroom."

Jeffrey shrugged. "They're just blowing off some steam."

"I know you went to Loehmann's during lunch, and by the looks of it, you didn't return empty handed. Being the friend I am, I bought some things for Tara you may not have thought about." She handed him a Duane Reade bag.

He peeked into it. "Oh. Right. I didn't think of that."

Mike still pranced around the office in the pink bra. "Whatcha got in the bag, Lizzie?" He pulled the plastic edges apart. "Ooh, cotton rockets. No wonder you've been so testy."

She stuck her tongue out at him. "They're not for me."

"Nice, Lizzy. So ladylike."

"We all can't be ladies like you."

Jeffrey stuck his fingers in the corners of his mouth and whistled. "Kids. Kids. Play nice.

Liz pointed to Mike "Well he started it!"

He ignored them as he picked through the bag. Liz was right. He didn't consider the personal items. Along with the tampons, he found citrus scented body wash and shampoo, body lotion, and assorted cosmetics.

"Thanks, Liz," he said, truly grateful.

"You're welcome."

"My, my. What have we here?" Scardino's form lingered in the doorway.

*What a disaster!* Jeffrey thought. Mike still sported a pink bra. Herb clutched a pair of panties in each hand, and he had a piece of pizza hanging from his mouth. He wiped his face and stood up from behind his desk.

"Sir."

"Lieutenant Corrigan," Captain Scardino replied coolly. "Is this how you're running your house now? What is this? Fucking Victoria's Secret?"

"No, Sir. Just a little light hearted fun," he said.

"Well, now that you're all dressed," he eyed Mike, who slipped off the pink bra and placed it back into the bag. "I'm going on down to the conference room to talk to some reporters. See you there," Scardino said and then turned down the hall, his shoes squeaking on the linoleum with every step.

*Great.* That's all he needed before a press conference, his own captain thoroughly fucking up the facts.

"Hurry up guys!" Jeffrey said as he gathered the contents of the bag. He was still out the door ahead of the rest of them.

On the way down the stairs, he mumbled to himself, "The man couldn't find his own asshole with a mirror and a GPS."

# Chapter Twelve

Wednesday, January 4, 2:00 p.m.

*T*he doorbell rang. Tara tidied her hair, took a deep breath, and opened the front door

"Hello, Tara. I'm Joe Corrigan, and this is Frank. I'm so sorry to have scared you the other day."

Heat rose to her cheeks. He didn't look nearly as frightening as she'd imagined him to be now.

"I'm Tara Ross." She shook their extended hands.

The men were pleasant enough. Early seventies and both were in great shape. Joe Corrigan was tall, clean shaven and had straight silver hair. It was like looking at Jeffrey—thirty years from now.

Frank was shorter and bald. His nose was Cary Grant classic, with the exception of a small, irregular bump on the bridge. His square chin imparted a look of defiance and determination, but when he smiled, he melted her heart. He was a lady's man, she could tell.

"I'm ready, boys. I do appreciate the ride to the station."

"It's no problem. I live only ten blocks from here, and Frank lives a street away from me. We're heading into the city anyway."

"I have my final oncology visit today at Sloan Kettering. I had CML." Frank informed her.

"Chronic myelogenous leukemia?" she asked, the words leaping from her mouth in reflex.

Frank raised an eyebrow. "Yes," he said warily.

"I'm so sorry, go on."

"I went for my yearly physical six months ago. They did some blood work. And bam, I get a call to come back. 'Cancer,' the doctor said."

Tara shut the door behind her, and they all crunched in the snow to Joe's black sedan.

Frank opened the door for her and helped her into the front seat next to Joe. Then he rounded the car and slid into the backseat.

Frank smacked the back of Joe's seat. "Let's go, already."

"Yeah. Yeah. Keep your britches on!"

Joe eased the car out of the driveway and onto the salted road.

"He scared the shit out of me, you know," Joe said. "Thirty-five years on the job. Kicked. Punched. Stabbed two times—"

"It was actually three times," Frank said.

"Okay, stabbed *three* times. Hit over the head with a two by four—"

"Yeah, that hurt. Fifteen stitches, right here." Tara looked into the back seat. Frank pointed to the back of his head. A faded linear scar traversed his skull.

"Wow. And I thought this was bad," she said and unzipped her jacket. She yanked open her turtleneck sweater revealing a two-inch scar, zigzagging across her right clavicle. "A patient dug her fingernail into me—right here." She tapped her scar with a forefinger.

"Holy cow," Frank said.

They traded "war stories" all the way to the precinct.

Joe parked a block from the station house. Together, they squished in the gray slush and slogged up the precinct stairs.

"Hey, look what the wind blew in!" the Desk Sergeant on duty cried out. The whole first floor began to applaud as though the two men were returning heroes. "If it ain't Joe Corrigan and Frank

Salvino, legends of the Bronx. I'll let Lieutenant Corrigan know you're here… with the lovely doctor." He winked at Tara.

"You're looking good, Frank," said a patrolman.

"Yeah, I got that Bruce Willis thing going on."

"You look like Kojak. Yeah. Yeah. Kojak. Who loves you Baby!" the officer joked.

Frank rubbed his baldhead appreciatively. Tara smiled, amazed that a man with a serious illness could be brave enough to joke about it.

"I'd go with Bruce Willis, Frank. The man is *Die Hard*, always has been," The Desk Sergeant called.

"Let's go Bruce. We need to get Tara to the third floor," Joe teased.

The thought of seeing Larkin again made her skin chill, but she was ready for payback.

Jeffrey heard the applause all the way from the third floor. He turned to Mike. "Dad and Frank are here."

"The dynamic duo," Mike joked.

And then Joe, Frank, and Tara strode into his office.

"Hey, Scrappy," Frank said to Scardino, who was still lurking around, much to Jeffrey's dismay.

Scardino's eyes narrowed, and he snorted. "Well if it isn't the geriatric Mutt and Jeff."

Joe turned to Frank and said, "I call Jeff. You get to be Mutt."

"No fair. You always get to be Jeff. I want to be Jeff," Frank said

Scardino raised his bushy eyebrows. "I don't have time for this bullshit. I have to get back to Police Plaza." he retorted and then skulked away.

Joe chuckled. "The House Mouse slips away."

"Here she is," Frank said.

Jeffrey beamed, proud Tara was coming forward to ID Larkin. That couldn't be easy for her. And despite only leaving her a few hours ago, his breath still hitched the minute she walked into his office.

Mike raised his hand, circled his palm. "Top of the morning, Mr. Corrigan,"

"Michael O'Malley-Price. You haven't called me Mr. Corrigan since the second grade. I hear you're going to be a daddy soon?"

"No shit," Frank said.

"No shit. I am."

"Scary."

"Tell me about it."

Joe shook his head. "I need to get Kojak here to his doctor's appointment. A lollipop awaits him. Tara, much luck to you, my dear. You'll do fine. Put that bastard away who punched you. I'd punch him myself, but they don't let us do that anymore." Jeffrey's dad shook her hand. "I enjoyed meeting you. Properly," he added with a raised brow.

"Adieu," Frank told her. He gently kissed the back of her hand, and whispered into Jeffrey's ear, "Too young for me, but for you …" He winked at Jeffrey.

Jeffrey grabbed Tara's hand. "Are you okay? Are you up to this?"

All Jeffrey had to do was to put that scum away, and he had Tara to ID the man who'd assaulted her.

Unruffled, Tara nodded confidently. "Let's go, I'm ready to do this."

Jeffrey gave her hand a squeeze and escorted her down the hall and into a room to stand in front of a thick window. The riding ADA, a young woman dressed in a navy suit, joined them. She nodded to Jeffrey and smiled while offering Tara a handshake.

"Dr. Ross, my name is Eileen Cranston. I'm the district attorney. I know this is difficult for you, but there will be several men to look at. They will not be able to hear or see you. Take your time and identify the man who assaulted you."

"I understand," Tara said.

The blinds went up.

She picked out Larkin easily. Jeffrey placed his arm around her shoulders. "Good job," he whispered.

"Jeffrey, I have something exciting to tell you. I spoke to—"

He interrupted her. "And I have some exciting news for you. Come with me back to my office."

"Okay."

Jeffrey's escorted Tara back to his office, his hand resting at the small of her back the whole way. She was about to meet the doctor that he was quite confident could jog her memory. He opened the door for her. "Tara, I'd like you to meet—"

"Marielle!" The woman stood from her chair. She rushed into the woman's arms.

Marielle hugged her. "Oh God. I'm so glad you're safe!"

Jeffrey froze in the doorway and furrowed his brow. He looked at Dr. Kane who rose from his chair and merely shrugged at him. Who was this woman and why hadn't anyone told him that she was in his office? Jeffrey joined Leo in the corner, while eyeing Tara and this strange woman as they embraced in reunion

"Who's that?" Jeffrey whispered.

"Marielle Kosto. Apparently, Tara's best friend, who has come to claim her. We arrived at the same time."

# Chapter Thirteen

Wednesday, January 4, 3:00 p.m.

*J*effrey's mouth went cotton, and his abs tensed. It was over. He was going to lose her already.

Tara spun around, apparently remembering they weren't alone. "Who's this?"

"Tara, this is Dr. Kane, the house psychiatrist and a friend of mine. I asked him to come and meet you. Leo's helped others retrieve their memories. I thought he might help you. That was my exciting news," he said.

Her eyes twinkled happily at him. His heart melted a bit. "My exciting news was about Marielle and I, finding each other," she said, breathless.

Leo nudged Jeffrey. "Marielle and I would like to speak with you. Alone."

Jeffrey blinked. "All right. Let's step outside of my office."

Leo said, "Tara, excuse us, please. We'll be right back."

Tara sighed. "Great. The cheese stands alone."

Once outside, Jeffrey began to pace circles around the group. He'd been utterly blindsided by this whole situation. *How could I have been so stupid?* Surely, Tara was bound to have remembered her best friend sooner or later. She was too smart—and sexy as hell, but that was beside the point—not to start solving this problem. He had underestimated this beautiful creature.

He narrowed his eyes at Marielle. She had really mucked up his plans.

Leo cleared his throat. "Let's keep this brief. Marielle and I talked while you were out, and we concluded that it's best to let Tara decide where she would like to stay, for now. She had originally planned to visit Marielle for a few days. I can reach out to another in psychiatrist, one in Brooklyn, who can treat her. Tara may feel more comfortable around someone she knows well and trusts."

Jeffrey held up his hands. "Whoa, wait! Tara seems to be doing well with me. Maybe moving her from one place to another is not such a good idea." *Oh, God. I don't want her to leave.*

Marielle frowned at him. "Well, let's ask Tara, shall we? Let her decide."

Leo turned to Marielle. "I know there are probably excellent psychiatric professionals near your neighborhood, but I believe I can best help her for now. I specialize in posttraumatic disorders, specifically memory recall. Perhaps we can all spend time with Tara. I think that would be good for her. Maybe even help her remember some things."

Jeffrey softly sighed. *Thank you, Leo!*

"Okay," Marielle said. "Anything to help her." She turned away and opened the door. Apparently, the conversation was now over.

Tara sat waiting, curled up in a chair reading one of Jeffrey's textbooks, Geberth's *Practical Homicide Investigation.*

Marielle peeked over the book and winced. "All those bloody bodies. Yuk. Why are you reading that? You'll give yourself nightmares."

"It's an interesting book. And I already have nightmares."

Jeffrey watched as Tara closed the book and set it in her lap. When she looked up, their eyes locked. Yes, she had nightmares, and he knew it.

She drew in a deep breath. "So, are you guys done talking about me?"

Marielle squatted down in front of Tara and grasped her hands. "We have no secrets from you, sweetie. We all agreed that Dr. Kane is the best specialist for you. I care about you. So, I'll let you decide if you want to come home with me today, or continue to stay with Jeffrey. Regardless, we're all going to be here for you."

Jeffrey gazed into Tara's eyes, desperately trying to read her response. He licked the inside of his lips.

*Please say something. I can't stand this much longer. Stay with me.*

Tara stared at Marielle. "You know you're my best friend. And that's not going to change. But I'm comfortable where I'm at right now. I'm going to stay at Jeffrey's house. I feel… safe there. And that way I'll be closer to my appointments with Dr. Kane. Please say you understand. I'll come visit you, often. I promise."

Jeffrey had held his breath awaiting her answer but now breathed out a grateful "Yes!"

"Okay," Marielle said softly.

Tara hugged her tightly." I'm sorry to have put you through all this."

"You owe me dinner and a couple drinks. Then we'll be even. And you will be seeing me… a lot. Remember, I still have the boxes you mailed me."

"Oh yeah." Tara smiled. "See? I'm getting better already."

"Hey, I can pick those boxes up for Tara sometime. It's no problem." Jeffrey said. "Marielle, you'll need to give me your address and a good time to stop by." He reached into his pants pocket and fished out his wallet. "Here's my card with my home and cell numbers. You can also call me at the station anytime."

"I'll call you," Tara said to Marielle again.

"And I'll call you. We'll have lunch this week. We definitely have some catching up to do," she said as she eyed Jeffrey speculatively." Bye, Sweetie." Marielle kissed Tara on the cheek.

Marielle glanced at Jeffrey and pointed to the door. "I'll need a moment with you, Lieutenant."

Jeffrey nodded. "Absolutely."

They stepped outside his office. Marielle's narrowed her eyes at him.

"Listen here. I don't know you from Adam, and Tara's vulnerable right now, but she trusts you. You hurt her, and you'll have to answer to me."

Jeffrey held his hands up in surrender. "I promise not to hurt her. And I'll make sure she's safe. You're a true friend; I know you want the best for her. We're on the same side here. Tara's side."

Marielle sighed. "I know. Now I get what Tara sees in you. We'll keep in close touch, yes?"

"For sure. I'll bring her by, often. "

Jeffrey held out his hand. They shook hands.

"I'll take good care of her."

Marielle shot a finger at him. "You better. I'll be calling her to make sure."

"Can I see you out?"

"Nah. Go back to Tara. I hope Dr. Kane's treatments work."

"I know they will. I'll keep you posted."

Jeffrey waved to Marielle as she walked away, then dashed to his office, barely feeling the ground beneath him. "Tara, are we still on for dinner?"

"I'm looking forward to it." Tara lowered her gaze. "Is Marielle all right?"

"Yes. And because I get you for dinner tonight, she'll take you to lunch later this week."

"Great." Tara pushed up out of her chair and hugged him. "Thank you so much, Jeffrey."

He couldn't stop smiling. As Tara pressed closer against him, he discovered that there was something else that he wouldn't be able to stop. "We better get going."

The phone on his desk buzzed.

He let her loose with a sigh. "Excuse me a second." He rummaged through the papers on his desk and retrieved his phone. "Corrigan here."

"Lieutenant Corrigan," the desk sergeant said. "I'm sending up a sixty-one. Cleaning lady found her boss and a woman dead in an apartment on West 67th. Responding unit confirms two dead at the scene."

# Chapter Fourteen

Wednesday, January 4, 3:47 p.m.

*J*effrey cradled the receiver on his shoulder. "Has CSU been notified?"

"They're on their way. So is the ME."

"Okay, thanks." He hung up the phone and called to Laurie, "Get Detectives Price, Malik, and Rivchak for me ... please." He frowned at Tara. "I'm so sorry. I have to go check out a double homicide. Stay here, and get to know Dr. Kane. I'll be back later. Then we'll go to Niko's. I promise."

"I'm sure I'll be in excellent hands here with Dr. Kane. Good luck."

With Jeffrey's door still wide open, Mike rapped on the doorframe. Jeffrey looked up. "We're ready," Herb informed him.

"Where's Rivchak?" Jeffrey asked.

"He's out there, flirting with Laurie," Mike said.

"Grab him, and let's get going."

The men snatched up their coats and rushed down the stairs to the first floor. Jeffrey gritted his teeth. After assuring the public, not an hour ago, that he'd use every tactic in his armamentarium to rid drug dealing from their streets, he was determined to curb his precinct's rising body count.

They walked briskly across the station house lobby, and just as they were about to exit out of the precinct door Jeffrey glanced up. There stood Scardino, coat buttoned and ready to go.

"I heard about the double homicide," Scardino said.

*Ah shit,* Jeffrey thought. *That's all I need.* He had to ditch Scardino, a known liability to every crime scene.

He nodded to his superior. "We're heading out now. I'm going to break in Rivchak right away. I've got it covered for now. I'll give you an update as soon as possible."

"I want to hear from you, Corrigan, by 5 p.m." his inept captain called.

"Yes, Sir." *Jerk off.*

Mike whispered in his ear," You see that outfit? Think his mother still dresses him?"

Jeffrey chuckled," Probably."

Mike scooted into the driver's seat of the black Crown Vic. Rivchak claimed the passenger side while Jeffrey and Herb slid into the backseat. Then the car pulled away from the curb, tires squealing.

Mike tapped the steering wheel. "Ah, sweet success. A crime scene that stands a chance sans Scardino."

Mike crammed the Crown Vic between two squad cars. There was a crunching sound followed by a high-pitched scrape.

*Dammit!*

He smacked the back of Mike's seat. "Shit. That makes the third squad car you've hit this month!"

"Ah come on, Lou. We've arrived in record time. This is a primo spot. Door to door service."

"More like fender to fender."

"Eh, take it out of my pay."

Jeffrey waggled his finger at him. "You jest, but that's exactly what might happen."

The four of them exited the car and jogged across the street to The Towers apartment building. Squad cars, CSU vehicles, and media trucks jammed the street. Herb jockeyed ahead of Paul, asserting his seniority.

"Who knew the man could run?" Mike said.

"Good afternoon, Lieutenant." Two uniformed officers stood outside the glass doors of The Towers. "Everyone is on the 15th floor, apartment 1501. We got Todeski with the doorman."

"Great. Make sure, no one in and no one out."

"Yes, Sir."

Jeffrey, Mike, Paul, and Herb entered the lobby. Jeffrey flashed his gold detective's shield at the doorman.

"Lieutenant Corrigan, NYPD. These are Detectives Price, Malik, and Rivchak. What time did you come on?"

"At seven this morning, Sir."

"Who was here before you?"

"That would be Reginald White."

"Hear anything? See anything? Anything out of the ordinary?"

"No, Sir."

"We're going to need the name of the owner of the building and where he or she can be reached."

"Yes, Sir. That would be Sharon Sullivan. Here's her card. She lives somewhere in Westchester County. I already called her, and she's on her way down."

"Okay. Thanks. Officer Todeski will ask you some more questions. We'll be on the 15th."

"Yes, Sir."

"Paul, I want you to talk to Sharon Sullivan and get a list of everyone who works here. Names, addresses, and phone numbers."

Paul sighed, audibly and snatched the card from the doorman's hand. "I'll get on it."

He squinted at Paul. "Yeah, you do that. All right let's roll. Your case, Detective Price."

They stepped into the elevator. Mike punched the number fifteen button, and the car ascended, making a *bing* with each passing floor

The elevator bobbed to a halt on fifteen, and the doors slid open on the fifteenth floor. The men piled out of the elevator and ventured down the hall to apartment 1501. Displaying their shields again, they dodged under the yellow crime scene tape and joined a dozen others milling about. As the CSU team processed the scene, taking photos and dusting for prints, a tall, slender dark-skinned woman sat on the living room couch, knees pressed together, nervously shifting them from side to side. Jeffrey smiled and nodded in her direction.

"Hey, Jeffrey," Marshall Woods, CSU's lead detective, called from across the room. "Good to see you, man. Hey, you didn't bring Scardino with you, did you?"

"Nah. Dodged that bullet."

"Whew! We might actually have a decent shot at solving this one. The DOA's are in the back bedroom—a man, and a woman. Both appear to have died from gunshot wounds. My team is sweeping the bedroom and finishing their photos. The ME is here, too. You guys want to take a crack at your photos before we move the bodies?"

"Yeah, we'll get in there. Herb go snap some photos. Mike, Paul, and I will be there in a minute. I'm going to get on the phone and get as many people down here as possible. There are twenty floors in this place, and I'm going to need more detectives to help canvass this building, let alone the neighborhood. Mike take Paul to the bedroom so he can get a feel for the action. And don't let him touch anything. He thinks he knows more than he actually does. Watch him. I'll be there shortly to help you out."

Jeffrey called the station and requested more detectives from his house as well as additional help from other precincts. Before heading to the bedroom, he introduced himself to the cleaning lady, who sat nervously on the couch.

Extending his hand to her, he said, "Hello. I'm Detective Lieutenant Corrigan of the NYPD."

The woman's hand trembled. " Marie Denault," she answered with a thick Haitian accent. Marie shook Jeffrey's hand.

"Wanna tell me what happened?"

"I've cleaned Mr. Thompson's apartment for two years. Never a problem. Then I get a call from Angelina. She said that I don't need to come no more. I am fired." She shook her head. "I don't know why. Mr. Thompson was very good to me. Then I decide to come and talk to him, maybe apologize if I do wrong. I have a key, but I knock first. No answer. So, I open the door and call for him. Still no answer."

She took in a jagged breath. "Go on," Jeffrey prompted.

"I see the bedroom door open a little and bed sheets on floor. I think I will make bed, clean a little. Make him happy. I went in the bedroom, and *Mon Dieu*, I see Mr. Thompson and a woman in bed, blood everywhere. They don't move. I run out and use my phone to call 911."

"I can imagine what a shock that was to you. I do need you to stay right here for now. Some officers may ask you additional questions about the apartment. Then we'll take you with us to the police station. We'll need to talk to you a little bit more there, too, while everything is fresh in your mind. We'll get you home safely."

"Okay."

"Good. We'll talk later."

That handled, Jeffrey headed to the bedroom. Herb had finished taking the first set of photos and now waited for the medical examiner to finish her preliminary assessment. Mike and Paul stood in a corner, speaking with Woods. Jeffrey crossed the room, and nodded to the ME, a woman named Emily Roseman. She glanced up at him and nodded back.

Dr. Roseman, at 36, was the youngest medical examiner in NYC. Her short brown hair with wispy bangs made her look even younger. He was always relieved to see her. He trusted her judgment. She was as pleasant as she was competent.

Jeffrey surveyed the victims. The woman stared back at him—her eyes vacant. He was sure her life ended well before the .45 slug ripped through her aorta. She appeared to be in her early twenties, naked, and face up amid bloodstained sheets. Blood congealed across her chest, and her blonde hair was matted with clumps of maroon. The man, also nude, lay face down, his forehead cradled in between her parted legs, his arms outstretched. A revolver rested in the curled fingers of his left hand.

Jeffrey nudged Emily. "So what do you think?"

"I haven't turned the man over yet, but the woman's corneas are cloudy. Her back has some lividity, but not totally fixed. There's no blanching to pressure. Taking into account the heat in this room, from their body temperature, and the beginnings of rigor mortis, I'd estimate TOD of six to eight hours, somewhere between seven and nine this morning. I emphasize 'estimate'. As you know, I'm reluctant to spout out a timeframe on the spot. The woman has a gunshot wound to her chest. She's lost most of her blood volume." She motioned for Jeffrey to help her. "Give me a hand here, and we'll turn the guy over."

Jeffrey donned latex gloves, and he and Emily turned the stiffened man to his back. Herb and Marshall continued snapping photos. Mike and Paul joined them at the bloody bedside.

The man was tall, about six feet, his body lean and muscular, now marred by a stippled bullet hole to the forehead. A condom sheathed his erect penis.

Herb raised an eyebrow. "Gunned done while going down."

Emily rolled her eyes. "Can we move along, please?"

Jeffrey examined the gun in the man's left hand and cocked his head at Mike, inquiring.

"Yeah, Lou. I see it. Paul, what do you make of the revolver in this vic's left hand?"

"Looks like he's clutching a .45 Colt."

"Look closer," Mike directed.

Emily and Jeffrey glanced knowingly at each other.

"Yep, he's definitely clutching a .45 Colt," Paul insisted.

"Detective Rivchak, what do you find unusual about it?" Jeffrey probed.

"Highly unlikely that a man's going to off himself while getting his rocks off. And most people are right handed."

"Two assumptions that are probably true. But what we're getting at is that if this guy shot the woman and himself then his left hand would have stiffened around the .45. Something called cadaveric spasm. It can't be duplicated. See how the .45 rests loosely in his hand? This is a definite plant. Also, the gunshot wounds of both vics have sooty deposits, not clean, and star shaped like a direct contact blast would be. Forehead GSW's aren't all suicides, and GSR's aren't conclusive. Anyone coming in contact with a recently discharged firearm could be positive, including us. But because we do not make assumptions, and all evidence collected is used to paint a picture of the crime, both vics' hands will be bagged and tested for GSR. They're all yours, Dr. Roseman."

Dr. Roseman outfitted the woman's and the man's hands with paper bags. She cocooned the bodies in zippered body bags, placed them on gurneys, and had them rolled away.

"I'll get you my autopsy findings as soon as possible, Lieutenant."

"Thanks Emily." He waved goodbye. Focusing his attention to the crime scene, he watched Marshall examine the bloody mattress.

"Lou, there's a lot stuff to go through. I see a bullet hole here. "He pointed to the burnt hole in the mattress. "With all the blood and possible body fluids to investigate, we're just going to load up the mattress and take it down to the lab."

"Sounds good."

Herb returned from the adjoining bathroom. "Hey Boss, I found an assortment of men's and women's toiletries and this bottle of pills." Herb shook the medicine bottle like a maraca. "Let's see what's in here." He opened the bottle and sprinkled the tablets in his palm. "Ah, little blue pills. Man, and by the looks of that guy he's got one hell of an erection that's gonna last more than four hours."

Herb read the label aloud, "May also cause an unsafe drop in blood pressure." Chuckling, he added, "Especially if used with bullet in the forehead."

"Good work. Bag it,"

Herb raised his other hand, hefting a plastic-wrapped object. "Now, here's really something worth bagging. A brick of coke wrapped and strapped under the toilet tank cover."

Paul licked his lips. "Shit. That's like...twenty-five grand, right there. Is there any more?" He lunged toward the bathroom.

Jeffrey gripped the back of Paul's shirt, harnessing him like a spoiled child. His biceps strained against his shirtsleeves as he reeled in Paul. "Hold it. That's Herb's area. The scene's processed systematically. Your sector is the bedroom—with Mike. You don't touch anything, or go anywhere, until we tell you to."

"Fine. Whatever. I got it. Now let go of my fucking shirt!"

"What was that? You little son of a bitch." He twisted Paul's shirt, wrinkling it beneath his curled fingers.

"Sir, I'm sorry."

Jeffrey twisted harder. "I can't hear you. What did you say?"

"I said I'm sorry, *Sir*."

"That's better." He released his hold on Paul, shoving him toward Mike.

Mike muttered, "The little prick had it coming."

Jeffrey scanned living room. "This guy's a definitely a dealer. By the looks of his apartment, I don't think he was pounding the pavement. My guess is that he spent more time at the gym than slinging. I'd say he was living large on his proceeds until someone froze his assets—permanently."

Mike nodded. "Yeah, I agree. Definitely got caught with his pants down."

Mike and Paul proceeded to the bedroom. Jeffrey followed them, tempted to shove his foot up Paul's ass.

Mike flipped open the wallet that he had found in the nightstand drawer. "Steven Thompson. Hmmm? According to his birth date...he's...39. Hey, Paul, look on the other side of the bed, will ya?"

"There are some women's clothes here on the floor: bra, panties, white silk blouse, jeans, and a pair of high-heeled boots," Paul said. "No wallet or purse. There's money stuffed in the front pocket of the jeans, four 100's and five 20's."

Mike ran his thumb across his mustache. "She doesn't look like a street hooker. Doesn't look familiar. Someone took the time, and money, to work on her. Hair styled. Straight white teeth. Impressive double D's. Probably high-end call girl. I'll run her prints once they're processed and see if she's ever been popped."

Jeffrey opened the double doors of the walk in closet. Designer men's clothes hung on one side and off the rack women's clothes, spaced in thirds, hung on the opposite side.

"Paul, what size are those jeans?"

Paul peered into the inside back of the jeans. "Size 4."

He shuffled through each partition of clothing. "Women's size 4, size 6, size 8. That's quite a spread."

"Exactly," Mike said. "Women keep all these sizes around...to cover 'their spread'. Amy has skinny clothes and fat clothes, and those for in between. Then she torments me with the question no man gets right, "Do these make me look fat?" Now that she's pregnant, it simplifies things. She looks fat in everything."

"There are four toothbrushes on the sink," Herb called out from the bathroom.

"If there are three women, where are the other two?" Jeffrey pondered.

Paul grinned. "Wow, three women. My kind of fantasy."

"Lucky for them, two of them skipped this party," Jeffrey said. "I briefly spoke to the cleaning lady. She said that a woman named Angelina told her that she was fired. I want you guys to take Marie with you down to the station for an interview. Find out more about this Angelina, and who else may be living here. I need to see how the canvass is going. Herb and I'll meet you back at the house." He waved to Marshall. "Hey, send me the CSU report once it's done, would you?"

"Sure thing, Corrigan. And it was great seeing you."

"Same here."

With the crime scene secured, Jeffrey and Herb walked to the elevator. Herb pressed the down button. Jeffrey waited beside him in silence. A door down the hall creaked open. Jeffrey placed his hand over the 9mm Glock at his side. "Get ready, Herb." They whipped around toward the sound. A woman with snowy hair and bright red lipstick craned her neck from her doorway. Herb and Jeffrey exhaled. Jeffrey relaxed the grip on his gun.

"Who's there?" the old lady called.

"NYPD. I'm Lieutenant Corrigan, and this is Detective Malik.

The woman pushed her door open. She clutched a yapping white Bijon Frise to her chest.

"I already talked to you guys."

"Yes, Ma'am. I'm sure you have." Jeffrey and Herb slowly approached her. "I'm the commander of the 27th Precinct homicide squad." Jeffrey cocked his head waiting for her to respond.

"Marjorie Crosdale."

"Very nice to meet you, Ms. Crosdale." Jeffrey extended his hand. Marjorie shook it. He patted the dog for good measure.

"And I'm Detective Malik." Herb extended his chubby hand too. The Bijon Frise growled and snapped at him, forcing him to retreat. He abandoned the handshake.

Jeffrey suppressed a chuckle. "Did you happen to hear or see anything unusual this morning?"

"There's always something suspicious going on in there. He's got people coming in and out of there like it's Grand Central. And the women! Always noise. Loud music. The walls shake day and night, if you know what I mean. I've complained to the board multiple times. But because he has all this money, he gets away with it. I'm just sick of it. I don't know why his wife takes it."

"Wife? Does she live there?"

She shook her head no. "They're separated. She's got a house upstate, in Katonah. Spends most of her time there. Steven's too busy with those other women."

"What's Steven's wife's name?"

"Madelyn."

"And when did you last see or speak to Ms. Thompson?"

"I saw her last night. They had an argument, as they usually do, and she left. I said hello. She said hello back."

"Was she upset or angry?"

"Not any more than she usually is, especially with his philandering. She was leaving for a vacation. And she needs one from him, a permanent one."

"How about this morning?" Jeffrey asked. "Did you see anyone this morning?"

"That tart, Angelina. He's cheating on his wife, and Angelina's all twisted up about him seeing some blonde. Serves her right. Now she knows how Madelyn felt."

Herb scratched his head. "Ms. Crosdale, I'm a little confused. Madelyn is his wife, but he's also seeing two other women, *and* he's still married?"

"Yeah, Pudgy, try and keep up with the story."

Jeffrey grinned but firmly corrected her. "This is Detective Malik. Please refer to him as such."

"I apologize Detective Malik."

"I appreciate that, Ms. Crosdale. Do you know Angelina's full name and where we might locate her?"

"Angelina Holtz. She practically lives here, even though the apartment belongs to Steven and Madelyn. She also works for him at his store in Williamsburg, Brooklyn. Thompson's Paints and Interior Design."

"Do you recall around what time you saw Ms. Holtz?"

"I saw her when I got my paper this morning, around 6:45."

Jeffrey let Herb continue to question Ms. Crosdale. She was warming up to him, and he didn't want to interfere with their developing rapport.

"Do you happen to know the name of the blonde woman?" Herb asked.

"No. She doesn't speak English. She stays inside the apartment a lot. Hardly ever comes out, and never without Steven."

"Can you describe her?"

"Young. In her twenties. Nice little figure. Big ones up here." Ms. Crosdale cupped one of her hands about six inches from her own saggy breast while hugging her dog with the other.

Jeffrey winced. Herb reached in his pocket and pulled out a Polaroid picture of the female victim. "Ma'am, is this the blonde woman you've seen in Steven Thompson's apartment?"

Marjorie Crosdale gasped. "Oh my God. Yes, that's her."

"No name?" Herb questioned.

"No, I don't know her name. Poor thing!"

Herb put the photo away. "You've been very helpful, Ma'am."

"Is it safe here? I don't have any place to go."

99

"You'll be fine," Herb reassured her. "This doesn't appear to be a random attack. Keep your doors locked. Here's my card. Call if you need anything or if you recall anymore. You have a good day."

"Good day to you Detective Malik, and to you Lieutenant Corrigan."

Herb couldn't help it. He reached out to pet the dog again. It growled.

Jeffrey guided Herb away, and they returned to the elevator.

"What is it with animals and me? Ophelia's parrot hates me, too."

Jeffrey patted him on his shoulder. "Maybe you should get fish."

Jeffrey bounded into his office.

Tara twisted in her chair and looked over her shoulder. "Hey, how did it go?"

He walked over and sat in a chair next to her. "It's going to be hard to untangle."

There's the money. The sex. The drugs. And an unidentified dead woman. He didn't want to think about it anymore. Jeffrey rested his hand on hers. After dealing with a double homicide and Rivchak, the tension between his shoulder blades released the second he touched her. He glanced and smiled at Tara "I'm looking forward to dinner."

She grinned back at him. "Me too."

He took a deep breath. At least she was happy. That had to be a good sign. Jeffrey turned his attention to Dr. Kane who sat in Jeffrey's chair behind his desk. Leo Kane pushed back in his chair and began to rock out of it.

Jeffrey waved his hand at Leo, motioning for him to sit. "Please, Dr. Kane. No need to get up. I'm quite comfortable here." He'd do anything to help Tara, including giving up his office for her sessions with Leo. "So, how were things here?"

"A very good start," Leo said. "Tara and I had a pleasant afternoon. Better than yours, I'd wager. But I'd like to take her to the hospital tomorrow."

Jeffrey swallowed hard, dreading the worst. "You're right. It's my fault. I should have insisted she get checked out that first day."

Leo shook his head. "It's all right, Lieutenant. I don't believe it's urgent, since I have a low index of suspicion for anything physically wrong with Dr. Ross, aside from the superficial eye injury that is healing well."

Tara cocked her eyebrow at Jeffrey. "See? I told you."

He squeezed her hand. "Yes, you did. But let's err on the side of caution. I think it's a good idea for you to get checked out. It would certainly make me feel better."

She winked. "Well, I'm all for making you feel better."

*Damn! How does she do that? Turn me on with one little zinger.* He quickly crossed his legs.

Leo cleared his throat. "To continue, I do believe that Tara has experienced a string of stressful events." He picked up a pen and tapped it on Jeffrey's desk. "Something traumatized her, pushed her over the edge." Leo narrowed his eyes and pointed the pen at Jeffrey. "I can't be sure, but I think Tara may be experiencing what's called *dissociative fugue*. She's blocking out some painful experiences."

Jeffrey looked at Tara, who sat speechless, staring at Leo. Jeffrey recalled her nightmare the other night. Someone bleeding. Something happened in that hospital. Not wanting to interfere with her treatment, he'd wait and see if she'd tell Leo about it. If not, he may have to.

Leo explained on, "It's a defense mechanism, a glitch in certain neurotransmitters, which are special chemicals in the brain needed for memory."

Jeffrey held up his hand. "Whoa, Doc. Neuro-what?"

Tara nudged him. "Neurotransmitters."

He scratched his head. *Thank God, she knows a bit of what's going on.*

"Right now, her fugue is protecting her from something. Fugue generally lasts a few days or weeks. It is a good sign that she's starting to remember some pieces of her life. I'll work with her. I've arranged for a CAT scan and some blood work for tomorrow morning." Finally, Leo rested the ballpoint on the desk. "Otherwise, we've decided to meet three times a week for now. I can come here, or Tara can come to my office. Whatever works best." Dr. Kane stood and began to gather his things. He smiled at Tara. "It was nice getting to know you today. We have a lot of work ahead of us. I'll see you in the morning."

"Bright and early. Good night, Dr. Kane. And thank you. I promise to work hard." Tara said.

"You're very welcome. Well, good evening to the both of you. Enjoy your dinner." Leo put on his coat, grabbed his hat and gloves, and left.

"I'd say that's progress," Jeffrey said, pleased they were finally alone.

"Yes, I'd say so." She stretched her arms over her head. It was sexy as hell. "I'm ready whenever you are."

"Hmm," he teased.

She grinned. *"For dinner."*

"Yeah, that too." He winked. "I need to get with Mike before we leave."

"No problem. I'll be here, reading. I'm on chapter two of *Practical Homicide Investigation."*

"Wait until you get to chapter five. It's a real page turner," he called out as he left his office.

Jeffrey fiddled with a paperweight on Mike's desk. "What did you find out so far?"

"Here's the deal. Cleaning lady has worked for Steven Thompson for two years. Said he was pleasant. Paid her well. She never saw him or anyone else doing any drugs. She did know about his women. She said Madelyn, his estranged wife, used to sleep over on occasion but not in the last four months. That's when he became involved with the blonde woman, the mystery lady. No one seems to know her name, or where she came from. Marie said this woman was very quiet, and almost seemed to hide, every time Marie came to clean. Then there's Angelina Holtz, who was living there before Marie started working for Steven. She described Holtz as in her late twenties with long black hair. She never liked her. So, when she got the call, last evening, that she was fired, she didn't believe it and wanted to speak with Thompson. That's how she ended up walking in on the scene. Oh, here's the weirdest part. We ran some of Steven Thompson's credit card statements. There's a charge to Delta Airlines for a one-way ticket from LaGuardia to Miami International for today. Paul checked the Delta flights that left today, and Holtz was on the roster for Delta flight 38, which left at 0755."

"Nice job, Mike." But the way Mike was smiling made Jeffrey think there was more to come. "What else, you got?"

"Believe it or not, there was another interesting person on that roster, Madelyn Thompson. But Madelyn has a returning ticket for next Friday. Angelina does not. We called Miami PD and briefed them on the situation."

"Good work. Paul pulling his share?"

"He's settling down. I'm watching him."

"I'm going to let Herb go home then. I'll approve both your and Paul's overtime. I'll be on my cell and home after eight. "

"Big plans?"

"I'm taking Tara to Niko's."

Mike winked. "Have a good night."

Jeffrey popped back into his office with a smile on his face. After dealing with the crud of society, he looked forward to spending a quiet evening with Tara. "Learn anything new?"

She shut the book. "Yes. It's very interesting. There are so many important details in processing a crime scene. Painstaking, isn't it?"

He nodded. "It is. You go to the head of the class."

Tara intrigued him. He used to hide crime scene photos from Cheryl, but Tara just jumped right in, devouring every gory detail with scientific hunger. *Where was she years ago?*

"Do I get an 'A' for today?"

"An A plus."

He grabbed her jacket and held it up for her. She slipped her arms into the sleeves and pulled up the zipper, then turned to face him. He placed her hat on her head, tugging gently on the orange braids just as he had two days ago. Was it only two days ago?

"There you go, Tara."

He buttoned his own coat and grasped the handles of the Loehmann's bag.

"What's that?" she asked.

"It's a surprise."

# Chapter Fifteen

Wednesday, January 4, 6:30 p.m.

*T*ara scooted out of his office and galloped along side of him. She had to see what Jeffrey was hiding inside the Lohemann's bag. And from the mischievous smile on his face, it must be good. "What's in the there?"

He swung the bag behind his back. "I'll show you after dinner."

"That's not fair. Now I *have* to look."

She bobbed her head from side to side, determined to snatch the bag from him. He towered over her, suspending it just out of her reach. Her fingertips brushed the bottom of the bag, like a cat batting a toy. The paper crinkled. He laughed and lifted it higher.

She shrugged her shoulders. "Okay, be like that."

"Okay, I will." He grinned. "You always want what you can't have."

*I'd like my memory back and you, not necessarily in that order.* "Do you want something you can't have?" *All you have to do is ask.*

He winked. "Maybe."

She strode forward, pretending not to notice him. He rounded her in the hall. Backpedaling, he slipped the handles of the bag over his wrist and playfully tugged at the orange braids of her hat.

"Hungry?" he asked.

"Starved."

"Then let's get going."

"Lead the way, And I'm going to find out what's in that bag before we reach the restaurant."

Jeffrey grinned. "Okay, You can certainly try."

"You're on, Lieutenant."

Like two kids, they jumped down the station house steps, and jogged along the salted sidewalk, their panting breath rising in the frigid night. She continued to swipe at the bag. He continued to bait her. She laughed, barely feeling the bruising cold air.

Half a block away from Niko's, he squeezed her hand and released the handles of the Loehmann's bag into her fingers.

"This is for you. And so is this." His face drew near. She closed her eyes. His lips brushed hers. He pressed harder, flesh to flesh. She pressed back. Their lips parted and they exhaled simultaneously, their heads haloed by the heat of their breath.

"You can go ahead and open the bag now," he said when they finally separated.

"I'll wait until after dinner."

He opened the door to Niko's, his hand gently pressing against her lower back as he guided her through the door.

"Let me help you with your jacket."

She pushed her shoulders back, letting him slide her jacket free, reveling in his chivalry.

"Table for two?" the hostess asked.

"Yes, please," Tara replied.

"This way."

They were seated at the front of the restaurant. Strings of lights, woven through grape vines, twinkled above them. She peered through the glass enclosure. The sidewalks of Broadway bustled with people. Couples huddled together. Some walked toy dogs, dressed in their tiny pet boutique sweaters. Others hurried along, clutching their Fairway grocery bags.

She smiled at him. "Thank you. I've always wanted to come here. I've passed by, but never stopped in. Now I know what I've been missing."

He winked. "Me too."

Warmth spread to her cheeks, and she fidgeted with her napkin. Jeffrey reached over and stilled her hands. She welcomed his touch—smooth and genuine—just the way he had held her hand in the holding cell that day. He was kind, comforting, smart, and sexy. If only she'd lost her memory years ago.

He lifted his hand from hers.

"Let's order."

They dined on Keftedes and cucumber salad. The waiter brought a bottle of Pinot Noir, a basket of bread, and a plate of spiced oil. Tara picked up a slice and whisked it through the oil, raising it to her mouth. She caught him staring at her, his eyes focused intently on her mouth.

"You're just waiting for me to dribble this all over myself, aren't you?"

"Nah," he teased.

Tara chewed slowly, with closed lips, and then daintily dabbed the corners of her mouth with her white linen napkin. She smiled at him. "See, no need to be embarrassed to eat with me."

He shook his head. "Never. Dining with you is an adventure, and a pleasure."

She held her index finger at her lips, hinting at the oily ooze trailing down his chin and laughed softly. "You did that on purpose."

"Maybe, maybe not." He swallowed, grabbed his napkin, wiped his mouth, and then cleared his throat. "I sometimes come here by myself for lunch or dinner. I sit in the back, have a nice meal, and then go back to the station, or maybe home. But this is much nicer. What a view! Broadway and a beautiful woman."

He reached into his wallet and pulled out her Metro Card.

"I know a couple guys in Transit. They scanned your card. You last used it four days ago at 11:36 a.m. at the Grand Central shuttle train turnstile and then you boarded the uptown number 1."

She furrowed her eyebrows. "I recall crossing over Broadway to Amsterdam. Larkin slammed into me. I thought that was the end of it. Hadn't even seen him following me. Then he showed up at La Vita Cafe. Sat his scumbag ass next to me. Well you know the rest. I feel so stupid. He had targeted me all along."

Jeffrey reached across the table and touched her hand. "You were vulnerable, confused…a good target." He grasped both of her hands. "But thank God you're alive. Don't feel bad. Everyone assumes drug dealers wear gold chains and have teeth to match and linger around shady corners. You'd be surprised how many are polished and respectable. Hell, some are business owners or even professionals. And Larkin didn't expect you to fight back. You held onto that case."

She shuddered. "I should have just given it to him. He could have killed me."

Tara lowered her head. She pushed a Greek meatball around her plate, prodding it with her fork. Jeffrey took the fork away from her, stabbed the meatball, and brought it to her lips.

"Eat," he said. "Enjoy your glass of wine. I'm driving tonight."

She met his gaze. "What if I never get home?"

"You will. Meanwhile, stay with me. And don't be disappointed. It'll come. Trust Leo. He deals with post-traumatic stress problems all the time. Every cop has had some scary stuff happen. Well, everyone but Captain Scardino. I think his mother more likely suffers from a post-traumatic problem. *Him.*"

Tara laughed so hard her cheeks ached as her Pinot Noir percolated through her. Her neck relaxed and her skin flushed.

"Are you okay?" he asked.

She glanced at him, squinting to keep his face in focus. *Buzzed after one glass of wine. I must not hold my liquor well.* "I'm fine. Just fine," she said with a slight slur.

Jeffrey confiscated her second glass of Pinot Noir. "No more wine for you. How about some coffee?"

She rolled her head back. "Coffee's good."

"I hope *everything* at this point is good for you. Tara? Are you listening to me?"

Resting her chin in the palm of her hand, she stared straight into his eyes. "Absolutely," she murmured.

"I have this weekend off, and had planned to go skiing. I want you to come with me. Do you ski?"

"Sure do," she slurred. *God, what did I just agree to? Do I know how to ski? I can't back out now. Two glasses are clearly my limit.*

"More coffee?" the waiter asked.

"No, thank you. Just the check, please," Jeffrey said.

Tara snapped her fingers at the waiter. "Yes, check please." She propped her elbows onto the table. Resting her chin in her palms, she gazed into those hazel eyes of his. "We're in a big hurry."

Jeffrey pulled his wallet from his back pocket and handed the waiter cash.

"Let's get your jacket on while you can still stand," he teased.

Tara pushed her chair back and stood before Jeffrey could reach her. "I got it," she said with a huge smile on her face. She leaned on the back of the chair, "Thanks for the great dinner."

"You're welcome." Jeffrey laughed softly. "Coffee's kicked in, huh?"

She smiled. "Yeah. Good coffee!"

They headed out of Niko's and walked the three blocks to his Mustang. Tara finally opened the Loehmann's bag and gently pushed through the clothes he'd picked out.

"Oh wow! Thank you," she said sincerely. She tugged on his coat sleeve. He lowered his face. She kissed him on the cheek.

"The things in the Duane Reade bag are from Liz. Hopefully, there's aspirin in there. You might need it in the morning."

She crinkled the plastic bag apart. "Tell her that I said thanks, again." Tara shook her head. "I'm so sorry I hit her."

"She's taken a lot worse."

# Chapter Sixteen

Thursday, January 5, 11:10 a.m. — Miami

*The* flight landed on time at Miami International. As the plane taxied to the gate, Angelina Holtz clicked on her cell phone and dialed the number Steven had given her.

"Hector, be outside Delta ground transportation. No delay. I need to be in Redlands in one hour."

"Yes ma'am," Hector responded. "I'm waiting for you. Bengal is on his way and will meet us there."

It was a warm, sunny, South Florida day in contrast to the frigid New York morning she left behind. She slipped the black overnight bag over her left shoulder, draped her tailored jacket over her right arm and strode through the gate, out to ground transportation.

Angelina gritted her teeth when she saw her. Madelyn Thompson stood curbside, her white Louis Vuitton suitcases by her side, tapping her toes in her Christian Louboutin strappy sandals.

*Could that bitch have been on my flight? How could I have missed her?*

Angelina clipped past her. Their eyes locked.

Madelyn smirked. "Making your Friday run for Steven while he's busy screwing Irina?"

"He's not fucking Irina anymore."

"Then he'll find someone else. You and I both know that. Except I'm not his slave.... or should I say mule."

Angelina could've slapped her, but she didn't want to waste her time and energy. She was on a tight schedule.

She dug the spiked heel of her black Manolo Blanik boot into the ground and twisted away, her long black hair nearly whipping Madelyn across her face.

"Bitch," Madelyn hissed, as Angelina slid into the passenger seat of Hector's blue metallic Taurus.

"Good morning, Miss Angelina."

"Hello Hector. Can you wait a minute before we leave?"

"I can, but I don't believe security will let us. We have to move along."

She watched Madelyn get into a cab, waiting until it pulled away before she signaled Hector to proceed. *Why is Stuart not with her? That's weird. They're usually grossly inseparable.*

"How's the restaurant on Calle Ocho doing?" Angelina asked.

"Business is booming—full house for lunch and dinner," said the dark skinned Cuban.

"And how's Daisy and your sons?"

"Very well, Miss Angelina."

"Ah, bueno. I'm glad to hear your business and family matters are excellent. Steven intended for you to do well. And of course, I wish you continued prosperity. You have my word that I will support your needs, just as I know you will do the same for me. Claro?"

"Claro."

Traffic was relatively light as they headed south on Dixie Highway. Every time she came to Miami, there was some new construction in progress. From Kendall to Cutler Ridge as well as Homestead, condos, banks, and shopping plazas blitzed former strawberry fields, orchards, and farm land. At least the Redlands retained some immunity to suburban sprawl, enough open fields for her purposes.

They were making excellent time. That helped her relax. Glancing at her watch, a Piaget that Steven had given her, she noted that it was

11:10. Angelina brimmed with heated satisfaction. Now that Steven and that Russian whore were eliminated, the thought of controlling the deals made her writhe in her seat like a cat, delightfully wriggling in the ecstasy of catnip.

Hector turned off the highway onto a side street leading to a dirt road.

"Right on schedule. I don't see any of the migrants. They must be in the shade, eating their lunches," Hector said.

The car rumbled down the road, surrounded by a cloud of brown, gritty sand. Hector pulled to a stop, facing a large, burnt grass field. A curtain of orange groves to the rear shielded them from unwanted attention. They got out of the car.

"Let's have a parade. Jorge is on time," Angelina said with no small amount of sarcasm.

Jorge's white van, displaying Thompson's Paints and Interiors in bold black lettering on the side, bounced up and down toward them. He pulled up next to them and exited the van. Angelina licked her lips and grinned. Five kilos of coke would soon be hers.

A whirring motor buzzed overhead, gradually getting louder over the next few minutes, heralding the drug runner's arrival. A white and blue Cessna appeared, just skirting the orange trees. It descended until tangential to the ground. The wheels touched down.

She squinted, shielding her eyes from the bright afternoon sun and clenched her teeth. *Dammit.*

Bengal cut the engines, sputtering the plane to a halt.

He dismounted from the plane, wearing his usual camouflage khakis and a tight army-green tee shirt that emphasized his muscular torso. His black hair was slicked back, banded in a tight, small ponytail. A pair of Ray-Bans rested across his tanned perfect nose, an unusual mixture of part Cuban and part Cherokee. Known only as Bengal, he was more like a snake, and as vain as he was adventurous. Traits Angelina would ordinarily admire if circumstances were different.

But she needed him—for now. An accomplished pilot, able to fly undetected from Jamaica, hired to smuggle cocaine brought in by fast boats from Columbia.

He slithered toward her, removing his 9mm semi-automatic pistol from the back of his pants, and motioned for Hector and Jorge to unload the cocaine from the cargo bay.

"Look man, I'm running the show here, not you. All of it better be there," Angelina said.

Bengal slid his Ray-Bans down his nose, exposing his dark eyes. He raised his eyebrows and pulled his lips into a tight, sinister smile.

"Whatever you say," he smirked.

He motioned, with gun in hand, to Angelina. She abhorred what was to come. They walked to the orange groves as Hector and Jorge transferred the cocaine from the Cessna to the van.

"This is good right here," he said.

Angelina reached into her bag. "Here's the fifteen grand, and, as agreed, ten ounces for yourself."

"And?" He clapped the back of her head, hard enough to make a sharp thumping sound. "Complete payment is due upon receipt."

She pulled back as Bengal, who always traveled commando, dropped trou. Grabbing her by the hair, he plunged her head down.

"Bite me like the last time, bitch, and I'll fucking blow your head off."

As he pistoned his way into her mouth, she heard him cock the gun that was pressed to the left side of her head. "Angie baby, I've missed you. Oooh, you give such good head."

She tried to steady herself; her knees sliding back as Bengal's hips shoved her small frame. He smelled of stale tobacco, rum, and day old sweat. He was breathing heavily, his short pants intermingled with moans. At least it would be over soon. Her head buzzed, and she squeezed her eyes shut, waiting for the wave of nausea to pass.

He pushed her free once he had spilled his load.

"You've outdone yourself Angie." Pulling up his pants, he tucked his gun away. He laughed and turned away. "See you next month," he mocked.

Angelina stood up and brushed the dirt from her slacks. Anger bubbled up to her face and wetness formed beneath her eyelids. She reached into her bag and felt for the .38 she'd stored in the glove compartment of Hector's car. Arms outstretched, she clutched the revolver with both hands and fired, striking him in the back of the head. He crumbled to the ground.

*That was satisfying*, she thought.

Putting the gun away, she pulled out a small bottle of mouthwash from her bag. She always came prepared for dealing with his lingering taste. Swishing her mouth clean, she spat where her knees had dented the ground and strode over to Bengal's prone form. He lay face down, motionless, his head resting in his warm blood. Kneeling over him, Angelina grabbed the cocaine and the fifteen grand and walked away.

She returned to find Hector and Jorge had finished loading the van, the bricks of cocaine stashed away inside paint cans.

"Where's Bengal?" Jorge asked.

"He's out there," she gestured toward the grove, "relieving himself. He's been paid. Jorge let's get going. We need to get back to New York." She kissed Hector on the cheek. "Bye Hector."

Taking her hand, he helped her into the van. "Bye Miss Angelina."

She liked that he called her Miss.

Jorge sped along the undulating dirt path, the drug filled paint cans clanking in the back. Angelina leaned against the open window, breathing the balmy afternoon air deep into her lungs, exhaling with renewed vigor. She reached for her cell and called Maurice.

"You finished?" she asked.

"Fuck no! Someone got there before me. You still owe me, Baby."

"I'm coming back tonight. We'll talk."

"Hey, I showed up. You owe me for my time. Don't hang up the phone, bitch—"

She snapped her phone closed.

"Jorge, we have a problem. Get me to the airport. I need to fly back now. You'll have to drive it alone. I'll meet you Sunday night at the warehouse. No speeding. No parkways. Don't draw any attention."

Jorge swerved the van, just barely making the exit to Miami International Airport.

Angelina righted herself in the black vinyl seat. "Jesus Christ, Jorge. This is exactly what I mean."

# Chapter Seventeen

Thursday, January 5, 7:00 a.m.

*T*ara squinted at the morning light peeking through the curtains. Her head ached, and her mouth was cotton dry. She pressed her hand to her forehead. Tara looked about the room. She had not slept in Jeffrey's bed after all.

And then she remembered. Last night. The dinner with Jeffrey. The wine. I'm hung over. What must he think? About to pull the covers over her head, she heard Jeffrey clear his throat.

"Good morning. Time to wake up," he said with wicked glee.

Oh no. There was no hiding now. "I'm so sorry about last night, Jeffrey. I must not usually drink. I hope I didn't embarrass you, or myself."

He laughed softly. "Apparently not, no, and I don't know. But I didn't want you to be late for your appointment with Leo. He's taking you over to the hospital this morning. Remember?"

"Yeah, I do." New memories were not a problem, but the past ones? They were a bitch.

"I left a towel and that bag of stuff Liz...Detective Shear...bought for you in the bathroom. I'll make us breakfast while you get ready." He grinned. "Would you like some aspirin with those eggs?"

Tara nodded. "That might be a good idea."

Leo Kane stood when Jeffrey and Tara entered Jeffrey's office. "I got here a bit early," he explained. "Laurie, your assistant, told me to have a seat in your office."

"That's fine. For a moment, I thought we were late." His hand, which had grasped Tara's tightly, slid free from hers. "Here she is." Jeffrey paused, thoughtful. "I can reschedule my day. I'll go with both of you to the hospital."

Tara looked into his eyes, so soft and full of concern. "No, don't. I'll be fine. I'm sure Dr. Kane and I will be back soon."

"All right. I'm sure you'll ace every test."

"I'm sure, too. Now, go on and lock up some criminals." Tara waved to Jeffrey as he stood in the door watching her leave. *He's a good man.*

Tara sat next to Leo in the hospital's radiology waiting room. She ripped off the Band-Aid the lab tech had placed across her upper arm, and stared at the puncture site. No blood, only a pinpoint remembrance.

She glanced at Leo. His face round and his hairline receding, Tara guessed he was in his late fifties. He wore dark brown corduroy pants and a matching jacket with mustard colored oval elbow patches. Clothes that screamed the '70's, but that's what Tara liked about him. He wasn't avant-garde. His calm, ocean blue eyes were the kind she imagined people were compelled to gaze into, including her.

Tara nudged him. "I don't know that I have insurance."

"It's all right. Jeffery found your insurance plan through your driver's license information. These detectives can find anything. Hard to be entirely anonymous in this age. And don't worry. I preregistered you." He turned his head and looked at her. "Do you want to be anonymous?"

She took a deep breath. "Sometimes."

A door opened, and a woman in short white lab coat stepped into the waiting room. "Tara Ross? Dr. Tara Ross?"

Tara stood.

She'd been told the CT scan, without contrast of her brain, would luckily not take long. Then she'd return to the precinct and to Jeffrey. That is if there wasn't anything physically wrong with her.

But before she could leave with the woman, the double doors to the emergency room next to Radiology swung open. Three people in blue scrubs pushed a gurney carrying a woman, huffing and puffing, out into the hallway.

"Take her straight to labor and delivery," one of them yelled.

Tara craned her neck and peered down the adjoining corridor. There they were—the secure doors to the hospital's labor and delivery area. She hadn't noticed them earlier, but now the doors to the maternity unit buzzed open.

Before the L&D doors shut her heart soared, rivaling that of the rapid-fire pop-pop-pop of fetal heart rate monitors echoing into the unit's hallway. Then the double doors clicked closed.

"Dr. Ross?"

Tara jerked her head. "Y…yes, I'm coming."

The whole time she lay on that table, getting her head scanned, she wondered whether anyone could read what was hammering away in her mind.

Tara scooted up the stairs to the Homicide Division on the third floor and ran into Jeffrey's office, leaving a panting Leo behind. Jeffrey shoved his chair back, stood, and ran around his desk to hug her.

"Well?" he asked.

Tara looked up at him. "The blood work and the CT scan are all normal." She grinned. "It's all in my head!"

# Chapter Eighteen

Saturday January 7, 8:00 a.m.

*C*leared from any physical reason for her memory loss, Tara couldn't wait to get away with Jeffrey for a day trip to the Catskills. She looked out the window of the SUV as Jeffrey drove to his brother's sporting goods store. *What if I've never skied?* she wondered.

The bell above the door clanged as they entered It's A Hit. Jeffrey flung his arms out and hustled toward Johnny.

"Hey, little brother!" Jeffrey said as he hugged Johnny, clapping him on the back. His brother nearly disappeared into Jeffrey's ski jacket.

"Good to see you too."

He parted from his brother's bear hug and placed his arm around her. "Johnny, this is Tara."

"Tara, it's a pleasure to meet you." Johnny shook her hand. His hand was smaller than Jeffrey's and his grip, firm but inviting. He was half a foot shorter than Jeffrey and had dark brown wavy hair, but the men shared the same eyes and facial expressions. She instantly liked him.

"We're heading up to the Catskills today, and Tara needs the works."

Johnny grinned at her. "It would be my pleasure to get you everything you need to go skiing with this pain in the ass."

Thank you," she said.

"Let's go in the back. I have the perfect pair of skis for you. I'll measure your foot, get you some boots, and set your bindings. You'll be good to go."

She followed Johnny into the back of the store. He had everything already laid out.

"Now, let's try these on," he instructed.

She easily snapped her ski boots closed, the snugness of them familiar.

He looked impressed. "Looks like you've skied before." Then he smiled at her. "You're all set. Have a good time."

She shook his hand. "Thanks again."

"You're welcome. And I do mean that. I haven't seen my brother this happy in years."

Funny thing was, she felt the same.

He walked her back out to the front where Jeffrey was flipping through the rack of running shorts. He looked up. "Ah there you guys are! All set?"

"Johnny went all out. Even if it turns out that I don't shine on the slopes, at least I'll look fabulous!"

Jeffrey winked at her. "You always look good to me. All right Tara. Let's hit the trails." He gave Johnny a thumbs up sign. "Thanks, bro."

Johnny pointed at him. "And don't scratch up my ride. You know I'm gonna check."

"Hey! Same goes for the Mustang!"

"Have fun. Don't hurt her!" Johnny called as they walked out the door.

"Never."

The snow sparkled in the morning sun, blanketing the mountains and clinging like puffy clouds on the evergreens. It was a beautiful day to ski.

Tara's knees quivered as she buckled her boots.

*Think hard, Tara. You must have done this before. Relax your body. It will come to you.*

Helmets on, they skied to the lift. She maneuvered in the snow gracefully. *Okay. See, not so bad. You can do this.*

In no time, they reached the top of the summit. Jeffrey pushed off the lift and moved to the edge of the slope.

"Ready?"

She peered at the abrupt drop. *Oh man, this is a black diamond trail. This is steep."*

He dug his ski poles into the powder and disappeared into a cloud of snow. "Let's go!" His words trailed after him.

"Oh crap. Oh crap, Oh crap," she yelled as she shot over the edge. She pictured herself, crumpled at the bottom of the hill, a ski pole piercing her leg, her brand new skis scattered miles up the mountain. *Wedge. Wedge. You can do it. Thank God, I missed that tree! Halfway down the mountain and I haven't fallen yet. Please Lord let me live.*

The world blurred by her and soon she could see Jeffrey, waiting at the bottom of the hill, ski poles dug into the fresh powder. She whizzed right by him, sliding to a stop.

Panting, she squealed like a little kid, "Again, again. Again." Certain that if she could handle that hill, she could handle anything.

"Wow. You *owned* that trail. I thought you'd take the intermediate one to the left."

"Intermediate trail?" she asked blankly. "You mean, I skied the pathway to hell with my heart squeezed into the back of my throat, and I could've taken the intermediate trail?"

He chuckled. "Well… yeah."

"You—!"

She dropped her poles and shoved him, her hands sinking deep into his padded chest. He toppled backward.

"Whoa," he yelled as he grabbed her hand. "Oh no you don't. You're going down with me."

Their tangled bodies thudded into the powder, shrouded by a cloud of crystalline flakes— their skis twisted into an odd macramé.

"Are you okay?" he asked, laughing.

"Great. Now get off me!" She teased, flinging a puff of snow at him.

"Oh. You wanna play, huh?"

"Uh oh," she said.

With each ride down the mountain, her heart raced, not from fear, but from exhilaration. No blood. No memories of screaming women. No dead babies. Life was good again.

Jeffrey hugged her as they entered the heated chalet. She didn't need the fireplace to warm her. She melted at his touch. As they defrosted their insides with hot chocolate, she rested her head on his shoulder.

"This has been the best day!"

He winked. "It's not over yet."

# Chapter Nineteen

Saturday, January 7, 4:30 p.m.

$O$nce he had loaded the skis, Jeffrey swung around the vehicle, climbed into the driver's seat, and started the engine. Switching on the heater, he glanced at her snow kissed pink cheeks. *God she was beautiful.*

He took a deep breath. There was no point in delaying his plan.

"I hope you won't be angry with me, but I want to drive by your house," he said.

She turned toward him and shook her head. "I'm not angry. Eventually, I'd have to go to the house. And I'm glad you'll be with me. Besides, I need my car. I remember leaving it there, but I'm not sure why."

He looked straight ahead, as he navigated out of the parking lot and onto the snowplowed road. "Maybe something will click for you, another memory."

Jeffrey wanted her to remember, he *did*, but he feared her clearing fog would somehow nudge him out of her life. For the first time since his divorce, he dreaded being alone.

They didn't talk much on the way to Brewster. Tara huddled in her seat. Her shoulder rubbed against the hand-rest, the slick of her ski jacket whooshing across the vinyl of the door. She tapped her toes.

He watched her fidget, pondering how she would react to her former home, hoping not to ruin a perfect day. But it was too late to turn around. He'd already said it. Backing out now would be selfish. She'd grow to resent him if he didn't give her every opportunity to prompt her memory. *But what if another man is waiting for her to return? Tara hadn't mentioned anyone. If there is, how could she forget about him? And where does that leave me?* Jeffrey gripped the steering wheel.

Turning right onto Pebble Road, Jeffrey drove to house number 210, and pulled into the driveway. A *For Sale* sign popped out from the snow covered lawn. A lockbox hung from the front door's brass knob. Her house, a sunny yellow colonial with deep green shutters, suited her, he thought. Bright, yet warm and inviting—just the way he saw her. He wondered why she blocked out such an idyllic place. Did something happen there that frightened her?

"Are you still okay?" he asked.

Tara didn't answer for a minute, just stared at the house.

"We can stay in here until you're ready, Tara. You don't have to get out. Or do you want to go home?" He regretted his words immediately. Jeffrey brushed his fingers through his hair. "I'm sorry, Tara. This is your home. I shouldn't—"

She turned to him and shook her head. "No. This is a house. It's not my home, not anymore."

He hugged her. "You do have a home, if you want it." Jeffrey let her rest her head on his shoulder, waiting for Tara to speak.

"Well, even if this isn't my home, *that* is my car," she finally said.

"Okay. Let's go get it."

They climbed out of Johnny's SUV and crunched in the snow of the unplowed driveway.

Her silver Toyota Avalon was parked in front of the two-car garage, blanketed beneath a foot of snow.

He pulled out a snow brush from the back of the Explorer and flung the mound of snow from the top of her car. After dusting the snow from her window, he peeked inside. Silver keys dangled from the ignition.

"I found your keys. You left them in your car." Jeffrey yanked the door open. It creaked as he loosened it from its frozen frame. "Your car door was unlocked. Good thing it wasn't stolen."

Tara blinked, looking a bit shocked. "I can't believe I did that."

Jeffrey reached inside her car and grasped the keys, ratcheting the one in the ignition free. He left the door ajar, crunched through the snow, and hugged her tight.

"It's all right, Tara. You must have been exhausted, or terribly distracted. I've left my keys in my car on more than one occasion." He handed Tara her car keys. "Go ahead and start it up. I'll check your mailbox."

He grabbed a week's worth of mail. The postman had left a change of address card.

Behind him, the car sputtered—then nothing.

Jeffrey slid into the passenger seat and examined the instrument panel.

"Empty, huh?" The orange arrow pointed at E.

Tara tapped her forehead on the steering wheel.

"No problem. Johnny has a gas can in the Explorer. He's notorious for running out of gas."

Jeffrey got out, opened her door, and pulled her to her feet, steadying her. The snow squeaked beneath their boots as they walked back to the Explorer. He lifted her up, tucking her safely into the raised bucket seat and then rounded the Explorer, plopping into the driver's seat. He pulled forward, on the lookout for a gas station.

Her nose nearly smudged the window, the warmth of her breath sticking in concentric circles to the glass. She mopped the moisture away with the tip of her mitten.

*Oh God, why now?* Today had been so perfect. She hoped that Jeffrey couldn't tell she was falling apart on the inside. The racing blur of snow topped evergreens slowed into focus as Jeffrey pulled the Explorer into a gas station and got out.

*"Dr. Ross, the last bag of blood is in."* The empty, collapsed bag hangs on the IV pole. *"I need more! Stat! Call the lab! I'm not going to lose her!"*

The car door slammed. Jeffrey buckled his seatbelt. "Gas can's full. Let's go get your car."

The car started readily now that it had gas.

Jeffrey tapped on the window. "Seems to run okay. Here's your mail. Follow me back to the house."

"I need to make one quick stop, and then I'll be home. I know the way."

Tara quickly pulled away before Jeffrey could protest, and stopped into the grocery store ten blocks from his house. Now it was her turn to surprise him. Tonight, she was going to give him a taste of her homemade pizza, and then... a taste of herself. She quickly gathered the ingredients, and feeling bold, grabbed a box of condoms, leaving the grocery store with a grin.

Parking behind the Explorer back at Jeffrey's house, Tara clutched her bag of groceries and bounded through the front door.

"I'm home."

"I'm glad." He reached for the grocery bag. "Let me take that for you."

Remembering the box of condoms, she hugged the bag close to her chest. "N...no," she stammered, "Uh, I'll take it in the kitchen. There's a surprise in there for you."

*Oh, God. Is there ever a surprise in there for you!*

# Chapter Twenty

Saturday, January 7, 6:30 p.m.

*T*ara stripped off her ski clothes and wriggled into a warm pair of jeans and a soft black sweater that Jeffrey had bought her, admiring the way it hugged the chill from her skin.

Humming, she headed to the kitchen. Peeking around the corner—Jeffrey wasn't anywhere in sight—she drew in a deep breath and crept across the tiled floor. Sliding a kitchen drawer open, she dropped the box of condoms inside, and then eased the drawer shut.

Homemade pizza and Jeffrey were on her mind—and how she'd enjoy both.

She arranged the ingredients on the kitchen counter and worked on the first course of the evening. Her hands sank into the tacky dough. The sticky white mixture oozed between her fingers. She thought of other things she'd like to massage. Her breath quickened, and her chest pulsed beneath her sweater. She wondered if he felt the same urgency too.

Jeffrey snuck into James's room. Having not stopped at a drug store, he was desperate. He rifled through his son's belongings wagering every college guy had condoms stashed somewhere. *Ah, yep. There it is!* Jeffrey's fingers curled around a box of Trojans hidden in James's underwear drawer. He paused.

He imagined Mike taunting him—"Do her. You know you want to." And Marielle admonishing him—"If you touch one hair…"

He took a deep breath, grabbed the box of condoms, and dashed into his bedroom, flinging the stolen goods into the nightstand drawer. Then he pulled the bed covers back and fluffed the pillows. He'd be ready if she was.

Jeffrey meandered into the kitchen, guided by her humming and the doughy smell of freshly baked pizza, leaning close enough to her as he passed, to inhale the sweet citrus of her hair.

"Smells delicious." He reached past her, into the fridge. "I have some Guinness in here, somewhere," he said.

He looked great, Tara noticed. His jeans were not too baggy. Not too tight. They framed his firm butt perfectly. He turned back, holding two bottles of Guinness, one in each hand. Jeffrey grinned at her and carried the beers to the kitchen table, setting them down. Tara pulled the steaming pizza from the oven, cut it into slices, and brought it to the table—a hot dinner for a hot man, and hopefully *her* for dessert.

Her stomach fluttered as she slid into her seat. Heat rushed from her heels to her scalp. Tara, curled her toes and clutched the underside of the table, willing the blush from her body.

He lifted his bottle of Guinness to her. "Here's to a fabulous meal, the gorgeous chef, and to a wonderful evening."

She raised her bottle too. "To a wonderful evening."

They clinked their bottles.

They polished off the pizza and bottles of Guinness in no time, and then stared at each other for a few seconds.

Jumping into nervous motion, Jeffrey cleared the table while she leaned over the sink, rinsing the dishes. She heard his footsteps as he approached her from behind.

Feeling the warmth of his breath on the nape of her neck, she teased, "Ordinarily I don't like people sneaking up behind me, but I'll make an exception for you."

He reached over, shut off the faucet, and whispered, "Those dishes can wait until morning. I don't think I can."

That's all it took.

The soapy dishcloth fell from her hand, splashing into the sink. She spun around. His hands hugged her hips. She wrapped her arms around his neck, giving in to his embrace. For this instant, she didn't want to ponder the past or the future. All she wanted was to be in this perfect moment.

She patted for the drawer behind her, yanked it open and reached inside, grabbing the box of condoms and hiding it behind her back as Jeffrey took her by the hand and led her to his bedroom.

Tara bounced the box of Trojans onto the bed while Jeffrey opened the nightstand drawer and pulled out his box. They looked at each other and laughed.

She smiled. "Well, we'll be set for quite some time."

"A long time, I hope."

He cupped her cheeks and kissed her lightly. Then he slid off his shirt, letting it crumple to the floor and then grasped the ends of her sweater, edging it over her head while she shimmied free. Tara stood in her pink bra, the bra he had purchased for her, the curves of her breasts billowing from the borders, the outline of her nipples jutting at the centers. Her chest pulsed at his every touch.

He slipped his long fingers beneath the straps and peeled them from her shoulders, then reached around and released the hooks. The straps tickled her arms as the bra skidded to the floor.

He shook his head. "Tara, you are so beautiful."

He dropped his jeans down to his ankles. Every bit of him was firm. Jeffrey's chest was athletically solid— his belly was flat, and his legs muscular. The soft brown curls on his chest funneled down his abdomen and, like an arrow, pointed directly to his saluting erection.

"Oh lieutenant!" she teased.

She stepped out of her jeans too and crawled beneath the covers. He slipped in next to her and ran his fingers through her hair.

Jeffrey gently rolled Tara to her back, covering her, slipping her feet under his own. He stretched for miles. She slid the soles of her feet along his legs.

The tension in her shoulders released as he nuzzled the slope of her neck, his nose tickling that sweet spot that made her stomach dip. His kisses trailed across her neck and then down to the curve each breast, pausing with wicked delay at her puckered nipples. Tara closed her eyes and sank her head back into the soft pillow at the warmth of his tongue, arching at every languid lick.

Jeffrey crept lower. She floated away as his breath wafted over belly.

"Oh so good," she murmured. Her fingers glided through his sandy, straight hair—joyful at his shiver. He stopped at her velvet triangle, kissing and then gently sucking until her whole body blissfully quivered. Jeffrey made his way up to her chin and then tilting his head back, he gazed down at her face.

She cupped his angular cheeks and drew his face to hers. Lips slightly parted, she pressed her mouth against his. Jeffrey's face was rugged, but his lips were full and soft, completely covering hers. Her hands slid from his face and rounded his broad back. Her palms swirled in circles, massaging his back.

Jeffrey stretched out his arm and blindly patted for a condom in the open drawer of the nightstand. He thumped around wildly, smacking the alarm clock in his heated search. It dropped off the table with a clang and dangled precariously by its cord over the open drawer.

"Shit," he murmured, but managed to extract a condom packet.

She laughed softly at him.

"Oh, you think this is funny?"

"Yes." She nodded.

He grinned and ripped the wrapper with his teeth, pulling out the flattened latex ring. He rolled on the condom without a hitch. She watched it unroll...and unroll. He was immense.

He moved toward her and kissed her, lightly then increasingly deeper. She brushed through the soft hairs of his chest and pressed her hand against him. His hand skimmed the underside of her breasts.

Tara softly gasped and wriggled beneath him.

He slowly parted her. She murmured something unintelligible and eased her hips forward. Her body arched against his. She clung to him, her toes pinching the sheets. Wrapping her legs around his waist, she pulled him even closer.

There was no stopping now as he filled her faster and faster until they pulsed together in their release. Her heart thumping, Tara exhaled. Jeffrey's chest rose and fell in rhythm with her breaths as she lay beneath him, sated, warm, and secure.

The phone rang.

"Crap," he muttered. Jeffrey stretched out his long arm and answered it without rolling away from Tara.

"Hello," he said with a sigh.

He listened patiently as Mike detailed his conversation with Madelyn Thompson.

"It sure will be a few interesting days. Good work, Mike."

He hung up the phone and returned it to its place on the nightstand.

Tara brushed Jeffrey's bangs from his face. "Is there a problem?" she asked.

"No. That was just Mike, updating me on information about the double homicide that we're investigating."

"Do you have to leave?"

"Leave you, like this? Never! Come here." Jeffrey drew her in closer, his body against hers, her delicious warm breasts pressed into his chest. He stroked her hair. Leaning into her, he kissed her forehead, nose, and then in a deliberately lazy pace settled his mouth onto her lips. They needn't hurry. They had all night.

# Chapter Twenty-One

Sunday, January 8, 7:35 a.m.

"*G*ood morning," Jeffrey said, nuzzling Tara's neck.

He pulled away from her and scooted to the edge of the bed. Grabbing her hand, he pulled her out from the warmth of their covers. "Let's go take a nice hot a shower...together."

Tara shook her head. "We'll never get out of here if we do."

He slipped his hands down the slope of her back, her skin so silky beneath his fingers, and cupped her butt, giving her cheeks a gentle goose. "It's a risk I'm willing to take," he said softly.

Jeffrey and Tara lingered in the shower, lazily lathering one another. After finally toweling off, they then quickly dressed, and wolfed down breakfast to make up for time lost, but well spent nonetheless.

"You ready?" he asked.

"Yep," she agreed, "You sure you don't mind taking me to Marielle's today? Williamsburg is out of your way. I can take the train."

"No, traffic is light today. Besides, I would drive you anyway." And he'd get to spend an extra hour with Tara before walking into a frenzied Sunday at the precinct.

"Okay," she thankfully relented.

Snatching their coats, Jeffrey and Tara leapt out the door and into Johnny's Explorer. The winter sun that had melted the snow banks and licked the icicles from the roof of his house warmed his cheeks. He leaned over and kissed her—a kiss that he needed to carry on his lips for the rest of his day.

Jeffrey parked the SUV at the curb in front of Marielle's apartment and kissed Tara goodbye. She slid out of the seat, and trotted up the building's brick stairs, meeting Marielle half way. They hugged and then turned and waved to Jeffrey.

"I'll take good care of her," Marielle called to Jeffrey.

Jeffrey watched them go inside, and then bowed his head over the steering wheel. *God he was falling for her.*

Grinning, he started the engine and, as he drove away, bound for the two-seven, his cell phone rang. Jeffrey glanced at the screen. It was his precinct number.

"Corrigan."

"Hey, Lou," Mike started right in. "You won't believe who showed up."

# Chapter Twenty-Two

Sunday, January 8, 11:30 a.m.

The desk sergeant poked his head over his New York Post. "Good morning Lieutenant. I wouldn't go up there if I were you. Just turn around and go home." He grunted and returned to his newspaper.

Jeffrey shrugged his shoulders and trudged up the stairs to Homicide on the 3rd floor. Five steps away, he heard scuffling followed by the familiar sound of bodies crashing into walls.

"Shit!"

He hadn't anticipated walking into a Superbowl Sunday showdown. Jeffrey rounded the corner following the shrieks of women. He sighed. *Another great day in the house.*

"Whore!" a red-haired woman yelled.

"Bitch!" the woman with long black hair screamed. "I'm gonna connect the freckles on your ugly face with my fingernails."

"I'm gonna pull out every strand of that black troll hair of yours, slowly, piece by piece!"

"Bring it, bitch," the black haired woman yelled, clearly in charge. She jammed the spiked heel of her black boot onto the top of the fire-haired woman's foot.

Jeffrey winced. *Ooh, that must have smarted!*

The redhead howled, jumping up and down on one of her high-heeled shoes. Jeffrey rubbed his chin.

*This is getting good.* The red haired woman charged and then hurled herself onto the other woman's back, clamping her freckled arms around her chest, and rode her piggyback style.

Jeffrey strolled up to Mike, who stood against the hallway wall sipping a cup of coffee while holding another cup of Joe in his other hand. Without a word, Mike handed him the cup.

"I knew you'd be coming in," he said. "Don't you just love girl on girl action?"

"Hmm," Jeffrey mumbled as he sipped his coffee.

Paul sauntered up to them. "What's going on?"

Jeffrey and Mike replied in unison, "Girl fight."

"Cool."

They watched the female melee, letting it go for a bit.

"Women, they're so brutal," Mike said.

The others nodded in agreement.

"Who *are* these people?" Jeffrey asked.

"The woman with the black hair," Mike began, "is Angelina Holtz. The woman riding her is Madelyn Thompson. And that guy over there, sitting on the bench, is Stuart Thompson, Steven's brother. Amazingly, all three showed up here at the same time."

Stuart Thompson, hair cropped short and gelled back, sat quietly on the hallway bench. Wearing a Brooks Brothers suit and tie, his folded hands rested in his lap. He never flinched once during the women's scuffle.

Liz Shear's running shoes thudded against the faded brown linoleum as she pummeled down the hall from Narcotics. Wearing her Nikes and gun belt, she sandwiched herself between the battling women. Her eyes tightened as someone yanked her ponytail.

"Hey, watch the hair!" Liz jutted her elbows out defensively, separating the skirmishing women. The three bent over, huffing, with Liz in the middle.

Pointing to Madelyn, she yelled, "You, over there," and then to Angelina, "and you, go over there." Liz glared at the men. "Don't make me come back here, boys."

Mike shrugged. "Okay. We won't."

Adjusting her gun belt, she strode back to Narcotics briskly, squeaking her rubber heals into the worn floor.

Madelyn, not to be ignored, stomped her feet. "I want my husband's body now!"

"Mrs. Thompson, I'm Detective Lieutenant Jeffrey Corrigan," Jeffrey calmly replied, "commanding officer of the homicide squad of this precinct. I'm sorry for your loss. Please come with me and we'll talk."

He led Madelyn to interview room one. Before he went in, he called out instructions to his men.

"Detective Price, please escort Mr. Thompson to room two and Detective Rivchak, please take Ms. Holtz to room three." Jeffrey crooked his finger at Madelyn. "Mrs. Thompson, if you please."

Stuart complied wordlessly.

Angelina grinned as she brushed past Rivchak, flipping her long black mane across her slender shoulders. Paul winked at her. Glancing at his reflection in the interview room window, he smoothed his hair back before entering. Jeffrey and Mike shook their heads.

Jeffrey closed the door.

"Please sit," he instructed Madelyn Thompson. He then sat across from her at the interview room table.

"I brought you some coffee." His gaze never wavered from her flushed face as he set the Styrofoam cup in front of her. Still staring straight at her, he straightened his tie.

"Thank you," she said. She fixed her hair and fidgeted with her leopard print dress. His first impression of her was that she was all fire on the outside, but weirdly vacant on the inside.

"Your husband's death is under investigation as a homicide, Ms. Thompson. His body is at the Medical Examiner's office and will not be released until the medical examiner's completed her final report.

He was identified by his housekeeper, and through other records including his driver's license. However, I can take you to see his body today."

Hands trembling, she nearly spilled her coffee as she asked, "Do you know who killed him?"

"No. That's what we are trying to find out."

*She'll sign a confession before I'm done with her, or I'll have her shoving the pen right into the killer's hand,* Jeffrey thought to himself.

"You seem quite nervous, Ms. Thompson."

"I'm still in shock."

Jeffrey lifted his brows, watching Madelyn fan herself with her hand. He always kept the heat cranked a little higher in his favorite interview room. Jeffrey had gotten used to the hellish temperature. That and he could always leave. He enjoyed watching his suspects squirm through the observation window while waiting for them to change their story. Jeffrey grinned. Frank had taught him that trick.

Madelyn swiped her hand across her forehead. "I go on vacation, and I get a call that my husband's dead."

Jeffrey drummed his fingers on the table. "Yes, that can certainly spoil a vacation. So, were you and Steven still married?"

"Yes, but I left him six months ago. I couldn't deal with his womanizing or his drugs. I thought he would tire of Angelina, but he didn't. Then he got involved with a prostitute. He was obsessed with her. He spent a lot of money fixing her up, you know, like in that movie *Pretty Woman.* His drug use and irresponsible spending started to hurt the business. Money was missing. Stuart was convinced that Steven had paid off an accountant to fix the books. Stuart and I decided that, for the longevity of the business, Steven needed to step aside until he could pull his life back together. He wouldn't relinquish his role, of course, even temporarily. To get even with us, he refused to file for separation let alone divorce."

Jeffrey dragged his notebook across the table, delighted at the sound of the metal spiral scraping across the Formica that made her wince ever so slightly. He scratched a few notes with his pen and then looked up at Madelyn.

"Were you and Stuart angry?" he asked.

She craned her neck, trying to get a look at his notes and Jeffrey pulled the notebook closer. Madelyn relaxed back into her chair with a huff.

"We weren't happy," she said.

"I asked you if you and Stuart were angry with Steven,"

"Yes, we were angry. I know what you're getting at."

He sipped his coffee, reveling in his intentional delay.

"Getting at? Hmm." And then he hammered at her, "That maybe you, or Stuart, were angry and that sometimes emotions get heated and lead to situations which get out of control?"

Madelyn jumped out of her chair. "You're dead wrong!"

He leaned back in his chair and lowered his voice. "Please, sit."

Madelyn plunked into her seat.

"I may be wrong, but Steven is definitely dead," Jeffrey said, probing for her response.

She shook her finger at him. "I don't like what you are implying, detective."

"Okay." He paused, and then continued. "When did you last see or speak to Steven?"

"I saw him the night before I left for the cruise."

"What time, on Thursday night, was that?"

"Around 8 p.m."

"Did you argue?"

"We had a difference of opinion. I wanted a divorce. He didn't want to give me one."

Jeffrey pressed on. "You said that you moved out six months ago. Where did you go?"

"I moved into Stuart's house in Katonah."

Jeffrey arched his eyebrows. "Do you and Stuart have an intimate relationship?"

Madelyn tapped her fingernails on the desk. "Of course. My marriage to that ass was long over."

"How did Steven feel about you sleeping with his brother?"

Madelyn gulped her coffee and then sat the cup on the table. "Humph! Steven couldn't care less. He was busy with his drugs,

Angelina, and that Russian prostitute. He *hated* Stuart. He wouldn't divorce me because he didn't want Stuart to have me."

Jeffrey tapped his pen on the table. "Really? So Steven didn't want out of the marriage to spite his brother?"

Madelyn rimmed her coffee cup with her red polished fingernail. "Steven was a spiteful man."

"Okay, so is the house in Katonah your permanent address?"

"Yes, but I don't own the house, yet. Stuart does. I still own the apartment with Steven. That bastard wouldn't sell it. Wouldn't give me my half. Well, in the end, looks like I won anyway."

"You wanted that apartment badly, huh?" Jeffrey pointed at her. "You could sell that for a mint. And now you can finally marry Stuart, you know, the man you *love*. Steven's sudden demise, oh I mean *murder*, worked out quite well for you."

Madelyn leaned towards him and narrowed her eyes. "I may not have loved him, but I didn't kill him."

Jeffrey shrugged. "Didn't say you did."

Madelyn shook her finger at him. "You implied it."

Jeffrey folded his hands on the table. "I can imply what I want until the truth is discovered, which in my experience eventually happens. He glanced at his watch and then stretched back in his chair placing his hands behind his head. "All right. Tell me about this prostitute. What did this woman you called 'Pretty Woman' look like? What was her name?" Now maybe he'd find out who the woman was, that was lying on that blood soaked mattress, eyes slit open as though she was taking one last fleeting glimpse at what her life had become, before her fate was sealed.

Madelyn hissed through her teeth. "Blonde. Early twenties. Didn't speak English. Steven mentioned that she was Russian. I don't recall her name. He got her from some pimp. By that point, I didn't care."

Jeffrey waited, but Madelyn offered no more. He sipped his coffee. "Tell me what you did on Friday."

"I woke up at 5 a.m. The limo picked me up about 5:45 to take me to LaGuardia. I had a flight to Miami. My cruise line was leaving from the Port of Miami that afternoon."

"Where was Stuart?"

"He had to meet with an accountant that morning. He took a later flight, and then met me in Miami."

"What time was his flight, and when did he meet you?"

"He took the 10:05. I met him about 3 p.m. Our cruise left at 4:30."

Jeffrey cocked his head. "Why didn't you take the same flight?"

"I told you, he had his meeting. I wanted to leave earlier to shop in Miami."

"So you left The Port of Miami on a cruise to the Bahamas with Stuart, the man you love, and the brother of your late husband."

"Uh uh. No you don't. You implied that Stuart and I were on a cruise leaving Miami when my husband is already dead."

"I said no such thing. I said Stuart is the brother of your late husband which is a fact." Jeffrey grinned and rubbed his chin. "Interesting how you zoomed in on that word "late"."

"You're trying to trick me. I'm done talking with you."

"We're nearly done." Jeffrey picked up a stack of papers he'd picked up off Herb's desk and tapped the edges on the desk. She didn't have to know they were his overtime reports. "I see that you are named as the beneficiary of Steven's life insurance policy and that you could collect up to five million dollars."

Madelyn thumped her fist onto the table. "*Possibly?*"

Jeffrey nodded. "That's right. Steven was found with a gun in his hand. If his death is ruled a suicide, then you get nothing."

"But you said this is a homicide investigation."

"Yes, precisely, an *investigation*." Jeffrey slid a paper and pen to her. "Okay, Madelyn. I need you to write down your address and phone number. This is an ongoing investigation. I'll take you to the Medical Examiner's office later this afternoon."

Madelyn snatched the paper and pen from Jeffrey. "Fine! I want Stuart to come with me to view Steven's body. I prefer to ride in my own car, if you don't mind, since I'm not under arrest." Madelyn dashed the pen across the paper and handed it back to Jeffrey.

"You are correct, Ms. Thompson. We'll leave for the New York City Medical Examiner's Office soon."

Madelyn snorted, "I'll be consulting with my lawyer."

Jeffrey nodded and then stood. "I think that would be wise. Make yourself comfortable, Ms. Thompson. I have a few things to wrap up, and then I'll be back for you. Can I get you another cup of coffee?"

Madelyn turned her head away from him. "No thank you," she said curtly.

Jeffrey closed the door. He peered through the observation window, watching Madelyn, seated in her chair, tapping the toe of her high -heeled shoe against the stone floor. He wondered how Mike was faring with Stuart's interrogation in the next room.

Jeffrey folded his arms across his chest, surprised by his wan face, reflected in the glass of interview room two. He frowned and turned up the speaker outside the room, while watching Mike rest his elbows on the table and lean toward Stuart Thompson. He had the optimal view, split down the middle, Mike on one side of the table and Stuart on the other, their reactions to one another clear.

"When did you and Madelyn become an item?" Mike asked. Jeffrey shook his head. Mike had his own unique interview style.

"We've have been in a committed relationship for over a year. She moved in with me six months ago."

Stuart sat motionless. Jeffrey hadn't even seen him blink.

"Before that, where was she living?"

"She was living in her apartment with Steven on West 67th, but frequently spent time with me in Katonah, until she formally moved in."

Mike squinted at Stuart. *Humph. This guy is dead from the neck up.*

"And who's idea was that?" Mike asked.

"Both of ours."

"I see. And Steven was cool with that. Come on!"

Stuart paused. Mike snapped his fingers in front of Stuart's face. "Earth calling Stuart."

"Steven was too busy with his drugs and women to notice," Stuart replied in an eerie automaton-like voice.

"What kind of drugs was he using?"

"Cocaine."

"Anything else?"

"Not that I'm aware of, but who knows."

Mike fingered his mustache. "Feel free to elaborate at any time, Stuart. Have you ever used cocaine or any drugs?"

Stuart glared at Mike. "Absolutely not!"

Jeffrey grinned. *Now, you got under that thick skin of his!*

Mike swung his fist in the air. "Now that's what I like, a little emotion. Tell me about your relationship with your brother."

Stuart leaned back in his chair and pressed his fingertips together into a tight steeple. "We're related, that's where it ends. We had a business relationship—equal ownership of Thompson's Paints and Interiors after my father died. I argued with him about his drug use and missing company money. I told him that I knew that he was stealing from the business."

Mike cocked his brow. He rested his elbows on the table and mirroring Stuart, he tee-peed his fingers, then paused for a good ten seconds before he asked, "Did you have proof of this?"

Stuart likewise paused. "Steven was involved in creative accounting. I'm in the process of tracking all the monies."

Mike leaned in towards Stuart. "Do you think he was crooked, or just incompetent?"

"Yes. And yes," Stuart answered flatly.

Mike frowned and pushed back his chair. 'Let's take a little break here. Maybe you're running on empty. Can I get you a coffee or anything to eat?"

Stuart clasped his hands together, "I can't have coffee. Caffeine doesn't agree with me. I have irritable bowel disease."

"How about some water?"

Stuart gave Mike a quick nod. "Yes. That would be fine."

Mike stepped out of the room, mocking Stuart in a monotonous voice once the door was closed. "Stuart, would you like me to slap you around? Yes. That would be fine."

He patted Jeffrey on the shoulder and said, "This guy's a real talker. We'll be here all day."

"Go get the guy a glass of water. Do you mind if I talk to him?"

"Be my guest."

Jeffrey walked into the room and extended his hand to Stuart. "Hello Mr. Thompson. I'm Lieutenant Corrigan."

Stuart didn't get up from his chair. He merely shook Jeffrey's hand.

Jeffrey sat and stared straight at Stuart. "So I hear that you are having an affair with your dead brother's wife."

Stuart rolled his manicured fingers across the black Formica table. "I've explained this ad nauseam to you guys. I don't want to, or need to, explain myself anymore. He didn't love her. She didn't love him. He wouldn't give her a divorce just to spite me. He fucked up the business. I fucked his wife. End of story."

Mike returned to the room, nearly spilling the glass of water at what he'd heard.

"The guy has a pulse after all," Mike whispered to Jeffrey. "Stuart, my man, I brought you water, a bagel, and an apple."

Stuart waved his hand dismissively. "I can't eat gluten."

"Glu...what?" Mike squinted.

"Gluten. Forget it. I'll just have the water. And I'll take the apple. Can I have a knife?"

"No, you can't," Mike said.

"Then I'd like to have this apple pared, seeded, and cut into wedges."

"Look, pal," Mike retorted.

Jeffrey jumped in. "Sure, we'll take care of that for you. Nice suit, by the way."

"Thank you. I always dress for official business."

Mike glanced at Jeffrey and raised his right eyebrow. "Ooh, we've been upgraded to official business."

"Go get the guy's apple peeled and then meet me outside room three," Jeffrey said.

Mike walked away, mumbling, "What am I? A fucking chef?"

With the break room door open, Jeffrey grinned as he eyed Mike remove a knife from the drawer and proceed to peel the apple. Jagged shards of red skin tumbled to the floor. He watched Mike return to room two and place a paper plate with the sliced apple on the table in front of Stuart. Jeffrey shook his head and laughed. Less than half of the apple remained after Mike finished paring it. Stuart stared at the irregular chunks of apple slices peppered with slivered brown seeds and frowned.

"Enjoy," Mike quipped, then hurried out the door and joined Jeffrey outside interview room three. "What's going on over here?"

Jeffrey rested his hands on his hips. "I'm going to give our 'star detective' about a minute more before I cut in on his crap ass job."

Paul squirmed in his chair as Angelina sat cross-legged, sucking seductively on the tip of a banana.

"Whoa!" Mike nudged Jeffrey. "She's mouthing that banana. That's so unfair. I'm second grade, and he's wet behind the ears. I get the apple-freak-robot-man, and he gets the banana-sucking porn star."

Jeffrey snickered.

"How long did you know Steven Thompson?" Paul asked.

"I met him two years ago, at a party. We hit it off and started seeing each other."

"Were you aware that he was married?"

Angelina snorted. "Sure."

"That was not an issue for either of you?"

"No, silly. Madelyn and Steven had drifted apart. I think she was really into his brother. He's more her type anyway."

Paul grinned and cocked his head. "And what type would that be?

"Uptight. Repressed. Steven liked to party." Angelina washed down her banana with a swig of orange juice, staring at Paul the whole time over the brim of her paper cup. "He was good in bed too."

"Did you move in with Steven?"

She set the cup down and traced her tongue along her bottom lip, never breaking eye contact with Paul. "Yes, shortly after we met."

"And was Steven using cocaine?"

"Yes."

"Were you?"

"On occasion. Mostly before or after sex. We both enjoyed it. Are you going to arrest me for using coke, Detective Rivchak?" she teased.

Paul shook his head. "No. Where was Steven getting money for his coke?

Angelina shifted in her chair, arching her back and rocking her hips. "His business was doing very well."

Mike poked Jeffrey with his elbow. "Shit! Will you look at that!"

Jeffrey widened his eyes. "Hell of an interview so far."

Paul loosened his tie.

Jeffrey shook his head. "I shouldn't have paired those two together. She's clearly in charge here." Jeffrey glanced at the clock on the wall. "I'll give Rivchak two more minutes to redeem himself."

Paul cleared his throat. "The paint business, you mean? Thompson Paints and Interior Design?"

Grinning, she replied, "Yeah, the business."

Jeffrey narrowed his eyes he watched Paul clicking his ballpoint pen repeatedly with his thumb. "Do you know where he was getting his coke from?"

Angelina's eyelids flickered. "No, he didn't discuss that with me."

"I understand that you just got back from Miami. Short trip. You must be exhausted."

"I'm fine. I was just... hungry." Angelina slowly brushed her lips with her finger.

Paul shifted uncomfortably in his chair.

Jeffrey pressed his lips tight and exhaled through his nose, Heat shot from his nostrils. "I'm cutting Rivchak off!"

Jeffrey twisted the door handle and pushed open the interview room door. Paul popped his eyes wide and shoved his chair back.

Jeffrey pointed to Paul, "Sit." Jeffrey sat down next to him.

"Hello, Ms. Holtz. I'm Lieutenant Corrigan." He offered her his hand but Angelina made no move to take it.

Instead, Angelina leaned back in her chair, crossed her legs, and folded her arms across her chest, right under her breasts, propping them up in obvious display. "Hello," she said curtly.

Jeffrey grinned at her. "Not bothering you, am I?"

She rolled her eyes. "Not yet."

He shot a glance to Scardino's idea of a bright, up and coming detective. And as always, Scardino had fucked him over. "Please, continue, Detective Rivchak."

Paul stared at him, giving Jeffrey a challenging, deadpan look.

*Yeah, keep it up, Rivchak. You'll be out my door as fast as you came in it.*

Paul turned his attention to Angelina. "Ms. Holtz, we were just talking about your return from Miami. Tell me, when did you leave New York?"

"I took the 7:55 a.m. Delta flight from LaGuardia to Miami International, Friday morning."

"Why did you go to Miami?"

Angelina unfolded her arms but kept her legs crossed. She leaned towards Paul and propped her elbow on the table. Angelina lowered her chin to her palm slowly, pausing in her pose for a few seconds, her eyes locked with Paul's. "My sister needed me. She had a miscarriage."

Jeffrey quickly asked, "Which hospital did your sister go to?"

Angelina glared at him and coolly answered, "She didn't. It was an early pregnancy. I gave her some Tylenol and stayed the night."

Jeffrey had nearly had enough of Angelina, and of Paul. His head pounded, but he needed to get through the interview Paul was flailing at. Jeffrey shoved a pen and paper across the table to Angelina. "Write your sister's name, address, and telephone number."

Angelina squinted at Jeffrey and then took up the pen. "This is the name of my brother-in-law's restaurant. My sister's name is Daisy. They just moved into a new house, so their phone isn't hooked up yet. Here's their cell number and the restaurant's phone and address."

Jeffrey shot back, "If you were in Miami, how did you know Steven was dead?"

"I didn't know until I came back to New York."

"Let me get this straight. Your sister has a miscarriage. You go to Miami to be with her, but you're back in New York a day later? She must have had a miraculous recovery."

Angelina leaned toward Jeffrey and gritted her teeth. "She was feeling better. There was nothing more that I could do for her. I had to get back to New York because I had a lot of inventory to do at the store before Monday morning. I stopped by the apartment, but it was designated as a crime scene. The doorman informed me that Steven was dead so I rushed over here to get some answers, and now you guys are giving me grief."

Paul responded, "We don't want to cause you any additional *grief*, Ms. Holtz. We just need to get some answers ourselves."

"Detective Rivchak knows how to treat me with respect, Lieutenant Corrigan. I'd rather just talk to him, if you don't mind."

"Yes, I do mind."

She sunk back into her chair. "Fine."

Paul continued his questioning. "Do you work at Thompson's Paints?"

"I'm the manager. The store is closed on the weekends, and that's when I do inventory."

"How's the business doing, financially?" Jeffrey asked.

"Well," she said curtly.

"No problems?"

"None that I am aware of."

Jeffrey arched his eyebrows. "As the manager, if there were problems, you should know. Right?"

"I'm not an accountant, Lieutenant. I file invoices. Supervise employees. Make work schedules. Do inventory."

"Who's your boss?"

"Steven."

"Not Steven *and* Stuart?"

"Stuart was not involved in the day to day business aspect. He lives in Katonah. He's hardly at the store. He just thinks he knows all about the business. He doesn't know shit."

"When did you last see or speak to Steven?" Paul asked.

"I saw him early Friday morning, about 6:30, before I left for Miami. He gave me my ticket."

"He bought the ticket for you?"

"Yes. He always took care of me."

Jeffrey leaned toward her. "You do know that Steven was also taking very good care of a beautiful young blonde?"

She smacked her palm on the table. "Beautiful, huh? You should have seen the bitch *before* Steven took pity on her. A low class foreign hooker. He had to fix her before he could fuck her."

"Fix her?" Jeffrey asked.

"Yeah. Hair dyed and styled, veneers for her teeth, a nose job, and breast implants."

"He certainly spent a lot of money on her makeover. Why?"

She tapped the floor with her boots. "Steven was a sex addict. Look. Madelyn is red headed. I have black hair. He wanted a blonde. And she was a real mess. She needed one hell of an overhaul."

Paul inquired, "What was her name?

"Some Russian name...Irina...something. I could never pronounce her last name. It started with an 'F'."

"And when did Steven get involved with her?"

"About seven months ago. It took her three months to recover from the plastic surgery. He enjoyed her *company* for the next four months. That's when Madelyn moved out. She wasn't going to play nurse to some hooker. I stayed, figuring that she was his pet project, a passing phase. He would complain to me that she wouldn't do coke with him and he knew I always would. And no one could communicate with her because she didn't speak English."

"Do you know where Irina came from?" Jeffrey asked.

Angelina smirked, "Not a clue."

"Ms. Holtz, I will ask you again. Do you *know* where Irina came from?"

She cleared her throat. "Steven got Irina through a pimp. She had been beaten, badly. He fixed her up. For all the time and money he spent on her, he didn't want to send her back to her pimp just for her to get beaten up again. Steven wanted to keep her 24/7, so he paid her pimp well. For God's sake! She was only a hooker!"

Jeffrey stared at Angelina. "Did you say *was*?"

"Yeah. It's not like anyone is going to miss her."

*Gotcha!* "I never told you that Irina was dead."

Angelina's green eyes bore directly into Jeffrey's own, searching eyes. "What? She's *not* dead?"

"She's at the morgue…lying next to your dead boyfriend," Jeffrey confirmed. When there was no flicker of any emotion at all he said, "I see that you're overwhelmed with grief. Okay, Ms. Holtz, this is an ongoing investigation. You may not return to the apartment because it is a sealed crime scene. After the apartment is released from crime scene status, you will be allowed to remove your personal effects. Do you have other living arrangements?"

Angelina tossed her hair behind her shoulders releasing the heavy perfume pulsing from her long, slender neck. "I have an apartment on West 84th."

Jeffrey wrinkled his nose as the overly floral scent filled the interview room. Tara kept her scent light, enticing, not the harsh kind that would burn in you in the throat like this crazy bitch.

Paul leaned in closer, completely intoxicated. "I thought you were living with Steven?" Paul asked.

"I was," she paused, flashing a wicked grin, "but sometimes I needed to get away, especially if Steven was planning on having Irina in his bed."

Jeffrey slid a piece of paper and a pen to Angelina. "Please write your full name, address, cell, and home phone numbers. We'll be talking to you again. Soon. "

"I can't wait."

"Goodbye Ms. Holtz." Jeffrey said, not bothering to shake her hand. "Paul, when you're finished with Ms. Holtz, I need to see you in my office."

"Yes Sir."

Jeffrey exited room three, rubbing his temples. He plodded down the hallway to his office. *I'm going to rip him a new one.*

Angelina wrote down the requested information, ripped off the top piece of paper, and slid it back to Detective Rivchak.

"Looks like you've been a naughty boy and need to go to the principal's office," she cooed.

Paul stood, placed his hand on his hip, and grinned. "It's cool. No worries."

"Hmm." She scribbled a note on another piece of paper. She tore it from the pad, folded it into quarters, stood, and walked toward Paul, crossing one leg in front of the other like a model walking a runway.

"Detective Rivchak, you're clearly ahead of the game." She traced the opening of his front pants pocket, snaked her hand inside, and released the note, her slender fingers lingering close to his zipper. He shuddered, and she whispered in his ear, "I'll tell you secrets that will make you crack this case. Don't open this note until you're alone. I'll see *you* later."

# Chapter Twenty-Three

Sunday, January 8, 1:15 p.m.

"*S*tay outside my office," Jeffrey said to Mike as he passed him in the hallway. "I need to speak to Paul then I'll call you in when I'm ready."

"I'll wait right here, Lou." Mike leaned against the wall. Propping his right heel to left ankle, he reached into his pocket, pulled out three blue Super Balls, and juggled them. Mike juggled after every interview. Catching all three balls in one hand, he rolled his eyes as Paul swaggered past him. Once Paul was inside Jeffrey's office, Jeffrey slammed his door.

Pointing his finger toward a chair, Jeffrey said, "Sit."

Paul complied.

"That interview was far from what I expect of you, of all my squad. And I don't want you to speak to Angelina Holtz alone, either. You let her take charge of the interview today. She was leading you, right by your dick. For now, I want you to stay in house. I want you to comb through all the records. Cell phone calls. Bank statements. Credit card transactions—both personal and business. Finish your report on the interview and then get started on those assignments. Clear?"

151

Paul nodded. "Crystal."

Jeffrey yanked his door open.

Mike pocketed his Super Balls, strode into Jeffrey's office, and plopped into a chair then raised his eyebrows at Paul. "That was an interesting morning. What do you make of Angelina Holtz?"

Jeffrey rolled a pencil across his desk, awaiting Paul's response.

"She definitely had motive, but we need to confirm her alibi. A screwy bunch, for sure."

Mike wagged his finger. "I wouldn't discount all three. It's really odd that Angelina, Madelyn, and Stuart all ended up in Miami and that they then showed up here together. That girl fight could have been staged."

Mike could be a renegade, but he was the sharpest detective on his squad. Jeffrey could always count on him. Although he had his doubts about Paul, he'd keep him paired with Mike, giving Paul a chance to redeem himself.

"Are you liking Stuart Thompson?" Jeffrey asked, looking at Mike.

Mike pulled two balls from his pocket, rolling them between his fingers. "He also had motive, and his alibi is shaky. Is he the gunman? I'm not sure. The guy has irritable bowel disease. He's afraid of his own asshole."

Paul stifled a snicker. Then all three roared.

"We need to review the building's security tapes," Jeffrey said when the laughter had subsided. "Mike, make sure that happens. Also, get a hold of all the canvass reports."

His phone buzzed. Jeffrey picked up the receiver, cradling it with his left shoulder while writing his notes with his right hand.

"Lieutenant Corrigan here."

He stopped writing and straightened up in his chair, grabbing the receiver with his left hand.

"Yes, Captain. I appreciate your reaching out. Really? Is she willing to make an ID? I understand. I'll brief my people. Thanks for the call. We'll be in touch. Goodbye, Captain Stanton."

He hung up the phone, paused and then picked it up again and buzzed Liz's desk. Three minutes later, she appeared in the doorway.

"What's up, Lou?" she asked.

"Come on in, Liz. Have a seat."

"Uh...no chairs left. I'll stand."

"Mike, get up. Let Liz have your chair."

Mike slowly rocked out of the chair, teasingly falling back into it several times.

"Hey, Price, if you don't get out of that chair, I'm gonna kick your balls down the hall," she said, half grinning.

"Ouch," he joked back, tucking his Super Balls away.

Liz sat. Mike stood behind her, leaning on the back of her chair.

"I just got off the phone with Captain John Stanton of Miami PD. His squad is investigating the shooting death of a drug runner found in a field along with an airplane containing traces of cocaine. A woman migrant worker who was in the orange groves saw a young woman with long black hair with a tan ponytailed man in khakis. She said the woman gave oral sex to the man and then shot him. She left with another man in a white van with black lettering. The worker also saw another car leave but couldn't describe it. Scared and illegal, she's fled the area, but she did tell what she saw to a Spanish speaking field hand, who then reported this to the police."

Mike fiddled with his mustache. "Gee, who do we know with long black hair who was recently in Miami? Hmm."

"Unfortunately, we don't have an ID. But perps always leave something behind at a crime scene and take some of the crime scene with them. Liz, I want you and Herb to go to Miami tomorrow morning and get together with the Miami homicide detectives working the drug runner case, and with the Fibbies who I'm sure have their claws into the case by now. Find out if anyone other than that migrant woman saw anything. I'll get you a picture of Angelina to take with you. You and Herb will leave from JFK airport. Miami PD will be waiting for you at Miami International."

Mike whined, "Hey, what about me? It's 30 degrees outside today. Why don't I get to go?"

"Because," Jeffrey said, "it's Herb's case and Liz is in Narcotics. And Amy needs you right now."

"No she doesn't. She has her mother." Mike rolled his eyes. "Besides, there's nothing I can do for her. All she does anyway is complain how big she is. How she can't sleep. Ya-da-ya-da-ya-da."

"That's really sensitive of you," Liz said.

"Yeah. Yeah. Go to Miami. I'll be thinking of you in your thong on the beach."

Liz smirked. "Go play with your blue balls."

Paul glanced between Mike and Liz. Jeffrey, though, was used to their banter. He knew neither was ever truly offended. Mike and Liz were like brother and sister, so he let it go. He still had to deal with Madelyn and Stuart.

Jeffrey dismissed his squad from his office. He stood from his chair, walked around his desk and strode to his doorway, peeking into the hallway. Laurie was busy typing at her computer. He scanned the bullpen for his detectives. They were nowhere in sight. Jeffrey frowned.

*They all must be out of the house, pursuing their cases and Rivchak better be busy with Steven Thompson's cell phone records.* As much as Rivchak chafed him, he'd continue to work on mentoring the naive detective, whipping out every wrong policy that Scardino had indoctrinated into him and then molding Rivchak into, at the very least, a promising detective.

Jeffrey shut his door. Before spending the next painful hour with a vacant Madelyn and stoic Stuart, he'd salvage the last few minutes of his exhausting morning listening to Tara's voice.

He returned to his desk. Jeffrey pulled out his cell from his back pocket and tapped "call" beneath her picture in his phone, smiling while he waited for her to answer.

"Hello there," she said.

He could tell by the lilt of her voice that she was smiling back at him.

Jeffrey leaned back in his chair, crossing one leg over the other, ankle to knee. "I've been thinking about that pizza all day."

"Just the pizza?" Tara teased.

Jeffrey grinned. "That and what followed."

"Ah, so I left you with a lasting memory. And guess what? I recall our evening, too."

"Now that's progress! I could go for some more pizza tonight."

He couldn't wait to rid of Madelyn and Stuart, and spend the evening with Tara. At least he didn't have to deal with Angelina, yet.

"We may want to expand our culinary adventures. Add some variety to the menu."

Jeffrey sighed, picturing her lips, her neck, and her perfectly round breasts. "I'm up for that. I'll definitely need to unwind...with you...after my day."

"Why? What happened?"

"I can't go into it now, but I'll tell you later, that is if I don't get distracted. Well, come to think about it, I doubt I'll get around to it."

"Leave your problems outside the door. I'll even help you do that."

"But before then, tell me what you and Marielle have planned for this afternoon."

"We're supposed to go out for lunch. Some Thai place nearby. I doubt we'll leave right away since Marielle wants to hang out and talk a while. Me? I'm starved, so maybe I can prod her along. But I'll save room for dinner. How about you? Had lunch?"

"Aspirin and coffee. But my head feels better now. No time to grab lunch. I'm off to the morgue with this weird couple we interviewed this morning." He smiled. "I'll hold off eating lunch and save myself for dinner and you later!"

"Make sure you bring your appetite, especially after the morgue."

Jeffrey laughed softly. "I won't disappoint you."

Tara laughed back. "You better not."

Someone knocked. Jeffrey shot his eyes to the door. "Just a sec, Tara" He lowered his cell from his year. "Yes?"

"Sir," Laurie called behind the door. "Ms. Thompson and uh...Mr. Thompson are waiting for you in the lobby."

Jeffrey rolled his eyes. "Tell them that I'll be right with them." He raised the phone back to his ear. "Sorry about that."

"Sounds like you're really busy."

"Never too busy for you. Enjoy your afternoon with Marielle."

"I will, and I'll enjoy my evening with you. See you later, Lieutenant."

Jeffrey hesitated but pressed the end call option on his cell, delaying trading Tara for Madelyn and Stuart. He massaged his chin, smiling as he pictured Tara chatting animatedly while lunching with Marielle in Brooklyn. It was good for her to get out of the house and not to have to come into the precinct today.

Stricken, Jeffrey grasped the edge of his desk.

*Brooklyn.* Thompson Paints was in Marielle's neighborhood. Maybe he was just being paranoid, but he'd seen it before—drug dealers lashing out at loved ones of investigating officers as payback. Suspecting Angelina's involvement in the drug trade, the twisted bitch's Brooklyn business was too close to Tara for his comfort. Jeffrey picked up the phone. He had one more call to make before leaving for the morgue.

Madelyn and Stuart sat on a bench in the precinct lobby, holding hands, and waiting.

Jeffrey walked over to them, "Are you ready to go see Steven's body?"

"Yes, we're ready," Stuart answered for them both.

"I'm parked out front. I'm driving a black Ford Explorer." Jeffrey said.

"Madelyn and I will be in my silver Mercedes."

Jeffrey's eyebrows shot up. These two oozed of money. "Okay. Follow me to the Medical Examiner's Office then."

He could see the black Benz in his rearview mirror. Stuart drove while Madelyn patted her bun with one hand, and applied red lipstick with the other. *That takes coordination,* he thought. When they pulled into the parking lot, Stuart parked the Mercedes neatly behind Jeffrey's Explorer right outside of the Medical Examiner's Office.

"Come with me." Jeffrey motioned to them. "I'll have you wait in the lobby while I get the medical examiner."

Stuart opened the door for Madelyn, who let out a forced sob and dabbed her cheekbones with a tissue.

Jeffrey shook his head and muttered, "Oh brother," convinced her performance strictly for dramatic purpose.

Stuart and Madelyn settled in the waiting room. She rested her head on Stuart's shoulder. He patted her hand. Jeffrey didn't know whether to applaud them or throw up. He stopped at the receptionist's desk.

"Hi, Lieutenant Corrigan. Haven't seen you in a while," the secretary greeted him. "Dr. Roseman is here today. She's in the middle of an autopsy. I'll buzz you in."

"Thanks."

Jeffrey walked into the autopsy suite as he had done so many times before as a detective, not even wrinkling his nose having become used to the pungent smell of the dead. "Hello, Emily."

Dr. Emily Roseman, dressed in a blue plastic apron and wearing latex gloves, waved to him over the body she was working on.

"Lieutenant Corrigan. I'm stuck here on a Sunday because of this." She gestured to the body, its rib cage parted like a grinning maw. "What's your excuse?" she teased.

"I bring you Steven Thompson's estranged—and very strange—wife, Madelyn, and his even stranger brother, Stuart. They're here to view Steven Thompson's body."

"I'll be with you in a minute then." Emily pushed her bottom lip out and puffed, trying to blow her bangs free from her eyes without having to use her blood-stained gloves. Giving up, she lifted the deep pink, cobblestoned liver from the metallic scale.

Jeffrey glimpsed at the bald, emaciated, waxy-looking man lying on the silver metal table sporting a "Y" incision from his sternum to his pubis.

"Fifty-five. Alcoholic." Emily said into the recorder, and then placed his lumpy cirrhotic liver on the scale.

Jeffrey raised his eyebrows. "And I was going to have a Guinness tonight."

Dr. Roseman untied her apron and snapped off her latex gloves. "You know what? I'll finish this later. He's not going anywhere." She tossed the soiled garments into the bin. "Regarding Steven Thompson. He took a single .45 caliber bullet to the forehead. The bullet ricocheted around his cranium, resulting in extensive damage to his brain. I recovered the bullet and already sent it to ballistics. I'd estimate he was shot from no further than four feet away. I'm sure Sarah in ballistics will confirm that for you. Tox screen was positive for cocaine.

"The female vic was shot once in the chest. Her aorta was severed, but no bullets were recovered. The shot went through and through. I spoke with Marshall of CSU. He said he recovered a .45 caliber bullet from the mattress. Tox screen was clean. She'd had some plastic surgery done recently. I recovered two saline breast implants that can be traced to the doctor that placed them for a positive ID. Her teeth had porcelain veneers and her hair was chemically lightened. Her original color was slightly darker, but she is a blonde. And she was ten weeks pregnant."

That stopped Jeffrey in his tracks. "Really?" he said, suddenly more interested than ever.

"We're in the process of a DNA analysis to see if Steven was the father. There was no semen in the vagina. Marshall confirmed that both vics hands tested negative for GSR. TOD for both is between 8 and 10 that morning. I'm officially ruling both as homicide. Have I made your day better?"

"Loads. Pregnant. There's a new twist." Jeffrey tried to stifle the feeling of elation that always came with a major element in a case being revealed, but couldn't quite do it.

"I'll have the techs get Steven's body ready to show. Let me get cleaned up, and I'll meet you and the oddball relatives in the lobby."

Jeffrey returned to the lobby and advised Madelyn and Stuart that they would be able to view Steven's body in just a few minutes. He warned them about Steven's facial disfigurement from the gunshot wound, and reiterated that Steven's body was not to be released to them yet, suggesting a memorial service in the meantime.

Madelyn gazed at Stuart. "What do you think? I would be okay with that."

Stuart replied, "Okay."

Jeffrey stood quietly, hands on hips, trying desperately to figure these two out. Not to mention, an oversexed Angelina and a pregnant Irina too. It was enough to make his head throb. He thought of Tara, hoping to relieve the tension in his neck, but he had to be careful. Too many thoughts of her and he risked tension elsewhere.

Dr. Roseman, now less macabre, walked into the lobby and introduced herself. Her bangs were neatly brushed to one side, and her short brown hair looked shampoo fresh. One would never have known that less than five minutes ago she was elbow deep in a chest cavity.

Jeffrey introduced her to Madelyn and Stuart.

Emily greeted them and then led the way to the morgue. They walked quietly, in single file, Madelyn and Stuart sandwiched between Dr. Roseman and Jeffrey.

A tech had already pulled the steel drawer open and had removed the sheet from Steven's body. Stuart remained eerily stoic as he viewed his brother's remains.

Madelyn tilted her head. "He doesn't look that bad. A little make-up will cover that bullet hole," she said thoughtfully.

Emily and Jeffrey exchanged a look.

"We're ready to go now," Stuart said, as though he'd received some unseen signal.

Emily nodded to the tech and the curtain closed. She turned to Madelyn and Stuart. "I'm sorry for your loss."

The Thompsons thanked Dr. Roseman, but didn't acknowledge Jeffrey, and then that strange pair left. No wailing. No tears.

"What weirdoes. They certainly gave you the cold shoulder," Emily observed.

"I'm crushed. I'd hoped that we could all be friends," he joked.

Emily cracked a smile. "Well, I'll let you know when I get the DNA analysis back."

"Thanks Emily." He shook her hand, relieved to end his workday.

# Chapter Twenty-Four

Sunday, January 8, 1:30 p.m.

*M*arielle paced across her living room carpet and then sank into the soft brown recliner. The springs squeaked as she rocked back. She paused and furrowed her forehead at Tara who sat huddled in the corner of Marielle's couch hugging a throw pillow to her chest. Tara hated sliding under anyone's microscope, including her best friend's.

*Here it comes.*

Marielle shook her head. "You did it, didn't you?"

Tara pressed the balls of her feet into the carpet burying them into the thick tan piles. "Yes. *We* did. Last night."

"Tara, you've known Jeffrey for a week."

"True. But it seems longer."

"Sweetie, a week ago you had no idea who you were. Maybe this isn't a good time to be making a major decision."

"I knew who I was…who I am!"

"Did you use protection?"

"Yes, mother! Of course."

Marielle leaned forward. The recliner groaned. "I worry about you."

Tara lowered the pillow to her lap. She looked at Marielle and smiled. "I know."

"Well…you *look* happy."

Tara grinned.

Marielle stood and grabbed Tara's hand, pulling her out of the couch. "Let's head out for lunch. We'll order Cosmopolitans—my treat. Then I want to stop by Thompson's Paints and Interiors. My neighbor got her window treatments there. They are gorgeous."

They grabbed their coats, plodded down Marielle's creaky old stairwell, and strode arm in arm all the way to the Thai Café.

Once seated, Tara peeked over her menu. "Marielle?"

Marielle lowered her menu. "What?"

"It wasn't just sex."

Marielle reached across the table and touched Tara's hand.

"I was married to Theo for fifteen years. That was sex. I have a chance now, to be in love. And not just because it's novel. And it's not lust. Not pity sex." Tara shook her head. "I can't explain it."

"You just have." Marielle paused. "Why do you remember Theo and not other things?"

Tara sighed. "I don't know. Dr. Kane told me that may happen. There's this gap, this hole I have to fill in."

"If you remember Theo, how about Edouard?"

Tara propped her elbow on the table and rested her chin in her palm. "Hmmm. Edouard? Ed – dou – ard?" She shook her head. "No, should I?"

Marielle grabbed the table's edges. "Oh God! How about Abbie?

"I remember her. She's safe. She's with Theo in Greece visiting his parents. And she's getting school credit, too." Tara's heart sank, and her stomach fluttered. "He promised she'd be back in the spring."

"He'll bring her back, sweetie."

Tara pulled her elbow off the table, grabbed her menu, and gritted her teeth. "He'd better. I agreed for three months. No longer. If he does keep her, I'm going to go get her!"

"And I'd go with you. But none of that's happened so let's enjoy the day and order lunch."

Tara unclenched her jaw. "You're right." She reached for Marielle's hand. "I love you."

"I love you, too. Now let go of my hand before those men who'd been staring at us get off."

Tara's heartbeat shot up. Her eyes widened. "What men?"

Marielle tilted her head towards the table diagonal to them, her eyes darting sideways.

Tara whipped her head toward the men in question. Both in suits with their coats draped over the backs of their chairs, they glanced back at her and smiled.

Larkin had smiled at her, too. Paranoia flooded her.

*Are these Larkin's men seeking me out after I ratted on their boss? This drug ring must be in every New York City borough. How far is their reach?*

She leaned over the table and whispered to Marielle. "I bet they're drug dealers."

"Tara, your imagination is getting to you. Our dealers don't look that nice! They're probably having a business lunch. People do that in Brooklyn."

Tara pressed her lips tightly.

Marielle dropped her menu and clutched Tara's hands. "Hey, I'm sorry. I know you must be extra sensitive since that creep followed you. I'm here. Nothing bad is going to happen."

She dropped her voice to a whisper. "But I identified Larkin. Jeffrey and the district attorney said he couldn't see me, but he had to know it was me. I mean, who else? Is there a string of women he assaulted that day?"

"Of course not. Tara, they're just here eating lunch, like we should be."

The waitress returned to take their orders.

"Two Chicken Pad Thai and two Cosmopolitans. And some more water, please," Marielle said.

"Very good," the waitress said, collecting the menus.

Tara stared at Marielle. "They're still watching us, aren't they?" Tara had to know. She had to be ready to run.

Marielle arched her eyebrows. "No. They're eating their noodles."

Tara broke her gaze when the server dropped off their plates. "Okay, P.I. Kosto. Let's eat. I'm being a noodle head."

The Pad Thai nipped at the tip of her tongue and warmed her belly. Had it tasted this delicious before?

A noodle fell onto the red napkin across her lap. *Ha! Foiled that noodle!* Reaching to discreetly pluck it off her napkin, Tara knocked her knife off the table with the back of her hand. The knife clattered to the floor. She bent over to retrieve it. As she grabbed the knife, her eyes wandered up to the mysterious men. One of them reached his hand into the side pocket of his jacket.

*"Gun!" the detective yells. Larkin, lay prone, his hands secured behind his back. He stares at me and smirks. "This isn't the end for you, bitch!"*

Tara clutched the knife, pointing it in their direction before giving it to the bus boy.

The waitress rushed over to Tara and Marielle's table. "Miss, I get you another knife."

Tara eyed the men. "No thanks. We're finished. We'd like the check please."

"Everything okay?" she asked.

"Absolutely. Best Pad Thai ever."

"I glad you enjoy."

The waitress brought the check while Marielle gulped the last of her martini. "Boy, you're in a hurry."

"Yeah, I can't wait to see this place and help you pick out your window treatments. And who knows? I might gently suggest a change in decor to Jeffrey. His house is a bit dated. Could use a woman's touch."

But all Tara truly wanted was to get out of this restaurant and away of these men's prying eyes, quickly, businessmen or not.

After Marielle picked up the tab, they meandered along the north side streets of the Williamsburg section of Brooklyn. Tara's face flushed as the winter sun warmed her cheeks, or maybe it was the curry and the Cosmopolitan, she wasn't sure which.

"Oh, here it is—Thompson's Paints and Interiors," Marielle said. "Oooh, look, the lights are on. There's someone in there." She tapped on the glass door as they peeked inside.

Angelina snarled. "Shit. I can't seem to get anything done today. First that stinking interview and now these morons."

The clanking of the cocaine filled metal paint cans coming from the back of the warehouse followed her as she made her way to the front door.

"Keep unloading," she yelled back to Jorge. "I'll get rid of these idiots." She walked to the glass door and unlocked it, opening it half way.

Angelina poked her head out the door. "We're closed."

"Oh. I really wanted to see what you have. My friend says you have the best," one of the ladies said.

Angelina paused and eyeballed the two women. She didn't recall them as buyers. But someone had referred them. A deal is a deal. She'd let them in. Angelina smiled. "Okay. Come in."

The women went straight to the mini-blind display. "Ooh. These may be the way to go," said the woman who had pleaded her way inside.

Angelina twisted her lips. *These bitches aren't here for coke.*

"You know, we're actually closed. And these things shouldn't be rushed." Angelina strode to the counter, her four-inch stilettos clacking against the hardwood floor. "Here's my card. Call me in the morning and we'll set up a private appointment."

"All right. I really appreciate your time," the woman said, glancing at the business card, "Ms. Holtz."

The annoying little asshole who had interrupted her tucked the card into her purse and smiled at her friend. "Hey, Tara. Maybe you can come back with me tomorrow, peruse what might look good in Jeffrey's house. Sounds like your dear detective's decor is criminal."

Angelina's ears perked. Now these losers were interesting. "So *Tara*, your boyfriend...husband...Jeffrey is a detective?"

Tara nodded with a proud smile. "Not husband. We're uh, seeing each other."

The stupid one rolled her eyes. Tara nudged her.

"Ah, I see. An inside joke."

"No, not really. But I'll mention you to him if he decides to redecorate."

Angelina grinned. "You do that, *Tara*."

Her grin melted the minute the two men in suits walked into Thompson's Paints and Interiors."

Angelina flicked her hand at them. "Gentlemen, we're closed."

"We'll come back tomorrow," said one. They turned and left as quickly as they came, followed shortly by the irksome women.

Angelina smiled to herself. *They didn't fool me one bit, fucking dicks hanging around. This is Corrigan's work, sending them over trying to scare me. Huh! I'll give Scardino a call. He'll know if she's Corrigan's woman or not.* She scratched her glassy, red fingernail across the counter. *I'll teach him the meaning of scared.*

"Hurry up." Tara grabbed Marielle's hand, yanking her best friend along the glistening sidewalk, their boots splashing through pooled lakes of melted snow. "Now do you think they're businessmen? They followed us from the restaurant."

Marielle panted alongside Tara. "Okay. I admit it's creepy. Here, I know a short cut. There's a deli up ahead. I go there all the time. There's an exit into a back alley. From there, we only have a short run to the back of my building. I have the key to the back with me. We'll dodge inside. The door automatically locks. We'll run upstairs to my apartment, lock the door, and call Jeffrey."

"Let's run for it." Tara agreed. Her feet near tangled with Marielle's. They burst through the deli.

"Habib, quick! Back door. Men chasing us," Marielle called.

"Go, Marielle! I call cops for you."

Marielle slammed her palms into the back door. They spilled into the alley and sprinted to her apartment.

"Hurry, Marielle. Get your key! The key! The key—"

"I got it."

Tara's heart raced. She looked back. "I don't see them."

Marielle turned her key in the lock. She pushed Tara in first and yanked the door shut. Already oxygen starved, Tara legs burned as they climbed the four flights to Marielle's apartment.

Marielle's hands shook, and she dropped her key.

Tara snatched it up and jammed it into the lock. She shoved the apartment door open, slamming it shut the second they were inside. Marielle clicked the deadbolts. They ran to the couch and collapsed.

"We made it." Tara gasped as she sucked air into her lungs. She stared at the window overlooking the street. Pushing off the couch, she ran to it and pulled its drape to the side.

There were the men, walking past the building.

She shoved the drape closed and waited. Then Tara's cell phone rang, playing Jeffrey's ring tone—the first four bars of *Van Halen's You Really Got Me.*

"Hi, Are you ready?"

Her chest squeezed. "Jeffrey. Men." She took a deep breath. Air stuttered into her lungs. "Men followed us!"

"Tara, calm down. They're my men. I'm working on some homicides. There might be some payback involved. I should have told you, but I reached out to detectives from a Brooklyn precinct. They were watching over you. I wanted to make sure you stay safe. They're down the block from Marielle's place. I'm coming to get you. It'll be okay."

Jeffrey crammed Johnny's SUV between two cars in front of Marielle's apartment building. He waved to the detectives down the block.

"Thanks," he called.

The suited men walked up to his vehicle. "No problem. We didn't mean to scare your girlfriend and her friend."

"It's fine now. Job well done. They're safe."

As they walked away, Jeffrey looked up at Marielle's apartment. There was Tara, peeking through the drapes. He waved to her and then trotted up the building's outside steps to ring the downstairs bell.

"She has to live in a walk–up," he muttered.

Marielle's voice crackled through the speaker, "Come on up."

He trudged up the four flights and knocked on the door. "It's me."

The deadbolts clicked.

Marielle opened the door. "Dammit, Jeffrey. You could have told us."

"Then you wouldn't have acted natural."

Tara nodded. "I went a bit over the edge."

Jeffrey hugged her, squeezing her to his chest and kissed her head. "I'm so sorry. It's the job. I don't want to drag you in the middle of this."

Marielle shot her hands to her hips. "Hey! Where's my hug and kiss?"

Jeffrey released Tara and hugged Marielle playfully. "Want to come stay with us?

"No I'll be fine. I'm a Brooklyn gal. I got connections."

"Yeah. Habib was awesome," Tara agreed.

Jeffrey grinned. "Yep. The Brooklyn Precinct got a call from him. It's straightened out though. So where are these boxes?"

Marielle pointed to her corridor.

"Holy crap!"

Tara rubbed his arm. "It's only a few. They're not heavy. They're probably the essentials: clothes, toiletries, etc."

Jeffrey squinted at the boxes. "You're whole bathroom's in there!"

Tara shrugged. "No, not everything."

"All right, let me have at it!"

Marielle lifted a box. "Oh, and I put your flash drive in this one."

Tara jerked her head. "Flash drive?"

"Yeah. Your back-up file for your book?"

Tara hesitated, staring at the box.

Jeffrey rested his hands on her shoulders. *What was in there that would cause her to freeze like that?*

"Oh... yes. Thank God. My back-up. I forgot about that."

"Marielle, I'll take this." He couldn't miss the worry stamped across Marielle's face. "It's okay. I'm sure it will take days to get through these boxes."

He'd mention the flashdrive to Leo too.

Jeffrey helped Tara with her jacket. Her hands still trembled. He should have told her about the tail.

Jeffrey plunked down the stairs balancing the stacked boxes against his chest.

He loaded her boxes into the Explorer praying he'd never have to move her possessions again. After Tara's belongings were secure in the back of the SUV, he opened her door. They both waved to Marielle as he pulled into the street.

He paused and gripped the steering wheel at the first red light. "I don't want you or Marielle going to Thompson's Paints. It's a good thing the detectives tailed you into that store. I can't tell you why right now. Trust me. Stay away."

"But—"

"Don't ask, please. I can't talk about it."

"Okay. I won't press. You'll tell me when you can?"

"Absolutely."

The last thing he wanted to do was spook Tara, especially if he had nothing solid to back his suspicions. "I need to stop at Johnny's and get my car back. We can swing by Ming's and pick up Chinese food for dinner if you like."

"Sounds good."

# Chapter Twenty-Five

## Sunday, January 8, 4:45 p.m.

*H*e pulled into Johnny's driveway and parked behind a car next to his Mustang. "Shit."

"What's the matter?"

He clutched the door handle. "Nothing. We'll just switch vehicles and get going."

She squinted at him. "What are you hiding?"

Jeffrey grabbed Tara's hand, pulling her along as they trotted up the porch steps. She'd not seen him act this way before, not at the station or at home. His clenched jaw made his cheekbones seem oddly angular. Something was up.

Jeffrey rapped on the front door. It groaned open. Johnny stuck his head out and shoved the Mustang's keys into Jeffrey's open palm.

"Hurry up. Evie's in the kitchen," he whispered. He smiled at Tara over his brother's shoulder.

"No, she's not," a woman said as she poked her head out from behind Johnny.

Jeffrey took a deep breath. He squeezed Tara's hand. "Tara, this is my sister, Evie."

Evie looked strikingly like Jeffrey—sandy blonde hair, hazel eyes and appeared about the same age. She was taller than Johnny but shorter than Jeffrey.

Tilting her head, Evie smirked and glanced at Tara first, then looked at Jeffrey, "So is this who you've been playing house with?"

Tara extended her hand to Jeffrey's sister. Evie's handshake was limp and uninviting. Tara took a step a back as Evie eyed her from head to boots.

Jeffrey cleared his throat and jingled his car keys, "It's late. We really have to get going. Goodnight Johnny." He nodded to his sister. "Goodnight, Evie."

Tara waved to Johnny and Evie. "Yes, goodnight. It was lovely meeting you, Evie."

Evie gave Tara a half-hearted wave back.

Jeffrey clutched Tara's hand and led her to his car, opened the passenger door, nudged Tara inside, and shut her door.

"Wait, Jeffrey!" Tara called, but he didn't respond. She shifted in her seat and looked out the back window of the Mustang. Jeffrey unloaded her boxes from Johnny's Explorer to the back of his car nonstop. He was clearly in a hurry to leave Johnny's house and apparently Evie was the reason why.

The trunk slammed. Tara fastened her seatbelt and waited, anticipating Jeffrey's sour mood. The driver's side door swung open, and Jeffrey slid inside the car.

Before he closed his door, he shouted, "See you all later."

He revved the engine, backed out of Johnny's driveway, and turned onto the street before Tara could get comfortable in her seat.

Tara glanced at Jeffrey who looked straight ahead at the road. "That was a whirlwind visit."

"Tara, I'm so sorry about how my sister treated you."

She rubbed his knee. "It's all right."

*Evie couldn't be that difficult to figure out,* Tara thought. She got on so well with his father and brother, and Joe and Johnny had reciprocated with equal affection for her. Sarcasm from a Corrigan was unexpected. She'd wanted to stay longer, pick at Evie's icy armor, but Jeffrey swooped in and bustled her out, before his sister could sling any more arrows.

The only sound in the Mustang was the shifting of gears until Jeffrey parked in front of Ming's. He paused at the steering wheel and turned his head toward Tara.

"Evie can be harsh sometimes, but she's not malicious. You should know that she's never fully accepted my mom's death. She was only sixteen. Judy—Frank's late wife who was my mother's best friend—tried to nurture her, but Evie resisted her efforts. She considered herself the woman of the Corrigan house. She took care of us, but she always had to have the last word with Johnny, me, and even my dad. My dad and Johnny tolerated her obsessive personality. I wasn't always as kind."

She leaned over and kissed him. The light from a passing car flashed across his face, reflecting the moisture in his eyes.

"I know you miss your mom, I'm sure her death was painful for everyone in your family, especially Evie. I can't expect her to accept me right away. We've become involved at lightning speed. I can hardly believe it myself. And I'm sure she sees me as quite unusual, if not bizarre."

He pressed his finger to her lips. "I know everything has happened so fast, but I don't care what Evie or anyone else thinks."

She stroked his cheek.

"I'll run inside and get our order." He cupped her face in his palms and softly said, "Don't go away."

Tara shut her eyes and kissed his cold fingers, hoping her breath would heat him as he had so often stirred her blood to her winter chilled skin, then looked into his questioning eyes and whispered, "I won't."

He lifted the collar of his coat and dodged into the restaurant. She smiled at his trail of huge footprints, pressed into the snowy sidewalk, all the way to Ming's door. The thought of his reassuring voice and protective glances prompted heat to radiate out from her cheeks. Yes, she was hungry but starved for his touch.

Minutes later, Jeffrey jogged from Ming's toting wire-handled, steamy, red and white paper cartons and slid into the car. Tara took the cartons and balanced the Chinese food containers on her lap.

"Aha. See? We're already expanding our culinary adventures."

Jeffrey placed his fingers under Tara's chin, gently tilted her head up, and pressed his lips to hers. The cardboard cartons began to slip from her lap. She grabbed their dinner with one hand saving them from the floorboard, Jeffrey's mouth still on hers. He slowly pulled away.

Jeffrey laughed softly. "We better leave before the cops come knocking on the steamed up windows."

"I don't want to end up in another holding cell. Of course, this time I'd be with you, so that wouldn't be so bad. A real mood breaker, though."

Jeffrey grinned and started the engine.

Jeffrey pulled into the driveway. Tara grabbed the cartons from Ming's while he unloaded her few boxes from the car. The smell of warm ginger tickled her nose, and her stomach growled as they scurried from the cold night air into his warm house. Soon she'd be snug in his arms.

She set their steaming dinner on the kitchen table and ambled behind him as he carried the boxes to James's room, set them down and shoved them against the edge of the bed.

Tara shrugged with a sheepish grin on her face. "Doesn't look like I'll be able to get past those boxes and into my bed. I may have to sleep elsewhere," she teased.

"I know a very comfortable place," he said as he pulled her hips to his.

She reached up, barely able to wrap her arms around his neck, but pulled away before he could kiss her.

"Go sit at the table. I just want to check something in one of the boxes. I'll go through the rest of my things later."

He waited for her. She didn't want to tell him to leave but...

Tara paused. Jeffrey still hadn't budged.

Tara turned toward him, explaining. "I'm scared I won't remember what's on the flash drive in this box."

"It's all right. Give it a try. No one is pushing you."

She reached into the box and pulled it out. "Marielle said it's a back-up file to the book I'd been writing."

"Wow. You truly amaze me. You're writing a book?"

Tara shrugged. "I guess so, but with my laptop smashed on the rails."

"No problem. Use my laptop. Perhaps it will all come back to you."

"I'm Mac. Your PC. We're incompatible," she said with a smile.

He took the flash drive from her and laid it carefully on the bed. Pulling her to him, he kissed her. "We're compatible. Now let's eat before it gets cold."

She squeezed his hand tightly, all the way to the kitchen.

Jeffrey pulled out a kitchen chair and as Tara sat, he eased her toward the table then handed her a pair of chopsticks. Dining with Tara was always an adventure. With a wicked grin on his face, he couldn't wait for Tara's version of dinner and theater. He reached into the cupboard and brought two plates back to the table.

Tara shook her head. "I don't do chopsticks. I make enough mess with the standard fork."

"Ah, come on. Chinese food is more fun with chopsticks." He handed them back to her.

She tapped the bamboo sticks on her plate, contemplating. "More fun for whom?"

He smiled but only answered, "Bon Appetite."

Jeffrey watched as she awkwardly scissored the wooden sticks, occasionally grasping a shrimp. She finally managed to raise one to her mouth. It popped free, though, and plopped right onto her chest.

She flicked the little pink, curled shrimp off her breasts.

He chuckled. This could get interesting!

"Oh, yeah! Laugh at me will ya? Well take this." She flung a shrimp at him and then a pea pod for good measure.

The shrimp bounced off his chest, but the pea pod stuck — right in his hair. He pulled the slick, green, lumpy bean from his sandy-colored strands and threw down his white napkin. "That's it! This means war!"

Two minutes later, shrimp and assorted vegetables peppered the table. They stared at each other, and the mess they had created. Jeffrey lowered his gaze to Tara's cleavage, that valley between her perfectly round breasts he longed to trace his finger along. "Truce?"

She smiled and nodded. "Truce."

He tossed his napkin onto the table. "I'm not hungry anymore."

Tara dotted her lips with her napkin. "Neither am I."

That did it. Jeffrey wove his long fingers carefully between Tara's tiny fingers and led her to the bedroom. He twirled her under his arm with the finesse of a ballroom dancer and lowered her onto his bed.

"Nice boxers," she teased. "These look familiar." She sat up and yanked them down to his ankles, pushed him onto the bed, and freed his boxers past his feet.

"They're the same pair you wore that day you attacked me in the bathroom."

She reached over to the nightstand, grabbed a condom packet, and tossed it to Jeffrey. He snapped it up, ripped the end open with his teeth, and held up the prized latex ring.

His mouth agape, he watched her whip off her own jeans and panties, squirm out of her sweater, and unhook her bra at lightning pace.

Jeffrey quickly rolled the condom onto his hardness. He prayed he could last.

*God help me. The woman is perfect.*

She clambered up and straddled him. Her knees pressed into his thighs. Jeffrey cupped his hands around her rounded breasts only to have them pushed away.

*Hey.*

Her fingers weaved into his as she thrust his hands over his head, pinning him into the mattress. His chest heaved. She rocked her pelvis, gently at first, then increasing with speed and intensity. Her breasts danced before his eyes, and she flung her head back.

"Mercy," he uttered. *Truce? What happened to that? Who cared?* He'd be more than willing to be her prisoner tonight. "Keep going!"

That last thrust finished him. He pulsed into her. She tightened around him and then collapsed onto his chest.

Cradling her head against him, he ran his fingers through Tara's hair, her heart rate slowing with his. Jeffrey's eyelids fluttered, sated with her taste and lulled by her scent.

But his "all is right with my world" ended the second the walls began to shake.

# Chapter Twenty-Six

Sunday, January 8, 6:30 p.m.

*J*effrey and Tara jerked apart. He lifted Tara off him and jumped out of bed, slid into his pants, zipping his fly while he moved toward the hall.

"Something hit the front door. Stay here and get dressed. I'm going to check it out." He grabbed his 9mm from the dresser and left the bedroom door open, not wanting to close her in if she had to run. It was 6:30 p.m. but it might as well been midnight.

He breathed hard as he scooted along the hallway wall, his Glock steadied in both hands. Rounding the corner of the living room, his eyes darted from one wall to another. Nothing came at him.

Then someone touched his back.

Jeffrey clenched his jaw and tightened the grip on his pistol.

"It's just me," Tara whispered.

Still looking straight ahead, he hissed, "I told you to stay back."

She gripped the waistband of his jeans and whispered back, "I was scared without you."

He went to squeeze her hands but found Tara's hands were not empty. "What the hell are you holding?"

"Your gun. I found your spare gun in your underwear drawer when I was searching for something to wear. It was underneath your boxers." Tara pointed it straight ahead, grasping the butt of the revolver with both hands. "I got your back."

"Tara!"

Jeffrey had forgotten about the revolver his father had given him as a gift. A .38, just like his dad's back in the day on the force.

"Don't worry. I won't shoot you, but I'll nail anyone who comes at us," Tara whispered.

"Do you know how to use a gun?"

"No, but how hard can it be?"

"You don't want to shoot at something or someone you don't have right in your sight. Give it to me."

"Hell no!"

"What?"

"I can do this, Jeffrey. What if something happens to you, or I get cornered."

She had a point, a good point.

Jeffrey reached over her small hands and cocked the hammer. "Don't squeeze the trigger unless I say so. Got it?"

"Yes."

He turned the porch light on. The front door groaned as he pushed it open. There were jagged pieces of brick scattered on the front steps beyond the scratched and dented door. Glock in one hand, he held the other one out in a protective barricade, prompting Tara to stay in the foyer. "Keep your finger off the trigger"

"All right. All right. Understood. Who's there? What hit the door?"

"I don't know, and someone threw a brick at the door."

Barefoot and shirtless, he didn't flinch as he stood on the frozen porch, the adrenaline that comes with protecting the woman you love above all else coursing through his veins, keeping him warm.

"Stay back, Tara," Jeffrey warned as he searched the front yard. No one around.

Something rustled in the bushes. His chest pounded.

"I'm ready, Jeffrey," Tara called out softly.

"Shhh."

A brown rabbit froze in front of him and then leapt away. *Shit! It's only an animal.*

Jeffrey trotted down to the driveway and unlocked his car, retrieving latex gloves that he carried around for crime scenes from the glove box. Snapping on the gloves, he picked up the broken pieces of brick, fitting them together like a jigsaw puzzle.

Painted in white, the top read, 'Stay away', the side, 'from' and the bottom, 'our bricks'.

Tara peeked from the doorway. "What's it say?"

"It's a message for me to look the other way on this case."

She cocked her head. "The other way?"

"The drug dealers don't want me to disturb their circulation in my precinct. My squad is investigating the murder one of their main suppliers. With Larkin locked up and Steven Thompson dead, there's going to be a play for the keys to cocaine kingdom. The wannabe kingpins are gently reminding me to stay out of their business."

Tara clutched his hand, his revolver still grasped in the other one and pulled him into the house. "I think you need to get a shirt on and some warm socks. You go change, and I'll make pot of coffee. And then I'll put your gun back where I found it. I don't think we'll be sleeping tonight."

Jeffrey placed the brick pieces into a paper bag, sealed it, and tucked his pistol into the back of his jeans. He kissed Tara on the forehead. "You're gutsy grabbing that gun, but I'll take it now." Jeffrey secured the bag and the .38 in his office and then went into the bedroom.

He glanced at their freshly rumpled sheets. Someone messed up his night and that really pissed him off. He threw on a sweatshirt and while pulling on his second sock a sudden thought gave him pause.

*Shit. They know where I live. I can't leave her here by herself tomorrow when I'm half an hour away at the precinct.*

"Coffee's ready," Tara called from the kitchen.

"I'll be right there." And then he picked up his phone, and called the one person he could trust to keep her safe.

"Hey Pop."

He had just hung up the phone when he saw Tara, standing in the bedroom doorway. He walked over to her and wrapped his arms around her, kissing her gently on her lips still warm from her coffee.

She nuzzled her head against his chest and whispered, "I love you."

"I love you too. And that's why you need to leave."

Jeffrey swallowed hard at those words. He didn't want to lose her, but this may be the only way to keep her.

# Chapter Twenty-Seven

Sunday, January 8, 6:45 p.m.

*A*ngelina leaned over the bar, showcasing her ample cleavage. She was a regular there. All the male bartenders looked forward to her visits, but the female bartenders dreaded them.

"Hey, Ricky," she called. "I'll have a dirty martini."

With a big smile on his face, the bartender replied, "Coming right up."

Pouting her lips, she asked, "Sweetheart, can I use your phone? My cell phone battery's dead." She had to be careful not to use her cell, since it was still on Steven's plan.

"Sure, go right ahead."

She rounded the bar while Ricky mixed her martini. She just prayed Hector would accept her collect call.

"Hello Miss Angelina," he said once the operator dropped off the line.

"Hector, darling, do me a favor. Some detectives are nosing around about my trip to Miami." She lowered her voice. "Here's the story. I came to Miami to be with my poor sister, Daisy—your wife—who had a miscarriage. We didn't take her to any hospital. She was doing fine, so I returned to New York promptly because I had inventory to do at the store. We never left the house. You just moved and don't have a telephone so that's why you use the restaurant phone. Got it?"

"No problem," Hector said.

"And since Bengal is out of the picture, I need you to get me another pilot if you want your business to stay afloat."

She hung up before he could tell her goodbye, and smiled at Ricky, motioning with her finger that she'd be there in just a minute, as he placed her dirty martini on a white napkin on the bar. Ricky nodded and turned his attention to a young couple, seated at the far end of the bar. She had one more call to make and could do it fast. Angelina tapped his number with the tips of her crimson lacquered nails.

"Hey, Maurice."

"Angie. So when are you coming to pay me, and bring me my supply?"

She smirked and narrowed her eyes. "I'll be by in about twenty minutes."

"See you then, Angie."

Before hanging up she shot her middle finger at the receiver. She despised being called Angie. Bengal used to call her that. Her mouth soured at the thought of him foisting himself upon her, yelling *"Angie, Angie, Angie"* in sickening satisfaction.

Now Maurice would join Bengal… after her dirty martini.

She tilted the glass to her mouth, finishing her cocktail in less than a minute. Angelina usually sipped her drink while flirting with Ricky, but tonight, she was in a hurry. She had to run home, get her .38 snub-nose, kill Maurice, stop at Zabar's to pick up dinner, and get ready for her date with Detective Rivchak, all before 7 p.m. Talk about murder!

"Can I get you another drink?" Ricky asked.

"Sorry. Big plans tonight. See you, Babe."

"It was a pleasure, as usual," he said as she twirled from the barstool. She strode out of Shane's, confident that Ricky was still gawking at her ass, all the way out the door, just the way she intended.

Hugging her black fur trimmed coat to her chest, Angelina scurried across Broadway, toward Amsterdam and West 70th Street, her .38 tucked into her Kate Spade purse. Her black Manolo boots beat out a rapid-fire tempo on the sidewalk.

For a pimp and drug dealer, Maurice Chiguard had certainly scaled the social ladder. She had met him five years earlier, when Maurice and she lived in adjacent apartments on the Lower East Side. He had introduced her to Steven Thompson.

Maurice was only five feet six inches, but when he wore his designer suits, neatly gelled his short brown hair, and manicured his nails, it made him appear larger in stature—and social status. He began to mingle with the wealthy. His clientele now included professionals, officials, and politicians.

And that pissed off Steven.

"No way was that little piece of shit going to compete with me," he'd say.

Angelina sighed. She and Steven were good together...until Irina. The stupid bitch definitely had it coming.

Lured from Russia to Trenton, New Jersey as a mail order bride, she was promised a genteel husband and citizenship upon arrival, but what she got was her passport confiscated, an 8 by 10 room with no windows, and a steady stream of sweaty men, crushing her into soiled sheets. After attempting to escape, she was beaten—severely. Considered a liability, she was sold to Maurice cheap.

But Steven *wanted* her.

That was his last mistake.

Throbbing heat filled the blood vessels in her temples. *How could he have touched that whore with the same hands that touched me?*

She gripped the door handle to Maurice's apartment building. Her fingernails pierced the heel of her hand until her knuckles blanched. She swung the door open, humming "Ding Dong the Bitch is dead" and rang the doorbell.

"It's Angelina," she announced into the intercom.

One of Maurice's girls answered. "Come on up."

Angelina pursed her lips. She was counting on Maurice being alone. The girl buzzed her into the building. She took the elevator to the 3rd floor and knocked on apartment 3A.

The woman that opened the door was wearing beige slacks and a white chiffon blouse.

"Going out for the evening?" Angelina asked.

"Yes. I have to meet a client in an hour. I never leave earlier than I have to. The customers only get what they paid for."

"Yeah. I'm all for giving people only what they deserve. Here's a fifty. Treat yourself to drink and then call a cab. Keep the change. I need to speak to Maurice—alone."

"He's in the tub. You guys can have all the privacy you want in the bathroom. I don't drink before a job. I need to be alert at all times, if you know what I mean."

The woman turned around and walked to the kitchen. Angelina grabbed a red tapestry throw pillow from the black leather sofa, sidled up to her, and pressed the pillow to her back. White feathers burst into the air as the woman thudded onto the green ceramic tile floor, blood seeping through the back of her white chiffon blouse.

"You should have taken the fifty. I have plans, darling. I can't spare an hour."

She stepped over the body and headed to the bathroom.

"Knock. Knock," she teased.

"Angie. Come on in. The water's fine," Maurice quipped through the door.

Her blood boiled. That's what Bengal had called her too, before his face smacked the parched Florida dirt. She forced a smile, draped her coat over her hands, and strode into the bathroom. She laid her coat on the commode, the revolver hidden between the folds.

Angelina massaged Maurice's neck. "I'll give you five grand for the attempt on Steven."

Maurice swiped the bubbles out of the tub. "You owe me fifteen grand, and I want a partnership."

"I'll sweeten the pot. Fifteen grand and a kilo bonus. No partners."

"No. Fifteen grand. Partnership. And I'll take the kilo, since you're so kindly offering." Maurice grabbed her hand. "We could be good together. I'll manage the women and my clientele. You keep your clientele. We get a supplier and split the proceeds. Or not. In which case, who knows—perhaps a leak to the cops about your anger control issues, or your jaunts out of town. Those homicide detectives are already looking at you. And wait until they discover Irina was pregnant. They're gonna be thinking about how pissed off you were when Steven admitted that he's the baby-daddy. I'll make sure that slips out. Motive. Motive. Motive," he crooned.

"Let's talk about motive." Angelina purred. "I recall you how pissed off *you* were about Irina's pregnancy. Steven had fixed her up beautifully, don't you think? She would have been gold to you. But he knocked her up, and that was going to cost you. She would be totally useless to you for weeks. Off the market. Lost revenue."

"The cops couldn't care less about me. Enough of them use my services."

Angelina bristled at the blackmail attempt, but she had the advantage. She had Ray, and "the boys", and soon... Paul. And now she had Maurice—vulnerable, egotistical, stupid Maurice.

"Okay. We'll work out a deal," she said slowly.

"I'm so glad you've reconsidered," he murmured and settled back into the water. He closed his eyes.

Her hands dug into his neck. She had to restrain herself from squeezing him too hard.

Instead, she swished her hand in the tub. "This water is a little chilly. Do you mind if I heat it up?"

"Go ahead and twist on the hot. Then come twist me." A smile that she'd come to hate slid across his face.

She cranked on the faucets and knelt behind him, nuzzling his neck. "I'll be right with you," she said in her best seductive voice.

Then she reached under her coat, freed her gun, and grabbed a towel. She slid it between the barrel of the .38 and the back of his head. His skull smacked against the porcelain of the tub and his arms draped over the sides. Waves of red diffused through the water.

Angelina glanced at her watch. It was 6:45. Paul was due to be at her apartment at 7:00.

She whispered to Maurice, "Hey, gotta go. Don't get up. I'll let myself out."

# Chapter Twenty-Eight

Sunday, January 8, 8:00 p.m.

"*I*'m glad you could come," Angelina said as she swung open the door, admitting Paul Rivchak to her apartment on W. 84th Street, also known as Edgar Allen Poe Street.

She came up behind him and pressed her head against his shoulder blade. He shuddered. She squeezed his ribs so tight he had to push against her fingers as he inhaled, prying them loose from his chest. She eased her grasp and laughed softly in his ear.

He spun around to face her. Angelina could see that his breathing had quickened, without her restraining touch. She thought maybe she spooked him a little. *Good.*

"Where can we go to talk?" he asked.

"I'm starved. Why don't we go to that Chinese place around the corner? They have great Dim Sum. Afterward, we can stop at Zabar's and pick up some desert."

"I'm not going to discuss a homicide investigation in a crowded restaurant," he told her.

"I agree. We'll eat and bring desert back to my place. Then we'll talk here." She grinned.

Paul relented. She knew he would. She always got her way.

Bearing red velvet cake, Angelina flicked on the lights once they were inside, illuminating her well appointed home.

"Thanks for dinner," she told Paul.

Her living room was pristine, her furnishings eclectic. A white suede sofa was set almost in the center of the living room with bright green and white polka dot throw pillows cradled in its corners. Two tiered glass end tables flanked the sofa, each with a brass lamp that boasted a fringed white shade on top and neatly stacked magazines on the surface. Three framed Andy Warhol prints hung on the off-white wall. One was of a dollar sign in red ink, and another had red, black, and white revolvers fanned across a pink background. A portrait of *Marilyn Monroe* silhouetted in shades of pink hung in the middle.

Paul stood, hands on hips. "Interesting choice of art."

She rubbed her shoulder against his arm. "I love Andy Warhol."

"I didn't know that managing a paint store paid so well."

"I do okay. Steven paid for most of this. I did buy the Andy Warhol prints. Let me take your jacket." Angelina pinched the collar of his black leather bomber jacket and whispered, "Nice. Buttery soft." Then she sniffed his neck. "Hmm, is that Hugo Boss you're wearing?"

He cleared his throat as she dragged his jacket from his shoulders. "Yes it is."

"You weren't wearing that earlier, in the interview room. I would have noticed."

Paul lurched forward, leaving Angelina clutching his jacket. "You're right. I wasn't. Speaking of earlier, what is it that you'd like to tell me?"

She tossed the black leather bomber onto the sofa. "Let's have some cake first, Relax a bit."

He squeezed her forearm. "Quit stalling Angelina. You're wasting my time."

She glared at him. *How dare he touch her?* His pupils widened, and he let her go.

"That's better. You're much too tense. Have a seat." She set the cake on the coffee table in front of Paul. "I'll be right back."

Angelina sashayed into the kitchen. She returned with a knife in one hand and two plates in the other, twirling the handle of the knife absently, the sharp silver edge gleaming in the lamplight. She could see his reflection in the blade. Angelina set the plates down, and scooted in next to Paul, bumping her hip into his.

Gripping the dark wooden handle of the knife with her slender fingers, she cut into the red velvet cake and scooped a slice onto each plate. Looking straight at him, she licked the cream frosting from her red polished fingernails. He studied her, tracing his tongue across his dry lips.

"I know who killed Steven," she said bluntly. *That should get him interested.*

He jerked his head back in surprise. "Who?"

"Maurice Chiguard."

Paul squinted. "Who's Maurice Chiguard? And why didn't you say this earlier?"

"Maurice is a pimp and a drug dealer. He would come to Steven's apartment to get his supply. He also owned Irina."

"*Owned* Irina? The blonde woman killed with Steven?"

"Maurice is involved in sex trafficking. He was furious when he found out Steven had gotten her pregnant."

His eyebrows shot up. "She was pregnant?"

"Yes, a few weeks. He just found out. Maurice also grew increasingly discontent with Steven's prices. Because he'd complained, Steven sold him some cut cocaine. When Maurice's clients realized that the coke had been cut with baking soda and soap shavings, he beat the shit out of Maurice. Nearly killed him."

Paul nodded. "I've seen that happen. People get fucked up like that. Surprised, he let him live. Probably left him for dead."

Angelina stroked Paul's arm. "It's a war out there. There are consequences when people step out of line."

She played with his fingers and continued. "After that, Maurice threatened to do business only with Larkin. So, Steven sent some guys to rough up Maurice. Threatened to kill him if he did any more business with Larkin. Maurice must have taken matters into his own hands after that and killed Steven and Irina."

Paul twisted his lips. "How do you know all this?"

"I heard them arguing the night before. Maurice had threatened to kill Steven. Steven was a powerful man. He'd laughed at Maurice. I think he viewed Maurice merely as an annoyance.

Angelina flicked her hair over her shoulder. She dug her fork into her slice of cake and lifted a piece of it to Paul's lips. "Here. Taste."

Paul opened his mouth. She gently fed him the forkful of cake. He closed his lips around the fork and Angelina slowly pulled the fork away, watching him swallow her offering with a smile.

"And I didn't mention this earlier today because I didn't care for your lieutenant. He was treating you like crap. I like you, Paul. And I want *you* to take credit for solving the case. More cake?"

He obliged and this time raised his own forkful of cake to his mouth, dragging it from the silver prongs with his lips. He chewed while gazing at her, thoughtful. Had she given away more than she'd planned?

He finished his dessert. "Thanks for everything, Angelina. This has been illuminating"

"The evening doesn't have to be over yet. Now that we have the business part out of the way, how about some pleasure?" She stroked him, under his chin, and down, through the vee of his gray sweater.

But he pulled away

"I'm sorry. I can't stay. You're still a person of interest, and this can get me in deep with internal affairs."

Angelina swung her legs beneath her and leaned toward Paul on her knees. "I know people. Trust me. You won't be harmed by this…association."

He placed his hands on her shoulders and gently pushed her back.

"Another time, Angelina. It really was nice spending time with you. I'll call you soon. I promise."

"I'll keep you to that. Are you sure you don't want to stay?"

He grabbed his jacket. "Thanks for the invite, but I gotta go.

"Goodbye Detective Rivchak."

"Bye, Ms. Holtz."

As soon as the door had swung closed, Angelina picked up the phone and dialed. He answered on the second ring.

"He's gone. I pinned it on Maurice. You know what they say, 'Dead men tell no tales.' "

She listened carefully to what needed to happen next. Wrapping this up was going to be a piece of cake. "Good night, Ray."

# Chapter Twenty-Nine

Monday, January 9, 7:45 a.m.

*J*effrey held up her jacket while Tara stretched her arms through the sleeves.

Her back pressed against his chest, even through the thickness of her down jacket. Tara sighed. She'd rather be spooning beneath the comforter of his bed—their bed—than brace for the frigid morning beyond his now dented door.

Once properly dressed, Tara whipped around to face him and tilted her head up. "I don't want to leave. What will I do all day?"

He started to zip her jacket, but she pulled away.

"Just for today. I need to find out who threw that brick. I would be worried sick if you were here by yourself," he said.

"I'm not a child!" She stomped her foot and yanked on the zipper. The metal teeth ground to a halt half way up. *Damn!* She grabbed the stalled tongue and yanked hard, freeing the jam. The zipper flew past her chest and nipped her neck. "I can handle anything that comes my way. I know where the gun is, and I'll use it if I have to!"

He grinned, plopped her hat on her head, and eased the zipper from her pinched neck. "I'm sure you can. You are the bravest woman I know. "

"Fine," she huffed, appeased. "But you can't keep me away forever."

"I wasn't intending to. Today you're going to be schooled in self-defense by the best." He popped his head out the front door and called to Frank, who sat in the silver Sebring that was idling in the driveway. "She's coming."

Jeffrey cupped her cheeks and kissed her. "Now go play nice," he teased. "Listen to everything my dad and Frank says. They taught me everything."

Tara twisted her lips. "What? You're sending me away without a packed lunch? No apple for the teachers?"

"My dad and Frank have that covered. Frank is going to take you to the gym. Then he'll take you to his house for lunch. You'll get to meet his wife, Myra. I know she's anxious to meet you. And you'll like her. She was a journalist. Then they'll take you to the shooting range. They're going to teach how to handle a revolver properly."

Frank rolled down his window and yelled, "Let's hit the road. I'm not getting any younger."

Tara reached up and tapped Jeffrey on his nose, "Looks like I have a schedule to keep."

He patted her behind. "Now run along."

She inched along the icy driveway and then Tara slid into Frank's car.

"Good morning, Tara. Pleasure to see you again."

"Good morning to you, too. I'm ready to go. Teach me everything I need to know."

Frank tapped his steering wheel. "Anxious, aren't you? Next stop, the boxing gym. I'm going to teach you how to defend yourself."

Tara and Frank entered the Gallant Gloves Gym. Tara scanned the men and women that were punching heavy bags, sparring in rings, and lifting weights. She'd never been inside a boxing club before.

"Wow. Look at those women." She shook her head. "I don't belong here, Frank. These people are *good*."

"No one's born a boxer, Tara. They were all beginners once." He gestured to a door in the far wall. "The woman's locker room is over there. Meet me at the weights when you're ready." Frank handed her a gym bag. "Compliments of Johnny, with Jeffrey's help, of course. He said he was an *expert* at shopping for you."

She giggled. "Yeah."

Once safely in the locker room, Tara changed into shorts and a tee shirt.

*I'm so out of my league.*

Curling her fingers into a fist, she drew a deep breath and ventured out of the locker room. *Bring on those perps! I'll be ready.*

With chin up Tara strode over to Frank.

"Okay, now we'll put some gloves on you."

She hesitated. "I'm not ready to get knocked on my ass."

"No sparring. I'm going to show you how to use a speed bag. It's a bag, not a person. The gloves are different too. These gloves are designed to cushion your hands."

Frank wrapped Tara's hands and fitted her with a pair of gloves. He showed her the proper stance and footwork.

"It must be all that dancing you've done." Frank said, pleased with how fast she was learning.

She nodded her head and replied, "Hmm, perhaps. I like this. When can I smack the bag?"

Frank chuckled, and then set to work demonstrating the correct rhythm of punching. Then he let her try. She progressed from slow and methodical punches, to quicker and more controlled, alternating jabs. There was so much to remember.

Jeffrey trudged past the desk sergeant.

"Top of the morning to you, Lou," he said.

Jeffrey grumbled, "More like the bottom."

Jeffrey thought about the brick. The obvious warning had to be coming from the inside. Aside from his friends, only his colleagues and superiors had access to his home address. And he had always refused to be listed in the phonebook. He examined every face that he walked by, looking for telltale downcast eyes, but no one reacted unusually.

Jeffrey frowned and nodded to Laurie as he walked by her and into his office. He sat at his desk, pulled out the top drawer, and picked up his bottle of Aspirin. It was too light. He shook the plastic bottle. Nothing. *Shit!* He chucked the empty bottle into the trashcan next to his desk.

Laurie approached him slowly and sat a cup of coffee on his desk. "Good morning, Boss," she said softly."

"Good morning, Laurie," Jeffrey grumbled

She glanced into his trashcan. "I thought I heard a ping. Empty huh?"

"Good ears. Yes."

"Not for nothing, Boss, but you're taking way too many of those. How about I get you some nice herbal tea instead?"

He grunted at her.

Laurie squinted. "Or not. I don't want to stress you any further but Lieutenant Blass from Narcotics would like to speak to you."

"Send him in."

Not five minutes later, Doug Blass stepped into his office and shut the door. Eyebrows knitted, he asked, "Did you happen to get a package last night?"

Jeffrey motioned to Doug. "Have a seat." He tapped his pen on the desk thoughtfully. "Yeah. A brick, hurled at my front door. How'd you know?"

"Me too. Was there a painted note on your brick?"

He nodded. "Yep."

Doug glanced at the closed door. "We've got to be careful. Someone's dirty in this house, and they know where we live... and who lives with us. I got a wife and two kids to look out for."

"I know," Jeffrey said. His eyes followed Doug's bouncing knees. He'd always accepted the job's risk, but it had been different since his divorce and James off to college. He had been alone for the last two years. No perp to worry about harming his family when he was away. Now he had Tara's welfare to consider. Beautiful, stubborn Tara.

Doug steadied his knees with his palms and rose from the chair. "Get ready to find dead rats in your desk drawers."

"We can't let that stop us. We can't have a dirty house."

"Time for some early spring cleaning," Doug joked.

"I'll bring the dust pan." Jeffrey stood and clapped him on the shoulder. "Catch you later."

As Doug left, Mike strolled into Jeffrey's office.

"Hey. How was your weekend?" Mike asked.

"You saw me Sunday. That was the extent of my weekend."

"Okay. Let me clarify. How was your *night*?"

"It was…good." Jeffrey didn't mention the brick incident or the possibility of corrupt cops in the house. And the hot sex was too personal to share, even with his best friend.

"So, did you try the handcuffs? Maybe a little role playing?"

He sighed. Mike's total inability to censor himself was at least entertaining.

"No handcuffs. She didn't need them. She had complete control."

Paul picked that moment to swagger into Jeffrey's office. Easing back into a chair, he stretched his legs and crossed his hands behind his head.

"Don't you ever knock before barging in?" Mike said, irritated.

"It's my office, Mike." Jeffrey chided, then repeated, "Don't you ever knock before barging in?"

Paul got up, knocked on the doorframe, and relaxed back into the chair. He brushed his blonde hair back, preening himself in front of Jeffrey and Mike. "I've solved the Thompson double homicide case," he announced.

Jeffrey and Mike stared at each other. Then at Paul.

"Really?" Jeffrey asked, skeptically. "Who did it?"

"Maurice Chiguard."

Jeffrey and Mike yelled out in unison, "Who?"

"A drug dealer and pimp who had it in for Steven Thompson and Irina" he waved his hand dismissively, "whatever her last name is."

Jeffrey narrowed his gaze. "And you know this because…?"

195

"Angelina Holtz told me, last night."

"Damn it, Paul!" Jeffrey tossed his pen down. "Didn't I order you *not* to speak to Angelina Holtz alone?"

"Yes Sir. But I took the initiative to follow up on a note that she slipped me after the interview."

"And you didn't bother to *discuss* this with me or Mike?" Paul sat silently, gritting his teeth. "That's a rhetorical question. You don't need to answer it because we all know the answer — *no*."

Paul shrugged. "You were gone by then."

Mike scooted his chair toward Paul. "I waved to you on the steps of the station house. There was your chance…right then."

"Okay. Angelina expressed that she only wanted to speak with me…alone."

Jeffrey squinted. "Where is this guy now?"

Paul looked down. "I don't know."

"What, she didn't tell you that, too?" Jeffrey slammed his fist on his desk. Paul sat, unshaken. "You solve a case, but you have no concrete evidence. The only card you have to play is the story of a woman, who is a person of interest in the case I might add, implicating a drug dealer and pimp. And you don't even bother to find out the suspect's whereabouts?"

Mike stood up. "Yeah. Yeah. I'll go search his history," he said to Jeffrey on his way out.

Jeffrey stared at the dingy white wall, refusing to acknowledge Paul's presence while they waited.

Mike returned with Maurice Chiguard's rap sheet. "According to BCI, Maurice Chiguard has been collared three times in the past — twice for possession of narcotics, and once for pimping prostitutes. Last known address — seven twenty one West 70th Street, Apartment 3A."

Jeffrey knocked on the door at apartment 3A. "Open up, please. NYPD. We need to speak to you, Mr. Chiguard." There was no answer. He called out again, "NYPD. Open the door."

"Get ready, "Jeffrey whispered.

He, Mike, and Paul placed their hands on their 9mm Glocks. Mike leaned forward, shoulder down, ready to slam his weight into the door.

"Hey! What are you doing?" A man called as he ambled toward them, his keys jingling from his belt.

Mike and Paul quickly flashed their shields.

"Detectives—NYPD," Mike said. "We need to speak to Mr. Chiguard."

"Fred Stansky, the super. And I need to talk to him too. Mrs. Lefkowicz, in the apartment below, called to complain about water dripping from her bathroom ceiling."

"I'm Detective Lieutenant Corrigan. We've identified ourselves twice. There's no answer. Can you let us in?"

"I got the keys right here," Fred said.

"Sir. Once you unlock this door, we need you to step aside."

"Okay, then. *You* fix the plumbing."

"We appreciate your cooperation. It's for your own safety," Jeffrey said firmly.

"I think we got ourselves a bather," Mike said.

"I think so too."

Fred fanned his keys, selected one and inserted it into the keyhole. With a twist and a click, the lock released.

He backed up.

Jeffrey, inched into the apartment, Mike and Paul close behind, their backs to each other, and their hands clutching their Glocks.

Mike called, "NYPD. Mr. Chiguard?"

His shoes squished across the soaked living room carpet. A pair of feet, wearing frosted pink, high-heeled shoes, poked past the kitchen door.

"Lou," Mike whispered. He tilted his head in the direction of the kitchen. Jeffery nodded. Mike walked over, his Glock steady in his hands. He took one look at the bloodied woman lying face down on the tiled floor and said, "This gal's DOA. Shot in the back."

Paul scanned the rest of the living room, his hands trembling as he clenched his pistol. Jeffrey slowly approached the bathroom, stepping over a puddle. Following the whoosh of running water, he shoved the bathroom door open. "Found him!"

Maurice's arms hung stiff over the curled edge of the tub, his head frozen to his shoulder. Jeffrey reached into his coat pocket and pulled out a pair of latex gloves. He twisted the faucets closed. Mike and Paul crowded into the bathroom behind him. "Don't touch anything. I'll put in a call to CSU and get some uniforms to guard the scene."

"Holy Mother of God!" The super had decided to join them. "What happened here?"

Mike asked, "Mr. Stansky, do you recognize this man?"

"Looks like Chiguard, but I usually see him wearing his face."

It was true. Shot at close range, Maurice Chiguard's face was half blown off.

"How about the woman in the kitchen?"

"Don't recognize her."

"Are there any surveillance cameras in this building?" Jeffrey asked.

"Yeah, but the hallway one on this floor is out for repair."

*Great.* "What do you know about Maurice Chiguard?"

"Quiet guy. No loud music or parties. None of the other tenants ever complained about him. He always paid his rent on time—in cash. Had a lot of lady friends. That's all I know."

"How long has he been a tenant in this building?"

"Three years."

Stansky shot his hands to his hips and stared at parts of Chiguard's brain, stuck in between the cracked porcelain tub. "Gonna be a bitch to rent this place out again."

Jeffrey nudged the super out of the bathroom. "Thank you for your help, Mr. Stansky," Jeffrey said. "I must insist you step outside. This apartment is now a crime scene and will be sealed off. I've turned off the faucets in the bathroom. That should take care of Mrs. Lefkowicz's dripping ceiling. If not, let me know, and we can get someone to supervise your repairs. Here's my card."

"Uh…are you guys going to take care of the bodies or should I call someone?" Stansky asked.

"We have special detectives that will be coming to process the apartment. The bodies will be removed by the medical examiner. Once that's complete, we'll notify you. Then you can make arrangements to have the apartment cleaned."

Fred Stansky looked around at the sopping mess and shook his head. "Gee, thanks." His keys jangled as he walked out the door.

Jeffrey surveyed the bathroom with Mike, looking for a murder weapon or any other clues. Paul now guarded the entrance to the apartment.

"I don't see any casings on the floor," Mike observed. "Who knows what's in the tub. Probably part of his face. They'll have to put him together like a Mr. Potato Head. Eye here. Nose there."

"I'm sure Dr. Roseman will have a good time," Jeffrey said.

Marshall Woods of CSU popped his head through the doorway of Maurice's bathroom. "Whoa, Jeffrey. Two doubles in one week."

"Yeah, I'm going to get hammered at CompStat."

"There's still time. We can make some progress before you walk the plank," Marshall said. "Emily pulled in behind me. She'll be right up. This guy looks kinda familiar. I think I saw him on the surveillance tapes from the Thompson case. Yeah. That's it. We scanned the tapes of the day of the murder, concentrating between 7a.m. and 9 a.m. for the estimated TOD." He pointed excitedly at Chiguard. "This guy was definitely on it, although he looked better at the time, and two other people, too. One was a woman with long black hair, and the other was some dude in a suit."

Mike glanced at Jeffrey. "Angelina and Stuart."

Paul had joined them in the bathroom now that they had reinforcements to guard the door. He held a .45 in his latex gloved hands. "I found this under Maurice's mattress. I'll bet this is the pistol that was used to shoot Steven and Irina."

Paul was too anxious to close out the Thompson case—too anxious to pin it on a dead drug dealer, Jeffrey thought. Something didn't fit. Was he covering for Angelina? Was he dirty? He still wanted to review every second of the surveillance tape and get the ballistics report on the .45 before he'd entertain Maurice as the perp.

"Marshall, send me that tape. I'm out of here. Mike, stay with Paul. I'll meet you guys later at the station." Jeffrey glanced at his watch. Tara and Frank were probably still at the gym. He'd take a ride out there, anxious to check out Tara's progress. Seeing her in those shorts and tight tee he had picked out at Johnny's store was an added bonus. And he needed a break from the homicide paperwork piling up on his desk.

Jeffrey entered the Gallant Gloves Gym, stopped at the vending machine, and bought a can of Coke. His throat was parched, and he had skipped lunch again. Cold and wet in his hand, he popped the lid off the soda. It hissed, and the bubbles tickled his nose as he sipped. Given his morning, he would have rather had a Guinness, but the Coke would do. He meandered into the gym and spotted Tara right away, marveling at her determination.

He watched her jab—right, right, left, left. The speed bag rocketed back and forth with increasing speed. For a split second, he saw her glance at him.

Her wandering eye cost her.

The bag smacked into her face. *Thwack!*

"Shit," he mouthed and ran toward her nearly dropping his can of Coke. Frank also leapt into motion.

Tara's cheeks were crimson. "Everyone saw that, didn't they?"

"Nah," Jeffrey said, shaking his head in empathy. "That bag suckered punched you." He gingerly touched her hot cheek.

"I'll be fine," she sputtered. "Serves me right for looking away."

Jeffrey pressed the cold can of Coke to her cheek. "Better?"

"Yeah, thanks." Tara looked up at him. "What are doing here? Not that I mind."

"I needed a break from yet another murder."

Tara stroked his arm. "I'm so sorry. Drug related again?"

Jeffrey nodded. But he was convinced Chiguard's murder was payback. He hoped Maurice's assassination wasn't a distraction from what may be coming his, and God forbid Tara's, way.

He took her hand. "I appreciate your touch, your concern for me, as always, but it's your cheek that needs attention."

"Eh. Just like my eye, it will heal."

Jeffrey kissed her lips. *She's such a resilient woman.*

"All right. Break it up," Frank said. "Get back to work, son. You're distracting my student."

"Okay, Frank. I'm leaving." Jeffrey gazed at Tara. The redness of her cheek was already fading. "Sip of my Coke?"

Tara took a gulp. "Thanks. Now go get some proper lunch. I'll see you tonight. I have a lot of work ahead of me, and so do you."

Frank eyed him.

"Yeah. Yeah. I'm going." Jeffrey kissed Tara again. Then he smiled at Frank, waving at him as he exited the gym.

Jeffrey hummed as he left the gym, relieved that Tara was under the tutelage of Frank. She'd at least have a fighting chance if anything happened.

He eased back into the seat of his Mustang, resting one hand on the steering wheel and the other on the gearshift. He started the engine with a roar and pulled out of the parking lot of the Gallant Gloves Gym heading back to the precinct and to his growing stack of folders. *Van Halen's Panama* played on the radio. Turning up the volume, he bobbed his head to the beat.

He glanced in his rearview mirror. A dark green Dodge Charger was tailing him.

*Asshole!*

The Charger veered to Jeffrey's left and accelerated. The passenger side of the speeding car scooted closer to Jeffrey's Mustang pushing his vehicle further and further to the right.

"Hey!" Jeffrey turned his head to glance at the lunatic driver, but before he could identify the culprit, the tires of his Mustang skated across ice, Jeffrey jerked in his seatbelt, the straps locking him in tight. Reaching over he grabbed the stick shift and put the car in 2$^{nd}$ gear, tapped the brakes, and prayed. The Mustang slid to a stop, the back end crunching into a blackened and crusty parkway snow bank. Vehicles slowed past him. Jeffrey's heart pounded.

He smacked the heel of his hand against the steering wheel. "Shit!"

As the Van Halen tune played on, he looked straight ahead. The Charger idled about fifty feet away. *That fucker waited, watching the whole time!* Jeffrey leaned forward and squinted. Without a computer or camera in his own vehicle, the best he could make out on the New York plate was a D, G, and a 7. Then the muscle car sped away.

# Chapter Thirty

Monday, January 9, 12:30 p.m.

*T*ara scooted out of Frank's car before he could open her door for her. Between the chilly afternoon air and Jeffrey's frosty Coke can remedy, her "boxing disaster" merely tingled. Frank's white ranch-style house blended in with the surrounding jagged snow plowed banks. The woman waving at a side door offered a pleasant contrast to the starkness.

As Tara and Frank plodded up his driveway, Tara could make out more of the smiling woman's striking features. Her shiny silver hair bobbed on her slender shoulders, neatly restrained with a black velvet hair band, and her sculpted cheekbones rested high on her oval face, accenting her placid blue eyes. A petite woman, a shade taller than Tara, she looked Audrey Hepburn classic, in a maroon cashmere sweater, black pencil pants, and black ballet flats.

"Hurry, Frank. It's freezing out there. For heaven's sake, get her in here where it's warm."

"We're coming." Frank hustled Tara into the warm kitchen and closed the door behind them. Both peeled off their coats. "Myra, this is Tara. She's, uh, staying with Jeffrey."

Myra smiled. "It's so nice to meet you. I've heard such lovely things about you. Jeffrey really lucked out. You're nothing like his ex, Cheryl, thank goodness!" She took Tara's hand. Oh, your hands are so cold. Frank put on a pot of coffee. How was your workout at the gym?"

"Pretty good, until I got hit in the face."

Myra rested her hand on her hip and pursed her lips at him. "Frank! You hit her in the face?"

Frank arched his thinning gray brows at Myra and shook his head "*No.* The speed bag did. She took her eye off it and *wham!*" He smacked his fist into his palm.

"It was my own fault. Jeffrey distracted me. I wasn't expecting him to show up."

Frank waggled his finger at Tara. "Remember, always expect the unexpected."

"Yes. I've learned my lesson."

"And after lunch, there will be more lessons." He turned to his wife to explain. "Joe and I are taking Tara to the firing range."

Myra's fingertips grazed Tara's cheek. "Honestly, Frank. You guys are making her into a mercenary." She clutched Tara's hand and led her toward the kitchen. "I've prepared a nice, hot lunch for us."

"She needs to learn how to defend herself." Frank explained. "Jeffrey's had some uninvited guests at the house."

Myra halted, forcing Tara to do the same. Frank skidded to a stop, nearly colliding into the women.

"Oh my God! Someone broke in? You've told him and told him to fix that basement window."

Tara squeezed Myra's hand and prodded her forward. "Frank is embellishing a bit. No one broke in. Someone threw a brick at the front door the other night. And you're right, Jeffrey should fix the basement window—not that it would make me any braver to go down there. His basement creeps me out."

"Usually, I think Frank's full of it with his stories, but this time I have to agree with him. If Jeffrey is stirring things up at the station, then you have to be prepared for some backlash."

This time, Tara halted in her tracks. Her hands shot to her hips. "I'll be ready. Don't worry."

Frank grinned. "The elf has spoken."

Myra, Frank, and Tara sat at the table. The walls of the kitchen were painted a warm, sunny yellow and the cabinetry matched the honey maple table and chairs perfectly. It was a pleasant change from the stark white of Jeffrey's kitchen.

Tara gazed about the room. "It's very cozy here. Jeffrey's kitchen is so... white."

"The house belonged to his grandmother," Frank explained. "He moved there about two years ago, after his divorce from Cheryl. He's a bit of a procrastinator. Jeffrey's been planning to fix it up a little, just hasn't gotten around to it. Just like the basement window."

He poured the coffee while Myra ladled her homemade minestrone into their bowls.

"Jeffrey mentioned that you write. What are you working on?" she asked.

"This may seem bizarre, but I can't completely recall. I know it was a story about a woman that was lost in the wilderness, but the number three train decimated my laptop last week. Fortunately, my friend, Marielle, found my back-up flash drive. I haven't gone through it yet."

"We have something in common, then. I was a columnist years back for Harper's Bazaar. I'm currently working on a book about women pilots."

Tara paused with the soupspoon inches from her lips. "That's amazing. I can't wait to read it when you're done."

"And I can't wait to read your story."

So far, everyone in Jeffrey's family—even the kind that came without the ties of blood—had welcomed her. Except for icy Evie. Even though the steaming soup had not yet passed her lips, warmth rippled through her chest.

"You may have a long wait. I need to get another laptop and review my draft first," Tara said.

"You're welcome to come here anytime. Our basement isn't scary at all. Frank has his pool table down there, and I have my laptop. You can use my computer anytime."

She nodded. "I would like that."

The phone rang. Frank cradled the receiver on his shoulder while finishing his minestrone. "Hello?" After a brief pause, he said, "She's ready. We'll pick you up on the way to the range."

Herb tottered into Jeffrey's office with cannoli cream crusted on his lips and plopped into a chair.

"Miami was great, Lou. Eighty-two degrees and sunny. Too bad we couldn't be outside that much."

Jeffrey brushed his lips with his finger, hoping Herb would get the hint about the telltale trail of pastry.

He didn't. "Good work, Herb. Where's Liz? I want you guys to brief me on the drug runner hit. I want to know more about the white van with New York plates, and get a possible ID on who was in that field."

"Liz will be up shortly. What have I missed?"

Jeffrey held up his fingers and began ticking things off. "Let's see. We're working a double homicide that may be related to the Thompson case involving a drug dealing pimp and one of his girls. Mike and Paul caught that one. Oh, and a brick smashed into my front door last night. And someone tried to pit maneuver me off the road about an hour ago. Otherwise, it's been pretty quiet." He didn't even mention that he had suspicions that Paul might be into the lead suspect.

Liz, Mike, and Paul lumbered through the door, childishly squeezing each other, as they vied to be first one inside, all three nearly falling to the floor as they popped through the doorway.

Jeffrey rolled his eyes. "Everyone. Sit!"

Mike winked at Liz and whispered, "Tan all over?"

She discreetly flipped him her middle finger. Mike grinned.

"While everyone's here, I'd like Liz and Herb to update us on the Miami drug runner case."

Liz cleared her throat. "Jose Marquez, known as Bengal, age 31. Found in a field in Redlands, south of Miami. Shot in the back of the head once with a .38. No weapon recovered. A Cessna was found about 500 yards from the body with traces of cocaine. There's an orange grove not far from the body, about twenty yards. That's where a female migrant worker described seeing a young white female with long black hair. Approximate age: Mid-twenties, engaged in oral sex with a man. The female then shot the man as he walked away and fled in a white van with bold black letters on one side. The migrant worker has since vanished, though she described the incident to a field hand who relayed her story. Miami's forensic unit was able to get a cast of tire tracks, two different kinds. One is presumably the van and the other, an unidentified vehicle. Also, casts of the vic's shoe prints and those of the female suspect are available."

"Thanks, Liz. I'll let you go back to Narcotics. Lieutenant Blass will need your report, too. He will also be briefing you on our conjoined effort to eliminate drug trafficking in our precinct. We are actively pursuing the Miami-New York connection in the drug trade, along with the feds, and the recent homicides of Steven Thompson and Maurice Chiguard. Vice will be pursuing the prostitution aspect of both cases."

Liz stood, stepping on Mike's foot on the way out.

"Ow," he cried.

She smiled. "Oops. Sorry."

"I bet."

"Mike," Jeffrey called, interrupting his and Liz's banter. "Grab those surveillance tapes and let's review them. Paul, you come with us. Herb, I want you to go to Williamsburg to interview Thompson's employees."

"I'm on it, Boss."

As Herb left, the rest of the guys headed to interview room four. Jeffrey couldn't help but notice that Paul winked at Laurie as he walked past her desk.

"Hello, Detective Rivchak," she gushed.

Jeffrey watched as she pretended to file some papers while eyeing Paul's rear.

While relieved that Laurie no longer lingered in his presence, he'd have to protect her from Paul's toying, self-centered gestures.

Once settled, they sat across from the screen. Laurie brought coffee, spilling Jeffrey's and Mike's overflowing Styrofoam cups, while setting Paul's cup down with the finesse of a geisha.

Paul smiled, displaying his perfectly straight teeth. Jeffrey and Mike rolled their eyes at each other.

"Hey, Laurie. What? No popcorn?" Mike asked.

"Let's get on with it," Jeffrey said.

Mike fast-forwarded the tape to the day before the murder. "Here we go. 7:06 p.m.-Thursday. Steven and Irina are leaving the apartment."

Paul leaned forward, tracking the image on the screen. "Her black fur coat is partially open. You can see she's wearing the silk blouse and jeans that I found on the floor."

Jeffrey nodded in approval.

"7:27. There's their neighbor, Marjorie Crossable, leaving her apartment with her dog."

Jeffrey chuckled. "That dog nearly chomped off Herb's fingers."

"Probably thought they were little sausages," Mike said.

The tape continued. Jeffrey observed, "8:12. Steven and Irina are back. 8:21. Mrs. Crosdale returning from her walk with her dog. Okay, there's Madelyn knocking on the door. 8:24. Door opens and closes. Madelyn stomps out the door at 8:35. Ah, Mrs. Crosdale peeking out of her door. Brief exchange—looks like hello and goodbye. Madelyn smacking elevator button. Gets in elevator...gone."

The screen flashed with images of an empty hallway until 6:45 a.m. the day of the murder. Then Angelina appeared on the screen. Jeffrey noted that Paul's eyes widened at the sight of her. She leaned on the doorframe of Steven's apartment, twisting her jet-black hair around her finger.

"Slow it up. What is she holding?" Jeffrey asked.

"Looks like a black travel bag," Mike said.

Jeffrey glanced at Paul. "Seen that before?"

"No. She had a small black purse that night we went to dinner." Jeffrey glared at him, but Paul just shrugged.

"Look," Mike said, drawing his attention back to the screen.

Angelina entered Steven's apartment and reemerged fifteen minutes later.

"She's not fidgeting anymore," Jeffrey noted. "She just flipped Marjorie Crosdale the bird. And look, the old bird is sticking her tongue out at her while snapping up her morning paper."

"Women can be so cruel," Mike said.

Jeffrey baited Paul. "It's probably not wise to piss off Angelina. I think she'd use more than a finger to get even. What do you think?"

"I think she's dramatic and unpredictable. Tense one minute and then a few seconds later practically wanting me to mount her."

Jeffrey's eyes narrowed. "You didn't!"

"Hell no... but I thought about it. What can I say? The chick is hot."

"Yeah. One day that hot chick is gonna turn on you. That woman is psycho! Mike said.

Paul shrugged. "I can take care of myself."

"Sure you can." Mike folded his hands behind his neck. "Well don't count on your brain when you're distracted by your dick. Steven Thompson was distracted by his dick and look what happened to him."

"I don't believe Angelina did it. She can be scary, but I like Maurice for the doer."

But Jeffrey couldn't reconcile Maurice as the perp. He was a guppy in shark-infested waters with the likes of Thompson and Larkin.

Mike lurched forward, pointing at the screen. "Here comes our man Stuart Thompson at 9:02. The guy's always wearing a suit. He looks irked...or constipated. Probably both...irked that he's constipated. I went through a lot of trouble to prepare that apple for him. But was he thankful? Nooo!"

Jeffrey tapped at the screen. "He's taking out a key. Oh, shit. Stop the tape. Right there. Look. He's wearing latex gloves. Didn't you and Paul find latex gloves in Stuart and Madelyn's garbage can?"

"Yeah we did Boss."

"Call the lab and find out if CSU is done processing the gloves."

"Will do," Mike said and left the room.

Jeffrey and Paul continued to watch.

"9:12." Jeffrey slammed his hand onto the table "There he is! Stuart's coming out of the apartment. "Freeze it right there, Paul. Zoom in. Gloves are off. Can't tell what's under his coat, but he has what looks like the top edge of plastic bag hanging out of his coat pocket. Ah shit! His coat is black. Hard to see any blood spatter. We have to get a hold of that coat." Jeffrey looked at Paul. "If he shot Steven and Irina at close range, there has to be serious blow back on that coat. Steven and Irina's blood has to be there." Jeffrey pumped his fist in the air. "He's an amateur. He has to have touched something."

Jeffrey drew a deep breath and sat back in his chair. *Better not celebrate too soon.*

"Roll the tape again, Paul."

Jeffrey pushed his glasses up the bridge of his nose. "Stop! Well here's something interesting. Here's your guy Maurice. 9:21 And he has a bulge in the back of his jacket. Why does *he* have a key to Steven's apartment? Thompson wouldn't have given this guy a key. But… Maurice and Angelina knew each other. Did she slip him a key? And he's in."

"Maybe he lifted a key…perhaps a spare," Paul mused. "I don't think Angelina plotted anything with Maurice. She said she only knew him casually, through Steven's dealings. And she heard him threaten to kill Steven."

Jeffrey cocked one eyebrow. "Do you really believe that?"

"Yes."

"Pinning the murder of her philandering lover on a small-time dead drug dealer is too convenient. She may not have pulled the trigger, but she's involved. She leaves the city and Maurice happens to come by two hours later. Coincidence?"

Paul shook his head. "I bet Chiguard is coming for his supply. It's Friday morning. He needs to stock up for the weekend. And dealers are always packing. Chiguard gets his supply and his revenge."

"Perhaps he's too late. Steven and Irina are dead before he gets there. And that somebody appears to be Stuart Thompson. It fits Paul. Maurice was taken out before he could turn what he saw into blackmail. Or Chiguard may have planned to boast to all the dealers, taking credit for the kill, upping his power, his machismo. Staking his claim as the new number one. But someone made sure none of that happened."

"Here he is leaving the apartment, six minutes later. Chiguard's closing the door. He's looking around like he's paranoid that someone heard something and called the cops. Though, we know that didn't happen. Maybe Stuart left without finishing the job," Paul offered.

Jeffrey, impressed by Paul's hypotheses, replied, "That's a decent observation. We need to find out if any prints, besides Steven's, were on the .45 recovered."

"I'll get with the lab," Paul said.

"And I'll make a call to the riding ADA. Stuart's presence at Steven's apartment is within the estimated TOD along with the latex gloves he's seen wearing. That's enough for a search warrant."

Mike returned. "The gloves are positive for GSR. DNA inside them doesn't match anyone in any of the data bases."

"Paul, you work on the gun prints. Mike and I are going to Katonah."

Tara's belly full and warm after Myra's hearty minestrone, she donned her jacket, hat, and mittens. Her cheek had dulled to a mild sting. "Okay Frank. Let's hit the road."

Frank slipped on his coat and gloves as well and then grinned. "You're like me. People like us don't give up. Let's go."

Tara and Frank got into his Sebring. Before he started the car, Frank turned toward her.

"Before we pick up Joe, I want to share something with you. Joe doesn't like me to talk about it, and Myra doesn't know."

Tara wrinkled her forehead. "What's that?"

"Forty-one years ago, my sister Maria was brutally raped and murdered on her way home after her evening shift as a nurse. My family was devastated, and her killer was never found." Frank gripped the steering wheel. "Five years later, Joe and I responded to a call. Two patrolmen had nabbed a guy, burying a body in the woods of Vancortlandt Park. During our search of his apartment, I found a locket that belonged to Maria. He'd kept it… as a trophy." He rubbed his eye. "I remember being frozen in place—my mind swirling with the implications. After that, there was… nothing. Joe told me my car was found in Boston. Boston PD brought me to a station house after they found me fast asleep on a park bench. My ID was on me. The police knew I was a cop, so they called my precinct. Spoke to Joe and he drove all the way to Boston to come get me." Frank looked at Tara and gently placed his hand over hers. "Then he took me home. Joe told me all of this later, because after finding the locket, I didn't recall anything. Still don't. The doctors weren't sure what to call it back then." He tapped her hand. "They diagnosed me with post traumatic stress disorder, but I'm not so sure. I snapped out of it eventually, but there was always something there, in my mind, gnawing at me." He turned to face Tara and quickly sniffed. "Just like you, I suppose. But I didn't know how to handle it, so I drank. Became an alcoholic. Joe covered for me. Saved my job. Got me some help. I've been sober thirty-nine years."

Frank gently touched her cheek. "Tara, dear, I am telling you this because you don't have to suffer like I did for all those years. I talked with Dr. Kane about ten years back. He helped me understand what happened to me. He's going to help you, too."

Tara looked into his moist eyes, getting misty herself. Strong-willed Frank, a boxer and a former cop who'd been trained not to shed a tear, laid out all that was so personal, so devastating to him, right before her. "I'm so sorry. Sorry that happened to you. Sorry about everything"

*Could this be happening to me?"*

Tara shifted in her seat, her palms growing moist beneath her mittens.

"You're awfully quiet. Are you okay?" Frank asked, breaking into her thoughts.

He touched her hand.

Tara jerked her head and blinked. "I'm fine Frank. Let's go. If you think I caught onto boxing pretty quickly, wait until I show you what I can do at the range." Frank laughed. Then started the car, backed out of the driveway, and onto the road.

"I know you've had some *limited* experience with guns, but Joe and I are going to teach you the proper way to handle a revolver. We'll have you stick with a .38. It's small and light, like you. Easy to shoot. Dependable. Less recoil."

"All right then. I'm ready."

Frank pulled the car alongside Joe's house.

Joe already stood at the end of his drive, his arms folded across his chest. "It's about time! How long does it take to drive two blocks?"

Frank pointed his thumb into the back seat. "Get in the car, Grumpy!"

Joe got in the backseat, leaned forward, and placed his hand on Tara's shoulder. "How are you, dear? Ready for me to teach you everything you need to know about a .38?"

"Oh yeah, I'm ready!"

As they entered the shooting range, one of the range instructors, greeted Frank and Joe.

"Who do you got with you?" he asked.

"This is Tara. She's staying with Jeffrey," Joe said. "He's had some meddlesome mooks messing with him. We'd all feel better if she knew how to handle a .38. Just want her prepared if she meets up with any scum."

"There's no one here right now. Perfect time. I'll set her up with goggles and ear gear. She gonna be using your .38?"

"Yeah," Frank said.

"Pick your lanes."

She followed Frank and Joe. "I can't wait to shoot one this time!"

Joe wrapped his arm around her. "All in good time. You want to learn right Not shoot helter-skelter."

She watched as the men unpacked their polished silver revolvers and opened a box of bullets, the silver conical heads lined up neatly in rows. Her eyes darted back and forth beneath the protective plastic eye-wear as she stood next to Frank. When Joe had loaded his .38, he aimed at the paper black silhouette of a man and fired all six rounds in succession.

Frank shrugged. "Hmm. Not bad."

"What you mean? I got him where it counts—six times!"

Frank winked at Tara. "I bet you can do better than that." He squeezed her hand. "Come here."

Frank handed her the revolver.

Tara steadied her hands as she palmed the grip of the .38, glaring at the target.

"Whoa! Wait now, kid. You gotta load it!" Frank pointed to a shelf in the booth. "Place the gun here. Not pointing at anyone!"

Tara laid the revolver on the shelf horizontally as instructed.

Frank picked up the gun. "Now watch. You push here, and the cylinder swings out."

Tara popped the cylinder open. Six empty holes faced her. One by one, Frank had her load each cylinder and then swing it closed.

He nodded approvingly. "This is a single *and* double action revolver, which means you can manually cock the hammer each time before you shoot, or cock it once and then shoot with each round uninterrupted. I want you to cock it manually first."

Focused on his instructions, she didn't flinch when the hammer clicked into place. *That was easy.*

"Now steady the gun with both hands—feet apart—just beneath your shoulders. Bend your knees a bit. That's it."

She repeated Frank's directives to herself, making a mental checklist. Tara gripped the handle and steadied her feet.

"How's this?"

"Good. We're going to use the target with black and white circles, twenty-five feet away. Each ring has a number. Aim at the middle. This 'V' shaped piece on the top is the site. Do your best to line it up with the target. When you're ready, squeeze the trigger."

She aimed and fired all six rounds.

*Pow-pow-pow-pow-pow-pow.*

Tara squinted to see what she had hit; the smoking barrel, and a warm gun butt in her palms. "Wow! Looks like I hit two fives, a seven, and a nine." She frowned. "But two of my bullets never hit the target."

Frank patted her on the back. "Hey! That's pretty darn good for a beginner. Think how much better you'd do with more practice."

Tara pumped her fist. "I'll do better next time."

"Damn straight you will. Pull the ejector rod and reload like I showed you. Do this again and again until you're out of ammo."

Twenty-four rounds later, she managed to hit the target consistently—mostly fives and sevens—but she got her dead on ten one glorious time. No mook was going to spook her.

"Mission accomplished," Joe finally pronounced. "She can handle herself. Between the boxing and the .38, this is one formidable lady. Let's call it a day, Frank."

Frank didn't resist. He wrapped his arm around Tara's shoulders. "Damn good job today, kid."

Joe ejected the casings from Frank's revolver and tucked it away in his black leather case. Then Joe emptied all but two bullets from his own .38. She watched him secure it in the ankle holster beneath his pant leg before they left the range.

Tara's eyelids fluttered as she fought to stay awake in the back seat of Frank's car. Two spry seniors had done her in today.

*Would you like to see your daughter, Bradley? Bradley's sobbing into his hands. Robert's staring at me, tears in his eyes. Bradley looks at me.*

*"Yes," he mutters between sobs.*

*The nursery nurse had wrapped the baby. No! I have to fix it. Fix the baby. Her skin is blue, her lips deep purple. I unwrap her. Swaddle her tighter. Unwrap her again, and again, and again!*

*No.* She tried to shake the memory free, but her head lolled to the side.

"We're here," Frank said as he turned into Jeffrey's driveway.

Then he hit the brake—hard.

Tara lurched forward, her shoulder pressed against the seatbelt. Her eyes shot wide open.

"Oh my God," she cried as she stared in disbelief at the shattered front window.

# Chapter Thirty-One

*J*effrey searched through the stack of files on his desk. "Damn it. It has to be here!" Searching for the Chiguard case, Jeffrey backhanded a pile of papers, sending them to the floor. One landed on top of his shoe. He kicked it across the room with juvenile satisfaction.

Laurie entered his office and stared at the papers scattered all over the floor. "Uh, Lieutenant Corrigan, Marshall Woods from CSU is here. He doesn't have an appointment. It's your call whether I should send him in." Laurie stepped over a file. "Now may not be a good time."

Jeffrey shook his head. "No. No. Send him right in."

They had gone through the police academy together. Marshall understood pressure, and Jeffrey wasn't going to hide his own stress from a friend.

Jeffrey squatted and began to rake his errant folders into one pile.

"Hey, Jeffrey."

Jeffrey looked up at Marshall. "Um, just cleaning off my desk."

"Well, that's one way to do it."

Marshall squatted next to Jeffrey and picked up the remaining papers.

Straightening Jeffrey motioned to a chair. "Take a seat, Marshall. So what can I do you for?"

"Sorry to barge in on you, but I thought I'd stop by since I'm having dinner tonight on this side of town."

Jeffrey raised his hand. "No problem. What do have for me?"

"Our vic, Maurice Chiguard, was shot by a .38. Single bullet right up to the back of his head. Makes me think he knew the assailant enough to let him, or her, approach him. The woman in the apartment had a prior for prostitution. I think she was probably in the wrong place at the wrong time. We've ID'd her as Sheila Knight, and it was obviously not a good night for her. Single, close range .38 caliber to the back. The .45 found in Maurice's apartment does *not* match the .45 in the Thompson case. And here's a cool one. We combed all through Thompson's mattress. We found a hair, but it's not human. The chromosomal count is feline. Thompson didn't have any pets, did he?"

"None that I'm aware of. No pets or any sign of pets at the scene. I hear you got some GSR and DNA from the latex gloves Mike sent you?"

"Correct."

"Interesting about the cat. Mike and I are headed to Katonah to pick up Stewart Thompson. Judge granted a warrant. I'm sure you'll be getting more evidence from us soon. Thank ballistics for me, for their speedy reply."

"Will do. Listen, I gotta run." Marshall glanced at his watch. "Picking up my date. Good luck with Stuart Thompson. I'll be waiting for your call."

Mike stood in the doorway of Jeffrey's office. "Hey, I just saw Marshall leaving. What's up?"

"He said negative on the .45 found at Maurice's place. But he recovered a cat hair from Thompson's mattress. Weird, huh? Did you see any evidence of pets?"

"Nope."

Jeffrey's cell vibrated across his desk and skidded off the edge. He caught the phone in his palm before it hit the floor.

"Gotcha!" He glanced at the number.

"It's Dad. I hope everything's all right." Jeffrey pressed his palm to his forehead. "Oh, God. Hope she didn't shoot herself or one of them at the range today," he said to Mike.

Mike shrugged. "I think your dad would be calling from the hospital if that happened."

Jeffrey pointed at Mike. "You're right. It's just that Tara can be bold when it comes to guns."

"Hey Pop." He bit his lower lip and listened intently. "Thank God," he breathed when his father was finished explaining what they'd come home to. "You did the right thing by calling White Plains PD. I'm just glad that Frank didn't go barreling in there armed and ready, and that everyone's okay. I'm on my way to Katonah to bring in a suspect and do a search right now. I can have someone else come up as soon as possible to relieve me, and I'll come home."

He paused.

"Thanks, Dad."

Jeffrey clipped his phone closed and rubbed his temples.

"Trouble?" Mike asked.

"Yeah. I was almost run off the Hutch the other day by a green Dodge Charger, a brick dented my front door last night, and now?" Jeffrey pushed out of his chair "My front window is smashed. My dad, Frank, and Tara are waiting for White Plains PD to arrive as we speak."

"Sorry, man. If someone knows where you live, you're either being followed, or it's someone from inside."

Jeffrey paced in front of his desk with his hands pressed into his hips. "That's my conclusion too. I'm going to call Marshall before he sits down to dinner and have him come up and do the search with you instead. Herb is busy interviewing the employees at Thompson's store in Williamsburg, and I want Paul to stay in house. I'll bring Stewart in myself."

"Your call, Lou. Whatever you want me to do it, I'll do it."

"Thanks."

Jeffrey stopped at Laurie's desk on the way out. "I'll be gone the rest of the afternoon. If Captain Scardino shows up, get rid of him. Tell him that I have a dentist appointment, or something."

He and Mike bolted down the hallway. "The last thing I need is for Captain Monkey Man crawling into my business,"

Mike clapped him on the back. "I hear you, brother."

Jeffrey and Mike's jaws dropped as they pulled up Stewart Thompson's winding driveway. A beautiful white and deep blue Victorian with a high-pitched roof, arched windows, and wrap-around porch faced them. Icicles clung to the sculpted façade.

"Wow. He isn't going to like Sing Sing," Mike observed.

"Yeah, the square footage just can't compare."

As Mike cut the engine, the downstairs window curtains stirred. A Siamese cat paced along the inside ledge. Jeffrey could see Madelyn's flaming red hair through the glistening glass, a beacon guiding their way. She scooped up the cat and poked her face between the curtains.

Mike pushed the little white round button centered in a lacy gold frame. A melodic chime played.

The blue double doors parted, and Madelyn peered through the crack, her loose bright tresses sweeping the edge of the door.

"Good afternoon, Lieutenant, Detective Price."

Jeffrey was impressed she knew them by name. "So nice to know we've made an impression. For official reasons, I am Detective Lieutenant Jeffrey Corrigan, and this is Detective Michael Price— NYPD. May we come in?"

She swung the door wide, "Yes, of course."

The men stepped into the wooden foyer. Jeffrey noticed the deep reds that flickered in Madelyn's hair from the light of the crystal chandelier dangling above them. Her red mane, free from its former constrictive bun, softened her freckled face.

"Have you come to tell me that I can have Steven's body?" Madelyn inquired.

"The autopsy is complete, and I'm sure that his body will be released to you shortly, but we're here to see Stuart. Is he home?" Jeffrey asked.

Madelyn hesitated. She looked at Mike and then darted her eyes to Jeffrey. "Yes. I'll go get him."

Madelyn climbed the staircase, hand on the thick banister, and returned with Stuart, plodding down the stairs behind her.

"He must sleep in that suit," Mike whispered.

If Stuart heard, he didn't acknowledge Mike's jibe. "Good afternoon detectives. How can I help you?"

"Good afternoon. Unfortunately, Mr. Thompson, we need to take you down to the precinct. We'll have to detain you for more questions regarding the murders of Steven Thompson and the woman found with him." Jeffrey said.

"I'll be glad to answer your questions here, but I'm not leaving."

Mike strode toward Stuart, stopping inches before his face. "Well, Stuart. We would be glad to ask you some more questions... at the station house."

Jeffrey walked up to Mike and rested his hand on his shoulder. "Look Stuart, we don't want to make this difficult. Fact is...we have you on surveillance video within the time frame of the murders."

Stuart's eyes narrowed. "So? That doesn't prove anything. I did on occasion visit my brother on business related matters." Stuart raised his palms. "Look, I've already told both of you everything I know."

Jeffrey leaned closer to him. "Not many people visit their brothers, whom they have an ongoing dispute with, wearing latex gloves. Let's do this the easy way, shall we? You're going to spend some extended time with us."

Stuart grimaced. "All right, fine. I'll come with you. Madelyn, call my attorney."

Her lips twitched. "I'll call him right away," she said, moving toward the phone in the foyer.

"We also have a search warrant for the premises," Mike said.

Madelyn thumped her socked foot on the wooden floor. "Absolutely not!"

Jeffrey reached into his coat pocket producing the paper. "Here is a court issued warrant. We can escort you to the living room while we search the premises."

Stuart pleaded, "Madelyn, do as the detectives say. It'll be fine." He turned to Jeffrey. "I'm ready to go."

Jeffrey could just make out the blue van with NYPD CSU lettered on the side through the sheer curtains as it pulled into Stuart's driveway. Mike peeked out the window.

"Marshall's here and looks like he brought Sarah Gonzalez from ballistics with him."

Mike straightened the sheers and walked over to Jeffrey. "Let us up here. Take Stuart on in. I'll catch a ride back with these guys, and get the paperwork started. You get back to your house. I'm sure things are buzzin' there."

He clapped Mike on the back. "Thanks. Remind Marshall to get a hair sample from the cat. And tell him that I'm sorry to have disrupted his dinner plans."

"I got it. I'll make sure everything's done right. Go on."

He escorted Stuart out the door and placed a hand on his head, guiding it as he slid him into the back seat of the Crown Vic. He glanced back at Stuart. It was a long ride from Katonah to Manhattan's twenty-seventh Precinct.

"So Stuart, what kind of music do you like?"

"Got any Rachmaninoff?"

"No. But I do have Van Halen." Jeffrey slid in a CD. Even Stuart bobbed his head to the beat of *Running With The Devil*.

# Chapter Thirty-Two

Monday, January 9, 5:05 p.m.

*The* Mustang's tires spiraled, sputtering in a fountain of snow as Jeffrey swung into the driveway, the car sliding to a stop. His dad and Sergeant Plantz from White Plains PD froze on the porch steps, their eyebrows arched to their hairlines and their eyes wide open, while Frank shot his arms out crucifix style, shielding Tara from the spray.

Jeffrey vaulted from his car, leaving the door rocking on its hinges, and sprinted toward Tara, his face wreathed in his adrenalized breath. He ran past Frank and hugged her.

"Are you okay?"

"I'm a little stunned at the moment. I'm not sure if I'm more surprised by the smashed window or your parking job."

He stroked her cheek. "I'm sorry." Lips pressed in a tight line, he exhaled through his nose.

"Son, what have you got your nose into?" Frank asked. "Is it worth it? I've told you before, but let me remind you. Never love the job. The job's a whore. It will never love you back." He tilted his head toward Tara and whispered. "But this woman will."

Jeffrey nodded. He loved and respected Frank as he did his own father. He and his late wife, Judy, never had children, and he'd fiercely guarded Jeffrey since childhood with a ferocity that rivaled his dad's.

Tara squeezed his hand. "Was it a brick again?"

"I'm going to find out right now."

Jeffrey took her hand and led her to the front porch where John Plantz was waiting. He extended his other hand to him. "Hey, John. I came as soon as I could."

John took his hand and shook it firmly. "Well, we've looked around inside. Nothing appears to be disturbed, but you'd be the better judge. We did recover a brick. Watch for the broken glass when you go in, and you have a nasty scratch across the living room floor. Sorry about that. Hey, what happened to your front door?"

"Another brick. Last night. I saved it in a bag. I didn't call you guys because I thought that would be the end of it and that I could handle things if need be. You know how it is."

Plantz nodded sympathetically. "Yeah, I hear you. We'll need that brick and your complaint now though."

"Absolutely. John, this is Dr. Tara Ross. She's staying with me. She was here last night as well if you need a statement."

Tara shook Sergeant Plantz's hand. Her voice crisp, she asked, "Did this brick have a message painted on it too?"

Plantz lifted his gaze from his notebook. "Yes. It said 'the next one's for you'." He eyed Jeffrey. "Someone's holding grudge, Lieutenant. Anyone in particular that you can think of?"

Jeffrey shook his head. "Too numerous to count. Lieutenant Blass and I are investigating two double homicides that appear to be drug related. He got a brick delivered to his house last night too, similar message. I'm unaware if he's reported it. You may want to contact him."

"Will do. He's at your precinct?"

"Yeah. Narcotics."

"We're gonna send some cars to patrol the area."

"Who's that?" Tara asked as a woman trudged toward them through the snowy lawn from the house next door to Jeffrey's, her hands tucked into the pockets of her white fur trimmed parka.

Strands of her silver hair blew across her rosy cheeks. She stopped at the bottom of the porch steps.

"Good afternoon Lieutenant Corrigan...officers."

"Sergeant Plantz, Tara, this is my neighbor, Carolyn Reese." Jeffrey waved her onto the porch.

Carolyn climbed up the porch steps and took a deep breath. "I saw the police cars with their flashing lights so I hurried over here. All this commotion got me to thinking about this crash I heard just after lunch." Carolyn shrugged. "I thought it was the garbage men rattling the cans into their truck." Gesturing with her open palm, she continued, "Of course then I scampered to put the trashcans out, and when I opened the door, Belle, my cat, ran right past me." Carolyn shook her head. "Little scamp."

She paused and grinned at Jeffrey's father. He nodded and grinned back, apparently unfazed by her longwinded story. Jeffrey rolled his hand, prodding Carolyn to finish her story while Plantz busily wrote Carolyn's account in his notebook

"Anyway while I was looking for my cat, I saw a dark green car speed away. The driver was wearing a black hooded sweatshirt like kids wear. So I thought it was some teenager, shook my fist at him, scooped up Belle and went back into my house. Didn't notice your window. I'm so sorry."

Jeffrey waved her apology away. "That's okay, Ms. Reese. This is a quiet neighborhood. No one would expect vandalism. This appears to be related to my work...if that makes you feel any better."

Jeffrey glanced at the sergeant. "Got all that, John?"

"Amazingly so," Plantz said with a grin and gave Carolyn his card.

"I'm going to go in and check the house. Thanks for coming out, John." Jeffrey shook Plantz's hand.

"We'll be watching the neighborhood from now on. Take care, Corrigan."

After Sergeant Plantz drove away, his father sauntered up to Carolyn Reese.

"Oh, how sweet!" Tara said. "He's giving her piece of paper. I bet he's giving her his phone number."

"Yeah how *sweet,*" Frank retorted, with no small amount of sarcasm. He yelled to Joe, "Let's get a move on. You'll call her later. She'll be thrilled."

His dad and Carolyn paused, and then shook hands.

Jeffrey was happy his dad was making a move. He'd been alone too long.

"Hold it right there. Don't move. Maybe a little to the left. Good. *Hold it,*" Tara commanded.

Jeffrey's long arms spanned the piece of plywood as he held it to the wooden window frame. Tara tried not to gawk at his contracted biceps, focusing instead on the job to be done. She reached into the makeshift tool belt that she'd fashioned out of a small a sandwich bag attached to a loop in her jeans, and pulled out silver nails two at a time, pounding them into the plywood edges. As she stretched over him to hammer the last nail, her breast grazed his arm.

She grinned. "Oops, sorry about that. It was an accident."

He winked. "Accidents happen. Make sure it happens again. I've never seen a woman hammer nails like that."

"Lots of practice with home repairs. You should see me with a table saw."

"Yikes!"

Tara never thought of driving nails as foreplay, however, between the physical exertion, the pounding of nails, and their bodies twisting and turning together in odd but inspiring ways, she could have screwed him right then and there on that couch.

His long arms wrapped around her waist, and he eased her down to him. They sank into the buttery soft leather. His arms and legs trapped her, luring her in to him in closer and closer.

Tara pulled away from his mouth to ask, "At the risk of sounding like Mae West, is that a gun in your pocket, or are you just happy to see me?"

"Both." He said with a smile and then removed his Glock and placed on the coffee table next to his .38. "Better?"

"Hmm. Let me see." She squeezed him, burrowing her head onto his solid but comfortable chest. "There's still something between us."

"I can take care of that," he whispered.

"Let me." She traced his firm belly, letting his fine hairs tickle the pads her fingers and then unzipped his pants. His warm hand swept up her sweater and rested at the curve of her breast. The steady, heated rise of her pulse in response to Jeffrey's deft maneuvers now rocketed to full throttle.

The doorbell rang.

"Shit!" he uttered. He smacked the couch with his palm. "Every single time!"

He quickly zipped his pants while she straightened her sweater. Jeffrey squinted through the peephole of the door. "It's just Ms. Reese."

Tara sighed with relief.

He opened the still-dented door. "Hey Ms. Reese? You okay?"

"I hate to bother you." Her cheeks pinked as she glanced between Tara and Jeffrey. Tara sheepishly smiled. "But my cat ran under your bushes. I didn't want to startle you, or have the police think I was an intruder poking around. So I thought I'd let you know I was here." Carolyn Reese stared down at her feet, pausing just long enough that Tara knew an 'and' was coming. "Plus Belle is so far under your bushes, I can't reach her."

"No problem. I'll get a flashlight," Jeffrey said.

"Oh thank you. She's not normally this skittish."

A few minutes later, they were all peering under the bushes that lined the porch. Jeffrey shone the flashlight into the dark. There sat Belle, curled far under a bush, well camouflaged by the white snow. If it weren't for the cat's gray patches, he'd never have seen her.

"Come here, kitty," he called softly. After too many minutes of cajoling, he finally got his fingers into her fur. "I got her."

He gently extracted Belle and handed her to Carolyn.

"Naughty kitty," Carolyn cooed.

"She's probably doing what's natural—hiding when scared," Tara explained. They all looked at each other in silence after her unsubtle reminder that someone out there wanted to do Jeffrey harm. "I didn't mean to spook anyone," she backtracked. "Cats get frightened for a variety of reasons. Maybe there was some animal…or something…"

She didn't get to continue. A White Plains squad car pulled into Jeffrey's drive.

"Everything okay, Lieutenant?" the officer asked.

Jeffrey waved to him. "Yeah. Fine. Trapped cat. Appreciate your watchful eyes."

"Our pleasure. We'll be around. Have a good night."

"Thanks," he called back as the patrol car reversed down the driveway.

"And thanks again Lieutenant Corrigan," Carolyn said.

"You can call me Jeffrey, Ms. Reese. And don't hesitate to call if you need anything. My dad doesn't live far from here either," he added, hoping she'd call on him next. His dad would love to play the hero for her.

Carolyn smiled at them. "Goodnight Jeffrey, Tara." She hefted the cat up against her shoulder and trudged home.

"Nice plug for Joe," Tara said, once they were back inside.

"He certainly deserves it." Jeffrey hugged her, picked her up and carried her back to the couch. "Come here, naughty kitty," he teased.

# Chapter Thirty-Three

Tuesday, January 10, 6:00 a.m.

Their legs had intertwined as they slept, curled together on the couch. Jeffrey slid his long legs free, wincing as Tara's legs flopped away.

She grumbled, "What time is it?"

He lifted his watch from the coffee table and strained his eyes to read it. "I don't have my glasses on, but it looks like six o'clock." He swept her hair from her cheek.

Tara's eyelids fluttered open. "Looks like we had made it through the night without incident."

He nuzzled her neck. "I wouldn't say *that*."

He swung his legs over the arms of the sofa, propped himself to an upright position, and stretched. His neck was stiff, but he had no regrets. Sleeping next to Tara was worth it all. He gazed at her as she rolled her shoulders and pointed her toes, stretching like a cat—a beautiful, sexy, nimble cat. He needed more of these rendezvous, the kind that left him stiff in more places than his neck.

He pecked her on her lips. "I'm going to take a shower. Join me?"

She yawned. "I'd love to, but I think I'll stay here and close my eyes for awhile longer. And anyway, if I did, you'd be a tardy commander."

He smiled. "True. But then again, I'm the boss."

She shooed him away. "Go. We have many more nights of twister ahead of us."

He kissed her, lingering his lips over hers. She made him forget all those missed years of truly connecting with a woman.

"Okay, I'll say goodbye before I leave."

After he had showered and shaved, he crept back to the couch and plunked a kiss on her forehead and then her lips.

"I gotta go. Remember, you have an appointment with Leo at ten. I called Dad. He'll be coming by this morning to house sit until the glass company arrives." He pressed a kiss on the end of her nose. "I love you," he whispered.

"Love you too," she whispered back sleepily.

"Why are we whispering?" he asked.

She chuckled. "Don't know."

"Bye, Babe. I'll see you later."

He pulled the door shut quietly and then skipped off the porch to his car. But Jeffrey halted when he saw Carolyn Reese fetching her morning paper, embarrassed by his childish glee.

"Good morning, Lieutenant," she waved.

"Good morning, Ms. Reese."

"Top of the morning to you, Laurie," Jeffrey crooned, his good mood surviving the drive in to work.

"Morning, Boss." Laurie grinned and muttered, "Someone's definitely gettin' some."

He playfully squinted at her. "Did you say something?"

She shook her head. "Nope." Letting the 'p' pop at the end.

He swung his briefcase onto his desk and trotted past her. "Gonna get a bagel and coffee. Can I get you anything?"

Laurie raised her eyebrows warily. "Uh, no thanks."

"Okay. Can you please get the squad? Tell them that I need them in my office in five minutes."

"I'll take care of it."

He sauntered back to his office a few minutes later, bagel in one hand, coffee in the other, and a smile on his face. Jeffrey eased back into his chair, propped his feet on his desk, and crossed his ankles. The coffee trickled down his throat, extra smooth and warm. *It just doesn't get any better than this*, he thought.

There was a knock on the door.

"Come on in."

Mike, Herb, and Paul filed into his office. Herb walked in with a gray parrot on his shoulder.

Jeffrey choked on his coffee. "What the—?"

"This is Milton, Ophelia's bird. Uh, you said it was okay to bring him, Lou." The parrot squawked in Herb's ear. He winced and cocked his head away from the bird. "It's just for today. Ophelia will be back from her hair stylist convention tomorrow."

"Yeah. Um. It's fine." He was in such a mellow mood that Herb could've brought an elephant to work.

Milton bobbed on Herb's shoulder. "Prrup". Liquid bird poop dribbled down Herb's shirt.

Jeffery roared with laughter. "At least you're wearing white."

"My standards are perhaps the lowest in the house, but I gotta say, even I find that gross," Mike said.

Paul turned his head away. "For Christ's sake, Herb, clean that shit up."

Milton squawked, "And fuck you too."

Jeffrey's jaw dropped, Mike slapped his knee, and Herb blushed.

"I'm so sorry, Lou," Herb said. "Ophelia'd been trying to teach Milton to talk. Nothing, not for months. Then one day he overheard the neighbors fighting. The guy yelled to his girlfriend 'yeah, and fuck you too' and for some reason, it stuck—Milton's first words."

This garnered another round of explosive laughter.

"Ophelia's beside herself. Sometimes he adds the 'yeah' and sometimes he doesn't. Go figure. He usually says it when he's nervous or tense, but sometimes, I swear he does it for the shock value. I told her to ignore it, like they tell you to do with kids, so that his profanity would eventually stop."

"Well, try to keep him calm. And for God's Sake don't let Scardino see him."

Herb plucked a tissue from the Kleenex box on Jeffrey's desk. He dabbed at his shirt then pulled back his hand quickly.

"Ouch! Damn bird bit me! He hates me. It's a good thing I love Ophelia."

Jeffrey needed to get this meeting back on track. That bird was a distraction. "So, Herb, what did you find out in Williamsburg?"

Herb smeared poop on his shirt as he wiped up Milton's mess. "The employees seemed to like Steven Thompson. They said he was a good boss. No complaints about Stuart Thompson, although his staff found him a bit stiff. That Angelina gal was there, prancing around in her high-heeled boots. There was also a white van in a gated lot behind the store."

"Good observation," Jeffrey commended. "Unfortunately for us, the migrant worker who reportedly saw someone matching the description of Angelina, as well as the white van, is long gone, and without her statement, I'm stuck. Not enough for a warrant. We do currently have Stuart Thompson in custody. But I want to keep Angelina under surveillance."

Paul's eyes darted between Herb and Jeffrey, but he said nothing.

The phone on his desk buzzed.

"I have the lab on line two," Laurie said over the intercom.

"Thanks."

For the first time in months, Jeffrey's desk was clear. He pressed the blinking button and cradled the receiver between his shoulder and ear while reviewing Herb's report.

"Corrigan here."

He made some notes as Marshall read him the results of the tests Jeffrey'd been waiting for. Jeffrey raised his fist in victory. This was all great news.

"Thanks Marshall," he said, hung up, and then turned to the eager faces across the desk from him. "The DNA from the gloves is a match to Stuart. Ballistics on the .45 that was recovered at his house were a positive match. Also, the cat hair found at the Thompson scene was a match for Stuart's cat. And we all know kitty didn't do it."

His squad whooped and hollered.

Mike stuck his fingers in the corners of his mouth and whistled.

Jeffrey lowered his hands with a huge smile. "Okay, calm down, guys. That's it. We've got enough to charge Stuart with the murder of Steven Thompson and Irina... Oh, shit, we still don't know her identity."

"Here's some more good news," Herb said gleefully. "I got with Emily Roseman at the ME's office. You may have noticed Irina had breast implants. We traced the serial number to the plastic surgeon that implanted them. He didn't want to show me his records, but when I mentioned subpoena and showed him Irina's picture, he cooperated. According to her medical record, her name is Irina Fedorchenko. I spoke to the Russian Consulate here in New York, and they were able to trace down her address in Russia—a small town fifty miles south of Moscow. Her relatives have been contacted, and arrangements are in the works to have her body shipped back home."

Jeffrey beamed. "Excellent work guys."

Mike punched Herb's arm. "Herbivore, buddy. Congrats."

Paul twisted his lips into his version of a smile, shook Herb's hand, and droned, "Yeah, congratulations."

Jeffrey shook his head at Paul's placating pleasantry. *Scardino sure saddled me with one conceited asshole.*

Tara panted as she swung into Jeffrey's empty office. "Hi, Leo. Sorry I'm a little late. I got stuck in traffic and then had to hunt down a parking spot."

She peeled off her coat and sank into the same chair she had claimed from the first day she met Jeffrey. She was positioned directly across from Dr. Kane. *Thank, God no couch,* she thought. Jeffrey had been gracious enough to let them use his office, saying he could spend more time perusing Paul's reports in a spare cubicle.

Leo tapped his watch. "You're actually right on time." He leaned back in Jeffrey's chair, crossed his legs, and smiled.

She's rather be sitting across from Jeffrey. But Tara recalled how Frank told her that Leo had helped him resolve his past trauma. She had to trust that would happen for her, as well.

"You look chipper this morning," Leo offered.

"I slept well. No nightmares. I think the daytime has been scary enough lately." In fact, she'd not had any nightmares since sleeping in the comfort of Jeffrey's arms.

"How so?"

"Oh. Well, Jeffrey's house was vandalized a few nights ago. Someone threw a brick at his door, and last night his window was shattered," her response came smoothly, with no hesitation. It was her nightmares she didn't want to discuss with him.

Leo's eyebrow's shot up. "He didn't mention anything about it to me."

"I think he's keeping this all low key. He thinks it's connected to his investigation of some drug related murders."

"This must be frightening for you."

"No," she said slowly. "I feel safe with him. His friend Frank taught me some boxing moves. And his dad, Joe, showed me how to fire a .38 at the range." She playfully shot her finger at Leo. "I did pretty well for a first timer."

Tara glanced at her watch while Leo scratched in his notebook. His notes were brief. She tapped her foot. Fifty more minutes of questions.

Leo lifted his gaze to her.

Tara frowned.

"You sounded very upbeat when you arrived, but your face is now telling a different story." Leo leaned in towards her.

Tara sighed "Well, yeah. It was a bit unnerving."

"Umm." Leo massaged his chin. That was just the kind of pensiveness from him Tara hoped to avoid. "Let's use this word 'unnerving' shall we?"

Tara swallowed past the lump rising in the back of her throat. "Okay"

"You've relayed external danger you've faced, but we've not really probed into what happened to you," Leo thumped his chest, "inside, that made you escape from your home...your practice...to Manhattan." He shook his head. "You were heading to Brooklyn, to your friend, Marielle's apartment," he prompted.

Tara held her breath for a few seconds and then exhaled through pursed lips. "There was a complication. My fault." Her knees trembled.

"A malpractice issue?"

Tara shook her head, "No."

"Why did you say it was your fault?"

Tara slapped her palm on Jeffrey's desk. "Because she was Robert's daughter! I begged off because I felt it was her decision. I should have pursued it. Had Robert talk her into a scheduled C section at 39 weeks, where I had failed to do so." Tara bit her bottom. "I was too exhausted and too preoccupied with my own crises, that I let it go!"

Leo remained silent.

Tara slid her hand off the desk and, with both palms, she steadied her trembling knees. "I'm so sorry, Dr. Kane. I don't know what came over me." She drew in a deep breath. "The words just came out." Her head pounded. "Can we please end a little early today? I'm not feeling well."

Leo nodded. "Okay."

Tara shrugged. Leo's hypnotic gaze trapped her. She couldn't avert her eyes. There was nowhere to hide. Her eyes began to sting. *Please don't cry. Please don't cry. Please don't cry*

"Actually, we've...you've...made considerable progress today. But I have some homework for you to do until we meet again."

Tara arched her eyebrows. "What would you like me to do?"

"I hear that you write."

"Sort of. I guess."

"I'd like you to write down what happened, you know, a little at a time. It could be as though it was a story. Maybe just the facts first. The storyline. Then fill in the characters. You get where I'm going this?"

Tara nodded. "I do."

Leo closed his notebook, smiled, and stood. He shook Tara's hand. "You can stop looking at your watch now."

Tara grinned. "I'm sorry about my outburst."

"Ah, catharsis, It does a mind good!"

"I'll see you the next week. Let's make it Thursday."

"I'd like that." *I need to know why I fled, what I made myself forget, but not today.* "I guess it's time to let Jeffrey have his office back," she said with a nervous laugh. "And I'll have my homework ready."

Leo reached for his coat.

"Thanks…for everything Dr. Kane."

"My pleasure. I'm here to guide you. You're finding your own way back now. So, what do have planned for the rest of today?"

"I'm going over to my friend Marielle's apartment."

"Enjoy your day then. Take care Tara." Leo tipped his hat. "Until next time."

"Until next time for sure."

Jeffrey knocked on the office door and then poked his head in. "All done?"

"Yes, we've just finished." Leo tipped his hat. "Adieu, Tara."

"Goodbye, Dr. Kane."

"See you later Leo."

Leo Kane nodded, and then furrowed his brow. "Yes. We'll speak later."

*Hmm, that was cryptic,* Jeffrey thought. Then he turned all his attention to Tara "You look a bit wiped out." he said. Jeffrey locked his eyes on hers. "Are you all right?"

She reached up and wrapped her arms around his neck. "I want to stay as long as I can with you."

"Well, that's good because I don't want to let you go." Jeffrey placed his hand beneath her chin and gently tilted Tara's head up. "Did something happen during your session with Leo?"

Tara bit her bottom lip. "I remembered something I'd rather not talk about right now." She gazed up at him. "If I go back to Brewster, will you still love me?"

Jeffrey swallowed hard. *What the hell happened in there?* He cupped her cheeks. "Of course" He bent over and kissed her, lingering at her lips.

*I'll never let you go,* he thought.

"I better walk you out before you ruin me for the day," he said against her mouth.

She slowly pulled away from him and cracked a smile. "I certainly wouldn't want to do that."

"Tara, you couldn't ruin my day if you tried."

Placing his hand on the small of her back, he escorted her into the squad room. Milton paced on his perch, stopping several times to preen, fan his feathers, and crane his neck. His black marble eyes zoomed to Tara. Milton squawked happily and wildly bounced his head in greeting.

"I get excited like that too when I see you," he whispered in her ear.

She smiled and approached the African Gray.

"He seems to gravitate toward women," Herb said. 'His name is Milton. He belongs to my girlfriend, Ophelia. I'm bird sitting while she's away."

"He's sweet."

Milton stretched toward her. She smoothed his silky feathers.

"What the hell is going on here?" Captain Ray Scardino yelled from the doorway. Scardino's eyes narrowed beneath his black furry uni-brow. "Corrigan! I need to speak to you *now*."

"Yes, sir. I'll meet you in my office."

Tara shrugged, patted Milton, and mouthed a kiss to Jeffrey. "I'm spending the afternoon with Marielle. I'll see you at home later."

He took a moment to delight in her words before he had to deal with Scardino. He would do anything to make her feel *at home* with him.

He wanted to share everything with her—especially his life. He never felt that way with Cheryl, but being with Tara was as effortless as breathing.

Tucking away his thoughts of her, he shuffled back to his office.

Ray Scardino sat crossed legged in his desk chair, drumming his fingers on the wooden armrest. "I don't have all day, Corrigan."

"Yes, sir. I apologize for the delay." Jeffrey sat in one of the other chairs, disoriented at being on the other side of the desk. He folded his hands on the desktop and leaned toward his captain. "You wanted to speak to me?"

"Yes. I wanted to congratulate you on the arrest of Stuart Thompson for the murder of his brother and that...uh...hooker."

Jeffrey gritted his teeth at the word. "Thank you sir, but the woman that was murdered Irina Fedorchenko, was a casualty of an international sex ring. Detective Malik went the extra mile to identify her and help bring her body back to her family. He's proven himself to be an invaluable member of my squad, closing out the Starbrights case in 48 hours and working hard alongside Miami PD and the Feds. And he worked as diligently on the Thompson case. I think Herb Malik deserves a citation for his excellence in detective skills. I also want to put him up for promotion to second grade."

"Ha! That fat slob?" Scardino scoffed. "Pat him on the back. Say, 'Atta boy' if you want. But second grade? I don't think so."

Jeffrey eyed the captain's untucked and wrinkled, white shirt. *God, please give me the strength not to ram my fist down this moron's throat.* "Captain, I wish you would reconsider. Detective Malik deserves some recognition. I'm very pleased with his exceptional performance."

"How about Paul Rivchak's work. I hear he also gave an excellent performance on the Thompson case."

*Oh, yes. He can definitely perform.* "Detective Rivchak is improving. He needs direction. I'm sure that, in time, he'll hone his skills."

"Let him cut his teeth on bigger cases then."

Jeffrey shook his head. "Sir, he's already been involved in two doubles."

"Give him a chance to fly solo."

"None of my squad flies solo." He pounded his finger on his desk. "They're a team. I partner them up. We meet. Discuss cases. It's effective. It works."

"You're looking good for CompStat this week. I want you to EC the Chiguard case. You'll have a closed case, less paperwork, and you won't have to review it constantly. That'll free you up for more important cases. Corrigan, I don't want you to jam me up. EC the case and I'll approve Price's promotion to first grade."

"An exceptional clearance doesn't apply to the Chiguard double."

"Yes it does. Thompson was responsible for Maurice's demise."

"I don't have any proof that Thompson was behind the murder of Maurice and the woman in that apartment. Thompson was dead before Maurice."

"Corrigan, in case you didn't *understand* me. EC the case. You don't want any more bricks flying your way do you? And I'm sure you wouldn't risk your life or that of your lady friend over a skel and a whore."

Scardino stared at Jeffrey, his eyes gradually narrowing beneath his bristly brows.

Jeffrey's tightened his lips into a thin line.

"Your right." He nearly choked on the words. *How did Scardino know about the brick? I hadn't talked about it to him.* Jeffrey placated his boss. "I'll EC the case."

Ray Scardino rose and slapped him on the back. "Atta boy!"

Jeffrey forced a smile. *Touch me again, and I'll break your fuckin' arm.*

"Have a good day, Captain."

"I will. And Corrigan? I hear you're taking the captain's exam next week. Smart move."

*Yeah, a move right out of the precinct.*

# Chapter Thirty Four

Tuesday, January 10, 11:45 a.m.

$S$cardino stomped through the squad room, his black bushy eyebrows leading the way.

"Malik, I don't ever want to see that bird here again."

"Yes, Captain."

Milton squawked, "Yeah, and fuck you too."

Scardino whipped around and shot his finger at Jeffrey. "Get that bird out of this precinct! Now!" He turned around and headed into the stairwell.

Mike laughed so hard that tears rolled down his face. Jeffrey stood in his doorway, arms folded across his chest, trying to stifle a snicker. "Goodbye Captain."

Out of the corner of his eye, he spotted Dr. Leo Kane at the top of the stairwell, hunched over and wheezing. "Are you okay, Leo?"

"I just need to catch my breath. I'll be fine in about five minutes, an hour at the most."

Jeffrey waved him into his office with concern. "Sit down. I'll get you a glass of cold water."

Leo wheezed and collapsed into a chair. "Thanks."

He returned with water and plucked a tissue from the box on his desk, handing it to Leo. "Doctor, maybe you should see a doctor. I'm concerned about you."

"I can't delay it anymore. I have to lose weight." Leo dabbed at the droplets of sweat dotting the top of his bald head. A wreath of brown hair crowned the back of his head, catching any errant sweat beads before they dribbled down his neck. He drew a deep breath and looked straight at Jeffrey. "I'm concerned about *you*."

Leo finally stopped sweating.

Now it was Jeffrey's turn.

"Really?" Jeffrey shrugged. "About what? I can't complain. I'm a happy man."

"I see how you are with Tara and I know that you care deeply for her. I must caution you, though, that people that have experienced fugue, when they recover, often do not remember occurrences in their lives during the fugue state. Do you understand what I am telling you?"

Jeffrey nodded, shell-shocked by the possibility that what he had with Tara could all end.

"Tara *is* making progress. She's primed for recall. She remembers part of a tragic event that happened to her at the hospital. Jeffrey, it's only a matter of time when she pulls everything together." Leo leaned forward. "I've given Tara a special assignment, telling her to write down what had happened to her in a story format. I honestly believe that that's going to spark her memory. I just don't want to see you hurt when she finally regains her memory."

His stomach tightened. He had to make sure. "Do you mean to say that when she recovers, she might not remember me or what happened between us?"

"It's a possibility. However, it's not absolute. Fugue isn't that common, so we don't have a lot of data on it. I just wanted you to be aware that there has been a precedent."

Jeffrey sank into his chair, desolate. "You said that it wasn't absolute. I'm going to go with that. There's too much that's happened between us. She *can't* forget us. She won't."

"You're a detective, Corrigan. I know you understand the difference between possibility and probability. I just want you to be prepared."

Jeffrey leaned toward Leo. "I appreciate your concern. You are a good friend and a good doctor."

Dr. Kane smiled wanly at his compliment. "I also want to let you know I've arranged for Tara's partner in her practice to come to our meeting next Thursday."

"I look forward to meeting her."

"It's a him—Dr. Edouard LaCroix. And…he and Tara were involved professionally." Dr. Kane paused, "and personally."

His pulse quickened and his mouth went cotton. "La—what?"

"LaCroix. He's French."

"Okay. Bring on the Frenchman," Jeffrey said trying to sound nonchalant. "If it's going to help Tara, I'm all for it. I'm not worried. She's not mentioned him."

"Good. If you're sure, I'll arrange the meeting for Thursday. That will give you a few more days."

"A few more days for what?"

"To adjust to the idea."

He didn't want to *adjust.* He liked it the way it was now—he and Tara forging a future.

*Stop obsessing. You love her. She loves you. She can go back to practice medicine. Even with the Frenchman. That was the past. We have the present and the future.*

"Thanks for stopping by, Leo. Are you feeling better now?"

"Yes. Thank you. And Jeffrey…I'm your friend, but I'm also Tara's doctor."

Jeffrey nodded. "I know." He rose and clapped Leo on his back. "See you Thursday."

He handed him his hat and escorted him to the stairwell. After Leo's steps no longer echoed in his ears, Jeffrey trudged back to his office massaging the back of his neck.

*Why hadn't the Frenchman come forward before now? If he lost Tara, he wouldn't rest until he found her. How could this guy really love her? And*

242

*why would she ever want him back? Whatever happened between them, it was now in the past.*

Laurie softly knocked on his open door, bringing him back. "Are you all right, Boss? Can I get you anything?"

The corners of his lips twitched into a wistful half-smile. "No thanks. I'm fine."

She retreated and closed his door behind her.

Jeffrey reached into his desk drawer. Laurie had placed a new aspirin bottle in his drawer. He tapped two tablets from the container, and washed the bitter pills down with his cold coffee. Then he picked up his cell and stared at Tara's number in his contacts, but paused short of dialing.

*Hmm. She's with Marielle.* He clamped his phone shut. *I gotta get out of here.*

He had EC'd the Chiguard case, but it wasn't over as far as he was concerned. He'd pursue surveillance of Angelina as planned, no matter what Scardino thought.

The station house was quiet, except for Milton's intermittent squawking, so he decided to take the rest of the day off. He trusted Mike to handle any problems. It was a balmy, forty-five degree, late winter day as Jeffrey slogged through the gray slush that coated the sidewalk to his car.

He climbed into his black Mustang, and as he pulled out of the precinct lot, there it was—a dark green Dodge Charger, same model and color as the car that had forced him off the road.

He swung his car around and circled the vehicle. Idling behind the Charger, Jeffrey reached into his glove box, retrieved a pen and notepad, and wrote down the license plate number, EXT 2265. No D, G, or 7.

He scratched his head. It had happened so fast. Maybe he got it wrong. He grabbed his cell and called Mike.

"Hey, Jeffrey…I mean Boss. Checking up on me already?"

"No. Run this plate on a late model green Dodge Charger." He looked at the paper, shook his head, and read off the letters and numbers.

"Is this the one that ran you off the parkway?"

"I don't know. Maybe. Just do it. I'll talk to you later."

"Will do."

He ended the call without saying goodbye and tossed the cell onto the passenger seat. Spinning his Mustang 180 degrees, he accelerated toward the lot's exit.

*Cool it, Corrigan. Slow down.* He eased to a stop and glanced in his rearview mirror. He couldn't believe his eyes.

Scardino was walking toward the Charger. Ten feet away from the car, his captain halted, as though he could feel Jeffrey's eyes on him, and stared back. Scardino grinned and then waved cheerily.

*That bastard!* Jeffrey waved back but didn't pull onto the road. He watched his captain walk past the Dodge and reach for the door handle of a white Honda four-door sedan.

Jeffrey shifted into drive and turned out of the lot. But, he didn't go far. Instead, he waited a block away. No white Honda left the precinct lot.

The Mustang's tires splashed through the wet, blackened grit of the roadway and a mixture of mud and salt pelted the sides of the car. Pushing thoughts of Scardino from his mind, he focused on Tara instead. Leo's prophetic warning gyrated in his head, grating away at him.

"Not true. Not true," he repeated like a mantra. "She can't forget about us."

Between his trip to Katonah and tending to his smashed window, he had procrastinated shopping for a new laptop for Tara. But today was perfect. Since she was tucked away with Marielle in Brooklyn, he had the whole afternoon to himself.

Hell, he'd take more than the afternoon off.

Jeffrey hadn't taken any vacation days in two years, not since the divorce, and he needed to get away from his grimy captain. Now was an opportune time to be with Tara. He'd surprise her, not only with a new laptop, but also with a home office of her own. He imagined the smile on her beautiful face when she returned from Marielle's to find a room of her own and his undivided attention.

"Fuck the Frenchman," he muttered.

Jeffrey parked his car in the driveway and grabbed the bag with Tara's new MacBook and the others too, filled with an assortment of office supplies. Admiring his new front window, he hummed as he thumbed through his key ring. He hadn't thought about Leo, Angelina, or Edouard LaCroix the whole afternoon, nor Scardino. He'd only thought of Tara.

Jeffrey unlocked his front door and found his dad and Carolyn canoodling on his couch. He cleared his throat and rattled the plastic bags, heralding his entrance.

His father's eyes darted to the door. "Oh...Jeffrey. I didn't expect you home... so soon."

"Apparently," he teased.

His father jumped off the couch. "Everything all right?"

"Fine. I'm taking a few days off," he explained. He quickly removed his coat and hung it up on the coat stand. This certainly was awkward. The last thing he expected today was to find his dad, wrestling with his neighbor, on his sofa. "Uh...I'll be in the study. Carry on."

Carolyn blushed, demure.

"The glass company just left," his dad told him, "and we'll just be on our way as well."

They picked up their coats and bolted out the front door.

Jeffrey peeked through his front window and watched them scurry across Carolyn's lawn and duck into her house. "Caught ya!"

After changing into jeans and navy blue tee shirt, he went to work on his study, boxing up his belongings and shifting things to accommodate her. This was Tara's room now.

He unpacked the MacBook and stocked the drawers with stickies and paperclips, and donated his stapler to her. Dusting off his printer, he strategically repositioned it, anticipating her movements. He wanted everything streamlined, perfect.

*Hmm. There's something missing—besides Tara.* He snapped his fingers.

Jeffrey unfolded the attic stairs and climbed up, smacking his head on a crossbeam. Once safely in the attic, he rooted through a box of his grandmother's old Christmas decorations, discovering a huge red bow. He blew on it. Particles of dust flickered in the ray of sunlight that filtered through the octagonal attic window.

Satisfied, he backed down the stairs and hung the big red bow on the study door. Then he paced back and forth across the living room floor, peeking out his new window every few minutes, waiting for Tara's arrival. He couldn't stop grinning when he saw her pull up in her silver Avalon.

"I'm home," she called as she crossed the threshold.

"Stay right there." He skidded down the hallway in his socks and plowed to a stop, smack in front of her.

Tara slid off her coat and squinted at him. "Something's up."

"No, just happy to see you. How was your afternoon with Marielle?" Jeffrey avoided asking her about her session with Leo. He didn't want to think about that. Not now. Not today.

"We had a good time." She circled him, keeping her eyes focused on his.

Jeffrey wagged his finger at her, trying hard not to break out in a smile. He wanted to prolong her excitement, hardly able to contain his own high. "You would be great at interrogations."

"Is there something I *need* to interrogate you about?"

He shrugged and then unable to keep it to himself any longer, he clasped her hand. "Follow me. Close your eyes." Then he led her to the study. "Okay, open them."

She blinked. "What is this?"

He pushed open the door. "Ta Da."

Tara stepped into the study and gasped. She ran her fingers across her new laptop.

He swung his palms about the room, his chest heaving with male pride. "Over here you have your printer and," he opened the desk drawers, "here are pens, pencils, and the like."

She twirled in place, a huge grin on her face. He plunked her into the black leather office chair and playfully spun her around, abruptly stopping her every few rotations to kiss her.

"What a great day," she said.

"Wait, it gets better."

He scooped her up and carried her to the bedroom. She bounced on the mattress as he let her go. Climbing on all fours toward her, he balanced over her, elbows propped on each side of her head, his lips a millimeter away from hers.

"What about dinner?" she mumbled.

He whispered, "Highly over rated."

# Chapter Thirty Five

Tuesday, January 10, 5:00 p.m.

"*F*ucking phone. Can't get anything done around here. Thompson's Paints and Interiors," Angelina droned.

"Hello, Ms. Holtz."

Angelina grinned. Here was one phone call she didn't mind answering. "Detective Rivchak, so nice to hear from you. And Ms. Holtz is my mother. I'm nothing like her. What can I do to you...I mean do for you?"

He paused. "I'd like to see you tonight."

She twirled a finger through her hair. "Are you trying to trap me, officer?"

Paul softly laughed. "No trap. Just want to talk to you some more."

"Well, *Paul*. Be at my place around eight."

Angelina hung up the phone before giving Paul the opportunity to back out. She tapped her fingernails on the counter. *I knew he'd call.* If she could secure him to her side, life would be sweet. She licked her lips in anticipation.

Angelina retrieved a paint can from the back and strode to what used to be Steven's office, but was now hers. She kicked the door shut and locked it

Steven had everything she needed stashed away—scale, spatula, pestle and mortar, bags and ties. She fashioned several "twists"—nimbly tying the corners of the cocaine filled plastic bags. Then she packaged a few eight balls and saved a half a kilo for Ray. Her fingers ached. It had been faster and easier with Steven. She stuffed the bundles into her black Louis Vuitton handbag and hurried out of the office, clicking the door closed behind her.

Entrusting Carl, the assistant manager, to lock up the store, she hustled onto the sidewalk. Her Blahnik boots clattered against the concrete. A passing UPS truck splattered her Chanel trousers and vintage velvet coat with sludge. Angelina saluted the driver with her middle finger. "Asshole!"

A dark green Charger slowed to the curb. She was about to give him a piece of her mind too, until the window rolled down, revealing a familiar face.

"Get in," Scardino commanded.

She did as he said, sliding into the passenger seat and clutching the Louis Vuitton bag close to her chest.

"What the hell happened to you?" Scardino said, taking in her sodden appearance.

"UPS target practice." Angelina pulled a monogrammed linen handkerchief with Steven's initials on it from her bag and dabbed at her spotted clothes.

"You got mine?"

She patted her bag. "Right here. Drop me off on Amsterdam and 112th. I have a few appointments to keep today. I'll slide yours under the seat."

"When are you seeing him again?" he asked. She couldn't help but notice how pushy he was being about it.

"Tonight. By morning, I'm sure he'll be reasonable. What about Corrigan?"

"Let's lay off him for a while. Make him comfortable. He's too busy thinking with his dick. When he makes captain, he'll be out of our way for good—way out—to Staten Island."

Jeffrey rolled onto his side and pulled Tara to his chest, their bodies nestled beneath layers of winter bedding, their skin in a halo of heat. He brushed back her bangs. "I'd like your professional opinion."

"Yes, each time," she teased.

He grinned. "Not that opinion, although the validation is nice. Does a woman having a miscarriage need to go to a hospital?"

She propped herself up on one elbow, looking worried. "Is this about someone you know that's having a problem?"

"No. I worked on a case where a woman gave an alibi that involved her staying with a sister-in-law who was having a miscarriage. The sister-in-law lives out of state. The woman couldn't name a local hospital because she said her sister-in-law didn't go. She said that the woman was feeling better by the time she got there, and didn't seek medical care. So she left her sister-in-law within twenty-four hours. Does this alibi wash?"

"That's hard to answer. A woman will usually call her doctor or go to an emergency room if she is bleeding heavily, in pain, or upset about the possible loss of a pregnancy. Not every woman will seek care. If it's an early pregnancy, the woman may just ride it out and choose to either see her doctor later or not even go at all. Women are different and so are their circumstances. It is *possible* that the woman is telling the truth about her sister-in-law's miscarriage."

He rubbed the morning crust from the corners of his eyelids. "Hmm. I thought it was unusual."

Tara yawned. "Your instinct was right though. Most women would at least call a doctor. And why would this woman involved in your case not stay with her sister-in-law longer, especially if she traveled a distance to be with her?"

He popped his eyes open. "Precisely."

She grinned and playfully swiped her finger across his nose. "So have you solved this case?"

Jeffrey shook his head. "Uh uh. The case is closed. The woman I mentioned was actually a suspect in this crime, but now I'm suspicious of her involvement in other cases."

"Other cases? Is she a repeat offender?"

"It appears so. She has no record, but I think she's been lucky so far. Or someone's protecting her." Jeffrey waved the discussion away. "That's enough talk about cases." He kissed her forehead. "I'm on vacation."

She cupped his cheeks in her hands. "I don't want to disrupt your time off. I know what it's like to forego time off and the stresses that accumulate with no relief." She inched toward him. "But I'd like you to come with me on Thursday when I see Leo."

He kissed her lips. "I'll be there. Leo mentioned you've made great strides lately. I'm happy for you."

She purred in his arms, her head nudging his chest. He swallowed hard and squeezed her closer. He couldn't tell her that he was counting the days until Thursday, the day she could remember it all, and just like that, slip away from him.

"Don't be afraid to fall. I'll be your soft place to land," he whispered.

Her deals done for the day, Angelina was free to play. She was the type that liked it rough and she was sure Paul would be up to the challenge.

Her apartment intercom buzzed.

Dressed in tight jeans and a black long sleeved Lycra tee with a plunging neckline that clung to the curves of breasts, Angelina was ready. She sauntered over to the intercom and pressed the button with her black polished fingernail.

"Come on up," she called in her well-perfected, sultry voice.

Angelina pressed her back against her door waiting for Paul's arrival, her arms folded.

His footsteps grew closer and then he knocked. Angelina opened her door. "I've looked forward to seeing you all day."

She crooked her finger, beckoning him into her apartment. Paul stepped inside. Angelina glanced at the bottle of wine Paul clutched in his hand.

Paul raised the bottle of Bordeaux. "I wasn't going to come empty-handed."

"How considerate of you. Red is my favorite color." She took the bottle from Paul. She tilted her head. "Come with me. I have a surprise for you in the kitchen."

Angelina pattered barefoot across the hardwood, looking back once and smiling at Paul, making sure he dutifully trailed after her.

After setting the wine bottle on the counter, Angelina peeled Paul's black leather jacket from his arms, pressing it to her nose. "I love the smell of leather." She draped his jacket over the back of a barstool.

"So what did you want to talk to me about?"

Paul leaned against the green marbled kitchen counter and cleared his throat. "Maurice Chiguard, the guy you said murdered Steven Thompson and that hooker, is dead. Shot in the back of the head while in his bathtub."

Angelina rested her hands on Paul's jacket. She widened her eyes. "Really? Well, it was only a matter of time before another dealer got to him, getting rid of any competition." She shrugged.

Paul creased his forehead. "I thought Chiguard was small time."

"Once he claimed he took out Steven, his status in the drug community would soon rocket. No one wants that kind of competition around. And what do you care, Paul? One less dealer for you and that lieutenant of yours to chase after. Corrigan should thank whoever did it." Angelina strode toward Paul. "Now that we've concluded the business part of the evening, why don't we just relax? You're not in a hurry, are you?"

Paul grinned. "Nope. I have all night."

"Then open that bottle of wine and pour us some." Angelina pointed to a cupboard, "Wine glasses are in there."

Paul filled their glasses while Angelina grabbed a spoon and stirred cheese bubbling in a fondue pot.

"Do you like brie?" she asked.

Paul stood next to her, holding the two glasses of wine and peeked into the pot. "What's that?"

Angelina quirked her lips. "Fondue, silly. I'm not domestic, but I can melt cheese."

She took a wine glass from Paul. "Here's to an interesting evening!" Angelina swirled the maroon wine in her glass and raised it to lips. "Salut!"

Paul raised his glass. "Salut!"

Angelina set her glass on the counter. "Oh, the bread's ready." She grabbed a potholder and pulled a baking sheet of toasted bread cubes from the oven. Angelina stabbed a piece of bread with a fork and dipped it into the heated brie. Puckering her lips, she blew on the steamy cheese coated bread and placed it into her mouth, pulling the gooey concoction off the fork with her lips. "Hmm. Now you try."

Paul twirled his piece of bread into the pot. Melted brie dribbled from his skewered toast. He licked the stringy cheese.

"Oh my, what a long tongue you have."

"The better to lick you with, my dear," he teased back.

Angelina poked her finger into Paul's chest. "Nice. Firm." She grinned and tugged at the starched collar of his white shirt, pecking the buttons of his shirt with her fingernails down to his belt buckle. Angelina slid her hand over his right hip. Paul reared back, his hand shielding the gun in his holster.

"That piece is off limits, but everything else is up for grabs."

"I enjoy loosening up. I work hard. I play even harder."

Paul stepped closer to her. "I understand. I like to work off a little tension myself."

Angelina poured the fondue into a small bowl and grabbed some toasted bread cubes, scattering them on a plate. "Why don't we take this into the living room where we'll be more comfortable?"

Paul grasped their wine glasses. She motioned for him to join her on her sofa.

Angelina placed the bowlful of fondue and the plate of bread on the coffee table. "You don't mind using your fingers, do you?"

Paul grinned. "I like using my fingers."

"Hmm. I like a man who is flexible." Angelina brought her glass to her lips and swallowed her wine while Paul finished half the plate of bread.

"This is really good."

Angelina set her glass down, now half empty, and sighed. "I'm not much of a cook. My mother was useless in the kitchen. Booze for breakfast... lunch...and dinner. A tuna or turkey sandwich in between, if she woke up."

He scratched his forehead. "I'm sorry. Was she an abusive alcoholic?"

Angelina darted her fork into a piece of bread. "She never touched me. Her words hurt enough. Called me a slut. Drinking was her way of dealing with my father and me." She raised her fork and narrowed her eyes. "My father visited my bed nightly, ever since I was ten. I took it for six years, and then I got the hell out of Jersey City." Angelina stared at her Brie covered cube. "My mother was never going to rescue me; and I'd kill the bastard if I stayed." She looked at Paul, daring him to judge her. "So I hitched my way to Manhattan."

Paul reached for her hand. She pulled her hand away at first, but then relented, letting Paul hold it. "Wow. That must have been frightening, and then leaving home at sixteen."

No man had touched her this gently. Not even Steven. Sex with him had been fast and furious, and that was what she had planned with Paul. Well, maybe not fast, but definitely furious.

Right now, ironically, she just wanted to talk. Angelina chewed and swallowed her bread. She shifted on the sofa, switched her crossed legs, and continued. "So once I reached New York I found roommates posted on a bulletin board in a Laundromat, and moved in with two other girls. I worked at a fast food joint.." Angelina laughed. "That was a disaster. I didn't have patience with people perusing the menu. Then I got a job at a bodega. The owner was good to me. Treated me to deli lunches. He'd been robbed several times so he had a .22 caliber revolver. Showed me how to use it in the basement. I liked him. One night he wasn't fast enough. Got shot in the chest and died. I never went back."

Paul squeezed her hand. "Shit. I thought high school in Dix Hills sucked."

Angelina yanked her hand away and swallowed her Bordeaux. She traced her tongue over her lips. Paul grabbed her by her shoulders, pulled her to him, and kissed her deep, burying his tongue in her mouth.

*Now, this is promising!* Angelina wriggled to an upright position and feverishly unbuttoned his shirt, popping the last three buttons across the room. She raked her fingernails down his chest, turned, and walked away, glancing back at Paul.

Paul vaulted over the coffee table, toppling the plate of bread to the floor.

*Ooh, he's acrobatic, too!*

"I get it," he called. "You want to be chased."

"Come and get me!"

Angelina dashed into her bedroom, stripped off her clothes, and lay naked on her side waiting for him to barrel straight for her bed. *Three, two, one.* Paul ran into her private sanctum. She smiled. *Right on time.*

Angelina drummed her fingernails on the brass headboard of her bed. Paul stripped off his shirt and jeans, his gun lost in the rubble of his clothes. He whipped off his briefs.

Angelina eyed his ampleness. *Excellent.* She patted the mattress. "Join me?"

Paul leapt into her bed.

She snatched his wrist, digging fingernails into his forearm.

"Wait!" Paul uttered.

"Nervous, my pet?"

He shook his head.

She laughed. "Well, there's still time to change that."

"No, it's just... I don't have a rubber on me."

"I got you covered." Angelina flipped back her hair and produced a latex ring from behind her left ear."

"That's amazing. Most people pull a coin out from the back of their ear."

"Party trick I learned from Steven."

Paul grinned. "I guess dealing wasn't his only talent."

"Ah, but from what I can see, you are definitely more *talented* than Steven."

*That ought to inspire him.*

Angelina flipped him to his back and palmed his solid chest. He arched his eyebrows, apparently stunned by her strength and her gymnastic flexibility. She straddled Paul and pressed her knees into his hips. She grabbed his hot dick and lowered herself onto it, watching his eyes roll upward, as she snaked her hips, pushing herself into him deeper and deeper.

Paul squeezed her breasts. "Magnificent," he murmured. He grasped her nipples between his thumbs and forefingers and twisted them gently at first and then harder, Angelina rolled of her head in pleasure. She'd have to reward him. Angelina reached back and pinched his scrotum.

"Whoa. Ease up there. Perhaps we need a, um, code word," he uttered.

"Code words are for cowards."

Angelina laughed and spun around, mounting him reverse cowboy style.

She bucked hard, delighted in his groans. Their skin slapped together. He couldn't hold back, succumbing to his explosion. Pressing her fingernails into his thighs, Angelina dismounted and crumpled into the mattress next to Paul, watching him shudder.

Paul's breathing slowed. He looked at her and uttered, "Thank God you didn't kill me!"

Angelina rolled to her side and propped her head up on her elbow and ran her finger from his chest to his navel "No. That would be a crime."

# Chapter Thirty Six

Wednesday, January 11, 1:12 a.m.

*A*ngelina shifted beneath the 800 thread count sheets, and downy feather comforter, proud she spared no expense in her bedroom. Paul stroked her hair and nuzzled his nose in her neck. Ordinarily, she kicked out her men right after she was done with them. Nevertheless, she actually liked Paul. And the poor guy was just laying there, limp and exhausted. She'd give him a break and let him stay the night.

Paul hugged her closer. "Man, you must have really been stressed. How taxing can working at a paint store be? "

She glared at him. "What did you say?" Maybe she would shove him out her door.

"Sorry, Ange. I guess customer service can be a bitch."

*Ange?* She could let that slide. At least he didn't make the mistake of calling her Angie.

Paul playfully ran his finger down her nose.

*Okay, now he's pushing it.*

"What if I told you that you're safe?"

Angelina snorted. "I'd tell you I don't scare easily, but I'm intrigued. Do you honestly think you're protecting me?"

"You can take care of yourself, I know that. I mean that you are no longer a suspect in Steven Thompson and Irina's deaths. Stuart has been arrested for their murders. I knew you didn't do it."

*Ah, Corrigan got him. Freedom! And I don't have to waste my money on Maurice. What a fucking fabulous day! Hmm. Now to make Paul out to be the hero.* Angelina turned to him and gazed into his baby blue eyes. *I should get an academy award for this shit.*

"You were the only one that believed me. Corrigan had it all wrong." She stroked his cheek. "And the way he dismissed you!"

Paul rolled up on his elbow. "Lieutenant Corrigan was doing his job. He's sharp and he's looking out for me. I was the one with the pissy attitude."

Angelina bolted upright in bed and wrinkled her forehead. "Did you even get credit for the case?"

Wrapping his arms around her shoulders, Paul lowered her back to his chest. "No. It was Price's case. He got the hit, and rightfully so. I got experience. I'm happy with that."

She pushed him away. "Why are doing this 360 on me?"

His eyes bulged. "Jesus, how exactly am I doing a 360 on you?"

Angelina whipped off the comforter, releasing the heat from their bodies into the cold of the bedroom and glared at Paul. She vaulted out of bed. *Un-fucking-believable. I'm going to have to work harder on him than I thought if he is gonna cling to this good cop shit.*

Angelina strode to the nightstand, lit a cigarette, and paced the room. She stopped and flicked her ashes into a crystal tray. "Last week you couldn't stand Corrigan. Now he's your hero? Is he going to watch your back? See you get the promotions you deserve? Or is he going to keep you as his 'go to' squad boy? Think about it. Who had the real confidence in you? Who put you on that squad?"

Paul slapped his palm on the sheet and shot up to face Angelina. "I told you. I didn't give the guy a chance. He let me take the hit for Maurice's case. I didn't see all the angles of it, but he gave it to me anyway. The case was cleared, but I got the hit. I'm going to work my cases. Eventually, I'll prove myself. Yes, Scardino is my hook, more like a crane, and he did get me into the detective squad despite my limited time in uniform compared to the other guys. There were far more deserving candidates than me. Now that I have the chance, I'm going to take every opportunity to be a better detective."

Angelina clapped. "Bravo," she spat. "Your new work ethic impresses me. You're going to spend *years* working your ass off working overtime. Will you get promoted? No. Oh, maybe every decade or so you'll move up a grade. Or you can be smart. Build your list of informants. Throw out the little fish to haul in the big one."

"I'll collect informants. It takes time to cultivate those relationships."

Angelina crawled across the bed towards Paul. "Well, Farmer Rivchak, I'll get you a crop of informants. Your very own, ripe for the picking."

He laughed. "You're going to get me informants?"

She shoved him onto his back. "I know a lot of people who would cooperate. I can get the coke. You sell it at a jacked price and get the 411 on who took whom down. You take the credit and get a little cash. Screw the overtime. You get yourself a nice apartment. Maybe even a house. And promotions? You'll be scaling that ladder."

Paul ran his fingers through her hair. "I don't know, Ange. I'm just starting to get the hang of being on the squad."

"Ah, come on Paul! Don't make this so difficult. Grab the opportunity I'm giving you! Your noble way will someday put a bullet hole in your head. I can give you people that will deal with you. No squealers. You keep them happy—and I'll see to that—and you get to walk away at the end of the day, cash in your pocket, and a promotion on your sleeve."

Paul drummed his fingers on the mattress. "I'll think about it."

"Don't think so hard, Baby. Just be hard." Angelina rolled on top of him. "I'm feeling energetic again." Angelina smiled and tugged at Paul's earlobe with her teeth. She already had him by his balls.

Tara eased her feet over the edge of the mattress and slid off the bed. A floorboard moaned as she stood. She pursed her lips and gazed at Jeffrey, hoping he wouldn't wake. He mumbled and rolled onto his side, swinging his arm over to embrace her.

Thinking fast, she shoved her pillow into position to catch his falling arm and waited. He snorted, smacked his lips, and flipped over to his other side. His eyes never opened.

Tiptoeing into his son's room, she shivered, searching for her warm clothes. Reaching into one her boxes, she pulled out a thermal top and soft flannel lounge pants and then smiled.

*Right where I put them.*

Tara wiggled her toes into a pair of white cotton socks — the ones Jeffrey bought her. She was now a mixture of past and present and it felt good.

She pushed the office door open, leaving it ajar, and switched on the light. Tara sat at her new desk. About to slip the flash drive into her laptop, she halted. First, she had to work on the assignment Leo had given. *Write it out. It's okay. It will only be on the screen. I can control what happens.*

Tara glanced behind her, making sure Jeffrey wasn't standing behind her. He loved her. Always told her everything would be fine. But would it? As Leo said, she was the one finding her way back. The work was hers and no one else's. Tara took a deep breath and brushed her sweaty palms across the sides of her pants.

Fingers to keyboard, she typed:

*A screaming woman. "Help me!" she called. The nurses rush her to the operating room while the surgeon secures her mask, speedily scrubbing her hands. That's me! Another surgeon arrives. I don't know who he is! He whips on his mask, scrubbing his hands next to me at the sink. "You warned her, Tara. You can't control everything."*

Tara's heart pounded in her throat. She jerked her hands from the keyboard. "Stop!"

Tara swirled the pads of her fingers over the mouse. She saved the file as NEWYEARSEVE.doc.

The words flashed away from the screen.

Tara sat in her chair, slowly breathing in and out. "Better now," she whispered.

She reached for her flash drive and inserted it into the USB port. There, on the screen, was her unfinished story. Tara scrolled through the pages. The words unfurled before her. It was all there, and best of all, the words were not a stranger to her like so much else. She'd unlocked something in her brain. "I remember this part. Now, to continue…"

The door creaked open and Tara jumped up from her chair.

Jeffrey leaned on the doorframe, looking sexy as hell. "I didn't mean to startle you. Your pillow trick didn't work for too long. It's soft like you, but no curves to hold on to." Scooting up behind her, he nuzzled her neck. "I need your curves."

"Next time, I'll stuff some rolled socks into the pillow case."

"Uh uh. Won't work." He brushed the hair from her forehead. "You're up late."

"Couldn't sleep so I thought I'd come in here and write."

Putting on his glasses, Jeffrey leaned over her shoulder and focused on the screen. She was glad that her book was open, and not her other work.

"Hey, that's good!"

Tara grinned. "You're biased."

"When it comes to you, yes." Jeffrey bent over and kissed her. He rubbed her shoulders "I'll leave you be."

Tara clutched his forearm. "Oh. No! You don't get to leave now. Not in the middle of my massage! "

"Okay." Jeffrey kneaded her shoulders.

"Ah, so good," Tara murmured.

"Hey, I got an idea, Wait here. I know what we can load up on your computer. I'll be right back."

*What's he up to?* she wondered.

Jeffrey returned with a digital camera. "Smile!"

Spinning in her chair away from the camera, she protested, "I'm not wearing make-up and my hair is sticking up. Stop it!"

Tara fled from the chair and escaped to the bathroom. She flicked a brush through her tangled locks, checked for blemishes, and tested a smile in the mirror. Feeling somewhat more presentable, she skipped back to the study.

"All right, I'm ready for my close-up, but if I don't like the picture, I get to delete it."

"Deal." He snapped a picture of her at her computer. "Let's call this one — Tara at work."

She snatched the camera from him. He turned to hide and she chased him down the hall. *Click-click.* She snickered. "This is Jeffrey on vacation, a rare moment worth capturing!"

"Hey! I'm in my underwear. You got to fix your hair. I get to put some clothes on."

She continued to pursue him. *Click-click.* She snorted, "This is Jeffrey's ass — on vacation."

"Okay. *That* gets deleted."

After managing to slip into jeans and a tee shirt, he gripped Tara's hand and led her to the living room.

"Let's take a picture of us." He propped the camera on the bookshelf and set the timer, then plopped on the sofa next to her, placing his arm around her shoulders. She kissed him.

The camera flashed.

Exhausted from their boisterous photo shoot, Jeffrey carried Tara back to the bedroom. He tucked her in and kissed her forehead. Hovering over her until she fell asleep, he wondered if their days really were finite, as Leo had suggested.

Returning to the study, he closed the door, powered up her Mac Book, and loaded the photos they'd made together onto her hard drive, placing them in a file he named 'Jeff and Tara'.

Brimming with satisfaction, he shut down the computer and peeked into the bedroom. Tara purred beneath the covers. He closed his eyes, trying to stem the throbbing pulse, rising up his neck. "Please don't leave," he murmured.

Unable to sleep, he meandered into the living room and plopped into the recliner.

*What if Leo's right?*

He glanced at the clock on the wall. 3:15 a.m.

Suddenly, there was a roar of an engine. Light flooded the room, piercing his sagging eyelids, and his eyes sprang open. Bolting from the chair, he pulled back the curtains. High beams assaulted his eyes. He squinted but couldn't identify the vehicle in front of his house and then it sped away.

# Chapter Thirty Seven

Wednesday, January 11, 6:30 a.m.

*A*ngelina cradled the cordless phone in the crook of her neck while she wiggled her red polished toes.

"He just left. I'm confident he'll fall in line. Sex, greed, and fear work every time. He'll be back for more." She stretched her legs. Paul's scent lingered on her sheets, a mix of Hugo Boss and musky sweat.

She listened with half an ear as he told her when and where to meet him. God the man was disgusting.

"I won't be able to stay long since I've plans with Paul again, the *all night kind*." She hoped that jealousy ate him alive. "I can hook you up with one, or even more, of Maurice's girls. With him gone, they're sort of... free agent. I've been considering helping them out," she told him, though her reasons for doing so weren't completely altruistic. Money was always her primary motivation in everything. "I think you'll have a good time with some of them. Much better than you would with Sugar." Even the name of that two-bit hooker tasted bad on her lips.

"See you then," She told him as he signed off, reminding her not to contact him for the rest of the day, as if she was as incompetent as he was.

She tossed the phone onto the bed, showered, and dressed. Slipping her stocking feet into a pair of tan Prada pumps, Angelina shoved her favorite black boots to the back of her closet.

*Won't need these anymore.*

She brushed her long, ebony hair while standing in front of her dresser mirror, smiling at her image. Puckering her lips, she blew herself a kiss, and skipped out the door. Sex with Paul invigorated her.

*He kept up well,* she mused. *Better than Steven.*

Angelina clattered down the stairs in her four-inch heels. The black, car service sedan she had called for earlier waited for her. She couldn't deal with a cabbie whining about the trek from Manhattan to Williamsburg today. She scooted into the back seat and dialed Paul's personal cell.

"You've reached Paul Rivchak. Leave a message. I'll call you back if I think you're worth it." *Beep.*

"Do you think I'm worth it? If so, meet me for dinner at Niko's at seven."

Tara stretched in bed and rolled over to hug Jeffrey only to find he wasn't lying next to her. *Where is he?*

Stumbling down the hallway and into the living room, she found him snoring with his mouth wide open and his head wedged between the sofa cushions. Tara's neck ached just looking at him.

She tiptoed toward the sofa and shook his shoulder.

Jeffrey stirred and wrestled his head from couch's grip.

Tara sat next to him and rubbed his thigh. "Good morning. What happened to you? I woke up and you were gone."

She desperately hoped she hadn't done something, said something in her sleep that made him leave her all alone.

Jeffrey kissed the end of her nose. "After you fell asleep on the couch, I carried you into bed but I couldn't sleep after that. Apparently, I passed out here. I guess I'm not used to vacation time."

She narrowed her eyes at him, but didn't press further.

Jeffrey stretched. "Hey, now that we're both awake, how about a morning run?"

Tara shrugged. "Sure. I'll give it a go."

His eyes twinkled. "I'll get my running shoes and take you to the South County Trailway. You'll love it."

She wasn't sure she'd "love" the trail, especially on a winter day, but what she did love was spending more time with Jeffrey.

Jeffrey parked the Mustang on the side of the road and pointed straight ahead. "The trail is beyond those trees." It was still cool for January, but it was a beautiful day and a run was going to do them both some good.

Tara and Jeffrey got out of the car. He clicked the remote on his key ring. The car doors beeped into lock position. Jeffrey dropped the keys into his short's pocket.

Jeffrey patted her on her rear. "Ready to stretch those beautiful legs?"

She smiled and nodded. "Absolutely."

Tara and Jeffrey edged their way carefully around some icy patches. She declined his extended hand, forging her own path. They finally hit the plowed and salted trail.

"Let's go," she called as she moved past him.

"I'll stay with you," he said, jogging up beside her.

His pace was quick, but Tara found her stride. Their chests heaved in rhythm, her feet scurrying double-time to catch his. She focused ahead, intent on completing three miles, even if it killed her.

Her feet bounced off the paved trail, her body airborne with each stride. The winter sun warmed her face as she ran mesmerized beneath the canopy of the snow-capped trees all in a backdrop of azure sky.

Panting, she glanced at Jeffrey. His arms rocked with purpose, his breathing steady. He was a gazelle in the suburban Serengeti.

When they reached the three-mile mark she puffed, "Go ahead. Stretch your legs. I'm gonna slow up."

"Are you sure?" he asked, jogging in place.

"I'm sure I'm pooped. Go." She smiled between pants. "I'll be puttering along."

"You gave me a run for my money today."

She laughed. "Flattery will get you everywhere, Detective Corrigan. Oh, go on. Really—go on." Tara shooed him away.

Awed by his tight gluts and his muscular calves that bulged beneath the spandex of his black running pants, she watched him disappear beyond the curve of the path.

Trotting at a comfortable pace, her pulse slowed and her breathing eased. Looking straight ahead, she heard the clap of running shoes, crunching on the salted asphalt behind her. The runner never made a shift to veer around her. He was so close that she swore his warm breath lingered on the back of her neck.

*Okay, just pass my pokey ass. Tailgating on the trail. Not nice. Pass, please,* she prayed.

The runner finally moved to her left. Her heart pounded in her ears and she shifted her gaze sideways. She couldn't see the runner's face. He—at least she *thought* it was a he—wore a black hooded sweatshirt and jeans. *Death in denim was out for a run.*

He body-checked her…hard.

Her feet flew up in the air, wildly in search of the ground, but there was no surface to touch. She landed in the ravine on her side and bounced onto her back, skidding down the embankment. Her diaphragm stunned, she sucked for air that didn't come. Her body tumbled down the cliff, accelerating over rocks and twigs.

Thankfully, her lungs finally filled with breath.

She tried to dig her heels into the dirt beneath the snow to slow her, but she skidded across the frozen ground. She grasped at a low-lying tree branch and her body halted.

Tara looked around, peering up at the trail for her assailant. No one. The woods were dead still except for the snapping of the tree branch she clung to, bicycling her feet, desperate for traction.

Sweating profusely beneath her running gear, she hung quietly on the branch, her eyes the only thing she dared to move. Her grip slipping, she had no choice. Tara wedged the heel of her shoe on a rock, and then on another and another. Grabbing onto branches and bushes, she inched herself out of the ravine and back onto the trail, brushing the ice and dirt from her pants, and pulling a twig from her hair. Her frozen hands burned, abraded from her climb. Tara took a deep breath and glanced down the ravine. She'd made it out with only scratches to show for it.

*There's no way I'm going to tell Jeffrey about this. He'll freak. He's had enough happen to him. He's on a much-needed vacation. Oh God, and here he comes now. Steady, Tara. Steady. Dear Lord, the man hardly looks rumpled—maybe a little sweat in his hair.*

Jeffrey slowed to a walk, bending a bit at the waist, and breathing deeply with his hands on his hips. "That felt good. Did you have a good work out?"

Tara tried to hide her skinned hands behind her back, but Jeffrey reached around her waist, pulling her hands into his.

His eyes widened. "What happened, Tara?"

She shrugged. "I'm such a klutz. I hit a patch of ice and down I went," she said with a shaky laugh "I'm fine, really."

"That was some tumble. You're sprouting wildlife." He pulled a twig from her hair. "Let's go home and get you cleaned up."

Tara and Jeffrey walked back to the car, his arm around her shoulder, her arm around his waist. The sun shone brightly and the wind had quit blowing. It was a gorgeous day, but all that was forgotten as they approached his parked car.

"Shit!" he yelled.

Shards of plastic and glass lay strewn on the pebbled ground in front of the smashed headlights.

# Chapter Thirty Eight

Wednesday, January 11, 4:30 p.m.

$\mathcal{T}$ara reached across the kitchen table and stroked Jeffrey's hand. "Scowling isn't going help."

She was right, of course. He could get his Mustang repaired, but what he couldn't fix immediately were the continued threats. He'd faced the personal assaults of disgruntled perps in the past, and as far as he was concerned, it was game on.

However, Tara's safety was nonnegotiable.

They were toying with him. Minor but annoying damage. But in his experience, the threats would soon escalate. Whoever was doing this would find out about her—that she was staying with him—if they didn't know already, and dangle her like a carrot to manipulate him.

He could kick himself for being so selfish, but now he had no choice. Jeffrey had to let her go…for now.

He propped his elbows on the kitchen table and sank his forehead into his hands. "I guess I should call my insurance company and get the car into the shop."

Placating Scardino, he'd green lighted the exceptional clearance of the Chiguard case, but he planned to probe the case again, once

Scardino preoccupied himself with far more mundane matters. Perhaps there were others beside the captain that had a vested interest in keeping the case closed, and they were intent on proving their point.

Tara leaned over him and massaged his shoulders. The pads of her fingers sank into his tense back, kneading his muscles into submission.

"Make your calls," she told him. "I'll follow you to the auto repair shop. Then let's forget about this whole mess and eat at Niko's tonight. I'll drive. You relax." She pecked a chain of kisses along the back of his neck, earlobe to earlobe.

He couldn't help but think about her words. He doubted she even noticed what she'd said.

*Was forgetting her forte? Did she always run from discomfort? Maybe she didn't know where to put her tormenting thoughts.*

He reached up and gripped her hands, swinging them to his lips and kissed every knuckle.

"Okay, I surrender. But I need to call Sergeant Plantz first."

Giving him a quick smooch, she bounded out of the kitchen. "Okay, I'm going to get ready for tonight," she called from the hallway.

He raked his hair into place and smiled. She was so full of life. And being with her made him feel alive for the first time in many years.

All of it could come crashing down.

Leo did give him fair warning. He ached at the thought of sending her off to safety tonight—possibly their last night together—but he had to have faith she'd be a part of his life forever.

Jeffrey called his insurance agent and then the body shop. He'd known Bud, the mechanic, for years, and was relieved he was available to work on his car soon.

His next call was to the White Plains PD. He paced the gold-flecked kitchen tiles while he waited to be connected to Sergeant Plantz.

"Hi John. It's Jeffrey Corrigan. I called to see if there's any news on processing the bricks. A long shot, I know."

His hope vanished as John gave him the bad news. No prints.

"I appreciate your efforts all the same. And... I wanted to let you know that my headlights were smashed today, while Tara and I were jogging on the South County Trail."

The phone buzzed angrily with Plantz's rapid-fire inquiries.

"No. No one was there when we got there, and no one when we returned. I'll file a report with the Westchester County Police. I've parked on that road, same place, many times. No problems. I'm sure someone tailed my car."

He glanced down the hallway before saying what he had to say next, cordless phone to his ear. He didn't see her, but he'd heard water running behind the closed bathroom door only moments before.

"Tara fell down a ravine. Got a few scrapes. She said she slipped on some ice and tumbled off the path. That's her story, but I'm not sticking to it."

John, always the reasonable one, tried to pacify him, but Jeffrey could only think of Tara's safety.

"Thanks, John. Let me know if you or the county guys come up with anything."

He hung up the phone and turned around. His jaw dropped.

Tara now stood at the kitchen doorway with her palms pressed into the wooden frame. Her black cotton wrap dress hugged her strong, slender arms and clung to her curves in all the right places, the edge of the bodice darting down the swell of her breasts, framing her cleavage in a perfect triangle, and her black high-heeled pumps accentuated her toned, balletic legs. Balancing on one foot without as much as a bobble, she slowly traced the back of her calf with the back of the other shoe.

The phone fell from his hand and clattered to the kitchen counter.

Tara grinned. "Ready to go?"

"I'll...uh...be right with you," he stammered.

He forgot all about his car.

Angelina drummed her red polished fingernails on the dark oak table of Shane's Bar. The galloping sound mounted with each irate sigh.

"Can't you follow directions? Do you recall what we discussed? Hmm?" she hissed.

"I took the car and wore the black hoodie," Detective Dave Willis said. "When I cruised by Corrigan's house, I saw him and the doctor leave, and followed them to the trail. I wanted to shake them up one more time."

She smacked his head with her palm and he let it loll to one side.

"You stupid shit! Corrigan closed Maurice's murder case at Scardino's request. You've pissed Corrigan off now, you moron. He's already suspicious. All I need is him getting some bright idea to probe into Maurice's murder again…no thanks to you. That puts me in a difficult position, you see? Let me remind you. I go down…you go down. Cops are prime prison targets, especially *ex*-narcotic detectives who skim off skel informants."

Willis and Detective Buck Gates scowled and slouched down the back of the bench like scolded children yet thankfully, Buck remained silent. Angelina sipped her dirty martini.

*Oh God.* Here came Scardino, walking into Shane's as if he owned the place.

Raising her arm, she motioned to him with a flex of her finger. He shoved into the bench next to her, knocking her arm. Her drink splashed onto the cuff of her white silk blouse.

"Watch it asshole," she muttered.

"Sorry about that." He signaled the waitress. "I'll get you another one."

"Another what? Another Gucci blouse?"

Scardino smirked. "What for? You have, like, *fifty* blouses. Go wash it off in the ladies room."

She squinted at him. "It's silk, you fool." *I don't know why I bother to explain. The slob's been wearing the same stinky crumpled shirt since last week.*

The waitress flipped a cork coaster onto the table and plunked a mug of beer in front of Scardino. He gulped through the foamy head, swiped his lips with the back of his hand, and belched. Angelina grimaced, wrinkling her nose in disgust.

Smacking his half- empty mug on the table, Ray asked, "So what was the take?"

Buck slid a thick mustard yellow envelope across the table. She snatched the envelope, crinkling it open beneath the table and rifled through the bills, doling out her thugs' respective shares, then dividing the remaining proceeds to Ray and herself. He tapped his foot after she handed him his money.

Angelina narrowed her gaze. "Fifty grand not enough? Of course, if you're ungrateful, then you're welcome to find another supplier — one less concerned with quality. I'd tell you to seek Maurice's advice, but he's dead," she said, hoping her reminder wasn't too subtle for these morons. "He expired from a bad case of blackmail. Go ahead take your chances. Others may not be as kind. Oh, and I failed to mention how sorry I'd be to see great detectives like you relocated… to Sing Sing. And Ray, don't count on your *rabbi* to save your incompetent ass. Goodnight, gentlemen."

She set her empty martini glass down, clutched her Kate Spade bag, and scooted off the bench. Scardino grabbed her hand at the last moment.

"Please, sit," he pleaded. Apparently, her message had gotten through.

She licked the inside of her cherry-red glossed lips, grinned, and swayed her hips back into bench. She had them by their balls, and oh, how she relished the tug.

"I'm so glad we get along," she said.

"We got Larkin, just like you wanted," Scardino said.

"Hmm. Yes, you did. Old news," Angelina replied. "Let's discuss present business. You two," she pointed at the two detectives across the table from her. "Lay off Corrigan and his woman. Apprise me directly of any activity *before* it happens. Also, I need a .22 caliber revolver. I don't care what model. And Paul Rivchak will be spending the night with me. He'll nose around. I don't want him finding my .38

and connect me to any of his murders. Get it somewhere. An evidence room. I don't care. I need it by tomorrow."

"We can take care of that for you," Buck told her.

Scardino gulped his beer and belched again. "Buck and I have more good news. " Tell her," Ray prompted him.

Buck hesitated, as though being called on to speak was not part of his plan. Angelina raised her eyebrows at him.

"Spit it out. I don't have all night." She thought of Paul. Golden haired, naked, sweaty Paul, writhing beneath her. Hot blood pumped through her dilated veins. She loosened the silk covered buttons of her blouse. "Hurry up."

"I tailed Phil Blass's kid home from school. I was wearing a mustache, bulky jacket, and ball cap. The kid's never seen me, but I didn't want him to be able to describe me to my own C.O.," he said.

Ray Scardino interjected, "The kid ran crying to his daddy. Blass's dick curled between his legs. He put in his notice. He's moving to Nassau County—trading one island for another. One less meddlesome C.O. and Corrigan's next, hopefully. He's taking his captain's exam next week. Then I'll get him transferred. He'll be out of our hair."

"Good work getting Blass out of the way, but kids are off limits. Even I have standards. Women, however, are fair game," Angelina said.

"I guess that includes Liz Shear?" Dave asked. "I overheard her asking Blass why she wasn't working anymore cases with us, always being partnered with Fenton instead. He told her that it was out of his hands and that he had no choice but to bend to Scardino orders. Then I heard them talking about how strange it was we were popping these dealers without signing out any narcotics to bait informants. And yesterday, I caught Shear rummaging through our files and checking out our drug vouchers."

"She's a problem. Deal with her, Ray," Angelina commanded.

She glanced over her shoulder and saw two women— some of Maurice's girls— sauntering toward them, their tight jean clad legs scissoring, one in front of the other. She grinned at Scardino.

"I have to go. I'm meeting Paul for dinner." She flicked Scardino on his shoulder with her manicured nails. "Enjoy your snack," and walked out of the bar.

Tara found a parking spot on West 73rd Street. Usually, the only time Jeffrey was a passenger in a car was when he let Mike drive him around in a precinct vehicle. Driving with Mike was like being in a bumper car at an amusement park. He would wedge into the smallest space he could find, ricocheting off every vehicle in his path. Jeffrey was happy that Tara was driving.

And she was certainly sexier than Mike.

Jeffrey hopped out, trotted around the Tara's silver Avalon, and opened the driver side door before she could open it on her own. One slim leg after another unfolded from the car. He reached for her hand.

Tara's sculpted calves contracted as she exited the car, the muscles glistening behind the veil of her sheer stockings, tight from the demands of dance. Her short brown hair was tucked behind her ears, revealing her blushed cheeks and soft brown eyes. His heart beat fast as he held her warm hand.

They walked the three blocks to Niko's, their footsteps echoing with each strike of the wet sidewalk. The stinging bite of winter winds had faded, but the night air remained brisk. He wrapped his arm around her shoulders.

"Stop," he said, twirling her toward him. Jeffrey lowered his face down to hers. "Do you remember this spot?"

"Yes." She grinned. "I remember. We kissed here for the first time, before we went through *that* door."

A misting of breath floated from her mouth. He breathed her in.

"Shall we make it a tradition then?"

"Absolutely. On this famed square of sidewalk," she followed the edge of the concrete with the toe of her shoe, "every time we come here."

"Every time," he murmured.

Jeffrey cupped Tara's cheeks, tenderly tilting her head back and waited, prolonging the moment. What he wanted to do was take her home—now—imprint every touch on her body so she'd always remember that he had been there. He lowered his mouth to hers, lingering at her lips, her delicately curved face enveloped in his palms, then he released her slowly.

Jeffrey grasped her hand. "We better go inside."

The hostess seated them at a table with a window view of Broadway.

She gazed up at the string of lights above the rows of tables. "It's just as I remembered. We were at that table across from us."

Jeffrey nodded. He could barely breathe. He wanted to jump out of his chair and embrace Tara. *She remembers,*

"You're right." Maybe if he emphasized every detail of their time together, she'd tuck it away in her memory, retrievable at will after her inevitable awakening.

Tara rested her hand on his. "I'm so sorry about your car, but I am having a wonderful evening."

He would give anything to have more evenings like this...with her.

The waiter brought them bread and a plate of oil. Jeffrey dipped his bread into the oil, and unable to keep his eyes of Tara, he brought it to his mouth. Oil oozed from his bottom lip.

Tara laughed. "Well there's a change! You making a mess with your food before I do!" She grabbed a linen napkin, leaned across the table, and dabbed his lips. Her sleeves inched up.

"Tara, what happened? Why did you hide this from me?" Jeffrey traced the branched red welts with his fingers.

"Honestly, it's no big deal. Like I told you, I ran off the side of the trail, skated across some ice, and slid down the ravine. A stupid, klutzy move."

Jeffrey shook his head. "What really happened?"

She rolled her eyes. "The only thing that still stings is my pride. And I've had worse dance injuries."

He stared into her eyes and muttered, "Uh huh."

"Yeah. Uh huh," she said. "Come to my ballet classes and you'll see. Jeffrey, let's forget about everything that happened earlier and order dinner."

He let go of her wrists. Tara pulled her sleeves back down.

Jeffrey leaned back in his chair, straining to peer behind the waiter as she recited the specials. He couldn't believe it. Rivchak and Angelina Holtz sat three tables away. How did he miss their entrance?

"Please take the lady's order, first," he told the waiter. He tossed the white linen napkin on the table and forced his chair back, and then he whispered to Tara, "Order for me, I'll have the moussaka and a Perrier. Excuse me a second."

He strode over to their table. "Detective Rivchak."

Paul peeked over his menu and arched his eyebrows. "Good evening, Lieutenant Corrigan. What a surprise," he said stiffly. I didn't see you come in."

Corrigan found himself feeling pleased at the shock apparent on Paul's face. "Likewise."

Angelina smirked at him, not even trying to hide her contempt. "Yes, it's *so* nice to see you again—Lieutenant. I hear we'll be calling you Captain soon. Congratulations in advance."

He glared at Paul. "I'm surprised too, quite frankly, seeing the two of you here…tonight."

"Well Angelina lives eight blocks uptown, so Niko's is very convenient."

Jeffrey ignored Angelina.

He focused his attention on his pain in the ass detective. "Since we're both here tonight I might as well tell you, Paul, that Lieutenant Blass will be filling in for me while I'm on vacation. He'll meet with you early in the morning. So don't give him a hard time and don't be late."

"I'll be there, Boss. But I guess you didn't hear. Lieutenant Blass is leaving. He's moving to Long Island. You may end up coming back earlier than you expected, since his notice was effective immediately. I hope your vacation isn't ruined."

Jeffrey blinked. "And you know this because…"

"I heard it from Captain Scardino—tonight, at Shane's Bar. We were having a few pre-dinner drinks there when we, uh, ran into him. Something about his kid being followed home from school. I guess he thought his family would be safer on Long Island. And the pay is better there too. It worked out for the best."

"It won't work out for the best for his squad. Lieutenant Blass has been a dedicated C.O. for six years. The narcotics division was strong under his command."

"No one's irreplaceable," Paul said smugly.

He leaned over the table, stopping inches from Paul's face. "Good people on the force are. You'll find that out, I'm sure."

Jeffrey caught Tara walking towards him out of the corner of his eye. *Clever woman. Coming to rescue me from this crappy encounter.* He extended his hand to her. Tara ducked under his arm, wrapping it around her waist, giving it a squeeze. "Good evening, everyone," she said cheerfully.

Tara nodded at Paul. "Detective Rivchak, nice seeing you again. I'm Tara Ross. We met briefly at the station."

"Yes we did. How are you tonight?"

She clutched Jeffrey's hand. "I'm well, thank you."

Angelina propped her elbow on the table and slowly sank her chin into her hand. "Ah, Tara Ross. I know you. You and that friend of yours stopped at my paint store last Sunday. Despite being closed, I did you both a favor and let you inside." Angelina drummed her fingers on her cheek. "Your friend never called for that private appointment."

Jeffrey glanced at Tara and crinkled his brow.

Tara smiled and shrugged. "Ms. Holtz, right?"

Angelina pulled her elbow from the table and shot her finger at Tara. "Good memory And I did not know your boyfriend was Lieutenant Corrigan. How about that! Small world, isn't it?"

Tara glanced at up at Jeffrey. "I guess so. Well, our dinner is waiting for us." Tara turned back to Angelina and Paul. "It was nice chatting with you."

Angelina sat back in her chair. "Looks like our dinner is arriving, too." Angelina gave Tara and Jeffrey an abbreviated wave. "Tah!"

Tara gave her a short wave back. "Have a pleasant evening...both of you."

Jeffrey grunted a goodbye and nudged the table as he pulled away from wide-eyed Paul and escorted Tara back to their table. He knew Paul and Angelina were watching.

He was watching them too.

They sat down at their table and Tara adjusted the napkin on her lap. "She's creepy."

"She's bad news." He took a deep breath. "Be careful of her. I didn't want to tell you but I think she's behind the murders I'm investigating"

"Wow! I get a bad vibe from her, too. I practically pulled Marielle from that store that day." Tara grinned. "I dumped the business card she gave us down the sewer." Tara cut into her food. "Marielle ended up getting her mini-blinds elsewhere." She took a bite of her shrimp, chewed, and swallowed. "And they're better blinds than what that bitch had!"

Jeffrey laughed, then he sighed. Only Tara could mend his sour mood. What if this was their last night together?

Jeffrey and Tara finished their dinner, none of it falling onto their laps. She gazed at him, smiled, and reached into her purse. "Here are my keys. Take me home."

Jeffrey grinned and raised his finger. "Check please!" He called to the waiter. He'd take her *home* and make love to her. There was no way Jeffrey was going to let Tara forget him.

# Chapter Thirty Nine

Wednesday, January 11, 10:30 p.m.

*T*ara nuzzled into his neck, inhaling his soapy clean scent. Hugging her, he pulled her closer to him. A wave of tranquility washed over her.

Jeffrey rolled to his side. He tucked the white down comforter under her back, careful to seal the warmth of their bodies from the cool air.

Tara rested her head on his solid chest. This was home, but there was something not quite right yet. She thought of Abbie. She'd be back from Greece soon. Tara had promised her daughter a new home, a more stable one.

Tara glanced up into Jeffrey's eyes. "Jeffrey, I need to go house hunting soon. I need a place for Abbie and me. She's coming home soon, hopefully for good." Tara stroked Jeffrey's chest in light circles. He shuddered, suppressing a laugh. Tara pulled off his chest and rolled to face him. "Sorry. Hit a ticklish spot, didn't I?"

He grinned. "Yep. But that's okay. I'll take that *torture* any day. Jeffrey pushed up on his elbow, propping his chin in the palm of his hand. He ran his finger down the slope of her nose and looked into her eyes.

"Stay here. Save your money. The house is paid off. I know it's dated, but I like it here, I was lonely until you came along. I'll build whatever you need. Fix anything the way you want. Abbie can stay in James's room. Tara, I want to build a life with you."

She kissed him. "I love you. I do want to stay. The house is wonderful—except for the basement. I've felt at home here ever since I set foot inside. You've never made me feel out of place and you've shared everything with me, including yourself. I couldn't have asked for anything better."

He touched his forehead to hers. "Me neither."

Tara ran her toes down his leg "Why don't we go out to lunch after my session with Leo tomorrow?"

Jeffrey hugged her tightly and showered her head with kisses.

"Well, that was enthusiastic. Not that I'm complaining, but it's only lunch." She laughed softly. "It's dinner that does us in!" Tara drew in a deep breath. "Jeffrey, there's something I want to tell you. Something I've been hiding from you."

Jeffrey looked down at her. His forehead wrinkled. "What is it, Tara?"

Tara's pulse bumped. She didn't want to burden him. With those murders, the vandalism, and that weasel of a captain of his, he had enough on his mind. But it was too late. She'd already alarmed him.

Tara swiped her moist palms on the bed sheets. "Leo gave me an assignment. To write down what had happened to me in story form." Tara inched away from Jeffrey, but her eyes still locked with his. "I was typing that into my laptop before you came in the other night."

"Tara, I know all about the assignment. Leo told me." He stroked her cheek. "Please tell me. What happened at the hospital? Did someone die?"

She swallowed hard. "Yes. A baby, the granddaughter of the Chief of Anesthesiology."

"Babe." Jeffrey embraced Tara and lowered her back onto the bed. "I'm so sorry. I know you did whatever you could."

She looked into his eyes. "I knew you'd understand." Jeffrey was everything she had dreamed of as a man, a partner. Her heartbeat eased as she lay in his arms.

"I do, and after seventeen years as a cop, dealing with death isn't any easier. Good people—when they suffer—that just rips me apart. With bad people, there's a sense of justice. But dead is dead."

Her eyes widened. "Did you ever kill anyone?"

"Twice." Jeffrey cleared his throat. "The first was some guy, fleeing from a robbery after he shot and killed the clerk. He had priors and no intention of going back to prison and knew we were going to catch him. He lost control of his vehicle and, with nothing to lose, chose suicide by cop. But not until he let loose two rounds. Missed me, but shot my partner in the thigh. So I took him down. My partner was taken to the hospital. I did my paperwork, saw my partner in the hospital, and then came home and puked.

"The other one was at a crime scene. A guy, high on crack, was hiding in the closet. I heard the door open, saw his weapon and I fired. It was so simple, so fast.

Jeffrey took a deep breath before continuing.

"Both shootings were ruled as justifiable. I got sick after the first one, never felt anything for the second."

She scooted in closer, snuggling against him and rubbed his back. "I'm sorry. I didn't mean to pry."

"I'll tell you anything you want. I don't mind. You and I are dedicated to saving people, but we're not always rewarded for doing what we love, are we?"

There was no reward for her that New Year's Eve. Alexis left with funeral arrangements and no hope for having another child.

"Tara?"

She jerked her head, back into the present. Back to Jeffrey's embrace.

"I know what you mean." Tara stroked his cheek. "You're good man, Lieutenant Corrigan. And you'll be a good captain."

# Chapter Forty

Thursday, January 12, 10:15 a.m.

*J*effrey had slept poorly. Leo's prophecy pulsed in his head all night. Fatigued, he let Tara drive them to her last appointment with Dr. Kane.

"You're quiet this morning. Is everything all right?"

Jeffrey flicked the corner of the white envelope in his hand containing Tara's assignment Leo had given her. She had printed it from her computer and he had sealed her thoughts in an envelope, tempted to read its contents, but didn't. "Yes, fine," he mumbled.

Jeffrey's knees abutted his elbows as he shifted his weight in the gray leather seat of her car. "Damn seat!" he exploded.

Tara glanced at him. He pressed his lip into a half-hearted smile, fighting the tension in his jaw. "Push the seat back," she said as though it was the most obvious thing in the world.

He looked straight ahead and grumbled, "It's as far back as it goes."

For the first time they'd been together, he didn't want to talk to her; afraid he'd stutter or worse— tear up. Actions typical of a wounded lover, but not befitting of a commanding officer.

Leo'd told him Edouard, Tara's partner and *boyfriend* would be there. *Will she recognize him?* Jeffrey clenched his fingers into a fist. His stomach tightened. *So what if she does? It's over between them.*

Tara parked two blocks from the station house. Jeffrey walked along side her, holding her hand in silence. Feeling maudlin, he held her back before the entrance and kissed her.

"I want you to remember that I'll always be your soft place to land, Tara. I love you."

She winked at him. "I love you too."

Holding hands, they climbed the stairs to the third floor. Dr. Leo Kane stood at the doorway to Jeffrey's office.

"Hello Tara, Jeffrey. Tara, there's someone I want you to meet today. He's waiting in interview room two."

Tara handed the white envelope to Leo. "I finished it."

"Very good, Tara. Let's see how well you've done your homework."

Jeffrey stared hard at Leo and then lowered his eyes. *Please, no.*

The three of them walked to room two. He watched Leo turn the brass knob and open the door. Jeffrey grasped her hand. There he was, Edouard LaCroix. *Hmmm. A compact kinda guy.*

Tara squinted, "Edouard?"

"Yes, it's me, Tara. Don't you recognize me?"

She paused for what Jeffrey thought was an eternity." *Yes! She doesn't know him.*

Tara and Edouard locked eyes.

"I just got back from the conference in Las Vegas," Edouard told her. "Then I got this call from Dr. Kane. He explained what happened. I'm happy you're safe. But it's time to go home, now—to Brewster." Edouard leaned back and held out his arms, stiffly.

Leo walked over to Jeffrey. Jeffrey loosened his grip on Tara, letting her go free. *There she goes. She has her memory back. Just as I had hoped for all along. Right where she had left off, with him, and not with me.* Jeffrey sniffed, holding back the moisture creeping to eyes.

Tara jumped into Edouard's waiting arms. "Of course I know you, silly. I missed you."

He patted her back. "I missed you too."

"I'm ready when you are. I need to get a good night's sleep. I'm sure there's a stack of charts waiting for me on my desk. Gone one day, and the piles grow."

"One day?" he whispered to Leo. Leo just gave him a sympathetic look.

Jeffrey shook his head. *Unbelievable.* His Tara was gone. This was someone else. He couldn't believe that she'd be attracted to this cold son of a bitch. His stomach clenched.

Leo whispered back, "Tara has picked up where she left off— memory wise. She has no recollection of the last two weeks. It's only been a day to her."

*This is unreal.* Jeffrey massaged his temples. *Leo warned me. And like a fool, I didn't truly believe him.*

Edouard took her hand. "The girls in the office can't wait to see you, Tara."

"Oh, I'm sure. I'll go in an hour early tomorrow and work my way through the charts and messages. The office nurse's going to love getting all those charts back to dispo."

She cupped Edouard's face and kissed him.

"Okay, Tara." Edouard said, looking uncomfortable, "Let's not hold everybody up here. I'm parked the next block over."

Jeffrey stepped back and gritted his teeth. It was as if someone had punched him in the chest. His heart raced and his eyes burned. It was the only way he could stay in that room.

"Oh, Edouard," she said, almost as an afterthought, "This is Dr. Kane. He made sure I was okay after being chased by an insane drug dealer. And, this is Lieutenant Corrigan. He was kind enough to get me out of the holding cell so I didn't have to hang out with ladies of the night. What a bizarre tale! I'm so glad it's over and that they called you to come get me."

Jeffrey nudged Leo. "Why does she know our names?" He asked softly.

Leo rested his hand on Jeffrey's shoulder. "She'll recognize us briefly, but only superficially. Then as she gets reoriented, she won't remember we exist." He patted Jeffrey on his back. "We'll fade away from her memory."

Jeffrey's mouth dropped open. *She only recognizes my title, not me, not... us.*

"Let's get your things," Edouard said, prodding Tara toward the door.

Tara rattled on about everything. "I had sent my boxes to Marielle's house but I changed my mind. I *do* want to move in with you, Edouard. We can call Marielle in the morning and give her the news. God, I'm so tired."

Tara shook Leo's hand and thanked him. She then extended her hand to Jeffrey. He took it, but didn't want to let go.

"Thank you for everything, Lieutenant Corrigan."

Jeffrey cleared his throat and pressed his heels into the floor, hard. "It was my pleasure."

Edouard clutched her hand. "Yes, yes. Thank you everyone for taking such good care of my Tara, but we really need to get going."

Jeffrey took a deep breath. "Um, Dr. La Croix?"

Edouard turned to face him. "Yes?"

Jeffrey motioned for him to step closer.

Edouard let go of Tara's hand. "One second, dear, and we'll be on our way."

"Tara's, I mean Dr. Ross's, car is parked nearby. I'll make arrangements for it to be delivered, just tell me where."

Edouard grinned. He handed Jeffrey his card. "My house." Edouard grabbed Tara's hand. "Come, love."

Then she was gone.

# Chapter Forty One

Thursday, January 12, 11:50 a.m.

*H*is head would have smacked the floor, if it weren't for his desk breaking the fall. He pressed his forehead into his palms. His office was dark, the way he wanted it; the slats of the vertical blinds clamped tight against the windowpane, the door shut—a barricade to the bustle on the other side.

His head throbbed. His chest heaved. And his heart pounded—hard—colliding with the buttons of his shirt. Jeffrey didn't want anyone to see him, weak and broken.

He should have known better. Leo had warned him, yet he convinced himself that it all would work out. That he would be a part of Tara's life, a hybrid of old and new. They'd be happy together.

That's what he'd thought.

He thumped his forehead with the heel of his palm and muttered, "You're a fool. You blew it. She's gone."

The knock on his door interrupted the buzzing in his head.

*Shit. Not now.*

He shuffled to the door, sighed, and twisted the dull brass knob. It creaked with age. Leo Kane stood before him, his face grim, and his eyes apologetic.

"I didn't want it to end this way for you," he told him.

Jeffrey leaned against the doorframe. His eyes shifted from the floor to Leo's face. "You warned me. I didn't listen. Or rather, I didn't want to hear. It's done. I don't want to talk right now, Leo. Maybe later."

"I understand. I do want to say something though."

Jeffrey gazed upward, avoiding eye contact with the doctor, fighting back the sting of hurt and humiliation.

"Humph. No offense, Leo, but make it quick."

"You made Tara feel safe enough to put the pieces of her life together. You helped her. And I know right now it's hell for you to let her go. We still don't know much about fugue. It's rare. I think, for her, it fell under the category of post-traumatic stress; something, in working with cops, I'm more familiar with. There's the possibility that in time, she will recall your relationship. You should know that."

"Thanks. That makes everything better. Not to be rude, but I need to move on with my day."

"I thought you were on vacation."

"Well, I'm back. Catch you later, Leo."

Jeffrey pushed the door closed. What he really wanted to do was bolt out of the station house and run as fast as he could in any direction. Run until he was out of breath. Exhausted to the point of numbness. Nature's drug. But it would be no use. He couldn't purge her from his thoughts. She was there, permanently.

He had just flopped down into his chair when he heard a knock on his door, again.

*Ah, come on.*

"Enter," he yelled.

Mike slipped through the door and clicked it closed. "Jeffrey, man, I heard. I saw her leave with the Frenchman. Not a good trade. I'm sorry, buddy."

He nodded. "Thanks."

Mike sat "She'll be back, man." He pounded his chest with his fist. "I know it in here."

"I want to believe that, but I think it's my turn to block things out."

"It's really dark in here." Mike looked around, bewildered.

"That's the way I like it."

"Okay." Mike cleared his throat. "I hate to bring this up, especially with everything that's happened to you this morning, but I ran that license plate number and guess what I found."

Jeffrey tapped his fingers on his desk. "I don't want to guess. Just tell me."

"The plate's registered to Maurice Chiguard."

"You're telling me that a dead man ran me off the road and then parked in our lot?"

Mike grinned. "Appears to be, unless… your ghost is Rivchak's flavor of the month, Angelina. She's toying with you, Jeffrey. I know it."

Jeffrey shook his head. "Mmm. I don't think so. It happened so quickly, but from the back, it looked like a man. Besides, that's not her style. Maybe she stole it or borrowed it from a dealer, but she'd get someone else to do it. That's how she stays out of the system. That and I'm pretty sure she has her own inside hook. I'll let anti-crime handle the grand theft auto."

Mike shifted in his chair and rubbed his mustache. "There's something else I need to tell you, Boss. I took Liz to the emergency room last night."

"What? Why didn't you call me?"

"Walking out to my car last night, I found Liz on the ground. She claimed she slipped on some ice and fell. Fractured her clavicle and dislocated her right arm. Her injuries didn't make sense. And then, the ER doc questioned *me*. Liz's arm had bruises consistent with someone grabbing it. I noticed him glancing at my hands the whole time. I told him that Liz and I are colleagues, and that I found her lying next to her car. He verified that, but Jeffrey, I don't believe she fell. Someone assaulted her. She denies it. She ain't talkin'. Liz is out today, probably will be for a while. Word is that Scardino already transferred her downstairs to anti-crime, desk duty given her messed up arm."

*Women,* Jeffrey thought. *First Tara denies being shoved down a ravine, and now Liz.* He leaned over his desk.

"Liz is lying to you because I would bet my ass she knows her attacker. Mike, get the lot surveillance tapes."

"Already tried, first thing this morning. The camera wasn't working." Mike arched his eyebrows. "But, the deli across the street has surveillance video. We just might get a glimpse as to what really went down."

"I like your thinking."

"Thanks, Boss. That's where I'll be going today. And I've been craving their hot buffet." He pushed back his chair and stood. "You look like shit. Get out of here. You still have vacation time."

"I don't want to go home just yet. It'll be too quiet. I'll drive myself insane."

"I got an idea. Let's get hammered tonight. Amy's visiting her mother in Albany. I'll bring the Guinness and crash at your place."

Jeffrey massaged the back of his neck. "All right. That sounds good."

Mike blinked. "That was easy."

"I just want to forget." He shuffled the papers on his desk and sighed.

"No you don't. Maybe you want to forget today, but not her."

Mike wasn't wordy but damn it, he was right. Since childhood, his ideas usually spawned trouble for Jeffrey, with Mike usually walking away unscathed. But Mike was his best friend. Tara had been his confidante, his lover. Now she belonged to someone else.

Jeffrey's phone buzzed. Still staring at Mike, he picked up the receiver.

"Lieutenant, I have woman on the line named Marielle," Laurie said. "Shall I put her through?"

Jeffrey tightened his grip on the receiver until his fingers blanched. "Yeah, go ahead."

Mike walked to the door. He shot his index finger at Jeffrey and mouthed, "Later."

He grinned and returned the finger pop. Then he pressed the phone to his ear. "Hey, Marielle."

"Hello, Lieutenant," Marielle said. "I spoke to Dr. Kane and then to Tara. I just wanted to say I'm sorry this happened to you two. We may have had our differences in the beginning, but I was only looking out for her. She loves you, though I guess she doesn't know that. As much as it kills me to say so, because I know it doesn't matter, but I think you two should be together."

"She *loved* me. She doesn't even know who I am anymore."

"Give her some time to sort things out."

He traced his tongue around his parched lips and shook his head. "I don't know that I can. What exactly can I do for you, Marielle?"

"I need to pick up Tara's things. She thinks that they're all at my house."

"I'll be home tonight. I'll have them ready."

Where else was he going to be? Jeffrey's heart sank to the bottom of his chest at the thought of repacking Tara's belongings. *Oh God, she's not coming back.*

"Okay, I'll stop by. And don't give up on her, Jeffrey."

"See you later, Marielle."

He hung up the phone. His head throbbed, but there was no quick fix. Perhaps no fix at all. Tara was where she needed to be. It would be selfish, if not destructive, to pull her back. He'd have to deal with the hole in his chest that she'd quite innocently left behind. It wasn't her fault. She'd been through her own hell.

Someone pounded on his door.

"No one's home," he yelled, frustrated.

Laurie smacked the door open. "Alright. That's enough, Boss."

She marched past him and snapped the window blinds open. Jeffrey squinted.

"I'm going to get you a cup of coffee and a cannoli. That is if Detective Malik hasn't eaten the last one."

When Laurie returned, she placed a cup of coffee and the pastry on his desk. Standing with her hands on her ample hips, she said, "If you want to pout, then go home. If you're going to stay, then work on something. It's none of my business, but I know this is a bitch for you. And you're not going to feel better for a long time. You're going to have to grapple with this at your own pace. It's not constructive to stay in the dark. Now, what can I do for you?"

"Get me Detective Malik."

She smiled. "Right away, Boss."

---

Herb Malik trotted into Jeffrey's office and flopped into a chair. He lifted his tie for Jeffrey's approval.

"Everyone makes fun of my knitted ties and scarves. It's true, Ophelia can't knit anything symmetrical, but she loves me. Accepts me for who I am." Herb punched his finger into his chest." And because of that, I wear everything she makes with pride. I know what I look like, but *she* makes me feel good." He then pointed to Jeffrey. "I like to imagine that's how you felt…feel about Tara. How boring would it be without the zigzags of life?"

"Well said, my friend. Is that squawking I hear?"

"Yeah, Lou. Ophelia's earlier flight was cancelled. She'll be back later today. I had to bring Milton into work for one more day. I'm sorry. I didn't want to bother you, not with everything going on."

"It's all right." In fact, he welcomed the distraction.

"Thanks. I'll do my best to hide him from Captain Scardino."

"Screw, Scardino. He was the one that demanded that I EC the Maurice Chiguard case."

Herb lurched forward in his chair, shocked. "That's bogus. That case doesn't meet the criteria for exceptional clearance."

"Damn right it doesn't. So Mike and I are going to review the crime scene, the evidence collected, and the autopsies again. I want you to contact Miami. Get a copy of the footprints found at the scene of the drug runner's homicide. Also, see if anyone can locate the female migrant worker that witnessed what happened. I'll call Captain Stanton in Miami and inquire how the case is going. I know Angelina Holtz is involved, but I need something on her. The whole miscarriage alibi is a dead end."

"I'm pretty sure Rivchak is banging her. Let's see what he can come up with."

"I'll play that card when I'm ready. Now's not the time. Let's keep this between you, me, and Mike for now."

"Will do."

Herb returned to his desk, leaving Jeffrey's office door ajar in the wake of his departure. Jeffrey leaned in his chair. Through the crack, he could see Paul's desk easily. He watched Rivchak, his hair tousled and necktie loose, pretend to work at his desk—acting as if he hadn't come in two hours late.

*Who does he think he is?*

He shoved back his chair and gritted his teeth, ready for confrontation. He needed a good blow out. He was going to find out where the guy had been and what—and who—he'd been doing. The floor vibrated with each strike of his size twelve black oxfords.

He stopped, bent over, and spanned his arms across the top of Paul's desk, easily grabbing the corners of Rivchak's desk in his broad hands.

"In my office, *now*," he growled.

Office wide, papers stopped shuffling. No phones rang. The clock on the wall ticked like a metronome. Even Milton had gone silent.

Paul glared at him and grabbed the papers on his desk. He clutched them into his balled fist, the crinkling noise echoing throughout the room. He ushered Paul into his office and slammed the door.

"I expect you to have respect for the job and the squad. Rolling out of a whore's bed and strutting into work late because of it shows neither."

Paul inhaled and then let his breath escape through his parted lips. He cleared his throat.

"Lieutenant Corrigan, I've spent the last three hours having the body parts of a Dr. David Longacre scraped off the block between West 78th and 79th. The man took a dive from his office window early this morning. I guess dentistry is depressing. If I was in the wrong because I preferred to get what was left of him off the sidewalk before the rush-hour lookie-loos and school kids could get a good view, then I'm sorry." Paul shook his fist and narrowed his eyes. "I had to go to his home to tell his wife and kids that daddy won't be coming home from the office today. It was my turn to catch. You were on vacation. I got the 61 from Sergeant Mackey. And yes, I was in the neighborhood because I did spend the night with Angelina." Paul smacked his report on Jeffrey's desk. "She's *not* a whore. I didn't pay to fuck her."

Jeffrey gripped the edge of his desk, clenched his teeth, and snapped his eyes shut for a few seconds. When he opened them, Rivchak was still standing there, staring at him, his hands pressed to his sides.

"I apologize for my outburst, Lieutenant," Paul offered respectfully. "I heard about Tara. She's a classy lady. I hope things work out for you two."

Jeffrey pinched the bridge of his nose. The grind of the day had caught up with him. His judgment askew, he knew he had to step away before he made a mistake.

He looked at Paul. "Good work. You can go now."

Jeffrey extended his hand and Paul shook it.

*Bang-Bang-Bang.*

They jumped apart and exchanged worried looks. Gunfire was coming from the locker room.

Jeffrey shot out of his office. "Shit. Someone's firearm discharged in the locker room. That's all I need—more paperwork. And we just got the old holes patched."

He rushed into the locker room, Mike and Herb at his heels. The room was empty.

Mike pointed to a scratched green locker, hammering noises vibrating through its rusted slots. "It's coming from inside here."

*Bang-Bang-Bang.*

Jeffrey's eyes darted about the room. "Whose locker is this?"

"No one's. It's been empty for at least the last year. Mine's right next to it," Herb said.

"Then why is there a lock on it? Mike, go get a bolt cutter."

Mike dashed out and returned with the cutter. Jeffrey snapped the lock, lifted the latch, and opened the locker door to reveal Milton, running in frantic circles.

"Oh my God. Milton!" Herb cried out. He reached in to pick him up, but the African Gray nipped at him in terror.

"Back off quietly, guys," Jeffrey said. He slowly reached into the locker. "Come here boy. I'm not going to hurt you. Atta boy. Good Milton."

He stroked the quivering bird, now perched on his sleeved arm. Milton clamped his claws tightly onto his forearm, but didn't hurt him. His feathers were ruffled and his black shiny eyes popped from the sides of his head in terror.

Jeffrey narrowed his eyes. "Anyone seen Scardino around?"

"No, Lou. Not today" Herb said and then glanced at the frightened bird. "I'll call home right now and see if Ophelia's back from the airport."

"Okay. I'll keep Milton with me."

They filed out of the locker room.

"Hey!" Herb cried out from his desk, phone in hand. He stared at his desk in a state of bewilderment.

"What's up?" Jeffrey asked.

"The footprint copy I got from Miami. It was here on my desk a minute ago. Now…it's gone."

# Chapter Forty Two

Thursday, January 12, 6:15 p.m.

*T*ara's head sank into the down pillow. The linen hugged her ears. Certainly, a soft place to land, but something was missing. It just didn't make sense. How long had she been gone? She knew she had taken some time off, Edouard had insisted. And he was right, of course. She needed the time to recoup.

His house didn't feel comfortable—not like home. The bed was strange. She shifted on the sheets, trying to get comfortable. Still not right. It was his house. Not really hers.

She shook her head. It was her decision to move in with him. Divorced, Tara wanted to move on, take her and Edouard's relationship to the next level.

They'd known each other for years. An unspoken fondness between them all that time. And now, love. She loved him, right? Of course she did. What wasn't there to love about him? Doting. Hardworking. Attractive. She tried, but "sexy" didn't come to mind. She repeated the mantra.

*Doting. Hardworking. Attractive. Se—*

Edouard poked his head into the bedroom from around the doorway. "Comfortable darling?"

She jerked to her elbows. "Yes. Fine."

He stood at the foot of the bed and cradled her feet, massaging them. "I didn't mean to startle you."

Tara curled away. "I'm sorry. It's been a long day. You caught me dozing."

"Understandable. You needed the rest. Are you hungry?"

"Starved."

"Where would you like to go?"

"I'm not up to going out. How about we call for some Chinese? Or pizza?"

He wrinkled his nose. "You know I can't eat that greasy stuff."

"Then how about some Thai?"

"Okay. I'll order dinner and let you freshen up."

After he left, Tara pulled back the sheets and stood, listening for his footsteps. She peeked around the bedroom door making sure he wasn't in sight. Then she berated herself for the awful thought. She should want to be with him right now, right?

She tiptoed into the bathroom and eased the door shut. Leaning over the sink, she cupped her hands and splashed her face. The cold water made her shudder. Icy droplets dribbled down her neck.

She pressed the thick hand towel to her face. Everything was going to be all right. They would have a nice dinner. She'd get a good night's sleep and then be ready to tackle the office in the morning. Tara dressed, and then walked into the dining room. The food was laid out and fine china adorned the table.

*Fine china for take-out?*

"We can just curl up on the sofa and eat," she offered.

"Darling, I never eat in the living room. That's what a dining room is for. Now, sit. Enjoy."

She stifled a pout and sat down as he pushed in her chair. He rounded the table, sat, and flipped a linen napkin across his lap.

"Bon appetite."

She unfolded her napkin and draped it in her lap. At least he decided to let her use chopsticks. By the third bite, the noodles slipped from her chopsticks and landed smack between her legs, completely missing the napkin. Not even a rebound.

She plucked at the limp pasta on her jeans and snickered, but she was laughing alone. Edouard didn't find the accident funny at all. Instead, he jumped from his chair and ran into the kitchen, returning with a napkin dampened with Seltzer.

"Hurry. Get up. Get up before it stains."

She bolted out of her chair. Gob smacked, Tara watched him dab furiously at the upholstery.

"I'm so sorry," she muttered.

"It's okay. It's Scotch Garded."

She scratched her head. "Well…uh…thank God for that."

Edouard put the soiled napkin in a hamper and returned to the dining room. She hadn't moved, still rooted to the spot.

He cupped her flushed cheeks in the palms of his hands. "I didn't mean to get so upset. Accidents happen. I have my own quirks. I'm not mad at you, Tara. I love you."

He kissed her, but Tara wasn't moved by his touch. They finished their dinner in silence.

Jeffrey jogged down the hallway, zipping the fly of his jeans and pulled on a worn blue Yankee tee shirt.

"Yeah, I'm coming," he yelled as the doorbell sounded again. He opened the door wide.

Mike greeted him with a huge grin, a twelve -pack of Guinness in one hand and a steaming cardboard box balancing in the other.

"Don't ever say I come empty handed. Cheese pie and beer, to wash it down."

"Come on in."

Jeffrey plopped onto the couch while Mike threw the box of pizza onto the coffee table and then deposited the beer into the fridge. "The house is the exactly the same as I remembered it. You haven't changed anything," Mike called from the kitchen.

"Maybe it's a comfort thing. Besides, Tara liked the house, except for the basement. I told her I was going to build it out. Not much point to it now…that I'm by myself. Even James doesn't stay here very long. He's carving out his own life now. But I don't want to sell Grandma's house. Feels wrong."

Mike sauntered back into the living room, two frosted beer bottles in tow. He handed one to Jeffrey and slumped into the recliner. Jeffrey pressed his back against the leather sofa and propped his socked feet on the coffee table next to the pizza box.

Mike flipped open the lid and picked up a slice of pizza. The gooey cheese slid off the crust and plopped into his lap.

"Shit."

As he went to wipe the melted cheese off his jeans, he tipped the hand holding the bottle of Guinness and doused himself.

Jeffrey roared with laughter.

Mike reminded him of Tara right now. She was always a good sport—capable of laughing at herself. That's one of the things that he loved about her.

He stopped laughing. Now his chest ached. He didn't want to look at her boxes, sealed and ready to go by the door.

"Washer's in the basement," he said to Mike. "You're gonna need it."

Mike hobbled bow-legged, holding his wet jeans away from his crotch. Jeffrey shook his head. *The man's not even drunk yet.*

He sipped his Guinness, tilted his head back, and closed his eyes. *Where was she now?* The last thing he wanted to do right now was to go to bed without her.

A pounding sound, coming from the kitchen, disrupted his self-pity. He swung his legs off the coffee table and hoisted himself from the sofa. He was going to have to get around to fixing that basement door. His dad had planed it, years ago, but it was obstinate—steadfast in barricading the exit from the dank abyss it guarded.

He yanked the door open.

Mike stood there in nothing but a navy tee shirt, white BVD's, black socks, and a frown.

Jeffrey grinned.

"Yeah, yeah, very funny. That door never stuck like that when we were kids."

"It did too. Grandma used to place a rock at the bottom of the frame when anyone went downstairs into the basement."

The old wooden planks creaked as Mike ascended the last two steps. Jeffrey shut the door. Cheese pizza and cold beer beckoned them back to their respective slumped positions. Mike devoured two of the slices while Jeffrey still picked at his first.

"Something wrong with the pizza? It's from Sal's. You always liked their pie."

"No. It's all right. Tara made me homemade pizza, you know? Everything is bland in comparison. No offense."

"None taken. I'm not Sal. You've mentioned Tara twice since I've been here. You wanna talk about it?"

Jeffrey popped the top off his beer. "Nah."

"Ohkaaaay. So, what happened between you and Rivchak today?"

"I was all set to ream him a new one. Accuse him of fucking Angelina, making it a priority over the job. Turns out he was working a case. Did a decent job, too. Went over his report. Confirmed it all." Jeffrey flung his hand up, making a mock cursive sign in the air, spilling beer from the bottle in his hand. "Signed it off. I misjudged him, at least on this account. I think he'll work out, but I don't like him banging Holtz. Nothing I can do about it now though. She's a psycho bitch. He doesn't know what he's getting himself into. He's young, inexperienced. There's a lot of bad shit out there to tempt him."

Mike scratched his belly. "Not that I care for him, Scardino being his rabbi and all; now there's a strike against him in my book. But, we are our brother's keeper. We should try to keep him from going to the dark side."

"All right, Obi Wan."

"Can you picture it? Scardino as Darth Vader." Mike cupped his hands over his mouth and with a deep breathy voice, he parodied, "Paul… I am your father."

They laughed and swigged their beers.

Jeffrey prayed for the numbness to set in. He knew, deep down, that he had to take responsibility for his own pain. He couldn't blame

Tara. He couldn't blame Edouard, as much as he wanted to. Not Leo, either.

He blamed himself.

He had fallen so hard, so fast. He thought she had journeyed to that place with him. And he wanted to believe that. But it was out of his control now.

Jeffrey took a sip of his beer and looked at his best friend, slouched in his recliner in his underwear. He sighed and then belched.

"Liz belongs in Narcotics, not Anti-Crime, Mike. Scardino shoved her out. I'm sure he'll celebrate when I'm captain and leave the two-seven—probably get hard *and* even change his shirt."

Mike nodded.

"So, did the deli camera catch anything?"

Mike smacked his forehead. "Oh, man, I forgot to tell you. Liz didn't fall like she said. It's fuzzy, but there's definitely someone else. The camera caught an image of the assailant twisting her arm and slamming her into her car. I sent the tape, which the deli owner was happy to give us since he knows Liz, to our video techs. They'll clean it up and, hopefully, we can get a good look at him."

"That's great news. God knows I needed some today."

"You know what? I swear I saw a Dodge Charger in the background too. But you know Liz. She isn't changing her story. Something *bad's* happening on the inside." Mike tossed his crust into the box. "And, don't you think it's weird how those footprints disappeared from Herb's desk. It's like… I think the bird in the locker was a distraction," Mike said.

"You're probably right. But, I think it was also meant to scare Herb. Someone doesn't want us, or Liz for that matter, nosing in the Miami case. They'd rather us leave it to the guys down south, let them falter around with it. Chiguard, the Dodge Charger, Steven Thompson, Miami. They all have one thing in common—Angelina Holtz. She may not have pulled the trigger on Thompson, but I bet you that she *wanted* to. And Angelina looks like the kind of woman who always gets what she wants. She and Chiguard had *something* going too, but Stuart Thompson must have conveniently fucked up their plans."

"Yeah, and that bogus trip to Miami." Mike shook his head. "If you think like I do, that Angelina is connected with all three cases, then why did you EC the Chiguard case? You've always out maneuvered Scardino, but this time...."

Jeffrey sighed. "You were going to find out next week. You're being promoted to first grade. I agreed to EC the case so Scardino wouldn't block your promotion. I couldn't let that happen. You deserve it."

Setting his beer on the coffee table, Mike paused. "While I appreciate it, don't do something you don't agree with on my account."

"You deserve the promotion. Your record speaks for itself. And the Chief of D's is behind you too. They barely tolerate Scardino at the Puzzle Palace. As far as the case, big fucking deal. It's better this way. We'll catch them off their guard eventually."

Mike's eyes gleamed in anticipation. He knew how much it meant for Mike to get first grade, and the bump in salary was perfect timing, with a baby on the way. Jeffrey watched him gobble down his third piece of pizza and top off his second beer. His best friend was a clown, but a good man.

"Why do I have the pleasure of getting drunk with you this evening?" he asked.

Mike frowned and waved his hand dismissively. "Amy and I had a *disagreement*. She went to visit her mother—who hates me. I'm staying with you to lend you my support, obviously, and to see to it that you forget that today existed."

"What was the fight about?"

"She's upset that I don't want to go to childbirth classes."

Jeffrey sipped his beer and then pointed the bottle at Mike. "You should go."

"Jeff, I don't want to see any movie where a woman is drenched in sweat and screaming at the top her lungs, pushing a bloodied head the size of a bowling ball out between her legs. Childbirth should be left to women, the way God intended. Besides, Amy's mother and sister, neither of whom have anything nice to say about me, will be there for her."

"So don't watch the damn movie. But you've got to be there—for Amy and for yourself. Who does Amy *really* want to be there? I'm sure it's you and not her mother. I've met the woman. Look. Just stand next to her, up by her head. You don't have to look at all the messy stuff. And I'm sure you won't have to cut the umbilical cord if you don't want to. This is the birth of your first child, Mike."

"Cut what? Uh. No way." Mike shook his head. "One slip of the scissors and I'll cut off something important. The kid'll be impaired for life. And I'm doing other stuff too, you know. We're closing on a house upstate, in Purdy's. A small apartment in the Bronx is no place to raise a kid. I need time to fix up the place for Amy and the baby."

Jeffrey raised his beer bottle. "Congratulations on the house, man."

"I didn't want to say anything until the loan was approved. And you were preoccupied with Tara, your car getting smashed, your house being bricked."

Jeffrey chortled. "Stop cheering me up, will ya?"

Mike tossed him a Guinness. "Have another beer."

The chilled, wet bottle nearly slipped from his fingers but he caught it.

Mike grinned and shot him a thumbs up. "Nice save."

Drinking was a band-aid solution, a stopgap for a fresh wound. He was raw, exposed, and he needed that Band-Aid *now*—the biggest one in the box.

Jeffrey finished his third Guinness, catching up with Mike. His lips were going numb. And it didn't matter, because he wasn't going to feel her breath upon them any time soon. He slammed the empty bottle on the edge of the coffee table. It wobbled around and vibrated to a stop.

He stared at it. A fourth would be a bad idea. *Oh, what the hell* "Hey, Mike. I'm headin' in the kitchen. You wanna another?"

Mike snorted and smacked his lips. His eyelids sagged. "Nah."

"Well, that's good, 'cause I can't get my ass out of this couch." Jeffrey swayed and fell, the armrest blocking him from pitching to the floor.

A pair of headlights danced across the living room wall, followed by the crackling of tires in the driveway.

"Hey, Mike. We got company. Look alive."

Jeffrey's stomach tightened. It was probably Marielle, coming to get Tara's boxes.

The doorbell rang.

He took a deep breath, clamored out of the sofa, and opened the door. He squinted to focus, and winced when he saw his sister, standing on his porch with her arms folded across her chest.

"Evie. What're you doing here?"

"I heard about what happened."

He smacked his palm on the doorway. "God, does everybody know my business?"

"Yes," Mike and Evie replied in unison.

Mike rocked out of the recliner and stood up.

Evie glared at him. "Ah, for Pete's sake Price. Put on some pants before I go blind!"

Mike air blew three kisses in her direction. "Like what you see do you?"

Evie shot Mike a glare. "Yeah. I'll have nightmares tonight. Jeffrey, I warned you about her. I don't know why you insisted on playing house with her."

Jeffrey leaned on the doorframe of his dented door, partly to hold himself up, and partly to keep Evie from getting inside. If he let her in, he'd never get rid of her. "*Her* is Tara. And we weren't playing *house*. I fell in love with her, Evie. You'll be glad to know it's over. You're my sister, and I love you, but it's none of your business. Goodbye Evie."

He gently pushed her away and shut the door in her face. He knew better than to give his sister a platform. She'd never shut up.

She rapped on the door, persistent.

He shouted through the closed door, "Goodnight, Evie."

"Arrgh," he heard her say, but he didn't hear her descend the stairs or the car start.

Like two schoolboys, Jeffrey and Mike ran to the sofa, knelt side-by-side, and peeked out the living room window.

"Shit. She's going over to Carolyn's house. I bet she's looking for Dad. Evie always has to have the last word. She couldn't get one here, so she's going over there to bark at my dad. She can't stand that Dad's seeing someone, finally."

Carolyn's porch light came on. He could see his dad standing with the door cracked open. He couldn't hear the conversation, but it was brief. The door closed. Evie got back into her car and drove away.

Jeffrey high-fived Mike. "He sent her packing!"

They had just settled back into drinking when another car pulled into the driveway.

"I thought this was a private party. How many invites did you send?"

"*That* must be Marielle. I told her she could pick up Tara's things tonight."

He peeked out the window. It was Marielle. He opened the door before she could ring the bell.

"Hey, Jeffrey."

He shook her hand. "I have all her things boxed up and ready to go."

Marielle whispered to him, "There's a man standing in your living room in his underwear."

He chuckled and whispered back, "I know. He's harmless."

Mike hid behind the recliner and smiled. Jeffrey and Marielle loaded the boxes into her car, and then she walked up to him and hugged him.

"Call her."

He shook his head. His throat dry, he couldn't answer with any clarity. Instead, Jeffrey waved as the car pulled away.

Mike came out from behind the recliner. "You're a detective. You can lie to catch someone. Catch her. Tell her that there's some paperwork she needs to sign, or something. Make up some bogus form. Hell, we can retrieve info from a hard drive, even when

someone thinks he's deleted everything. The mind's more complex —
but not all that different. The memories gotta go somewhere. You just
need to retrieve them."

"I'll think about it," Jeffrey said and switched on the television.
Basketball season had ended and baseball hadn't begun so they
watched an Italian soccer game. Mike fell asleep after the first thirty
minutes.

Jeffrey went into the bathroom. He had packed everything of
Tara's except the citrus scented shower gel that Liz had bought her.
She wouldn't miss it anyway.

He popped it open and breathed it in, recalling how the scent
would linger on her skin for hours. He'd inhale it when he nuzzled
her neck. It permeated the sheets.

He'd sleep on the couch tonight, he decided.

Then he remembered how frantic, but silly, she looked with his
boxers at her ankles as she swung the toilet plunger at him. He sat on
the edge of the tub and laughed.

Then he cried.

# Chapter Forty Three

Thursday, January 12, 9:45 p.m.

*T*ara heard him gargling. Then came spitting, followed by running water.

*God, his house echoed.*

She'd been here numerous times in the past, but never noticed the hollowness. Then again, her perspective had never been from his bed. They'd always stayed at her place.

She rolled from side to side. Head propped on one elbow, her champagne silk teddy strap tumbled down her shoulder.

*No, that's not quite right. Switch.*

She rested her head on her outstretched arm, curling her legs to the right then to the left—toes always pointed, a habit of years of ballet.

*Criminy Tara, strike a pose and let's get this over with.*

Edouard's hands clung to the doorframe and he leaned into the bedroom, biceps contracted, abs flat, wispy brown curls of his chest hair, shiny. The band of his black silk boxers rested below his navel. He removed his wireless frames and set them on the dresser.

His eyes roamed her body, head to toe. "You look incredible."

"Thank you." She curled her toes. *What a time to be polite.*

He left the lights on. The hairs on his chest and legs tickled her as he shimmied his way from her ankles to her neck. She inhaled him. He smelled of Dior Fahrenheit 32, his favorite. She tilted her head back in response, offering her neck.

She was surprised to feel so...uninspired. His kisses and embrace were welcomed before. So what was wrong? She ran her fingers through his wavy hair.

His hardness pressed into her belly.

Why was this so difficult tonight? Nothing. Nothing. Nothing. Absolutely no chemistry. Maybe she'd just fake it.

His moist kisses trailed down between her breasts and onto her belly. The muscles in her back stiffened.

He stopped and whispered, "Maybe later?"

To her relief, he headed back north. He held her close, showering his attention on her breasts. It felt so awkward that she could hardly stand it. It was like they were in a cartoon. He was Pepe Le Pew, le skunk romantique, and she was the white striped cat, wriggling free from his amorous grasp. The harder he kissed her, the more she bicycled her way free.

"I'm sorry. It's been a long day. I'm exhausted. It's not you."

He stroked her cheek. "Understandable, Darling. Too much too soon, huh?"

"Yes. Tomorrow, I promise."

"Tomorrow, that is, if you're not too tired after packing."

Rolling him off her, Tara sat straight up in bed and squeaked, "Packing?"

"Yes. We're leaving for France this weekend. You're going to meet my parents—in Paris. We've had this planned for weeks."

She blinked, hoping to recall any conversation about travel.

*France?*

The fall off the couch roused him. Jeffrey tried to lick his lips but his tongue was pasted to the roof of his mouth. He could have spit sand.

Mike's BVD clad butt was the first thing that came into focus. He was lying face down on the floor, snoring and mumbling. How he'd gotten from the recliner to the floor was not something Jeffrey dared to venture. He nudged Mike's behind with his foot.

"Get up," he rasped. "It's morning."

"Huh?"

Jeffrey clutched his hands to his head and hoped the pressure would dull the pounding. There was a knock at the door. He winced at the sound.

Mike smacked his lips and stretched. "Didn't we have enough company last night?"

"It's a new day," Jeffrey mumbled.

He opened the front door and found his father, standing with his arms folded across his chest, eyes narrowed.

"Tie one on last night?"

"Yep. Come in, Pop."

His dad panned the living room. An oil-stained cardboard box leaned half off the coffee table, teetering toward the floor, the tongue of a lone flattened slice of cheese pizza hanging from a battered edge. Empty Guinness bottles were strewn about the floor, one on the table on its side, facing his dad like a canon. The living room looked like a war zone, the remains of an assault on the male ego. Mike stumbled to his feet.

His dad shot his hands to his hips. "Michael O'Malley Price. What the devil are you wearing?"

Mike fingered his mustache. In his best Eddy Haskell voice, he said, "Good morning, Mr. Corrigan…Sir. As his best friend, I spent the night comforting Jeffrey at his darkest hour. Distraught by his suffering, I soiled my clothes during dinner. Your son was generous to offer his washer to immediately remedy my stained pants. He's just that kinda guy. We were so immersed in our conversation that I was remiss in placing my pants into the dryer." Mike walked over to Jeffrey. He clapped him on the back. "But what's really important is that Jeffrey had the undivided attention of his best friend."

His father rolled his eyes. "Michael, go get some pants on."

"I'm gonna hit the shower, get dressed, and high tail it to the station house. It was a pleasure to see you, Mr. Corrigan."

Then his father glanced at Jeffrey. "I have no idea how the two of you became friends."

Mike winked. "He was just lucky, I guess."

Jeffrey shook his head. "Look at you and Frank."

His dad nodded. "Point taken. The body shop called. They left a message on your machine, but when you didn't call them back yesterday, they called me as a backup number."

Jeffrey smacked his forehead with his palm. He had forgotten to call his mechanic back distraught with losing Tara." Sorry, Pop."

"Understandable. I can drive you to pick up your car. I'll be next door when you're ready. And you're welcome to have dinner with us tonight. You shouldn't spend so much time alone."

"Thanks. I'll think about it."

His father put his arm around Jeffrey's shoulders and looked straight into his son's eyes. "Don't lock yourself away. Call her or move on. See you later."

"Bye, Pop."

Jeffrey thought about what his father said. Maybe Mike's rouse about using phony paperwork as an excuse to see Tara would work. He couldn't believe that he was considering one of Mike's crazy ideas. This was the same guy that, in the fifth grade at St. Cecelia's parochial school, convinced him to tape a sign on the back of Sister Mary Catherine's habit that read, "I'm not wearing any underwear." That misguided mission landed him in Father Donahue's office, and then at the whipping hand of his mother, Maureen, the disciplinarian of the family and a devout Catholic. He swore he'd never again entertain one of Mike's schemes.

Of course, that didn't hold.

Mike had convinced him to participate in many more harebrained schemes throughout their childhood, and well into their adult years— his brainstorming increasing in complexity.

Whistling, Mike strolled into the living room, now squeaky clean, shaven, and dressed in his suit and tie.

*How does he do that—go from stumbling about, hung over in his BVD's, to swaggering around in creased pants, looking refreshed and ready to put in a full day's work?*

"I'm going to review the crime scene notes, the pics, and the autopsy reports on Maurice Chiguard and the hooker vic today. I'll have Herb call Miami and get an update on the drug runner case and another copy of the footprints." Mike paused. "If that meets your approval...unless...uh...you prefer to handle things from another angle."

Jeffrey nodded and flipped up his thumb. "It's a well thought out plan. I'll meet you and Herb at the station this afternoon to review your progress."

Mike saluted him before bolting out the front door, but it was not in jest. He saluted back, appreciative of Mike's respect and solidarity.

Jeffrey dragged his feet down the hallway toward the bathroom. His body was leaden and uncooperative, and it wasn't the because of the drink. It was Tara's absence. It weighed heavily upon him.

A shower might make him respectable on the outside, but his insides would remain a mess. Stumbling down the hall, he saw the door to the study ajar.

He stopped, swaying, and balanced himself against the doorframe. Jeffrey batted at the cockeyed red bow that remained affixed to the door. He ripped it off the door, threw it to the floor, and then yanked at his hair, ashamed of his childish behavior. Jeffrey pushed the door open. And there it was; the perfect excuse to see her again. Her laptop.

# Chapter Forty Four

Friday, January 13, 11:15 a.m.

*T*he morning in the office went smoothly. Tara was able to dispo half of her charts. Pleased with her accomplishments, she was just about to join the staff for lunch and sugary cake when Julie stepped into her office.

She cleared her throat announcing her presence and peered at Tara from around a mountain of charts. "A Lieutenant Corrigan, from the NYPD, is here to see you. Should I show him in? I can tell him you're not here if you'd prefer."

Heat rose up her cheeks. *Why am I acting like this?* "No. Please bring him in," she said, trying to ignore her dampening palms.

Jeffrey Corrigan walked into her office, clutching a black soft zippered case under his arm. Tara jumped out her chair, bumping into the stack of files, sending them toppling to the floor. He chuckled, set the laptop case on her desk, and bent over to help retrieve the scattered charts.

She stammered, "I…I got it."

Their foreheads collided as they reached for the errant folders, their noses bumping as their heads reared back in surprise. Tara chuckled, dropping the charts that they had gathered.

He laughed. "I'm not helping, am I?"

"I think we're doing a bang up job," she teased.

Tara let Jeffrey scoop up the remaining charts, plopping them on top of her desk. His long fingers eclipsed her petite hand, as he helped her to her feet, the creases of his palm somehow familiar. She teetered back, steadying herself with her other hand on the edge of her desk.

"Are you okay?"

"Y…yes. I'm fine. Thank you."

She pressed her back against her desk, covering the glistening trail left behind by her sweaty palm.

He let loose of her hand, and they stared at each other for a long moment.

"I brought your laptop. We, uh, held it for fingerprints."

She tilted her head. "I thought my laptop was damaged."

"No. This one is good as new."

They both held onto the laptop. *Why is he stalling?* He finally let go.

Tara hugged the computer to her chest. "This means so much to me."

He smiled. "I know it does."

She couldn't help but notice that she loved the way the corners of his eyes crinkled. His scent was so clean, not cluttered with cologne. She wanted to edge closer to him, but refrained. And his light blue shirt and navy striped tie—she'd seen him wear that before, she was certain of it.

*He probably wore that the day he pulled her out of the holding cell,* she told herself

No. No. She *remembered*. He was wearing a white shirt with a green shamrock printed tie.

Sparkles of light flickered before her eyes. Her knuckles blanched as she clutched her laptop tightly.

She blinked.

Then her knees buckled.

Jeffrey grabbed her shoulders pulling her safely into his arms. *His embrace feels so right,* she thought. But how could it? She barely knew him.

Edouard walked into her office and cleared his throat. "Ah, Lieutenant Corrigan. I was unaware of your visit. Nice to see you, *so soon*."

Jeffrey steadied Tara, let go of her and then extended his hand to Edouard. "Dr. LaCroix."

"Lieutenant Corrigan was kind enough to drop off my laptop," Tara explained." I skipped breakfast, and must have become somewhat hypoglycemic. Good thing he was here before I hit the ground."

"Yes, how fortunate that he was there to catch you."

"Please, Lieutenant. Won't you join us for lunch?" Tara said.

Edouard wrapped his arm around her in a surprisingly possessive gesture. She turned her head away from the heaviness of his cologne.

"Thank you for the invitation, Dr. Ross, but I need to get back to the station." He winked at her. *Oh my gosh, he's flirting with me!* "My desk looks as bad as yours right now."

"Yes, we're all very busy here. We won't hold you up, Lieutenant. Thanks for stopping by," Edouard said, dismissing him.

"Goodbye Tara."

Tara waved at him, staring into his eyes. "Goodbye, Lieutenant Corrigan, and thank you," she said softly.

He smiled back at her, nodded at Edouard, and then left.

"That was nice," Tara told Edouard.

But he had no words for her as he pulled her to the break room. She lagged behind at arm's length, glancing back out the window, watching Jeffrey drive away in his Mustang.

"Have some cake, Darling. The girls brought it in, just for you."

Jeffrey rolled a pencil on his desktop, numb from Tara's failure to recognize him as anyone but a NYPD lieutenant doing his job. The vibration from the ridges of the yellow pencil beneath his finger pads reminded him that he could still feel— at least physically.

He shot the pencil across the room.

The lead left a charcoal streak down the dingy white wall of his office. Jeffrey chided himself for behaving like a moody adolescent, snorted, and then asked Laurie to gather Mike and Herb for a meeting in his office.

Mike slinked in, juggling his blue Super Balls. He caught all three in one hand and flopped down in a chair. "So did she go for the phony paperwork?"

Jeffrey lowered his gaze and shook his head. "No."

"You should've let me draft them up. I'd make it look real official."

"I didn't try the bogus papers. She left her laptop at my house. I returned it."

Mike leaned forward. "And?"

"And... nothing. She only knew me as Lieutenant Corrigan. She did mention that she thought her computer was damaged. I was hoping she would remember more, but when I told her we held it for prints, she believed me."

"Nice cover. Too bad, she didn't remember. But it's only been a day. Give her time."

"Nah. It's not gonna happen, man. Let's get on with nabbing Angelina Holtz."

Herb tottered in, sporting a powdered sugar mustache, and flopped into a chair next to Mike. "I got another copy of the footprints, since the first one disappeared."

Mike rolled one of his Super Balls in his hand. "Yeah, that was weird."

Herb wiped his mouth with the back of his hand. "Then I talked to the guys in Miami. No new developments on the dead drug runner case. The vic was a well-known pilot. Even used to have a flight school in the Florida Keys. Miami P.D. and the Feds had been trying to catch up with him, but the guy was skilled in getting in and out under the radar." Herb sighed. "And as for the migrant woman witness, she's still nowhere to be found. Probably over the border in Mexico by now." He shook his head. "No way to trace her and doubtful she'd show on her own. Interestingly, I talked to Hector Suarez, who Angelina said was her brother-in-law. He confirmed her story about being in Miami because of her sister's miscarriage, but his answers seemed rehearsed."

Jeffrey narrowed his eyes. "I knew she was lying!"

Herb continued. "Her sister gave the same concocted account. But just like you Boss, I think it's a ruse, and they're not her relatives at all, but no one I interviewed has a criminal record."

Jeffrey nodded to Herb. "Good work. What do you have on your end, Mike?"

"I picked through the crime scene report on Chiguard's apartment. Marshall and his CSU team did a thorough job. I reviewed the autopsy findings with Dr. Roseman. COD remains lead poisoning for both Maurice and the hooker. No bodies were moved or staged.

"I also went over all the fingerprints. Our friend, Angelina, has no priors. I'm not sure how she's evaded the system unless someone on the inside has her back. I took the liberty of comparing her prints on the cup she used here during questioning, to every print found at Maurice's apartment. And guess what? There's a match. Her prints *are* in the apartment, but none in the bathroom where Maurice's body was discovered. She's definitely been in that apartment. That's enough to pick her up for further questioning."

Mike slapped his palm against his knee. "Oh, and that tape we were discussing, with our best resolution, the guy who assaulted Liz was wearing a Richard Nixon mask, so no visual." Mike shook his head. "What a freak! A green Dodge Charger was picked up as well, but only a side view. The driver had a hoodie on, pulled low—no ID. No luck on locating the vehicle yet.

"Liz is still out on medical leave. She didn't answer her phone, so I stopped by. She said the pain pills make her sleepy. She didn't want to talk much. Everyone's concerned about her. Sector cars have stepped up patrolling her neighborhood."

"We'll watch over her. And as for Angelina," Jeffrey slapped his desktop, "we'll bring in her in and tell her that there's a woman boarding a plane, as we speak, in Miami—headed to New York to ID her in the shooting of the drug runner." Jeffrey raised his fist. "Smoke her out! Let's see how nervous she gets. Chiguard and the woman at his apartment were shot at close range. Whoever pulled the trigger would have serious blow back on their clothes. If Angelina was involved, she had to have dumped the bloody clothes somewhere or perhaps stashed them away; paranoid her discarded clothing could be retrieved." Jeffrey scanned his squad. "Were all the dumpsters checked?"

"Yeah, Lou. We did a pretty wide canvas. No clothes or weapons found. We can search again, but the trash has been long since picked up," Mike said.

Jeffrey paced in front of his team, his hands on his hips. He halted. "Here's the plan. Mike and I'll go to Williamsburg. Pay a visit to Thompson Paints. Snoop around. If she's not there, we'll head to her apartment. Herb, you check out the dumpsters, in case some were missed by the city."

Herb protested, "Why do I get dumpster duty?"

"You're sounding like Mike. You have a fresh eye. You may see something we missed. Oh, and payback for the parrot."

"Okay Boss. I'm on it."

His preoccupation with zeroing in on Angelina had temporarily distracted him from thoughts of Tara. But like a submerged buoy, she popped back to the surface of his mind — floating there.

She couldn't remember.

He can't forget.

Jeffrey parked the Crown Vic two blocks from Thompson's Paints. He'd insisted on driving—not in the mood for Mike's creative parking techniques and driving busied his mind. The late afternoon light filtered through the windows of the store. Except for a couple perusing fabric swatches with an employee, Jeffrey and Mike were alone and had the full attention of the man behind the counter. Dressed in creased black pants, a mint-colored shirt, and dark green tie, he smiled and greeted them.

"Good afternoon. Can I help you, gentlemen?"

Jeffrey flashed his shield. "NYPD. We're here to speak with Angelina Holtz."

The man's smile melted. "I'm Carl Taylor, assistant manager. Is there something *I* can help you with?"

Mike grinned. "The precinct *could* use new blinds, but we're here to see Ms. Holtz."

"She's not here today."

"Do you know where we can find her?"

"She was here this morning and mentioned she was taking the rest of the day off. She's probably at her apartment. She's been under a lot of stress since Steven's murder. We all have. We're still in shock that Stuart would do such a thing."

"Yeah, we're all cracked up about it too." Mike peered past Carl. "Mind if we look around?"

"Not a problem, detectives. You've seen our lobby." Carl led them down a back hall. "The store also contains a warehouse. Back here are all our paints. Our quality is unsurpassed. Our base paint comes all the way from Miami. We can tint to any specification."

Jeffrey's eyes widened. "Miami?"

"Yes," he said proudly. "We have a van and contract with a driver for monthly trips."

Jeffrey craned his neck past the juvenile assistant, looking for the warehouse entrance. "So, *Carl*, the late Mr. Thompson would make these *long* trips to Miami with Ms. Holtz?

Carl nodded dimly. "Yes. Mr. Thompson—Steven, not Stuart—felt that was the most cost effective option. And either he or Ms. Holtz would go down with Jorge, our driver. Steven was busy the last few months, so Angelina went. They were never gone at the same time. One always stayed to manage the store."

Jeffrey rolled his eyes. Dealing with Carl, now he could understand why. "That's interesting. Most companies receive shipments instead of the owners picking the product up directly." Jeffrey cocked an eyebrow. "Didn't you find that odd—the trips?"

"No sir. Steven wasn't conventional in the least. I didn't question his decisions. He was a good employer. Gave out a lot of bonuses. That's all anybody cared about."

Jeffrey pointed to a locked door. "What's behind here?"

"Those are the paints that are strictly for contractor use. Only Steven and Angelina have the keys to that room. They preferred to handle those large accounts on their own."

Jeffrey stared down the hallway. *Is she hiding in there? Is Carl covering for her? Nah. she's not that dumb.*

Although Carl was her assistant, he was fairly convinced the guy was nine pins shy of a strike. "How about this door?"

"That was Steven Thompson's office. Now it's Ms. Holtz's. She locks it when she's not here."

"Uh huh. And where can we find Jorge, the driver?"

Carl rocked on his heels and looked at the floor. "Look, I don't want to get anyone in trouble."

Mike moved close enough to breathe in Carl's face. "You can get someone in trouble now, or you can incriminate yourself and we can ride to the station house. Then you can clear everything up there. What's it going to be?"

Carl pulled a crumpled tissue from his pocket and dabbed his sweaty forehead. "I don't know where Jorge lives. They pay him under the table. He shows up, drives to Miami, comes back to unload, and then he's gone until they need him again."

*Man, this guy's too easy,* Jeffrey thought. He wished all his interviews were as sweet as this one. "When did you last see Jorge?"

"A…about two weeks ago."

"So the last run to Miami was two weeks ago?"

"Yes."

"Was Ms. Holtz on that run?"

"Yes."

The Steven and Irina's murders were the first homicides to cross his desk— January 5th—two weeks ago. Jeffrey's pulse quickened. Tara was in his office that day.

Mike slapped Carl on the back. "Thank you for your cooperation, Carl, and the tour. I just moved into a new place and I'm sure I'll need some paint."

"I'll be happy to get you exactly what you want."

Carl had perked up at the possibility of a sale. Even the perspiration dotting his face was drying.

"I'm sure of that." Mike put his arm around Carl. "I think we hit it off quite well, don't you?"

Carl blushed. "Yeah, we have s…sir."

"Say Carl, do you keep that van on premises?"

"Yes, we do. It's right back here on our lot."

Jeffrey shook his head and grinned at Mike. Mike winked back.

"Come on, Lieutenant. Let's go check out this van."

Carl led them to a gated lot. "Here it is."

Jeffrey and Mike, their mouths agape, stared at the white van with Thompson Paints and Interior Design, Inc. in bold letters on displayed on the side.

*Bingo.*

They were so close to closing in on Angelina. He'd break her down. Catch her in her web of lies. He had enough to get a warrant to search her apartment and Thompson Paints.

If only he could get the vehicle impounded, he might get soil samples from the wheel wells and have a forensic geologist compare it to dirt at the Redlands crime scene.

With Carl Taylor's testimony placing her in that van within the last 2 weeks, he could nail her at the scene without the migrant woman's ID.

*Thank you, Carl.*

Mike's cell phone rang.

"Shit," he muttered.

"What's the matter?" Jeffrey asked.

"Amy's water just broke."

# Chapter Forty Five

Friday, January 13, 3:42 p.m.

*J*effrey grabbed Mike's arm. "Don't panic. Get in the car and I'll drive you home."

"Amy's at the house in Purdy's. That's over an hour's drive." Mike's nostrils flared, gulping oxygen with every frightened breath.

"Slow down, man, or you're going to pass out."

Mike dabbed the sweat from his brow. "She said her contractions are five minutes apart. That's bad, isn't it?"

"I think that's normal. Didn't you go to childbirth classes?"

"Uh, twice."

"Shit, Mike. Okay, tell her to get to the nearest hospital. Call her on her cell."

Mike fumbled with his cell.

"Aw, Aimes, please stop crying. I'm on my way. Call an ambulance." Mike hung up and yelled at Jeffrey, "She won't take an ambulance!"

"Calm down. Don't yell. You'll make things worse. I'll call Pop. He's closer to Purdy's than we are. He can get there faster and drive her to the hospital. We'll meet them there."

"Thanks."

While Mike called back to relay the plan to Amy, Jeffrey called his dad who was happy to help.

"We got it covered, buddy."

Jeffrey spun the car onto the highway ramp and glanced at Mike. He could see Mike's abs tighten and his pale, sweaty cheeks puff with each forced breath. He knew what was coming.

"Not in the car!" He pulled the Crown Vic off the parkway.

Mike jumped out, bent over, and stumbled a few paces. Jeffrey shook his head as he watched Mike's body jerk with each hurl. When he had emptied his stomach, Mike dragged his feet back to the car and plopped into the seat.

"Better?"

"Yeah."

"Dr. Ross, we have a 38 week primigravida with ruptured membranes and contractions coming up from the ER. Just moved to the area. Prenatal care was in the City. Her records are being faxed," the L&D nurse said.

"Thanks." *Oh hooray! I'll be busy tonight. No ducking Edouard.*

The wheelchair swung around the corner. The woman finished panting through a contraction and then smiled. She pushed back her wavy brown hair and extended her hand.

Tara glanced at the preliminary chart. "Hi Amy. I'm Dr. Ross, the OB on call this evening. Let's get you in a room. When did your labor start?"

"Thanks, Dr. Ross. My water broke about an hour ago."

Tara couldn't help but notice the composed man following along behind the wheelchair. He looked familiar. Tara guessed he was in his late sixties or early seventies.

"I'm Joe Corrigan," he offered, noticing the way she was evaluating him. "Friend of the family. The father is on his way."

She shook Joe's hand. "Nice to meet you. You are a good friend indeed, Mr. Corrigan."

*Joe Corrigan. Why do I know that name?*

She pushed the thoughts away and escorted Amy to a room and helped her into a dry hospital gown.

The nurse strapped the fetal Doppler and tocometer around Amy's rounded belly with elastic pink and blue bands. "This one monitors the baby's heart rate and this one keeps track of your contractions," she explained to her patient.

Tara examined Amy.

"You're four centimeters dilated. The baby's heart rate is excellent and you are contracting every five minutes. How're you feeling?"

"Nervous but okay. My husband should be here soon."

"You seem to be coping well. Would you like any pain medication?"

"I can breathe through the contractions for now. I'll wait for my husband."

"Sure. I'll be right outside the door. The nurses will take good care of you."

"Thank you, Dr. Ross. I'm so glad you're here."

"You're welcome, and it's my pleasure."

Tara sat at the nurse's station perusing Amy's prenatal records. Then she called Edouard to let him know she'd be busy *all night* with a laboring patient. She'd finished reading Amy's records and started on her admission paperwork when she heard a rumbling from the far end of the hallway.

The thumping footsteps grew louder.

She peered around the desk and saw a mustached man flailing toward the desk. He skidded to a stop and smacked his outstretched hands on the counter of the nurse's station.

Between gasping breaths, he said, "Hi...I'm...Mike Price...My wife...Amy...is in labor.

She stood to shake his hand, and there, behind him, was Lieutenant Corrigan.

"Oh!" Tara and Jeffrey stared at each other, their jaws dropping simultaneously.

"Hi Doc. I'm Mike Price. My wife, Amy, is in labor," Mike repeated, this time smoother.

"Nice to meet you, Mr. Price. I'm Dr. Tara Ross."

Mike shifted from foot to foot. "Yeah. Yeah. I know. And you can call me Mike. You always have."

*Did he say he knew me?*

"Well, Mike, let me show you to Amy's room." She gazed at Jeffrey, nodded, and smiled. "Lieutenant Corrigan."

He grinned and nodded in return. "Dr. Ross."

Heat rose to her face. Her stomach tingled.

*Please stop. You're acting like schoolgirl.*

Tara led Mike to labor room five. "Your husband's here," she called from the doorway.

Amy peered over her pregnant belly. "You don't look so good, Mike."

Tara agreed but didn't say so. His pallor had morphed to a light shade of green. She pointed to a chair. "Sit here next to Amy. Hold her hand. Breathe with her."

"Yeah. That's a good idea. I'll just... sit."

Mike plopped into the chair and took a swig of Amy's ice. Tara shook her head and left the room to find the lieutenant. She ambled down the labor and delivery hallway, Amy's chart in her hands.

There he was, standing at the nurse's station, towering over the counter.

*Thank God, he hadn't left.*

"It's so weird to see you so soon again. I mean...it's *nice* to see you," she said. *What a lame opener,* she thought.

"Yeah. Imagine that, meeting up like this. Kind of unexpected."

She couldn't stop staring at him. "Uh huh."

A stack of papers fell through her fingers and scattered to the floor. They bent over and collided craniums—again.

"Déjà vu. Didn't we do this earlier?"

He laughed. "Yes, we did."

He brushed the bangs from her forehead. Her heart quickened at his touch.

"Are you okay, Doc?"

"I'm fine."

She gathered the papers and tapped them together on the desk.

"I'm headed to the waiting room then, to take care of rubbernecking family and friends. I'll see you later."

*God, I truly hope so.*

Jeffrey tripped over his long legs, catching himself on the counter and blushed.

"Ow, Ow, Ow," Amy screamed, her cries echoing down the hall.

"I guess it's time for the epidural," Tara said with a smile.

Mike bolted out of the room and smacked into Jeffrey, looking like a cat dropped in a bathtub.

"Oh, no. You're going back in there." He shoved Mike back toward the room.

Mike pleaded, "Please, don't make me."

"Amy doesn't have a choice. Neither do you."

Tara giggled. She gave Jeffrey the thumbs up sign. He smiled and shrugged.

*Damn, those hazel eyes. And that...*

"Ow. Ow. Shit."

Tara stopped gawking and turned her attention to screaming Amy. She covered the distance from the nurse's station to room five quickly.

"Would you like an epidural?"

Amy's long locks were matted to her sweaty face. "Yes, *please.*"

Mike, now stationed at her side, bent his knees and winced as she grasped at him. "Amy, you're crushing my hand."

Amy twisted her head toward him and growled, "I could really give a fuck right now, Mike."

Mike's eyes widened, his bottom lip drooped theatrically. The nurse patted him on the back helpfully.

"Don't take it personally. Laboring women are allowed to say anything they want, especially things they don't mean."

Dr. Robert Upton, the on-call anesthesiologist, entered the room. Tara swallowed hard. She hadn't seen him since the night of Alexis's emergency surgery. He approached her and her heart went cold.

He whispered into her ear, "Glad you're back, Tara. And thank you... for everything."

She squeezed his hand.

Robert leaned over the bed's side rails and tilted his head toward Amy. "So you'd like an epidural?"

"Yes," Amy and Mike chimed together.

Mike stood up to watch Dr. Upton paint dark orange circles on Amy's back. He winced when the anesthesiologist poked a tiny needle into her back. Then came the long, skinny needle of the epidural. Tara looked to Mike just in time to see his eyes roll up into his head, but no one could catch him before he crumpled to the polished wooden floor.

*Ka-thunk.*

The nurse snapped a smelling salt capsule, waving it above his mustache. Mike jerked awake.

"Welcome back, Sport."

Blood oozed from a cut below his hairline. He'd sliced his forehead on the bottom edge of the bed.

"You're going to need stitches," Tara informed him. "We'll call for a wheelchair to take you down to the ER."

"I can walk," Mike said.

A chorus of "No" echoed through the room.

An ER nurse pushed Mike's wheelchair out of labor room five.

Jeffrey was still stifling a laugh when she reappeared in the hall.

"What happened in there?"

"Mike got a little lightheaded, fell, and gashed his forehead. It happens," Tara said with a smile.

"I didn't fall. I tripped," Mike called as he rolled away.

Jeffrey roared. "What? Did Amy trip you?"

"Ha Ha. Very funny. I need to get stitches. Do me a favor, Jeffrey. Stay with Amy."

She smiled then cleared her throat. "That'll work. Amy will be ready to push by the time you come back. And meantime, Lieutenant Corrigan can sit with her." *And with me.*

"Go get your face fixed. I got you covered," Jeffrey said.

Mike waved as the elevator door closed.

Tara ushered Jeffrey into the labor room, sneaking a peek at his tight, athletic behind. The nurse raised her eyebrows, grinned, and very subtly excused herself, leaving Tara with the handsome lieutenant.

Amy, comfortable and exhausted, snored in the bed. He leaned back in the chair next to Amy's bed, exhaled, and crossed his long legs. She sat on an exam stool and wheeled herself to the foot of the bed, closer to him but still at a safe distance.

"Hard day?" she asked.

"Long, but not as long as yours. You're still working, I'm not. I admire you."

She believed his genuineness. He wasn't playing her. She could see it in his eyes. She wanted to edge closer. But didn't.

"Do you have children, Lieutenant?"

"Yes, I have a son. James. He's a freshman at Columbia. And it's Jeffrey, my name is Jeffrey."

"Well, *Jeffrey*, you and your wife must be proud." *Ooh, that definitely sounded like fishing.*

"Yes. I and my *ex-wife* are proud."

*Smooth, Tara. He picked up on that.*

"How's your daughter doing?"

She squinted. "What?"

"Uh, I...um, guessed you have a daughter. I apologize."

"No need. I do have a daughter, Abbie. She's fifteen and in Greece with her father, my ex."

Tara was at ease with him. He didn't feel like a stranger. She could have spent the whole night talking with him.

He uncrossed his legs, sat forward, and rested his hands on his knees. "That's great, Tara. I mean Dr. Ross."

She smiled. "Tara is fine."

After far too short of a time, Mike ambled into the room. Blue nylon sutures decorated his forehead. He bowed his head, shamed. "I'm ready to behave."

"That would be boring." Jeffrey pointed at Mike's forehead. "Very colorful. I like it."

Amy roused, startled. "I feel pressure."

Jeffrey looked away as Tara peeked under Amy's sheets.

"That's because your baby is crowning."

Mike poked his head up from behind Tara. "Aimes, the baby's coming!"

The nurse returned and together, she and Tara guided Amy's legs into the stirrups. Another nurse rushed in and flipped the heater switch on the infant warmer.

"I'm going to step out," Jeffrey said.

"Oh no you don't! Don't you dare go, Jeffrey Corrigan. You need to keep an eye on Mike," Amy joked.

"He'll do just fine."

"Please stay," Mike begged.

"That's up to Dr. Ross."

"I don't mind. This is an intimate group compared to some other deliveries."

Mike held Amy's hand. It looked like they were keeping each other afloat.

Tara grinned, pleased that he'd risen to the occasion. Jeffrey stood in the corner, looking out of place, facing the head of the bed.

"Okay, Amy. Give me a steady push."

"Oh my God, Aimes. It's coming!"

A tiny head popped out. Tara suctioned the baby's nose and mouth.

"What is it?" Mike called.

Tara chuckled. "I can't tell by the ears. Don't push, Amy. I need to loosen the umbilical cord from around the baby's neck."

Mike clutched the side rails. "Is everything okay?"

"Yes, everything is fine. Now, give me one more push."

One shoulder slipped out. With a gentle upward tug, she guided the slick baby into her arms. "It's… a girl!"

"Aimes, oh Amy, she's beautiful!" Mike cried.

"Would you like to cut the umbilical cord?"

"Yeah, sure. What do I do?"

"Take these scissors and cut between these two clamps."

Beaming, Mike severed his daughter's umbilical cord easily. He kissed Amy and nodded at Tara. "Thank you, Dr. Ross."

"You're so welcome."

Tara looked up at Jeffrey.

A huge grin on his face, he mouthed, "I love you."
She tilted her head, smiled, and mouthed back, "What?"

# Chapter Forty Six

Friday, January 13, 7:06 p.m.

*J*effrey clicked the door of labor room five closed. He'd let Mike and Amy have their moment of glory with Christina Marie O'Malley Price, all seven pounds and nine ounces of her.

He stretched his arms, almost grazing the white speckled panels of the drop ceiling, and yawned. Following the sound of scratching pen to paper, he found Tara, scribbling on a mountain of forms. Her staggering paperwork rivaled his own pile.

Those three words, *I love you*, had shot right out of his mouth. No thought. No premeditation.

But maybe she didn't understand. Or worse, she thought he was some freak. She *did* smile.

He tried to dodge reliving the embarrassing encounter and head for the waiting room, but his feet remained pressed into the hospital tile.

*Just one more minute with her.*

Tara looked up from her papers. "I see you, Lieutenant Corrigan."

He was caught.

*Okay, act casual*, he thought.

But with her, casual was not what he desired.

"I forgot how intense childbirth could be—all the emotions. You were excellent in there, especially with Mike. They were lucky to have you."

*I was lucky to have you too.* "I guess it's routine...for you?"

"No, not routine. Maybe some are more noteworthy. This one, I won't forget. And Mike will be a good father."

He nodded. "I keep telling him that."

"I'm finished with my paperwork. Would you like to get some dinner in the cafeteria? It wouldn't be anything great, hospital food...as such."

*I'd eat cardboard to be with you.*

"I'd like that. I need to stop at the waiting room and catch everyone up on the details before the family descends on Amy and Mike. I'll meet you at the elevators?"

Just then, Edouard rounded the corner. "She can't make it. Lieutenant Corrigan," he said with a smile that did not look sincere. "I just can't seem to shake you today."

Jeffrey gritted his teeth. "I was here for the birth of my friend's daughter. Tara did a wonderful job with the delivery."

Edouard put his arm around Tara's shoulders. "Yes, she is wonderful." He pressed Tara to his chest. "But I'm afraid Tara won't be able to share dinner with you, because she's going to France, with me, tonight."

She blinked up at him. "I thought we were leaving next weekend."

"I moved our trip up. My parents are anxious to meet you. I packed your bags and have your passport." He tapped his chest pocket. "Hurry along. Our plane leaves in three hours."

*What the hell happened? A shot at a second chance, and now she's going to France? With him? Fucked by the Frenchman, again!*

"I'm sorry, Jeffrey. We'll do dinner when I come back." She bit her lower lip.

"I understand, Dr. Ross. You know where to find me."

Edouard grabbed her arm. "Let's go, darling. Hurry up and change out your scrubs. We're going to miss our flight. I paid a *fortune* to reschedule our trip. Nora is going to cover call for us while we're gone."

Jeffrey took a deep breath, trying to release the tension in his blanched fists. "Don't tug at her like that." The sight of him, manhandling her, chafed.

Edouard's eyebrow arched past the rim of his glasses. "Excuse me, Lieutenant?"

"I said—"

Edouard interrupted him. "I know what you said."

"Edouard," Tara chided.

Edouard prodded Tara forward and she began to move, somewhat reluctantly. He sidled up to Jeffrey and whispered, "I know what you're up to. Stay away from her. It's for her own good—and yours."

Jeffrey glared at Edouard. "Or is it for your own?"

The studded lights of the runway glowed parallel, an illuminated guide for pilots against the black background. She sat in the JFK airport terminal, watching the caravan of luggage being loaded into the belly of the jet.

Edouard approached her, carrying two cardboard corseted cups of coffee.

"Here you go, Darling."

"Thanks. You know, you didn't need to be so rude."

"I thought you'd enjoy some coffee."

"You know what I mean. You were rude to Lieutenant Corrigan back in the hospital."

Edouard gulped his coffee and stared straight ahead. "I'm sorry you thought I was offensive, but the guy is stalking you."

She sputtered. Coffee sprayed the front of her blue blouse. She grabbed a napkin and dabbed at the dots. "He kindly returned my laptop this morning. Then he brought his friend to the hospital. He didn't plan his friend's wife's labor. It was a coincidence. That hardly constitutes stalking."

"He was leering at you."

*He was gazing. I was gawking.*

"No he wasn't."

"Yes he was."

She turned away from him. "I don't want to talk about this anymore."

Edouard folded his arms across his chest. "Fine. Neither do I."

Finishing her coffee in silence, Tara flipped open her laptop.

*Hooray. Wi-Fi.*

"I'm going to email Abbie. I want her know that she can reach me. I can't wait for her to live with us."

"We need to discuss this, further Tara. You know I think your daughter is a hormonal handful. I was counting on time alone, with you." Edouard ran his hand up her thigh and along the zipper of her jeans. Thank God, no one was sitting across from them. Tara shifted away from him in her chair. He continued anyway. "Let her stay with her father. She can visit. And if you want her to stay, there are plenty of first rate private schools here and in France that will keep her in line."

Her jaw dropped. "She's fifteen-years-old. She's supposed to be hormonal. No private schools, Edouard. I have joint custody. She can't go live in another country. And neither could I, if that is what you are saying."

Edouard patted her knee. "We'll talk some more...later. It's almost time to board. You're tired. You'll sleep on the plane. Everything will look different once you've rested."

She clenched her teeth. There was no point in arguing with him.

She emailed Abbie, and then she perused her documents folder, making sure everything was there.

Edouard glanced over her shoulder. "We'll be boarding soon. No time for that silly story you're working on. Save it, darling."

Her eyes narrowed. "Silly?"

"Oh, jeez. That's not what I meant. It's a nice little hobby. I just want you to keep things in perspective."

"Uh huh," she muttered.

*This trip is turning into a nightmare.*

He traced the tips of his manicured fingernails along his coffee cup while she clicked on the documents icon on her computer screen. She slid the mouse to Photos. She missed her daughter so much; she'd certainly welcome Abbie's smiling face over his sour demeanor.

*Oh God.*

There they were—she and Jeffrey—photo after photo.

Skiing.

Laughing.

Embracing.

Her brain tilted and her heart rocketed out of her chest. She slammed the laptop closed and bolted from her chair.

"I have to go."

"What's the matter?" Edouard asked, climbing out of his chair and making shift to follow her.

Tara's head was spinning. "I have to go. I can't go to France with you."

"For God's sake, you're not making sense. Sit down, Tara. You're making a scene."

"I remember. I remember it *all*. I'm sorry, Edouard. I can't stay with you."

She clutched her purse and laptop. Her feet pounded the carpeting as she ran through the terminal.

"Where are you going?" he yelled from somewhere behind her.

Backpedaling, she called out, "To get perspective!"

# Chapter Forty Seven

Friday, January 13, 9:30 p.m.

*Clink. Clink. Clink.* Frank tapped his wine glass.

"Attention. I'd like everyone to raise their glasses in a toast to my partner, and best friend Joe Corrigan and to his lovely bride-to-be, Carolyn Reese. May they spend the years together in health and happiness."

"Here. Here," everyone shouted.

Jeffrey blinked. Was he so preoccupied with the loss of Tara and the chase for Angelina that he'd missed his father's engagement? After so many years of the family urging, his dad finally did it. He just had to do it in his own time and find the right woman, a daunting task in shadow of his mom. He was happy for him, if this was the real deal. The man had paid his dues.

Jeffrey scooted his chair closer to Carolyn's dining room table. He'd accepted the dinner invitation, with no forewarning of a full on Corrigan clan gathering.

Everyone was paired off: Joe and Carolyn, Frank and Myra, Johnny, Cindy, and their three kids and of course, Evie, and her husband Andrew, with their twin sons. James was a bigger surprise. He grinned at his son from across the table.

All were accounted for, except Tara.

Sated by a home cooked meal, the men retired to the living room, bottles of Guinness awaiting them. Well into the fourth chorus of *When Irish Eyes Are Smiling*, the doorbell rang.

Jeffrey rocked out of the sofa. "I'll get it."

He opened the door. Mike stood on Carolyn's porch with a smile on his face.

"Hey! It's the proud daddy, and looks like he's brought loads of baby pics," Jeffrey called back to the assembled Corrigans.

"Michael O'Malley Price. Get in here, son," his father yelled from the living room.

"You're dad's a bit happy. He just called me son."

Jeffrey rolled his eyes. "Newly engaged."

"*Wow*. That's great. I stopped by your house and saw all the cars. Figured you were over here. Came by to tell you Judge Cerzone signed off on the two warrants, Thompson Paints and Interiors, and Angelina's apartment."

He punched Mike's arm. "Strong work."

"The judge just had a granddaughter." Mike crossed his fingers. "We're like this. Let's ride first thing in the morning, get this over with."

"Anything else, I need to know?"

"Herb, bless his garbage picking soul, didn't come up with a thing."

"Bless his garbage picking soul? You *are* a changed man."

Mike hung up his jacket. "Yeppers. I'm gonna do Barbies and baseball. And I'm gonna teach her to juggle."

"I can go with Herb tomorrow since Amy's in the hospital," Jeffrey offered.

"Nah. She's staying another day because they're monitoring Christina's bilirubin levels."

Jeffrey cocked his head. "Everything okay?"

"Yeah, good." Mike raised his thumb.

"Come on in, Mike. Have a beer," Jeffrey's father said.

"Talk about a changed man," Mike said sotto voce.

His dad tossed Mike a bottle of beer and then motioned to Jeffrey, pointing to the hallway. Frank, always watching, followed at some unseen signal.

The men paused in the corridor, away from the family festivities.

His father touched his arm. "I was going to tell you about me and Carolyn sooner. It just happened so fast."

Jeffrey clapped him on the shoulder. "It's great, Pop. I'm happy for you, honestly."

"Listen, don't give up. Tara's the right woman for you. I know what it's like to lose someone you love."

Jeffrey shook his head. "Tara's alive, Pop. Mom died. You can't compare."

"Love is love," his dad said. "Like I've taught you, you gotta expect the unexpected."

Frank leaned toward him and whispered, "Cry if you need to. There's no shame in that."

He wanted to, badly, but he'd wait until he was home alone.

"Thanks." He hugged them all. "But I'm going to get another beer."

Frank tilted his empty wine glass. "And I'm going to get another cranberry juice."

Everyone had gathered in the living room. Mike sat, crammed into the couch, surrounded by Jeffrey's dad, Frank, and Jeffrey. They clinked their Guinness bottles together and sang in honor of Christine Marie O'Malley Price:

> *Over in Killarney*
> *Many years ago,*
> *Me Mither sang a song to me*
> *In tones so sweet and low.*
> *Just a simple little ditty,*
> *In her good auld Irish way,*
> *And I'd give the world if she could sing*
> *That song to me this day.*
> *"Too-ra-loo-ra-loo-ral, Too-ra-loo-ra-li,*
> *Too-ra-loo-ra-loo-ral, hush now, don't you cry!*

*Too-ra-loo-ra-loo-ral, Too-ra-loo-ra-li,*
*Too-ra-loo-ra-loo-ral, that's an Irish lullaby.*

Jeffrey's eyes stung with tears. Memories of his mom, and now Tara, bubbled mercilessly in his mind. It was one *too-ra-loo* too many. He bid all farewell and couldn't have bolted out the door any faster.

The muted pounding of Mike's rubber-soled shoes in pursuit behind him brought him up short. Mike halted several paces back.

Jeffrey didn't turn around. "Back off, Mike. I'm not feeling it, right now. I'll see you in the morning."

"All right, Boss. Bright and early."

After Mike retreated, Jeffrey sighed. He froze in the front porch light.

"Shit."

Blinded by headlight beams, he stood there, illuminated, yet completely lost. He squinted at the vehicle, still rolling toward him. The brakes squealed, sliding across the gravel. The engine ceased, and the headlights faded.

Marielle emerged from the opened driver's side door.

Then the other door rocked open.

Jeffrey's lips tumbled open in surprise.

*Tara.*

# Chapter Forty Eight

*H*e pressed her close. "What happened to France?"

Tara reached up, cupping his face into her palms, and smiled. "Oh, it's still there I imagine, a country over the sea — without me."

"Hmm. Their loss, my gain."

"I couldn't put it together, but I had all the pieces, I knew it fit. Then I saw the photos and it all snapped into place." She kissed him. "You downloaded them, didn't you? You wanted me to remember."

"Yes." He grinned.

"It worked."

"As intended," he whispered.

She closed her eyes and tilted her head back, anticipating the softness of his lips, the warmth of his breath. Her arms clung to his neck. She lingered there, appreciating every angle of his jaw. The gentle pressure of his hands at the small of her back guided her closer.

"Ahem." Marielle cleared her throat. "I'm going to be going now. Let you guys take this inside. I'm off to Brooklyn. I'll be up half the night, replaying this in my mind. Unbelievable." She hugged Tara. "Thank God you didn't go to France. That's not on my GPS."

She waved and winked at Jeffrey. "See you, lover boy."

339

Tara and Jeffrey didn't wait for her to leave before they hurried out of the spotlight of the garden.

The house was just as she left it, except for a few stray beer bottles and a pair of black crumpled socks, stuffed in a corner.

Jeffrey gathered the bottles, blushed, and apologized for the chaos. He left Mike's socks in their resting place.

Tara wrinkled her nose. "I think those need to be *buried*."

He chuckled. "I'll have Mike make the funeral arrangements. They're his socks. Just be thankful he didn't leave his underwear. There is one room untouched by all this…mess." He took her by the hand and led her to the bedroom. "No one's been here. Not even me."

"Jeffrey, Edouard and I didn't…"

He kissed her hard. She forgot what she was going to say. Her knees buckled and he nuzzled her down to the mattress. The coolness of the cotton sheets gave way to the heat of their friction.

How she missed the weight of him, his thighs pressed against hers. She wrapped her legs around his waist, drawing him closer. Her fingers clutched his hair, her knuckles pressed into the nape of his neck. Their chests heaved in rhythm. Her belly tensed against his.

She shoved her head to his shoulder.

A moment of breathlessness followed by an embraced collapse.

Nothing could have been clearer.

Angelina nestled into the crook of Paul's arm. It had been a shitty day. Deals left unsealed. *Was there new competition? Did Scardino and his lackeys think that I wouldn't notice a subtle skimming? And that pissy news about Steven's estate, giving Madelyn his half of the business. No way I'm going to be under* her *thumb. Damn Stuart too. But he needed the best defense attorney money could buy, even if that meant selling his share of the business to Madelyn. Lucky bitch also has the insurance bucks to take over the place.*

She didn't have the energy to wrestle sexually with Paul. Was she getting soft? Better not be. She could've loved Steven. Wanted to love him. But men had been brutal to her, physically and emotionally. It was a waste to love them, to love Paul. She would rather be equally brutal.

Gritting her teeth, Angelina rolled over and dug her toenails into Paul's leg.

He bounced her to her back, pinning her hands above her head, and straddled her.

She wanted to buck him off, bite his earlobe while humming in his ear, but the impulse passed. She let his hands stray to her breasts and circle their contours. He slid on top of her and showered her neck with kisses. Simple kisses.

*What's a girl to do but enjoy the moment?*

Then she yanked his hair.

# Chapter Forty Nine

Saturday, January 14, 8:30 a.m.

*A*ngelina crawled out of bed in the dim morning light and stared at Paul, who lay prone in the wrinkled sheets, snoring, beckoning her to attack him in his vulnerability, but she snuck into the bathroom instead. She'd shower and dress first.

Twenty minutes later, he hadn't moved. Barefoot, she moved to the living room. She had to know. He'd come by, looking for her, wanting to warn her about Corrigan's new efforts to snare her. Paul had been waiting for her. If he had searched her apartment...

She had to be sure that his protectiveness over her hadn't blurred with his disturbingly strong sense of duty to the NYPD. Still, she was pleased he had wanted to keep her safe. Having someone else on the force that cared about her best interests was important.

She pulled open the top drawer of her desk and noticed the .22 Ruger displaced from its origin.

*Good boy. You found my decoy.*

She pattered back to the bedroom and opened the closet. Her eyes narrowed. The spacing of her neatly pressed trousers had been tampered with, she was certain of it. One pant leg intertwined with another.

Heat rose to her face.

*Bastard.*

She yanked the hangers to the right; searching for the black duffle bag that she'd kept the clothes in that she'd worn when she killed Maurice. She grabbed it and her eyes found the difference immediately. The zipper was closed on the right; she *always* closed it to the left.

Angelina tossed the duffle to the side. And her black Manolo Blanik boots? *Moved!* Reaching into one boot, she plucked out the .38 S&W and glared into the bedroom.

*You weren't supposed to do this. Damn it, Paul.*

Angelina swiped at the tears welling up in the corners of her eyes. She had broken her own rules, allowed herself to have feelings for a man, but love was a superfluous emotion that only slowed her down.

She took a deep breath, arranged the hangers back to their places, keeping the gun and the boots in hand.

He'd left her little choice.

Pulling on her black slacks, she buttoned her pink silk blouse and donned the boots. After brushing her black mane fifty strokes, she applied her make-up. Tucking the .38 into the waistband of her trousers, she walked to the edge of the bed. For the first time, she found killing difficult.

"Get up, Paul," she said grimly.

He mumbled and rolled over. "Good morning, Babe. I must have overslept."

"Get out of the bed."

Paul rubbed his eyes. "Okaaaay."

He swung his feet over the side of the bed, stood, and tottered over to her, arms open.

She recoiled. "I'm not playing with you Paul."

"What's the matter?"

She narrowed her eyes. "You found my gun."

"Yeah, the .22. So what. I don't have a problem with you having a gun. But please don't tell me about the permit thing, 'cause I don't want to know. I'll look the other way. I'm not going to say anything about the coke you've got stashed either. I was going to talk to you

343

last night but… we got busy." He gyrated his hips at her. "I can get you help. We'll work it out."

She backed away from him. "I don't need your help. You went into my closet, Paul. And I was talking about my .38, not the .22."

"I did go into your closet." He stood there naked, raking his fingers through his mussed hair. "And you do need my help. I saw the bloody clothes and the gun, Angelina." Paul shook his head. "I know all about Miami. Guess what? I scored a copy of the footprints taken from a crime scene in a field, and I matched them to your boots. I don't have to tell you what happened next, but we can fix this before my lieutenant gets to you." He took a step closer to her. "Corrigan's a good man. I don't want to jam him up on this. I understand why you did it." He reached for her again. "I want this to be over with too, for both of us."

"Why didn't you tell me earlier?" She pushed him. "You were working me all along!"

"No, I wasn't. I found all this yesterday. I needed a day, to think things through. I wasn't working you. I was *protecting* you."

She paused, the steel pressed cold to her back. "I was going to tell you about L.A. today, tell you I was leaving. Madelyn's taking over the store. I'm moving on. Paul, I want you to come with me. You don't have to be involved in my business. Join the LAPD. Scardino won't risk his career to turn on us. He'll find another supplier."

For every step he took forward, she dropped back two.

"I don't want to go to L.A., Ange. I want to stay here."

"You're choosing Corrigan and the NYPD over me?"

Paul shook his head. "No. I'm choosing you both. Angelina. You are better than this."

Pressing her palm to his chest, she shoved him back. "He's gotten to you. Convinced you to turn on me. He's taken you away from me."

Paul's eyes widened. "Ange, Babe. I'm not abandoning you." He raised his arms, ready to embrace her. "We can untangle this mess. Get back on track. And he hasn't taken you away from me. I love you."

Angelina squeezed her eyes closed, fighting tears, reached behind her back, and cocked the hammer of the gun.

"And I love you too. We could have been good together, Paul."

She drew the .38 and pulled the trigger.

He tumbled to the floor, naked, his hand to his right side, blood oozing between his fingers.

Angelina lowered her hand, the smoking barrel of the gun at her side.

"I'm so sorry, Paul."

She bent down, picked up the black duffle bag, and walked out the door.

# Chapter Fifty

Saturday, January 14, 10:20 a.m.

*T*ara stretched across the bed. Jeffrey had long ago left for work, but his scent lingered, pressed into the linens. She hugged his pillow. How lucky was she? She was back into his heart and his home.

She rose and showered, dancing under the spray of the water. Her clothes were on the way to France, but Jeffrey had saved a pair of her jeans and a navy v-neck tee. Her heart made a giddy jump thinking of how he must have known she'd be back in his life.

As she zipped up her jeans, she heard the rattling of glass bottles from outside.

Tara ran into the living room, knelt onto the leather sofa, drew back the curtains, and saw Joe, hoisting an over-full plastic recycle bin. Rocketing off the sofa, Tara slipped on her running shoes and took a deep breath. She wanted to surprise him.

Creeping out the front door, she tiptoed down the porch stair and yelled, "Hey Joe! What do you know?"

He dropped the bin.

The clanking of the glass bottles resonated through the quiet neighborhood morning. He grinned so wide that she could see his teeth from yards away. The older man swept a stray gray lock from the tip of his eyebrow and danced a jig.

"I can't believe my eyes. And they're still pretty damn good without the specs at my age. Tara Ross. Sweetheart." He stomped his feet again. "I knew it. I told him not to give up on you. Come here girl."

She galloped across the lawn and reached up to hug him. Joe stood at 6'2", his muscles taut for a man of seventy-two. If Joe was any indication of how Jeffrey would look in the future, she'd have to work hard to keep up.

"Come in the house. I want you to meet Carolyn."

"I remember Carolyn. We met the night her cat ran under the porch."

Carolyn, who'd appeared at all the noise, clapped her hand to her mouth and waved Tara and Joe up to the porch.

Skipping two steps, Tara leaped onto the porch and hugged Carolyn. "Congratulations. I hear you and Joe are getting married."

Carolyn patted Tara's back. "Thank you. You missed our party last night."

Tara blushed. "Late for yours, on time for mine. Jeffrey and I are going out to dinner tonight to celebrate before his big day— promotion to captain. Then we'll all be together for the promotion ceremony on Friday."

"We're so proud of him," Carolyn said.

"Since my wardrobe is in France, I need to shop for a dress for tonight." Tara glanced at Joe. "And my car is at Edouard's house and Jeffrey's already left. Um…May I …"

Joe nodded. "Say no more. Take my car." He winked at Carolyn. "I won't need it this morning."

Tara kissed him on the cheek. "Thank you."

"You're welcome. You're family now."

Carolyn nudged him with her elbow.

*What do they know that I don't?* Tara thought.

She thanked them again and bounded back to the house, her feet leaping off the ground with every step. She couldn't wait to see

Jeffrey again. Abbie was coming on Friday morning, just in time to be at the promotions ceremony and to meet Jeffrey.

*Everything is going to work out. I'm so lucky.*

Her cell rang. It was Jeffrey. She couldn't stop grinning.

"Good morning," he murmured.

"Good morning to you too."

She could hear the whooshing of passing cars, horns beeping, and muffled yells in the background.

"Mike and I are on our way to serve the warrants and pick up a suspect. I'll stop by the house at two. Grab some lunch. Grab you!"

"I'll be waiting."

Jeffrey wanted Angelina cornered, but he needed to do this right. He wanted to make sure no one on his squad transgressed. No cowboy antics. One wrong move and the charges wouldn't stick. Angelina would be free to deal and destroy once again.

Today would be the last time he'd lead the squad he had raised. Jeffrey admired their growth, dedication, and perseverance. He would miss them, but his promotion to captain would lead him away to another precinct, someone else to step in his place.

He'd divided the squad into teams. Herb and Detective Fillmore were on their way to Thompson's Paints and Interiors in Williamsburg. Impounding that van would be key.

He and Mike were supposed to rein in Angelina at her apartment, a thorough search to follow, while she was being processed down at the station.

Mike drove the Crown Vic north on Broadway. Jeffrey's mind lapsed into thoughts of last night. Images, memories of Tara swirled in his head, heightening his senses. He could hear her voice and his skin tingled at the thought of her touch. He smelled and tasted her. Then he bucked forward in the seat as Mike slammed the breaks.

"Shit, Mike."

"Red light, Lou."

"Have Amy drive when Christina's in the car, will ya?"

Mike smacked the steering wheel with his palms and muttered, "There must be a moron convention down here."

Jeffrey had called Paul's cell several times that morning. No answer. No response to the multiple voicemails he left either. He wanted Paul to stay back at the precinct. He didn't want him involved in Angelina's case. His stomach tightened. What if Paul was there with her...in bed?

He'd warned him. The man's career was about to implode before it ever got off the ground. He should have kept a more vigilant eye on him, tightened the reins.

Mike made a left turn on Edgar Allan Poe Street and parked the car. Jeffrey braced himself for the collision.

For once...nothing.

They got out of the Crown Vic. He circled the car. No tires on the curb. No fenders dented. Not even a scratch.

He nodded his head and said, "Unbelievable."

"Let's roll, Lou."

They trotted up the three flights of stairs to apartment 4F. The door was ajar. Jeffrey licked his lips. Seventeen years on the job sharpened his intuition. Something was wrong He grabbed his Glock and proceeded with caution, circling the apartment together with Mike, eyes searching.

"NYPD," Jeffrey called.

Silence.

Then a gurgle came from the bedroom. Mike spun around, scanning the apartment. He walked backward behind Jeffrey, protecting his partner.

"Oh, shit!" Jeffrey's eyes wildly searched the room, his mind desperately deciphering dream from reality. His heart rocketed to his throat.

Paul lay naked, crumpled in a crimson pool on the floor, bloody sheets at his head. He had fallen to his side, his cell phone three inches from his fingertips.

"Oh my God," Mike said.

"Mike, get back into the living room. Guard every door. I'll call for an ambulance and back up."

He grabbed his radio. "10-13. Officer down." He choked. He repeated. "Officer down. 10-13. I need a bus and back up at 205 West 84th- 4F."

He rolled his detective over. Paul's eyelids flickered. Blood cascaded from his right side.

"Paul! Paul! It's Jeffrey. Hang on, man. Ambulance is on the way. You'll be okay."

He knew, deep down, that the extent of Paul's injury was probably beyond salvage. He wrapped Paul's torso tightly with the sheets, trying to stem the flow and covered his naked body. He cradled his Paul's head.

"Who did this to you?" He had to know.

Paul struggled to move his lips.

"Angelina," he rasped. "Gone. Don't go home."

He sputtered, sucking in air.

"Scardino, dirty." His eyes opened and he looked at Jeffrey. "I'm sorry, Lou."

The weight of his body sank into Jeffrey's arms, gone limp...empty.

"No! *No!*" Jeffrey screamed.

He started CPR. His own chest squeezed with each compression of Paul's sternum.

A multitude of uniforms and paramedics arrived. Paul was gurneyed out, life support ceremoniously continued, at least until he would be officially pronounced dead in a St. Lukes-Roosevelt trauma room.

"Mike, stay here. I'm leaving you in charge of the scene. Paul said something. I have to go. I have to get to Tara."

# Chapter Fifty One

Saturday, January 14, Noon.

$\mathcal{T}$ara hung the red dress in the closet, aligning the matching pumps beneath it. She'd found the perfect outfit in fewer than four hours and two stores! Tonight they would dine at Niko's. Today was going to be the best day.

Angelina parked the dark green Charger a block from Jeffrey's house, close enough to reach it quickly, but far away enough to blend into the neighborhood. She unzipped the black duffle bag, assuring herself she brought everything necessary. *Rope—check. Duct tape— check. Thirty-eight S&W—check.* She shifted the knotted plastic bag containing her blood-spattered blouse and patted the clean white cotton tee shirt, jeans, and a denim jacket neatly folded on top of ballet flats.

So not her, but that was the point.

Surely, an APB had already been issued by now, but she was prepared. She had stopped at Maurice's apartment and lifted the floorboard behind his dresser; that's where he hid licenses and passports.

She recalled Irina's passport as she flipped through the array of ID's, looking for anyone bearing a resemblance to her, picking out Melanie Waters' driver's license for herself. She could definitely pass as Melanie, same cheekbones and green eyes, except for the shoulder length blonde hair.

Good ole Maurice.

He had kept a variety of wigs for his women—just to change it up for his clients. Same pussy—different girl. She scored the perfect blonde wig and had it, waiting, with all the other things she needed to escape. Once she blew Corrigan away, she'd for Westchester County Airport, a small, uncomplicated airport, then slip away to L.A. — city of sunshine and opportunity.

Angelina bobbed her head to the right and then to the left, pressed up against a hedge to stay out of sight. No one around. Fabulous. She rounded the house. And there it was—appearing like a sign from God—the basement window, its rickety wooden frame rocking with the breeze.

*Oh, man! This is too good to be true.*

Slipping the black duffle through the opening, she lowered it gently onto the washer and then slithered through the window, her boots leading the way. The door above creaked open.

*Shit. I need more time. Why is he home so early? Or is that someone else?*

She quickly crouched behind the boiler.

Tara swallowed hard, but her laundry needed to be done. Pressing the bed sheets to her chest, cold tingles snaked down her spine. She shivered and hesitated.

*Damn that basement!*

Peering around the wadded sheets, she focused on the wooden stairs. No banister for balance, she inched down the wooden planks, step by step. Her heart fluttered with every drop. Wisps of her short brown hair dipped into the moisture dotting her neck. When she estimated she had reached the bottom step, she extended her foot and tapped it like a blind man's cane searching for the concrete floor, then stepped down and exhaled.

*Whew. I made it.*

She spotted a detergent box, jutting half way off the shelf mounted high above the washer. Plopping the sheets on top of the washer, she scanned the basement for something to stand on, eventually snatching up a small wooden stool sitting in the corner.

She jerked back.

She could have sworn something had moved behind the boiler. Tara sighed. Convinced it was just her overactive imagination, she set the stool beneath the shelf, mumbling about her short stature.

The uneven legs of the stool rocked as she stretched for the detergent. Then it slipped out from beneath her feet. Airborne, she instinctively bicycled her feet, but tumbled forward, smacking her chin on the white enamel corner of the washer.

Her head whipped back. She crumbled to the floor, her body cracking hard against the concrete. Everything went blurry, then black.

Angelina laughed as she smashed the wooden stool into the gray brick wall. The legs snapped from its smooth round base, scattering to the floor like toothpicks.

*The bitch didn't even hear me! That was an awesome punt — kicked it out right out from under her itty, bitty, little feet.* She glanced at Tara who hadn't moved. *It would be a pity if she were dead. Where's the fun in that?* Then she saw Tara's chest rise and fall. *Alright. Game on.*

*Ka-thunk. Ka-thunk. Ka-thunk.* Tara's head throbbed. Warmth trickled down her neck. She struggled to open her eyes, willing them to focus. The silver band of duct tape across her mouth pinched her lips, smothering her screams and her hands were tied behind her back, unable to cushion the blows to her head.

She gazed up. She had seen her—this woman—somewhere before. The woman with long jet-black hair. Then Tara realized the woman dragging her up the basement steps was Angelina Holtz.

"Damn good thing you're tiny," she said, huffing and puffing. "I wasn't expecting *you*. Funny how plans change. But this is better—two for one. Now let's get you settled upstairs and wait for your man."

She pulled Tara to the top of the stairs.

"He should fix that basement window, don't you think? We'll leave a note for the next homeowners. It would be the courteous thing to do."

Angelina twisted the doorknob and pushed but the door didn't budge. She pushed again, harder. Nothing. She rattled it, finally kicking it open with her black boots. The spiked heel of her left boot buckled and snapped.

"Fuck! These are $700 Manolo Blaniks."

She flung Tara across the kitchen floor, and then duct taped her boot heel together, and stormed into the living room.

*Try to stay calm. The woman is clearly insane. Cooperate. Give her time to cool off.*

Tara scanned the kitchen. She wriggled on the floor, able to loosen her bonds somewhat until she could see the clock on the wall. One o'clock. Jeffrey said two. She wanted him to come through the door but begged God that he stayed away.

Angelina returned to the kitchen.

Tara held her hands behind her back, pretending that her bonds were secure. Exhaling through her nose, she flung her legs into a pike position and performed the best "kip up" she'd ever done. She bounced to her feet and swung her leg toward Angelina's face.

A *grand battement*, right to her chin.

As Angelina toppled back to the kitchen floor, Tara ran—fast. Ran right into the bathroom.

*Great, Tara! No time to screw up!*

Angelina thundered like an angry mule down the hallway. Tara grabbed the plunger. This time she squeezed the pink rubber end in both hands, just like Jeffrey had said, and whirled the wooden handle

180 degrees as her attacker breached the door. The dowel whooshed through the air before cracking Angelina on her forehead.

Angelina shook her head. Tara didn't give her a chance to recover. She curled her right hand into a fist, cocked it behind her ear, just as Frank had taught her, and shot her knuckles to Angelina's cheek. Spit spewed from Angelina's mouth. Her green eyes glowed fury.

*Damn. This woman doesn't go down easy. Plan C don't fail me now.*

Tara vaulted out of the bathroom and skidded into the bedroom. She flung open Jeffrey's top drawer and patted through his underwear, reaching around the cold steel of his .38.

Then pain ripped through her fingers, vibrating up her arm and to her shoulder. Her teeth ached from the agony. The revolver dropped from her hand.

Angelina pushed the drawer closed harder, until Tara's bones cracked, and then grinned. "You're scrawny but you have spunk. I love a challenge."

She dragged Tara by her hair away from the dresser. Pressing the muzzle of her revolver into Tara's cheek, she stopped in the kitchen to grab a chair, and then pulled them into the living room.

Angelina drew the living room curtains closed. She hoisted Tara onto the chair and roped her to it, yanking the rope at Tara's wrists hard, then binding her feet, and wrapping an extra piece of duct tape around her mouth.

"Pity you didn't have me over sooner. The right window treatments would've brightened up this room. Too bad that I can't help you out with that, but I'll be off to L.A. and you'll be dead. Timing is everything, don't you think?"

Tara nodded.

"I'm glad you agree. You're quite reasonable. I like that. Now, I told Sheila to leave the day I killed Maurice. Even gave her money for a drink." Angelina sighed. "But unlike you, she wasn't reasonable. She had to go. And I'm sorry to say, so will you." She strode up to Tara and ran her fingernail along Tara's swollen cheek right above the rim of duct tape. "But, I'm going to do it in front of your boyfriend. Nothing personal. It's just to heighten the effect for him."

She wanted Angelina to keep talking. She raised her eyebrow, hoping to encourage her monologue.

"You're fun to talk to, you know that? I've always wanted a girlfriend. Girlfriend to girlfriend, our choices in men suck. Up until Paul, no man ever treated me well. Your boyfriend fucked that up." Angelina poked her finger into Tara's chest, repeatedly, harder and harder, knocking the breath from Tara. Tara struggled to gasp beneath the duct tape. She couldn't get enough air. Angelina droned on. "The only man I ever loved is gone. Love sucks, you know? Now if you didn't love the lieutenant, you wouldn't be in this situation. It's all about the choices we make."

Angelina grinned and strode across the living room toward the fireplace, grabbing her black duffle bag along the way. Unzipping the bag, she yanked out her bloodstained blouse and turned toward Tara.

"I hate to do this. Now there's a crime—burning a Chanel."

Opening the flue, she tossed the blouse into the fireplace. She flicked her lighter until the flame grew tall and orange.

She bent over and then paused. "Oh, this hurts. A moment of silence for Coco Chanel. Bye-bye. I'll miss you."

The blouse burst into flames.

Angelina left the room.

*Where did she go?* Tara thought.

She wiggled in the chair. If she could only loosen her hands again. She concentrated on stretching the tape, applying constant pressure. Beads of sweat dotted her forehead as she heard Angelina's footsteps, the unevenness of her heels.

Angelina teetered on her broken high-heeled boot and plopped down into the leather recliner.

"I hope you don't mind. I borrowed some of your nail polish I grabbed from the bedroom. Angelina grinned. "Well at least I hope it's *yours*. Nice color, My nails desperately need attention." She filed her nails and brushed the pale pink polish across them. "I prefer red but this is a nice, basic color. And I have time to dry too. Right in time for your boyfriend's five o'clock entrance."

*She doesn't know Jeffrey's coming home early.*

Tara glanced at the antique clock on the shelf. One thirty.

*Thirty more minutes. Think, Tara. Think.*

There was a knock at the back door.

Angelina shot out of the chair. "Who the hell could that be?"

Tara shrugged. Her heart raced.

*Was Jeffrey early? Why would he knock at the backdoor? It's someone else. Someone innocent. Oh God, please don't let it be Carolyn.*

A key scraped into the lock and the door creaked open.

"Tara, are you here, hon? I need the car keys."

*Oh, my God. It's Joe. No Joe. Go away Joe.*

Tara bounced up and down in the chair, shaking her head. "Mmmm. Mmmm."

Joe walked into the living room. Tara blinked her eyes wildly.

"What the..."

Angelina's arm swung up and rocketed down, slamming the butt of her .38 to the back of Joe's head. Tears streamed down Tara's cheeks as he collapsed to the floor. Long minutes passed and he didn't move.

The clock chimed one forty-five.

Jeffrey's eyes shot past the blue and red strobe on the dash of the Crown Vic as he sped down the Cross County Parkway, cognizant of the stream of vehicles in his path, Paul's dried blood still caked across his chest, He dialed Tara's cell, again.

Still no answer.

His dad didn't answer his cell, home phone, or Carolyn's phone either. Something was horribly wrong.

Frank, luckily, did answer.

"Frank, can you get to my house right away? I have a psychotic female suspect loose with a vendetta. If she runs across Tara, she'll have no qualms about taking her out. I'm on the Cross County now. I'll get there as fast as I can."

"I'm at the gym. I'm leaving now."

He called the White Plains PD, describing Angelina, warning them of a possible hostage situation at his house. The department had already received the APB from his unit. Sergeant Plantz reassured him that they were on their way.

*Tara, what did I do? I just got you back. I never thought at what cost.*

"Aw shucks. You must know the guy," Angelina said.

Tara squinted, trying to block the tears. Joe lay motionless, prone on the floor. Blood rolled down the curve of his skull and seeped into his gray cotton shirt. She bucked her legs, rocking the chair.

"Uh-Uh-Uh," Angelina said, wagging her finger at her. "Don't piss me off."

She approached her. Tara didn't flinch.

Angelina peeled the tape from her mouth.

"Did you want to say something?" she taunted.

Tara spat into Angelina's face.

Unfazed, Angelina wiped her face and then said, "I would be very afraid." She took a deep breath, and then backhanded Tara across her face.

The sting was warm, but the adrenaline dampened her pain. She glared at Angelina. Her left eye throbbed angrily.

"You're tough. I like that." Angelina stretched the tape back around her mouth. "Now sit here quietly and contemplate what you've done."

Angelina swung the chamber of her .38 Smith and Wesson open.

"Hmm, four left. I only need two. I'm an excellent shot, you know. And since I like you—girlfriend to girlfriend—I'll spare your head. Make you look nice. They won't have to patch you up or keep your casket closed. One to the heart. Dramatic but quick. Simple. No fuss. No muss. Easily covered up by a pretty dress. Unfortunately, it will be closed casket for your boyfriend."

Tara glanced at the clock. Five minutes. Jeffrey's early arrival might catch Angelina off balance. Her eyes flicked back to Joe. He still hadn't moved.

*Please don't die on me, Joe.*

Her eyes widened. She remembered that Joe carried his .38 in his ankle holster. It was worth a try.

Tara had worked the rope at her wrists apart enough to slide her hands free.

Tires crunched the gravel of the driveway. Angelina bolted to the window and pulled the drapes open. The clock chimed twice.

"Oh, my gosh. Your boyfriend's early." She clapped gleefully. "Well, let's get the party started."

Tara gritted her teeth and leaned sideways, the momentum enough to crash the chair to the floor. In one swift movement, she flung her arms forward, reached under Joe's pant leg, grabbed his .38, cocked the hammer, and aimed at Angelina's head.

Angelina heard the noise and spun around.

They both got off a shot. Blood spattered the drapes. Angelina jerked back.

Tara closed her eyes. She heard the crash of glass and the thud of a body. When she opened them, Jeffrey was standing over her, his shirt bloodied.

*Oh, my God. I shot him,* she thought, and then fainted.

The crunching of glass roused her.

"Don't move, Sweetheart."

*It's Jeffrey's voice. He's alive.*

Then she heard Joe, mumbling. There were people everywhere: uniformed officers, paramedics, men in suits and ties. Red and blue lights glowed through the window. A woman with a White Plains CSU windbreaker dusted glass shards from her body. Tara scanned the living room. Someone was covering a body. Strands of black hair snaked from beneath the sheet.

*Thank God. It's not Joe.*

She heard, "One, two, three." Someone rolled her onto a backboard. It was stiff and cold, but she was alive. Joe was on a board next to her.

She glimpsed at the sea of curious onlookers, gathered in the street, their mouths moving, but their words garbled.

Jeffrey knelt over her and stroked her hair. He kissed her forehead. "I'll see you at the hospital."

She tried to smile, but the pain in her face made her wince. The medics carried her out. It was over.

Before the ambulance door clicked shut, she heard yelling.

Jeffrey clapped the ambulance door, signaling for the driver to pull away. He glanced up and couldn't believe his eyes. Ray Scardino piled out of a blue and white.

"That bastard," he mumbled.

"I heard what happened. Is the White Plains CSU here? We'll get the scene secured," Scardino ordered.

Jeffrey's nostrils flared and his fists curled. *What balls! Is he that stupid?*

As he strode toward him, Mike squealed the tires of an unmarked Chevy Impala into the driveway. Frank, right behind him, screeched his Sebring to a halt. The two men sprinted up the driveway and tackled Scardino to the ground.

"What the hell?" Scardino yelled.

Frank secured Scardino's hands behind his back while Mike cuffed the Captain's wrists.

Mike panted. "We're on to you, Scardino. We searched your apartment and found the Richard Nixon mask you wore while assaulting Detective Liz Shear, along with a gram of coke. And that green Dodge Charger parked just down the road, you know, the hot one you and Holtz have been cruising around in, we got you on tape getting into it after you beat and threatened Detective Shear." Mike jerked the captain to his feet. "Ray Scardino, you're under arrest for assaulting an officer, conspiracy to harm an officer and a civilian, vandalism, possession and sale of narcotics, auto theft, corruption of subordinate officers, and tampering with evidence."

He read Scardino his Miranda rights and ducked him into a blue and white. He high-fived the officers that had worked with him, and brought Scardino to the scene. It was probably the first time everyone *wanted* Ray Scardino on a crime scene.

Frank jogged over to Jeffrey and hugged him.

"How you doing, son?"

"Holding up. Hell of a day. Tara took her out." He shook his head in awe. "She saved me...and Pop."

"Joe and I taught her the technicalities, but the bravery is all hers. Go to her. Everything's under control here."

Jeffrey and Frank embraced. Frank swiped a tear from his cheek. "Go on. Get out of here."

Mike trudged toward him. Jeffrey wanted, more than anything to be with Tara, but he hesitated.

"Okay, just this once," Mike joked and embraced his best friend. "All right, that's enough," Mike said. They parted and he cleared his throat. "You should know, Paul was pronounced dead in the ER. And you were right about the license plate of the Charger that ran you off the road. There was a D, G, and a seven—specifically DTG 9237. We found that plate in Scardino's apartment. He must have switched it with the one on Maurice Chiguard's car. I just wanted you to know."

"Thanks Mike."

"I gotta get going. Process our ex-captain," he said with a grin.

Jeffrey tapped his best friend on his shoulder. "I'm proud to have served with you."

Mike saluted him. "Likewise."

# Chapter Fifty Two

Friday, January 20, 11:00 a.m.

"*H*e looked good. Peaceful," Mike said.

Jeffrey nodded. *What else was there to say?* He thought.

He stood with Mike, Herb, and Liz, her arm in a sling, all dressed in their crisp police blues, across from Paul's parents and a group of unfamiliar people who he surmised were friends and relatives. They had followed the mourners from the church to the cemetery.

An open casket service, the funeral director succeeded in capturing Paul's youthful looks. A disgraced cop, he was dressed in a civilian blue suit, the only one of Jeffrey's squad not in uniform.

Jeffrey shifted his weight. His shiny black shoes pressed into the soft spring dirt. The snow long melted, thin green blades of grass poked through the earth. It was a sunny day but he was sure Mr. and Mrs. Rivchak hadn't noticed. He reached into his pocket and traced the edges of Paul's detective badge. The property of the police department, he'd turn it, the shield number assigned to the next newly minted detective.

His mouth was parched, and he swallowed. *I should've been a better boss, put a tighter rein on him. I was so wrapped up in solving cases and power struggles with Scardino, that I let Paul spiral away. He was narcissistic. Too young. Used by Scardino. But he was smart. And he was just getting it—how to be a member of the squad.*

He watched Mrs. Rivchak dab her tears with a crumpled wad of tissue, as the minister eulogized Paul, noting his accomplishments from his childhood to his days as a police officer.

Jeffrey's neck throbbed against the collar of his uniform. No brass attended. No taps. No bag pipes. No officer's funeral.

He glanced at Liz, standing at attention, her injured arm pressed to her chest. The squad saluted Paul one last time as his coffin was lowered into the ground. He narrowed his eyes. *May Scardino rot in hell for this.*

Friday, January 20 2:00 p.m.
Promotions Ceremony

The voices of the crowd collided. Heads turned and bobbed. Family and friends hugged and kissed. The auditorium at One Police Plaza was full. People milled about the neat rows of spectator seats, excusing themselves as they stepped over those already seated.

Jeffrey, Mike, Herb, and Liz huddled in a corner. They'd made it from the cemetery to the promotions ceremony on time, but it had been a hectic morning. Tara and his father had been discharged from the hospital.

Frank insisted on driving Tara to the airport to greet Abbie who arrived well before spring. Thrilled that Tara and her ex-husband had come to agreement on custody. Frank told Tara he could hardly wait to meet her daughter.

Liz bit her lower lip. Jeffrey came over to her and hugged her. "No one's angry at you. You were right to cooperate with Internal Affairs. You're not a rat, Liz. Buck Gates and Dave Willis have to take responsibility for their part. They'll serve their time."

"Their ex-narcotic cops, Jeffrey. They'll be brutalized in prison."

"Gates and Willis will be watched as best as we can. As hard as it is to say, these now ex-detectives are criminals, Liz. It's gonna be okay. I'll give you absolution, if that will help. Oh. And congratulations, Detective Sergeant Elizabeth Shear, new commanding officer of Narcotics."

She embraced Jeffrey. "I'll miss you, Detective Lieutenant Jeffrey Corrigan...ooh... I mean Captain Corrigan."

A deep voice resonated over the microphone.

"Everyone, move to your seats and please stand for The Pledge of Allegiance.

He looked sharp in his dress blues. White gloves and gleaming gold medals in a background of deep blue. His policeman's cap covered his dark blonde hair. No locks escaped. He had cut it, she noted.

Tara smiled and thought, *Plenty on top to rake my fingertips through.*

"Which one is he?" Abbie asked.

Tara leaned over and whispered, "First row, third man from the left."

Abbie nodded approvingly, "Nice...Mom."

She squeezed Abbie's hand. "Yes, he is."

Faded red bands still circled her wrists. At least her head no longer ached, despite her purple bruised left eye. She brushed her short hair with her fingers to the back of her head, the pads bumping along the suture line. She gazed over at Joe, no more worse for the wear than she was.

He winked back and clutched Carolyn's hand.

Then she caught Frank peering at her. He gave her the thumbs up sign, followed by a gestured knuckle punch.

He pointed at her and mouthed, "Tomorrow."

His wife, Myra, rested her palm on Frank's knee and rolled her eyes.

Tara smiled. Then inhaled deeply. So much had happened. The past was behind her but not to be forgotten. She had so much to look forward to now—life with Jeffrey. She had Abbie and a wonderful network of extended family and friends. She and Edouard had even spoken, with great civility.

Tara wasn't sure what was next for her, but whatever it was, she knew she'd always have a soft place to land.

Baby Christina cooed in Amy's arms. Her miniature fingers grasped at Tara's extended finger.

"Congratulations on Mike's promotion to Detective first grade," She told Amy.

"I may tease him a lot, but I'm so proud of him. And he's so good with Christina."

Abbie nudged Tara with her elbow. "Mom. Mom. Who's that sitting next to Mr. Corrigan?"

"Oh, um." Tara squinted up at the stage. "That's James, Jeffrey's son."

"Wow! He's *hot.*"

Tara patted Abbie's knee. "Ceremony's starting, dear."

The crowd hushed. Commissioner Donahue stepped up to the podium and welcomed all the guests. One by one, the officers received their new ranks. Mike trotted across the stage with a huge grin on his face. Muted giggles filled the room—those who knew him couldn't help it. He saluted the commissioner and exited down the stage stairs—shenanigans in check. Herb and Liz were next.

Jeffrey beamed at his squad. He had given them his best over the last seven years. And they had given theirs—tenfold. He wished Paul had been there to share the squad's day of glory.

"And being promoted from lieutenant to captain is Captain Jeffrey Franklin Corrigan," Commissioner Donahue said.

He rose and marched across the stage. He tapped the brim of his cap as he saluted.

"The New York City Police Department is proud to have a man of your caliber leading the way."

The commissioner shook Jeffrey's hand and handed him a certificate and a new shield.

Jeffrey took a deep breath, "Thank you, Sir."

He turned to exit the podium. Automatically, his eyes searched for her. There she was, next to Abbie, her face brilliant, glowing, despite her bruised eye. All was right. He smiled. She was just the way he had found her—bruised and beautiful.

## *The End*

## Tanya Goodwin

Tanya Goodwin writes romantic suspense with a twist of medicine and mystery. Her experiences as a physician are reflective in her characters, and her stories are based on medical professionals and events that have crossed her path. When not writing, she's still delivering babies. Tanya is a member of Romance Writers of America, Mystery Writers of America, and Sisters in Crime.

# DISCOVER MORE
# FINE FICTION

## Visit

# www.mitchellmorrispublishinginc.com

MITCHELL MORRIS is a registered trademark of Celeris Publishing Group, Inc.
Port Richey, FL